Death in Dixie

Death in Dixie

Edited by
Frank D. McSherry Jr., Charles G. Waugh,
and Martin H. Greenberg

BARNES
&NOBLE
BOOKS
NEW YORK

Originally published as Sunshine Crime

Copyright © 1987 by Martin Harry Greenberg and Charles G. Waugh

This edition published by Barnes & Noble Inc.,
by arrangement with Rutledge Hill Press Inc.

1996 Barnes & Noble Books

ISBN 0-7607-0229-2

Printed and bound in the United States of America

00 M 9 8 7 6 5 4 3 2

QF

Table of Contents

To Live or Die in Dixie

There's buckwheat cakes and Injun batter—
Just to make the fat man fatter—
—"Dixie," D. D. Emmons

Perhaps no part of the United States is more romantic than the South.

Consider its image: the rolling bluegrass hills of Kentucky; the reddish brown tobacco fields of the Carolinas; the long white coast of Florida; the mighty Mississippi River, Father of Waters, irrigating rich, black farmlands; the mountains of West Virginia where you can walk through clouds.

The lore and legend, in fiction and film: green-eyed Scarlett O'Hara strolling in hoopskirts across the lawns of Tara, with the slave quarters in the rear; Colonel Sartoris, seeing his gracious world of privilege collapse in the flames of the Civil War; Tom Sawyer and Huckleberry Finn on a paddlewheel steamer on the sparkling river.

Could crime exist in these sunshine states?

Of course. No matter how close the rolling planet comes to the sun, one half of it is always in darkness.

The stories of mystery, crime, and detection gathered here are each set in a different state of the South, largely by authors southern born and bred. Chosen for their quality as fiction, the stories provide not only the thrill of murder mysteries, but also a deep insight into the people of each state, how they live, and the land and cities they live in under the hot southern sky.

It's not surprising that the South should have a group of characteristics that form a bond among the individual states. (By the South, we mean more than just the eleven states forming the Confederacy; we've included the Union border states of Kentucky and West Virginia—it seceded from the South during the war and fought on the side of the North.) However, the states of the South have something more in common than their location on a map or their climate. No other comparably-sized part of the United States has had it so rough. From the Indian Wars of the Colonial days of Kentucky's "Dark and Bloody Ground," to the Revolution when a vicious guerilla war raged between American partisans under General Francis Marion, the "Swamp Fox," against American Loyalists and British Regulars, to the Civil War, waged almost entirely on southern territory, the South has suffered more than any other section. In contrast, the North experienced only two invasions during the Civil War, the Antietam and Gettysburg campaigns, each lasting only a few weeks.

The South's suffering has long been symbolized by the path of deliberate destruction, sixty miles wide and three hundred miles long, which General William Sherman's army cut on its march to the sea:

Bring the good old bugle, boys, we'll sing another song,
Sing it with a spirit that will start the world along;
Sing it as we used to sing it fifty thousand strong
As we went marching through Georgia.

No other section of the nation has seen its social structure so altered by force, the defenders of its old order slaughtered. (And shed no tears for it, either, with its aristocracy, slavery, and impoverished whites.) No other Americans have been decisively defeated in war and forced to suffer an occupying army on their land for years.

No wonder the South considers itself a unique region. It is bound together by experiences that are largely unique to it.

But all that is in the past. Slowly a new South is forming, with much of the old hate, bitterness and prejudice conquered. Its wounds are being cured, and while its shining shape is not yet clear, the best of the Old South remains and is preserved in its people and literature. Perhaps this accounts for the southern characteristic often seen in these stories: the humorous touch. People who suffer greatly experience life's humor and irony more vividly.

But this is not only a regional anthology. These stories have another characteristic, one that appeals to all. Everybody loves a good mystery.

So be our guest. Sit in the warm sunshine and enjoy these gripping, entertaining tales of sunshine crime.

—Frank G. McSherry, Jr.
McAlester, Oklahoma

Acknowledgements

Death in Dixie

The flim-flam preacher man discovered that when you wave a Bible before a good ole boy, the wind from it often blows out his pilot light. . . .

ONE

When the Lord Calls
Gloria Norris

When the Lord calls you—BAM—it comes like a bolt out of the blue. I was winding up that guest pastorate down in south Mississippi, and the wife was serving us nothing but buttermilk and cornbread on what the congregation was still giving when He looked down and decided He would help. I wasn't expecting that letter one bit when I went down to the little store that has the post office at the back behind a little wire-mesh booth. I only went every other day because old Jackson behind the counter would every time ask me when was I paying up what I owed him—imagine that, after all I'd did for this town. And believe me, I'm just one lone preacher, not a whole tribe like that Angel Martinez that needs a whole bus to haul around his group. Do you know that Angel takes around one feller that does nothing but play a trumpet number to inspire the congregation before Angel gets up to preach? No, I'm just serving God alone. But He picked me for His call, although I am short and fat and all that's left of my hair is a band of gray running around a bare round bulb of a scalp shiny as a china doorknob.

"I guess it's a good thing the other feller put the stamp on this letter for you," says old Jackson, sourpussing through the mesh window. "You'd of asked me to put the three cents on your bill too."

"God loves the cheerful giver, Brother Jackson. It's all in the hands of the congregation to pay their minister." And I took my letter and walked out slow, not letting his glare hurry me. I doubt his salvation very much.

I open up the letter and this Mr. Harvey Giles is writing Would I come up to a place called Alcoma to hold their meeting the very next day. "We've heard a lot about you and are real anxious to hear your message, which we hear has inspired so many and call collect because we need you right away." I wonder how in the world they

1

heard about me when I ain't even heard of that town. But he put in only two dollars for traveling. He must have thought I had wings and was going to fly; the two dollars was for a place to piss on the way. So I tuck the letter in my pocket and don't know that I would go.

Then the Lord hit me with another sign. I was walking along that hot street, when one of the church deacons, Lamson, he's got the Chevrolet agency, new and used cars, comes out of the bank and grabs my arm. "Brother Benson, looks like you just about wore out that Ford car of yours."

I laugh and say: "Yes, the Lord has put some mileage on that old car."

He says: "Well, I got a nice little used Chevy down on my lot, just about 50,000 miles on it, and I tell you what, you drive your old one in today and drive that one out, and I'll take care of the difference."

I couldn't believe it. You couldn't get five dollars for my old car, a 1932 sedan, seventeen years old. When I start to tell him what a man of the Lord he is, he cuts me off. "No, it's not anything like what you deserve because you have done more than any man I've known in my fifty years to bring Jesus alive and walking the streets of this town. You come on down and get your car." Now I never realized it but he's a man that's really got Jesus in his heart. My old car had a carburetor that's about to go, tires wore down thin as a dime, and the lights and back doors not either one working.

So I come in home at the guest parsonage, knowing now I would go; I've already called them and I got this shiny black Chevy, and I tell the wife to get the kids packing, the Lord's called me to north Mississippi.

Then she acts up the way she did. She starts pulling her hair and turning all colors. I don't know what started her off. Everywhere we've lived they say she's a good preacher's wife, never raises her voice. But she screams out at me in the kitchen. *"Why you need to drag us off again? You don't need us when you got all the deacons' wives and their innocent little daughters to run after and lick over like a dog. You don't need me when you got the choir soprano to take in the back of the church every afternoon."*

"What's the matter with you?" I said. "Have you ever known me to turn my back when the Lord calls me? Here they've heard about me and need me to come hold their meeting. You expect me to say no?"

"Oh the *Lord* calls you," she commences to scream. I don't know to this day what got into her. Maybe the female change starting. She rolls her head back with her eyes squeezed shut and the neck veins

2

all popped out. *"The Lord calls you to save the soul of every little gal that's got hot pants."*

I slapped her then. She was insulting the Lord's call in me. I figured she would shut up in a little while, but she went on all night crying.

The next morning I go in the kitchen where she's getting breakfast all red-eyed and quiet as a beat horse and I say brisk, pretending I've overlooked her acting up: "I'm ready to go serve my Master, are you?"

Well, she commences screaming again and throwing things at me. The upshot is that around ten o'clock I'm in the black Chevy with my black suit and two dress shirts driving up the highway alone. And after I done nothing but be a good husband for twenty-eight years, she's gone off to her mother's with the five kids and left me. I was so riled I was driving too fast. I says as I barrel over those red-clay hills We'll just see who will crawl back. We'll just see. It sure won't be me that does the crawling, I got the Lord's work to do and I can't stop for any woman's devilment.

Whoo-wee, it was a hot trip; by noon I was getting mighty hot. But I didn't stop even for a cool drink of water, just kept going up the blistering highway over the red-clay hills with their longleaf pine, sweating like I'm plowing a mule in that August heat.

I hadn't got far when I realize that Lamson's car give off too much heat. It ran okay but it give off more heat than any car I ever saw. And when you carry around a little weight like I do, you suffer with the heat. I passed through Jackson around two, but I still didn't let myself stop.

By four-thirty I hit Grenada and pull in at a City Service station to get seventy-five cents' worth of gas. I figured that would get me there and I would get the rest of my gas free from Giles. I drink two Co-Colas and a Orange Crush and feel a little better, but I hustle on to get on the back roads to Alcoma, cause you don't get on those after dark without getting lost.

It was around five-thirty I set to wondering was I on the right road. I was bumping slow down a old gravel hill road, winding around so you meet yourself coming back, the dust pouring out behind me. Lucky I met a old man walking down the road.

"Howdy, I'm Brother Benson and I'm on my way to Alcoma to preach the Baptist revival, am I going the right way?"

He looks at me like I just broke out of the penitentiary. It's like pulling teeth but I drag out of him that I'm totally out of my way. I have to go back several miles, turn at a mailbox that says Brown, go to a forked oak tree and turn right, go on for two or three miles, past a negro church and several miles more I'll hit the road that'll take me on into Alcoma.

Just past that mailbox I feel it. *Thump, thump, thump.* I brake it easy but the car nearbout pulled off into the ditch. I barely rassled it back. It was the right front tire, flat as a pancake, and not a soul in sight when the dust died down in that sun that was still beating down so it could fry your brains.

I jacked the front up and rassled the old bolts off and just about got the spare on when a colored boy come along, walking barefoot in the dust. I stand back and wipe my face while he finished it up. He says: "You ain't gone use that tire again." Says: "It wadn't nothin' but a recap tire anyway. Like the rest of um you got. You not gone run long on any of them."

That Lamson never told me the car had recaps. I could have taken the tires on my old car; they were better. Now how in the world am I gonna buy tires, the prices they are nowadays? I wonder about that Lamson's salvation.

When I get back in, I'm so wore out and fried down that I almost forget to thank the boy, but I say I'll pray for you, son, and he says Yassuh. Looking after me like he expected to get paid for that little bit of work.

Then the road gets narrower and hardly any gravel left on it, the yellow bitterweeds growing up from the side ditches and leaning in to slap the sides of the car like a curtain parting and then around a bend and up a hill and I'm to the Alcoma Baptist Church.

What there is of it. I get out and look at it, old and leaning in like it might collapse any minute, set up on high concrete triangles. And bitterweed growing right up and around the church steps like no-body set foot there for years. Out back in the cemetery they'd growed wild and high as your thigh.

I come all this way while she ran off to her mother's, and this is what I come for. I will be lucky to get my eats. I sit on the steps mopping my head. It's just a couples of miles up the road to Alcoma and Giles' house where no doubt they'll have some ice tea for me and I can get cooled off, but right then I can't go on. I was wrung out like a dishrag.

But the Lord gave me a third sign. He took pity on this sick and weary pilgrim. I watched the sun setting down behind the treetops, slanting through gold in the trees He made, turning them gold on top over the green, the trees making a long shade now, creating a cool spot on the earth for His creatures. God shows Hisself in shade trees. And His exaltation filled my weary heart. I know He is here watching over me. I praise Him for His being. Without which this mortal life of pain would be worse than nothing. I praise Him and He fills me with joy in my heart. Everything else drops away—her and being wore out and the heat and the recaps and the disappointment of Alcoma Baptist Church—it is all nothing. I feel it just the way I felt when He first came into my heart. The whole world dropped away and I cried to the rafters *God lives, Jesus is my Savior, lucky me.*

After that came a call stronger, frightening, but impossible to deny. I was bald since I was twenty-five and I carry around a lot of weight and most women can look over the top of my head. But He chose me. It's me that brings the light to them. They must listen to me. Yes, she must put away her personal feelings about the choir soprano and, yes, I will admit it was not always singing we were doing in the back of the church, but she is flaunting God not to realize that in sum I am doing His will. And it's not just her; there are those in the church that are misguided, that cannot heed the light I bring then I must gird myself and force God's light on them. It cannot be like this all the time. Many times I must force myself to preach, not feeling it, but must force the words out, carrying on His work blindly, as the mule must plow for his master, to the end of the row till he says stop. But I have faith He sees into my heart and when I have reached my limit, He gives me exaltation, so I can go on with His work.

So when I got back in the car, I swear I will show her I am on God's bidness. Who knows, I might prize some money out of these cheap farmers and make them build a new Alcoma brick church, with me as permanent minister. And no fooling this week with any choir soprano, I promise her.

It was like a confirmation after I drove on through Alcoma's one street of stores facing the railroad track and got to Giles' big brick house at the edge of town. Had nearbout a acre of yard in front and another acre in back. And that back was just lined up like a John Deere army with shiny new green tractors and seeders and discers. His garage had a pickup and a big blue Buick for the wife. And he's the man that's the head deacon of that old rundown church.

Giles hisself comes to the door. He's a red-faced man, short and big-bellied. "Well," he says, "we been expecting you since five o'clock, Brother."

"Well," I says smiling and sticking out my hand, "I didn't have anybody but the Lord to help me get here. How are *you*, dear lady,"

I says to Mrs. Giles, a little thin lady in a flowered dress hurrying up to greet me.

"Wecome, welcome," she says, making up for Giles. "We're just so thrilled to have you. Why, where's Mrs. Benson and your childrun? We were expecting them too."

"Oh, her dear mother," I say quick, "was taken sick sudden. She had to go nurse her mother; she was heartbroken at not getting to come."

She runs off to the kitchen to get me that ice tea and Giles and I sit down in his big living room.

He says several polite things about how happy they are to have me and it was him that insisted they bring me up.

But I let him know I'm not any deacon's preacher. I tell him I was expecting a church in much better repair. I tell him about those bitterweeds needing mowing first thing in the morning. And I say seems like there's a lot of reviving to be done here.

Mrs. Giles comes in with my tea, but it's no time to relax. I say we should start off by praying.

They bow their heads and I pray, finishing up ". . . and let those that have no obligation to You be brought into Thy fold, and let those that already *have* a obligation *see* it. Amen."

Giles' face looks redder when he raises his head and says to Mrs. Giles, "Hadn't you better go see about supper?" "I sure *had*," she says, jumps up, her flowered dress sailing behind her. "I sure hope Brother Benson likes oven-smothered pork chops," she calls, smiling back at me.

"There's nothing I'd rather eat," I say, "short of heavenly manna."

Giles looks so mad, I better back down. "Now," I say reasonable, "I'm sure you deserve a lot of credit just for holding this old church together. You must have a idea of who in the community we should see, who we should concentrate on bringing into the church and who has backslid as well."

He names off some, and I listen close. "Well, that sounds like a good start. But I have often found that the action of one man is what gets a good revival started. Is there one man in a *position* to start the revival off big?" I ask, naturally meaning him, he could give five hundred dollars if he would.

"Yes," Giles says, "there is. A old high-school buddy of mine, a well-to-do drunkard."

I decide right then not to wear myself out on Giles. You'd do as well to get up a running start and butt your head into his brick house as to make him see the light. I passed on to this drunkard.

"Was he a Baptist before he fell away?" I ask.

"No, he's Presbyterian. But they give up on him years ago."

"Is that right? No one at all concerned about his soul. You won't find that among us."

"I've been right concerned about him," Giles says. "Went to school with him. His daddy was the druggist here and his mama was from a fine family. Gene Paul has the drugstore building and a big piece of land alongside the railroad he could sell any day for a big price. But he don't care about nothing. Been drinking for thirty years. I wouldn't be surprised if he was to be found dead any morning. It gets you to worrying about your duty when you see somebody that was a school friend walking around in danger of Hellfire."

"Well," I says slow, like I might, and I might not, agree with him. "It would be the thing for us to visit him. It's more than one drunkard I've been graced to bring to God. And sounds like he would be a good addition to the church as far as its cash needs go."

Giles clears his throat. "About your pay, Brother Benson, there's a lot of members who aren't able to give much . . . We'll have to see how much we can give you when we see how much collection we get during the revival."

Uh-oh. I been waiting for this. They all want salvation but they want it cheap. I would preach for nothing but I got a family to think about. And now some tires too.

"That's between you and your conscience. But I normally get three fourths of the weeks's collection and a guarantee of one hundred dollars."

He turns it off as best he can. But after supper we talk some more and settle it: if I can get this drunkard in the church I'll get two hundred and fifty dollars. If I don't I will only get seventy-five dollars. But he knows hisself that is so little that I make him tag onto it that either way he'll throw in a set of tires from all those he's got laying around in his backyard.

I have rarely preached better. Right that first night when I stepped up to the pulpit a charge went through me. That very night a bunch that had been away from God yielded and came down to the altar and received Him through me. The next night a bigger crowd, and people joining right and left. The third night the church was about to bust with the crowd and Giles was counting that collecting plate. I was filled with joy, His power running through me. I even told Giles I could get this drunkard if only he would produce him.

He was downright apologetic because he couldn't get hold of him for me to visit for three straight days. Finally he come rushing in and says Gene Paul promised to see us this afternoon around three after I've taken dinner with one of the church families. And that's when this durn little Rachel got in to mess me up.

I was taking dinner with one of the deacons that's got a farm a few miles north in the reddest, poorest hills, not much to be got out of without breaking your back. Johnson's a good man, one you can count on to do his share in the church, however little his tithe may amount to, and I was glad to partake of their Christian companionship before taking on the drunkard.

We were sitting in the front room while his wife worked on the dinner, me and Johnson and his married daughter and her young husband that lived with them. They all praised my preaching and then a young girl with long black hair come in.

"Brother Benson, this is my baby girl Rachel," Johnson says. "She's the apple of her daddy's eye."

I noticed her the night before out in the congregation. Short skirts and knees pointing opposite directions, a little devil's workshop.

Seeing her up close, she is pretty as a movie star—white skin and long black hair and big brown eyes with long, curly lashes like a doll's. She's thirteen, fourteen, just turning into a woman. Her arms still slender like a little girl's and her face still has baby fat in the cheeks. But her body is all swollen out in the breasts and hips and behind like a grown woman's. Naturally she's in between, don't know what to make of her body changing and consequently acts like she's mad at the whole world, looking at me with this little frown and her lips poked out pouting. But I know what she's waiting for if she don't.

I take her hand and say: "Honey, I can see you've got Jesus in your heart just by your pretty brown eyes."

Her married sister, over to one side, cuts in: "We hadn't noticed Jesus in her that much ourselves."

The girl cuts *her* eyes around furious at her daddy and he shifts around and looks at the young husband, Alvin. He turns red like he just swallowed a whole chili pepper.

Johnson swallows his big red Adam's apple. "Preacher, we got . . . uh . . . a problem in our family, and I reckon we *need* some counsel from a man of God—"

Right then Johnson's wife rushes in—she's still holding a bowl of hot rice straight from the kitchen—shouting "It's all on the table now, y'all come and eat, *come and eat!*", hustling the two gals to the table and smiling big at me and when she gets near her husband she hisses: *"You keep your big mouth shut, don't go telling one word of that."*

Well, I'm used to wrought-up situations, called upon as I am to counsel the dying and troubled, so I didn't let it worry me. The two girls sit on opposite sides of the table looking away from each other so there's no chance of one having to use the same eyespace as the other. They push their food around, not even pretending to take a bite. I sit alongside Rachel, Betty sits by Alvin, and the Johnsons at each end.

Everybody stays quiet as the dead except Mrs. Johnson who keeps passing me things and saying "Now do try some of my peach pickles, Brother Benson," and "We sure would be grateful for some rain." Old Johnson is bending over his plate eating like a horse.

The young husband across of me is a big strapping fellow, two heads taller than me, big wide shoulders and hips skinny as a fencepost. Slate-blue eyes and light-brown hair in little curls that dips down on his forehead. A fine figure of a man to the ladies no doubt. But he hadn't got nothing to say for hisself. I could talk circles around him.

I carry on with Mrs. Johnson like nothing is wrong. I'll be glad to give my help, but meanwhile I'll enjoy my dinner. It was fried chicken and some right good gravy for the rice and biscuits, nice and hot, and tomatoes and greens just picked that morning from the garden.

We hadn't got all the way to dessert, I was just on my second helpings, when Rachel busts it up. She jumps up with tears in her big brown doll's eyes and shouts, "Oh, Daddy, I love him, I *love* him!"

Betty jumps up and shouts back, "But he's *my* husband and if you ever do again what you did yesterday out by the woodpile I'll snatch you baldheaded!"

Rachel runs acrying to the bedroom and Betty skitters out to the kitchen, her eyes boiling with tears.

It's Mrs. Johnson I feel sorriest for. She'd rather her house burn down as for scandal to come out before the visiting preacher. She looks at me like a drowning person. Old Johnson glares at Alvin like he's ready to shoot him for meddling around with his baby girl.

I'm not going to get that dessert. I sit Johnson back down and ask him what happened at the woodpile.

"Maybe it's my fault, Brother Benson; I won't let Rachel go out yet with boys. I can't see any of them being good enough for her."

9

"I see, and she's bucking against that?" The more he stammers out, the more I say Oh, brother, it sure is your fault. Old Johnson won't let Rachel even go to church with a boy. So what does that leave for a young girl, discovering herself, but look around at home? And she sees this big handsome older man that pets her and teases her and generally acts like she is God's gift to the world, just like her mama and daddy do.

And she's no doubt caught sight of him kissing Betty in the kitchen when he pretends to go get something, and seen those sick-calf looks he gives his wife those nights when he says he's so tired he's going to bed early and asks does she want to too. And no doubt she and this Betty have always fought over things like sisters do and Rachel can't stand the idea of her sister having something she don't.

Rachel had been trailing Alvin, giggling at little private things they talk about. The day before, when Rachel came home from school, she shoots out to the woodpile where Alvin's got his shirt off chopping wood. She worms closer and closer, him with his muscles rippling over his chest while he chops. All of a sudden she grabs him around the neck and kisses him right on the lips.

I can bet what this Alvin would of done next, but Betty is looking out the kitchen window. She screams like a rattler bit her and hollers her mother out in the yard and the whole house has been screaming and crying ever since.

"We don't know what to do," says Johnson, patting his wife that's crying into a dishtowel. "I can't turn my daughter and her husband out. But I'm not going to see Rachel unhappy or taken advantage of."

"You're lucky," I says, "because I've run into just this situation before, and I appreciate all sides of it. You leave it to me to talk to Rachel."

I go back to ber bedroom and ease the door open. She looks up from the bed she's crying on, her eyes spitting fire, her long black hair tumbling all over her breasts. When I sit down and scold her a little, Miss Spitfire comes right back.

"I don't care what you say, I love him," she sasses me and tosses that hair back from her breasts all heaving up.

"But does *he* love you?" I cut back. Her lips goes to trembling and she crumples up, I know how to handle these little gals.

"Now you're not only in the wrong coveting your dear sister's husband, but you're embarrassing yourself as a woman running after a man that don't care about you."

Rachel fires her eyes. Oh, I can't help but feel a urge.

"I don't have to listen to you," she snaps at me. Now ninety-nine percent of the people you let me talk to them two minutes, and they'll be respecting me and Yes, Preachering. This little Rachel could use a lesson.

I close my eyes and pray loud: "Lord, help this little girl to see she is putting herself in danger of Hellfire."

I move over and sit by her on the bed and take her hand. I talk to her soft about how God loves her even though she's doing wrong. She lets me hold her hand but looks down at the pillow. I can see the curliness of her long dark eyelashes against that soft baby-fat cheek and the swell of her blouse and Lordamercy my breathing sounds loud in this little gal's bedroom. Just then Johnson barges in, looking at me hard on the bed.

"Rachel and I are having a good talk, Brother Johnson," I says. "I believe she's feeling sorry for what she done."

"Is that right, honey?" says Johnson squatting down, patting his old work-calloused hand on her little soft white one.

"It's him talking, not me," she shrills out. "I didn't ask him to come meddling around."

I wait for Johnson to bring this little gal in line for talking disrespectful to the preacher, but he's spoiled her rotten. He just herds me right out of there. But Mrs. Johnson is apologizing all the way out the door, and I say "I just hope I helped *some*" before Johnson thanks me too. I drive back to Alcoma and all the way this little gal's got me thinking what I shouldn't. Oh the devil can hide in the prettiest little face.

Giles drives me over to the drunkard's in his big Buick, him in fresh work clothes he's put on for the visit and me still in my morning tie and carrying my Bible. We bounce up this dirt road that goes by a closed-up big two-story house to a old cookhouse at the back. Gene Paul is sitting on the porch tilted back in a cane chair, a shriveled drunk's face he has and a big shock of white hair. I could see that face behind a bank president's desk; he was born to wealth.

Coming up the walk with Giles I boom out: "I've come to bring you the Lord's word, Mr. Wescott."

"*Pres*cott," hisses Giles.

Well, that was the way it went. My mind couldn't focus on this Wescott-Prescott. It was wandering off to eyelashes just when I should be focusing on him.

This drunkard looks like he's already had a drink for the day. He looks sly at Giles.

"So you're running the Baptist Church, Harvey. I bet you got it all down on your books as a tax deduction."

Harvey looks like he spit on his mother. "You can say what you like to me, Gene Paul. The fact is, I done brought this preacher to see you out of concern."

I open up my Bible and pretend like it just fell to the place where I'm reading from. "Here is a message I didn't select, but God selected for you. *And the day shall come when he shall separate the lambs from the goats, the lambs on one side, the goats on the other.* I don't want you to do nothing right now, Mr. Wescott, I just want you to give us a chanct by joining up tonight for some Christian companionship. Open yourself up and let God Hisself speak to your heart.

"Nobody cares for you like God, and you're shutting Him out," I says. "And He loves you better than a mother." Wescott sits back and tears all of a sudden swell in his red drunk's eyes. If I hadn't had that durn little Rachel on my mind, I would have talked mother more—maybe he's lost his recent. But I close off too fast. "Won't you just come tonight?"

He don't say he will or won't, and when we are bouncing back out in the Buick Giles says sharp: "Well, I guess *that* was a waste of time. I don't know about giving you those tires after all."

"You just aren't trusting enough in the Lord," I snap back. But I was feeling as low as ever I have. My mind wandered from His task after all those signs.

Gene Paul doesn't show up that night. But afterward old Johnson asks me if I'll come out the next afternoon to see Rachel. She's setting in her room and won't touch a bite to eat. Oh, I know these tricks. I tell him I got too much of the Lord's work to do. But the next afternoon when I'm preparing in my room at Giles' for the last night of the meeting and one last blowout sermon, praying Gene Paul shows up, I keep thinking on that little gal. Like somebody else is inside me, I get up and go to my car and drive out to Johnson's.

The pa and ma greet me like I'm their long lost son and take me right to Miss Rachel's bedroom. I tap on the door and call out sweet: "It's Brother Benson, can I come in?"

"No. I told you the other day I don't want your meddling."

"Well, I'll just step in anyway, because your mama and daddy are worried sick and somebody's got to talk to you."

I close the door on Johnson's face. She's sitting in a green chenille bathrobe in the middle of her bed, a pout on her pretty lips, black hair hanging long and loose.

"Your mama's worried you not eating."

"Not going to eat. I'm going to run away."

"All by yourself?"

"No. None of your business."

"You not running away with your own sister's husband?"

She shoots me a look like she could sizzle me in a frying pan and pour me out to the dogs. "I will if I want to."

"You mean he's told you he'll run away with you?" I say real soft and understanding. If he has, she won't tell me.

"You leave me alone!" She throws herself on the pillow and busts out crying. So I know Alvin is innocent, all the mooning's on her side alone. I feel sorry for the poor man, his wife mad as hell at him.

I put my hand on her back and she don't move it. Lordamercy, it's been a long time since I've had my hand on such a pretty girl.

I am getting hot as a pistol. I don't know what I'm doing but I know I got to get us out of there. "Now Rachel, I'm going to leave and let you get dressed and I'm going to drive you into church myself. The Lord may show you the error of your ways there."

"I'm not going anywhere," she sobs.

"I'll just put a nice hot sandwich in my car and you eat it while I drive you in and we'll talk on the way about how you're grieving the Lord mooning after your sister's husband."

Her sobs slow down. I know these little gals—they can't go without more than three meals. I can feel her thinking this would be a good way to eat without losing face in front of Betty and still keep her ma and pa and Alvin all worrying about her.

I don't even wait for a reply. "She'll be out soon and ride into church with me," I tell Mr. and Mrs. Johnson. And sure enough she comes out dressed. But going out the door she shoots this at me: "Daddy, I guess you don't care if I ride by myself with the preacher. He's too old and ugly for even you to worry about."

She oughtn't to said that last. It makes me so mad I lose what judgment I have left. I got to have her, no matter my promise to the wife. She eats up that sandwich like a hungry dog and driving along I eye those little roads that run off to nothing but a cow pasture all along the winding hill road.

"Rachel, tell me, is Alvin the only man you're sweet on?"

She looks furious out at those dark little roads to nowhere we're passing.

"I bet there's lots of cute boys in your class at school. Bet they're all sweet on a pretty little gal like you. Idn't there one of them you like too?"

13

"They're all wormy sapsuckers."

I can't help busting out laughing. This Rachel may be only thirteen years old but she is already some woman. I can see those poor wormy sapsuckers, all of them too green to know how to treat this beauty of beauties that keeps them all squeezing their pants under their desks and blushing and acting like young goats, too dumb to know how to treat a woman. Let me show you how this old and ugly man can talk to make a woman hot.

"Rachel, you are just on your way to becoming a beautiful woman, but you're not there yet. Let Brother Benson tell you what he knows you do at night."

"I go to sleep."

"But not before you take off your clothes and look in the mirror at that pretty body naked. That's natural for a little girl that's going to grow up and be a beautiful woman, one that makes men sick just to sidle up to her."

She looks over at me, interested. How did I know that? "And sometimes you touch yourself, on your breasts and elsewhere because they are so new to you, and you like to make those little shocks go through you."

"What kind of preacher are you?" Rachel asks, but her voice ain't mad anymore. She is awed.

"I know what you think about at night. When you're lying there touching yourself. And I know you want to go dancing with boys, but we Baptists don't hold with that."

"I don't see no harm in it," she says, still awed. "A lot of girls do."

"Why, Rachel, if you was to dance with a boy, your breasts— excuse me for using the word, but I'm speaking as your minister— your breasts would rub up against that boy and excite him. And you would want to rub some more and some more. Idn't that what you think about every night?"

"O Lord," she screams, "I can't stand it, I can't stand it, kiss me, I want a man to kiss me."

She set me on fire. I reached over with the car still going over those hills and I set my hand right under her dress between her white thighs and squeezed like the whole world was there.

She screams and throws herself against me, throwing her arms around my neck and kissing me, and the car is already slipping on the shoulder. "Get off," I squeal, "get off—I can't see!" but it is too late. I rassle the car all the way down to the bottom of the ditch where it rams against the gully wall and throws me against the wheel like my lungs was knocked out. And I jump out of the car and it hits me what folly I've done.

She busts out of the car and charges over to me. "Oh, you dirty old man. You reached under my dress," she squeals out.

"What are you talking about?" I said. "You are lucky it was me you met tonight instead of some other man. A man of God that could ease you natural but in God's way."

"You dirty old man! I'm going to tell my daddy on you!"

Whatever heat I had wilts right inside me. This is one of the worse situations I been in. I cain't even jump in my car, stuck in the bottom of a gully, and hightail it out of Alcoma and north Missippi.

"My daddy's gonna get you!" She's crying and scrabbling up the gully bank to get up on the road. I grab her arm and try to pull her back.

"Don't you know *you're* the temptation!" I scream out desperate. "You're a vessel of the devil, girl, with your skirts raked up and your pouting lips." She kicks backward and hits me in the stomach, and I feel like heaving, but I hold on. I can already feel that Johnson's buckshot in my belly.

"You got to see you are a creature in *sin*. You are lucky it was me you met. I can show you you are disgusting in God's sight, and that you must repent."

She jumps almost to the top of the gully, but slips back down the side and falls on her knees, wore out and her head drooping. I clamp my hand on her head, desperate and talking automatic: "O Lord, show this little girl that she must learn what it is to be a godly woman. Show her You gave her natural desires, as You did to us weak men, but she must learn to express them in a way pleasing to you."

She lets out a scream: "O Jesus, I want Your holiness. Make what You will of me!"

My heart surges out. I can't believe I am being graced so easy. She has felt God's power and grace. And, yes, He has given it to me. My flesh is weak like other men's, I was tempted. If it just happened a little different I'd be the one kneeling on the ground begging God to forgive the old Adam in me.

"O holy Jesus," she cries out, "wash me white as snow, it's You I love."

I have seen this before, a little gal just full of womanhood coming on, and the right minister turning it into the proper love of Jesus. Sometimes the gal backslides right away, but I believe I've turned this spitfire for life. It's me she'll remember, not Alvin. She wears herself down crying and thanks me, wiping away her tears, for showing her God's truth. Then she gets down with me in the ditch—she's a real strong little girl—and we push that car right back onto the road.

Well, it seems like my night. Just like I knew in my heart he would, this drunkard Wescott sashays right into church. I preach hard, giving 'em my man dead in Tennessee and all I got, and I get him right up at the final invitational hymn, *Just As I Am*, but something happened and in all the crush of folks coming down to devote their lives to Jesus as I've revealed Him, Gene Paul slips away. A lost soul. I saw Giles looking all around for him and I figured he was going to try to weasel on even the seventy-five dollars and the tires, but I kept on smiling and blessing them all, including Rachel who was kissing Betty and still looking pretty as a doll, and old Johnson thanking me and saying is there anything I can do for you, and I think fast and say "Yes, I need some tires bad," and he says "You got 'em." So the next morning I left Alcoma with my new tires knowing the revival didn't come out just like I wanted, but I didn't feel bad over it because you learn that's just the way revivals are, sometimes they lift you up, and sometimes you just have to take them as they come. *Amen.*

Gloria Norris knows the people and land of her story's setting. Born and reared in Holcomb, Mississippi, she graduated magna cum laude from the University of Southern Mississippi. After receiving her Master's degree from Ohio State University, she worked as an editor in Chicago and New Orleans and now is a publishing executive. She is working on a sequel to "When the Lord Calls."

When the FBI, the state police, and the Texas Rangers find no clues about the robbers who shot up the town, a fourteen-year-old boy thinks he knows how to find them. . . .

TWO

The Homesick Buick

John D. MacDonald

To get to Leeman, Texas, you go southwest from Beaumont on Route 90 for approximately thirty miles and then turn right on a two-lane concrete farm road. Five minutes from the time you turn, you will reach Leeman. The main part of town is six lanes wide and five blocks long. If the hand of a careless giant should remove the six gas stations, the two theatres, Willows' Hardware Store, the Leeman National Bank, the two big air-conditioned five-and-dimes, the Sears store, four cafés, Rightsinger's dress shop, and The Leeman House, a twenty-room hotel, there would be very little left except the supermarket and four assorted drugstores.

On October 3rd, 1949, a Mr. Stanley Woods arrived by bus and carried his suitcase over to The Leeman House. In Leeman there is no social distinction of bus, train, or plane, since Leeman has neither airport facilities nor railroad station.

On all those who were questioned later, Mr. Stanley Woods seemed to have made very little impression. They all spoke of kind of a medium-size fella in his thirties, or it might be his forties. No, he wasn't fat, but he wasn't thin either. Blue eyes? Could be brown. Wore a grey suit, I think. Can't remember whether his glasses had rims or not. If they did have rims, they were probably gold.

But all were agreed that Mr. Stanley Woods radiated quiet confidence and the smell of money. According to the cards that were collected here and there, Mr. Woods represented the Groston Precision Tool Company of Atlanta, Georgia. He had deposited in the Leeman National a certified cheque for twelve hundred dollars and the bank had made the routine check of looking up the credit standing of Groston. It was Dun & Bradstreet double-A, but, of course, the company explained later that they had never heard of

17

Mr. Stanley Woods. Nor could the fake calling cards be traced. They were of a type of paper and type face which could be duplicated sixty or a hundred times in every big city in the country.

Mr. Woods' story, which all agreed on, was that he was ". . . nosing around to find a good location for a small plant. Decentralisation, you know. No, we don't want it right in town."

He rented Tod Bishner's car during the day. Tod works at the Shell station on the corner of Beaumont and Lone Star Streets and doesn't have any use for his Plymouth sedan during the day. Mr. Woods drove around all the roads leading out of town and, of course, real estate prices were jacked to a considerable degree during his stay.

Mr. Stanley Woods left Leeman rather suddenly on the morning of October 17th under unusual circumstances.

The first person to note a certain oddness was Miss Trilla Price on the switchboard at the phone company. Her local calls were all right but she couldn't place Charley Anderson's call to Houston, nor, when she tried, could she raise Beaumont. Charley was upset because he wanted to wangle an invitation to go visit his sister over the coming weekend.

That was at five minutes of nine. It was probably at the same time that a car with two men in it parked on Beaumont Street, diagonally across from the bank, and one of the two men lifted the hood and began to fiddle with the electrical system.

Nobody agrees from what direction the Buick came into town. There was a man and a girl in it and they parked near the drugstore. No one seems to know where the third car parked, or even what kind of car it was.

The girl and the man got out of the Buick slowly, just as Stanley Woods came down the street from the hotel.

In Leeman the bank is open on weekdays from nine until two. And so, at nine o'clock, C. F. Hethridge, who is, or was, the chief teller, raised the green shades on the inside of the bank doors and unlocked the doors. He greeted Mr. Woods, who went on over to the high counter at the east wall and began to ponder over his cheque book.

At this point, out on the street, a very peculiar thing happened. One of the two men in the first car strolled casually over and stood beside the Buick. The other man started the motor of the first car, drove down the street, and made a wide U-turn to swing in and park behind the Buick.

The girl and the man had gone over to Bob Kimball's window. Bob is second teller, and the only thing he can remember about the girl is that she was blond and a little hard-looking around the mouth, and that she wore a great big alligator shoulder-bag. The man with her made no impression on Bob at all, except that Bob thinks the man was on the heavy side.

Old Rod Harrigan, the bank guard, was standing beside the front door, yawning, and picking his teeth with a broken match.

At this point C. F. Hethridge heard the buzzer on the big time-vault and went over and swung the door wide and went in to get the money for the cages. He was out almost immediately, carrying Bob's tray over to him. The girl was saying something about cashing a cheque and Bob had asked her for identification. She had opened the big shoulder-bag as her escort strolled over to the guard. At the same moment the girl pulled out a small vicious-looking revolver and aimed it between Bob's eyes, her escort sapped old Rod Harrigan with such gusto that it was four that same afternoon before he came out of it enough to talk. And then, of course, he knew nothing.

C. F. Hethridge bolted for the vault and Bob, wondering whether he should step on the alarm, looked over the girl's shoulder just in time to see Stanley Woods aim carefully and bring Hethridge down with a slug through the head, catching him on the fly, so to speak.

Bob says that things were pretty confusing and that the sight of Hethridge dying so suddenly sort of took the heart out of him. Anyway, there was a third car and it contained three men, two of them equipped with empty black-leather suitcases. They went into the vault, acting as though they had been all through the bank fifty times. They stepped over Hethridge on the way in, and on the way out again.

About the only cash they overlooked was the cash right in front of Bob, in his teller's drawer.

As they all broke for the door, Bob dropped and pressed the alarm button. He said later that he held his hands over his eyes, though what good that would do him, he couldn't say.

Henry Willows is the real hero. He was fuddying around in his hardware store when he heard the alarm. With a reaction-time remarkable in a man close to seventy, he took a little twenty-two rifle, slapped a clip into it, trotted to his store door, and quickly analysed the situation. He saw Mr. Woods, whom he recognised, plus three strangers and a blonde woman coming out of the bank pretty fast. Three cars were lined up, each one with a driver. Two of the men coming out of the bank carried heavy suitcases. Henry levelled on the driver of the lead car, the Buick, and shot him in the left temple, killing him outright. The man slumped over the wheel, his body resting against the horn ring, which, of course, added its blare to the clanging of the bank alarm.

At that point a slug, later identified as having come from a Smith and Wesson Police Positive, smashed a neat hole in Henry's plate-glass store window, radiating cracks in all directions. Henry ducked, and by the time he got ready to take a second shot, the two other cars were gone. The Buick was still there. He saw Bob run out of the bank, and later on he told his wife that he had his finger on the trigger and his sights lined up before it came to him that it was Bob Kimball.

It was agreed that the two cars headed out toward Route 90 and, within two minutes, Hod Abrams and Lefty Quinn had roared out of town in the same direction in the only police car. They were followed by belligerent amateurs to whom Henry Willows had doled out firearms. But on the edge of town all cars ran into an odd obstacle. The road was liberally sprinkled with metal objects shaped exactly like the jacks that little girls pick up when they bounce a ball, except they were four times normal size and all the points were sharpened. No matter how a tyre hit one, it was certain to be punctured.

The police car swerved to a screaming stop, nearly tipping over. The Stein twins, boys of nineteen, managed to avoid the jacks in their souped-up heap until they were hitting eighty. When they finally hit one, the heap rolled over an estimated ten times, killing the twins outright.

So that made four dead. Hethridge, the Stein twins, and one unidentified bank robber.

Nobody wanted to touch the robber, and he stayed right where he was until the battery almost ran down and the horn squawked into silence. Hod Abrams commandeered a car, and he and Lefty rode back into town and took charge. They couldn't get word out by phone and within a very short time they found that some sharpshooter with a high-powered rifle had gone to work on the towers of local station WLEE and had put the station out of business.

Thus, by the time the Texas Rangers were alerted and ready to set up road blocks, indecision and confusion had permitted an entire hour to pass.

The Houston office of the FBI assigned a detail of men to the case and, from the Washington headquarters, two bank-robbery experts were dispatched by plane to Beaumont. Reporters came from

Houston and Beaumont and the two national press services, and Leeman found itself on the front pages all over the country because the planning behind the job seemed to fascinate the average joe.

Mr. Woods left town on that particular Thursday morning. The FBI from Houston was there by noon, and the Washington contingent arrived late Friday. Everyone was very confident. There was a corpse and a car to work on. These would certainly provide the necessary clues to indicate which outfit had pulled the job, even though the method of the robbery did not point to any particular group whose habits were known.

Investigation headquarters were set up in the local police station and Hod and Lefty, very important in the beginning, had to stand around outside trying to look as though they knew what was going on.

Hethridge, who had been a cold, reserved, unpopular man, had, within twenty-four hours, fifty stories invented about his human kindness and generosity. The Stein twins, heretofore considered to be trash who would be better off in prison, suddenly became proper sons of old Texas.

Special Agent Randolph A. Sternweister who, fifteen years before, had found a law office to be a dull place, was in charge of the case, being the senior of the two experts who had flown down from Washington. He was forty-one years old, a chain smoker, a chubby man with incongruous hollow cheeks and hair of a shade of gray which his wife, Clare, tells him is distinguished.

The corpse was the first clue. Age between thirty and thirty-two. Brown hair, thinning on top. Good teeth, with only four small cavities, two of them filled. Height, five foot eight and a quarter, weight a hundred and forty-eight. No distinguishing scars or tattoos. X-ray plates showed that the right arm had been fractured years before. His clothes were neither new nor old. The suit had been purchased in Chicago. The shirt, underwear, socks, and shoes were all national brands, in the medium-price range. In his pockets they found an almost full pack of cigarettes, a battered Zippo lighter, three fives and a one in a cheap, trick billclip, eighty-five cents in change, a book of matches advertising a nationally known laxative, a white bone button, two wooden kitchen matches with blue and white heads, and a pencilled map, on cheap notebook paper, of the main drag of Leeman—with no indication as to escape route. His fingerprint classification was teletyped to the Central Bureau files and the answer came back that there was no record of him. It was at this point that fellow workers noted that Mr. Sternweister became a shade irritable.

21

The next search of the corpse was more minute. No specific occupational callouses were found on his hands. The absence of laundry marks indicated that his linen, if it had been sent out, had been cleaned by a neighbourhood laundress. Since Willows had used a .22 hollow-point, the hydraulic pressure on the brain fluids had caused the eyes of Mr. X to bulge in a disconcerting fashion. A local undertaker, experienced in the damage caused by the average Texas automobile accident, replaced the bulging eyeballs and smoothed out the expression for a series of pictures which were sent to many points. The Chicago office reported that the clothing store which had sold the suit was large and that the daily traffic was such that no clerk could identify the customer from the picture; nor was the youngish man known to the Chicago police.

Fingernail scrapings were put in a labelled glassine envelope, as well as the dust vacuumed from pants cuffs and other portions of the clothing likely to collect dust. The excellent lab in Houston reported back that the dust and scrapings were negative to the extent that the man could not be tied down to any particular locality.

In the meantime the Buick had been the object of equal scrutiny. The outside was a mass of prints from the citizens of Leeman who had peered morbidly in at the man leaning against the horn ring. The plates were Mississippi licence plates and, in checking with the Bureau of Motor Vehicle Registration, it was found that the plates had been issued for a 1949 Mercury convertible which had been almost totally destroyed in a head-on collision in June, 1949. The motor number and serial number of the Buick were checked against central records and it was discovered that the Buick was one which disappeared from Chapel Hill, North Carolina, on the 5th July, 1949. The insurance company, having already replaced the vehicle, was anxious to take possession of the stolen car.

Pictures of Mr. X, relayed to Chapel Hill, North Carolina, and to myriad points in Mississippi, drew a large blank. In the meantime a careful dusting of the car had brought out six prints, all different. Two of them turned out to be on record. The first was on record through the cross-classification of Army prints. The man in question was found working in a gas station in Lake Charles, Louisiana. He had a very difficult two hours until a bright police officer had him demonstrate his procedure for brushing out the front of a car. Ex-Sergeant Golden braced his left hand against the dashboard in almost the precise place where the print had been found. He was given a picture of Mr. X to study. By that time he was so thoroughly annoyed at the forces of law and order that it was impossible to ascertain whether or not he had ever seen the man in question. But due to the apparent freshness of the print it was established—a reasonable assumption—that the gangsters had driven into Texas from the East.

The second print on record was an old print, visible when dust was carefully blown off the braces under the dismantled front seat. It belonged to a garage mechanic in Chapel Hill who once had a small misunderstanding with the forces of law and order and who was able to prove, through the garage work orders, that he had repaired the front-seat mechanism when it had jammed in April, 1949.

The samples of road dirt and dust taken from the fender well and the frame members proved nothing. The dust was proved, spectroscopically, to be from deep in the heart of Texas, and the valid assumption, after checking old weather reports, was that the car had come through some brisk thunderstorms en route.

Butts in the ashtray of the car showed that either two women, or one woman with two brands of lipstick, had ridden recently as a passenger. Both brands of lipstick were of shades which would go with a fair-complexioned blonde, and both brands were available in Woolworth's, Kress, Kresge, Walgreens—in fact, in every chain outfit of any importance.

One large crumb of stale whole-wheat bread was found on the floor mat, and even Sternweister could make little of that, despite the fact that the lab was able to report that the bread had been eaten in conjunction with liverwurst.

Attention was given to the oversized jacks which had so neatly punctured the tyres. An ex-OSS officer reported that similar items had been scattered on enemy roads in Burma during the late war and, after examining the samples, he stated confidently that the OSS merchandise had been better made. A competent machinist looked them over and stated with assurance that they had been made by cutting eighth-inch rod into short lengths, grinding them on a wheel, putting them in a jig, and spot-welding them. He said that the maker did not do much of a job on either the grinding or the welding, and that the jig itself was a little out of line. An analysis of the steel showed that it was a Jones & Laughlin product that could be bought in quantity at any wholesaler and in a great many hardware stores.

The auditors, after a careful examination of the situation at the bank, reported that the sum of exactly $94,725 had disappeared. They recommended that the balance remaining in Stanley Woods' account of $982.80 be considered as forfeited, thus reducing the lost to $93,742.20. The good citizens of Leeman preferred to think that Stanley had withdrawn his account.

Every person who had a glimpse of the gang was cross-examined. Sternweister was appalled at the difficulty involved in even establishing how many there had been. Woods, the blonde, and the stocky citizen were definite. And then there were two with suitcases—generally agreed upon. Total, so far—five. The big question was whether each car had a driver waiting. Some said no—that the last car in line had been empty. Willows insisted angrily that there had been a driver behind each wheel. Sternweister at last settled for a total of eight, seven of whom escaped.

No one had taken down a single licence number. But it was positively established that the other two cars had been either two- or four-door sedans in dark blue, black, green, or maroon, and that they had been either Buicks, Nashes, Oldsmobiles, Chryslers, Pontiacs, or Packards—or maybe Hudsons. And one lone woman held out for convertible Cadillacs. For each person that insisted that they had Mississippi registration, there was one equally insistent on Louisiana, Texas, Alabama, New Mexico, and Oklahoma. And one old lady said that she guessed she knew a California plate when she saw one.

On Saturday morning, nine days after the sudden blow to the FDIC, Randolph Sternweister paced back and forth in his suite at the hotel, which he shared with the number two man from the Washington end, one Buckley Weed. Weed was reading through the transcripts of the testimony of the witnesses, in vain hope of finding something to which insufficient importance had been given. Weed, though lean, a bit stooped, and only thirty-one, had, through osmosis, acquired most of the personal mannerisms of his superior. Sternweister had noticed this and for the past year had been on the verge of mentioning it. As Weed had acquired Sternweister's habit of lighting one cigarette off the last half-inch of the preceding one, any room in which the two of them remained for more than an hour took on the look and smell of any hotel room after a Legion convention.

"Nothing," Sternweister said. "Not one censored, unmentionable, unprintable, unspeakable thing! My God, if I ever want to kill anybody, I'll do it in the Pennsy Station at five-fifteen.

"The Bureau has cracked cases when the only thing it had to go on was a human hair or a milligram of dust. My God, we've got a whole automobile that weighs nearly two tons, and a whole corpse! They'll think we're down here learning to rope calves. You know what?"

"What, Ran?"

"I think this was done by a bunch of amateurs. There ought to be a law restricting the practice of crime to professionals. A bunch of wise amateurs. And you can bet your loudest argyles, my boy, that they established identity, hideout, the works, before they knocked off that vault. Right now, blast their souls, they're being seven average citizens in some average community, making no splash with that ninety-four grand. People didn't used to move around so much. Since the war they've been migrating all over the place. Strangers don't stick out like sore thumbs any more. See anything in those transcripts?"

"Nothing."

"Then stop rattling paper. I can't think. Since a week ago Thursday fifty-one stolen cars have been recovered in the south and southwest. And we don't know which two, if any, belonged to this mob. We don't even know which route they took away from here. Believe it or not—nobody saw 'em!"

As the two specialists stared bleakly at each other, a young man of fourteen named Pink Dee was sidling inconspicuously through the shadows in the rear of Louie's Garage. (Tow car service—open 24 hours.) Pink was considered to have been the least beautiful baby, the most unprepossessing child, in Leeman, and he gave frank promise of growing up to be a rather coarse joke on the entire human race. Born with a milk-blue skin, dead white hair, little reddish weak eyes, pipe-cleaner bones, narrow forehead, no chin, beaver teeth, a voice like an unoiled hinge, nature had made the usual compensation. His reaction-time was exceptional. Plenty of more rugged and more normal children had found out that Pink Dee could hit you by the time you had the word out of your mouth. The blow came from an outsize, knobbly fist at the end of a long thin arm, and he swung it with all the abandon of a bag of rocks on the end of a rope. The second important item about Pink Dee came to light when the Leeman School System started giving IQ's. Pink was higher than they were willing to admit the first time, as it did not seem proper that the only genius in Leeman should be old Homer Dee's only son. Pink caught on, and the second time he was rated he got it down into the cretin class. The third rating was ninety-nine and everybody seemed happy with that.

At fourteen Pink was six foot tall and weighed a hundred and twenty pounds. He peered at the world through heavy lenses and maintained, in the back room of his home on Fountain Street, myriad items of apparatus, some made, some purchased. There he investigated certain electrical and magnetic phenomena, having tired of building radios, and carried on a fairly virulent correspondence on the quantum theory with a Cal Tech professor who was under the impression that he was arguing with someone of more mature years.

Dressed in his khakis, the uniform of Texas, Pink moved through the shadows, inserted the key he had filched into the Buick door, and then into the ignition lock. He turned it on in order to activate the electrical gimmicks, and then turned on the car radio. As soon as it warmed up he pushed the selective buttons, carefully noting the dial. When he had the readings he tuned in to WLEE to check the accuracy of the dial. When WLEE roared into a farm report, Louie appeared and dragged Pink out by the thin scruff off his neck.

"What the hell?" Louie said.

Being unable to think of any adequate explanation, Pink wriggled away and loped out.

Pink's next stop was WLEE, where he was well known. He found the manual he wanted and spent the next twenty minutes with it.

Having been subjected to a certain amount of sarcasm from both Sternweister and Weed, Hod Abrams and Lefty Quinn were in no mood for the approach Pink Dee used.

"I demand to see the FBI," Pink said firmly, the effect soiled a bit by the fact that his voice change was so recent that the final syllable was a reversion to his childhood squeaky-hinge voice.

"He demands," Hod said to Lefty.

"Go away, Pink," Lefty growled, "before I stomp on your glasses."

"I am a citizen who wishes to speak to a member of a Federal agency," Pinky said with dignity.

"A citizen, maybe. A taxpayer, no. You give me trouble, kid, and I'm going to warm your pants right here in this lobby."

Maybe the potential indignity did it. Pink darted for the stairs leading up from the lobby. Hod went roaring up the stairs after him and Lefty grabbed the elevator. They both snared him outside Sternweister's suite and found that they had a job on their hands. Pink bucked and contorted like a picnic on which a hornet's nest had just fallen.

The door to the suite opened and both Sternweister and Weed glared out, their mouths open.

"Just . . . just a fresh . . . kid," Hod Abrams panted.

"I know where the crooks are!" Pink screamed.

"He's nuts," Lefty yelled.

"Wait a minute," Randolph Sternweister ordered sharply. They stopped dragging Pink but still clung to him. "I admit he doesn't look as though he knew his way home, but you can't tell. You two wait outside. Come in here, young man."

Pink marched erectly into the suite, selected the most comfortable chair, and sank into it, looking smug.

"Where are they?"

"Well, I don't know exactly . . ."

"Outside!" Weed said with a thumb motion.

". . . but I know how to find out."

"Oh, you know how to find out, eh? Keep talking, I haven't laughed in nine days," Sternweister said.

"Oh, I had to do a little checking first," Pink said in a lofty manner. "I stole the key to the Buick and got into it to test something."

"Kid, experts have been over that car, half-inch by half-inch."

"Please don't interrupt me, sir. And don't take that attitude. Because, if it turns out I have something, and I know I have, you're going to look as silly as anything."

Sternweister flushed and then turned pale. He held hard to the edge of a table. "Go ahead," he said thickly.

"I am making an assumption that the people who robbed our bank started out from some hideout and then went back to the same one. I am further assuming that they were in their hideout some time, while they were planning the robbery."

Weed and Sternweister exchanged glances. "Go on."

"So my plan has certain possible flaws based on these assumptions, but at least it uncovers one possible pattern of investigation. I know that the car was stolen from Chapel Hill. That was in the paper. And I know the dead man was in Chicago. So I checked Chicago and Chapel Hill a little while ago."

"Checked them?"

"At the radio station, of course. Modern car radios are easy to set to new stations by altering the push buttons. The current settings of the push buttons do not conform either to the Chicago or the Chapel Hill areas. There are six stations that the radio in the Buick is set for and . . ."

Sternweister sat down on the couch as though somebody had clubbed him behind the knees. "Agh!" he said.

"So all you have to do," Pink said calmly, "is to check areas against the push-button settings until you find an area *where all six frequencies are represented by radio stations in the immediate geographical vicinity*. It will take a bit of statistical work, of course, and a map of the country, and a supply of push pins should simplify things, I would imagine. Then, after the area is located, I would take the Buick there and, due to variations in individual sets and receiving conditions, you might be able to narrow it down to within a mile or two. Then by showing the photograph of the dead gangster around at bars and such places . . ."

And that was why, on the following Wednesday, a repainted Buick with new plates and containing two agents of the Bureau roamed through the small towns near Tampa on the West Florida Coast, and how they found that the car radio in the repainted Buick brought in Tampa, Clearwater, St. Pete, Orlando, Winter Haven, and Dunedin on the push buttons with remarkable clarity the closer they came to a little resort town called Tarpon Springs. On Thursday morning at four, the portable floodlights bathed three beach cottages in a white glare, and the metallic voice of the P.A. system said, "You are surrounded. Come out with your hands high. You are surrounded."

The shots, a few moments later, cracked with a thin bitterness against the heavier sighing of the Gulf of Mexico. Mr. Stanley Woods, or, as the blonde later stated, Mr. Grebbs Fainstock, was shot, with poetic justice, through the head, and that was the end of resistance.

On Pink Dee Day in Leeman, the president of the Leeman National Bank turned over the envelope containing the reward. It came to a bit less than six per cent of the recovered funds, and it is ample to guarantee, at some later date, a Cal Tech degree.

In December the Sternweisters bought a new car. When Claire demanded to know why Randolph insisted on delivery *sans* car radio, his only answer was a hollow laugh.

She feels that he has probably been working too hard.

Born a Yankee, bestselling writer John D. MacDonald was no carpetbagger; most of his enormously popular novels are based in Florida. Born in Sharon, Pennsylvania, on July 24, 1916, he was educated at Syracuse University (B.S., 1938) and Harvard University (M.B.A., 1939). His military service (1940–46) turned him to writing when his wife sold one of his letters home from Burma as a short story. Though his more than sixty novels have included science fiction, most of his work is hard-boiled crime and mystery, with his famous Travis McGee series starting in 1964 with The Deep Blue

Goodbye *and ending with* The Lonely Silver Rain *(1985) and his death in 1986. He has won many prizes, including France's Grand Prix de Litterateure Policiere (1964) and Mystery Writers of America Grandmaster Award (1971).*

In a world where political dirty tricks as old as Babylon are combined with state-of-the art computergraphics, the results can surprise even the most cynical. . . .

THREE

Access to Power
Doug Hornig

Sometimes I wish they held elections *every* year. For private investigators, election times are the best of times. I'm no exception. Though I operate out of Charlottesville, Virginia, which is well removed from the political fast lane, I can still count on it. Whenever a campaign starts to heat up, there are folks out there who are going to find a need for my services.

At the season's peak, it can seem like everyone wants you. The politicians want you, the campaign managers want you, the lawyers want you. Information is power nowhere more so than in politics, and I am in the information business. Not that these characters are going to get *too* close. I still engage in a somewhat unsavory occupation. I'm a lot like the mistresses some of the good old boys keep stashed away down at the shore. They're not for public display, but when they're desired it's with a rabid intensity.

In the old days, a few years ago, I had a monopoly on the area's investigative work. I was the only P.I. in the Charlottesville phonebook. Now I'm just one of several, but I'm currently the most famous. Or infamous, depending on your point of view. There have been a couple of cases which have, shall we say, generated publicity. So during election season I kind of expect something to turn up at my answering service every few days. (I still haven't gotten around to getting an office and I hate those machines that allow you to leave your message at the sound of the beep.) I expect to be told to phone such and such a pol, or one of the innumerable hangers-on who crowd around candidates these days. I *don't* expect the caller to have been a U.S. congressman.

But that's what the lady said. "Congressman Styles' office called. They'd like you to get in touch as soon as possible."

"Congressman Styles?"

"That's what they told me," she said. "I guess you're going big time, Swift."

"Highly visible fish, exceedingly small pond."

"Cute. Is this what passes for one of your philosophical moods?"

"You know," I said, "you may have the world's sweetest voice, but you have a very abrasive personality. You should work on that."

"'Bye, Swift," she said.

I called the number Styles' office had left. The congressman would like to meet with me himself, I was informed. Would tomorrow morning be convenient? I said that would be fine.

Congressman Stafford Styles didn't represent my district, but one of the adjacent ones. It wasn't that odd that he'd be contacting me. There weren't any large cities in his district. I was pretty well known in central Virginia. Even if there were any detectives on his home turf, he might shy away from using one.

Politically, Styles was a moderate. A real one. That's a rarity in Virginia politics. Usually "moderate" is merely a code word for someone whose idea of a rousing time would be dinner with Jesse Helms. The reason for this is that there is a formidable voting bloc out there on the right wing. Liberals are an endangered species almost everywhere in the state. True moderates can make it, but only if they're good and only if they don't seriously antagonize the conservatives.

Styles was good. He was an excellent campaigner and had won reelection three times by successively greater margins. In Washington, he worked hard. He brought federal funds into his district with some regularity. And so far he'd managed to avoid antagonizing anyone of importance. That was an impressive track record.

In addition to his accomplishments, he also *looked* like a successful politician, and that can be just as important. He was tall and had a first-rate tailor. Although only in his mid-forties, he had a full head of silver hair, of which he was proud. He liked it that people could say, "There's a guy who can't be bothered dyeing his hair." It's the distinguishing mark of all great pols that they can simultaneously appear to be almost royalty and yet as down-to-earth as any of us common types. Styles could pull it off. No doubt about it, he was a comer. He was beginning to be talked up for the Senate—by no means against his wishes.

I drove to his office, which was in a small town about an hour from Charlottesville. My feelings were neutral. From what I'd read, Styles seemed like a decent sort. But I'd learned back in my Boston days that you believe in trolls and elves before you ever trust a politician.

On the other hand, their money was good in exactly the same number of places as somebody else's.

I was fifteen minutes late for my meeting. Now, I don't consciously try to keep my elected officials waiting. And I'm sure they don't consciously try to steal my hard-earned green.

"I'm Loren Swift," I told the receptionist.

"You're late," she said. "The congressman is a busy person."

"Me, too. The governor, whatnot. I was a while getting away."

She gave me a sour look and made me sit. I waited for fifteen minutes. Fair enough. Then I was admitted to the inner office.

I'd never seen Styles in person before, but I wouldn't have failed to recognize him. He's one of those people who photograph just about like they are. The silver hair was in place, nicely coiffed and set. None of the facial features called attention to itself, with the possible exception of the jaw, which was square and strong. The only thing I wasn't prepared for was his height. He's very tall. Six-four or -five. That's half a foot or more on me. He also looked physically fit, like maybe he'd played some ball in school and had kept in shape.

We shook hands and introduced ourselves. I told him to call me Swift and he said I could call him Stafford if I wanted to.

"All right," I said. "I take it you didn't invite me here because you need someone to put on a straw boater and go around handing out campaign buttons."

"No, and I don't need another trombone player." He smiled. He had very even teeth. I smiled back. "Let me just say something, Swift."

"I'll save you the trouble," I said. "You want me to know that you're not accustomed to dealing with someone in my, ah, profession."

"But, of course—you would hear that a lot."

"Invariably. I try not to let it bother me."

"I'm sorry," he said. "I didn't mean to imply that I consider myself superior or something. It's that I don't know quite how to, well—"

"Congressman, it's simple. I do just about anything that's within the law. I charge two hundred a day plus expenses." When my client can afford it. He could. "Anything I become involved in is completely confidential. If you've checked me out, which I'm sure you have, you know that I have a reputation for keeping my mouth shut. That's all you really need to know. Next you tell me what kind of problem you have. If I think I can help you, I'll take the job. If I don't, I won't. Either way, I don't talk. How's that?"

He cleared his throat. "That's fine," he said. "Yes, we did check. You come highly recommended. But you have to understand that this matter is somewhat—sensitive."

"They all are, Stafford. The guy who works in a machine shop and wants to know if his wife is cheating, that's a sensitive matter to him. I'll treat you with the same consideration I'd give him."

"Yes, of course. But, well, in my case, in any public figure's case, the problem usually affects more than one or two people."

"Political fallout," I said.

"That's one way of putting it. What happens to me ultimately affects thousands of people in my district. I do a good job for them and I don't want to see them hurt. Are you surprised that I called in an out-of-towner?"

"Not really. I've done political work before. I assume that you'd rather your staff didn't know what was going on. Also that you're afraid a local person might not be impartial. Someone like me is a lot less likely to want to do you harm."

"Very astute," he said. "Politics is a tricky business. You need to take risks, but you need also to minimize the possibility that they'll come back to haunt you. Sometimes your best bet is a complete stranger."

"I understand, and I hope that I'll be able to help you. Could we get down to the job now?"

"Right. Well—this is an election year, as you know." I nodded. "And you are aware of who my opponent is?" I nodded again. "Just how much do you know about him?"

I told Styles what I knew about Elwin Beasley. That the man was as right wing as they come. That his political experience consisted of having served for one term on a county board of supervisors. That he'd been nominated only because he was backed by a coalition of fundamentalist Christian groups and that it was generally thought that his party had given up on defeating Styles but wanted Beasley's supporters in future campaigns and so were throwing them a sop here.

"That's pretty accurate," Styles said when I'd finished. "And you're correct in thinking that I didn't take Beasley's challenge too seriously. But something has—come up." He thought for a minute. "I suppose I have to trust you, don't I?"

He opened one of his desk drawers and took out a large manila envelope. He pulled an 8 × 10 photograph from the envelope and slid it across to me.

"This showed up in my mailbox at home last week," he said, "though it never went through the mail. There was no note, no return address, nothing. I think it's obvious where it came from. You're familiar with the gentleman?"

I nodded. The photograph was of Styles and a black man. The black man was a politically active minister from the southeastern part of the state. His politics were radical left. In fact, he'd been accused many times of being a Communist. He'd responded that he was only working on behalf of his people, but that his people's struggles were identical with those of oppressed people throughout the world. In an attempt to gain further leverage, the minister had threatened Styles' party with massive defections by black voters. These were voters that the party counted on. The party brass hated the minister. So did a large segment of the voting public. For a moderate white politician, then, any association with the activist clergyman was the kiss of death.

In the photograph, both Styles and the minister had broad smiles on their faces. They were embracing.

"You know the damage this could do," Styles said.

"Yeah," I said.

"I don't condone racism," he said. "My record is clean on that score. But there are certain political facts of life that have to be faced in Virginia."

"Shouldn't you have thought of that before you hugged him?"

"That's the point. I never did."

I looked again at the picture. I looked at it closely. I've seen a good number of doctored photos in my time. Most of them are so crude that it's obvious. Others are more cleanly done, but you can still usually tell. This one looked absolutely real.

"Congressman," I said, "you're going to have to level with me."

"I am," he said. "The thing is a fake."

"It doesn't look like one to me."

"I'm telling you the truth. I've never even met the man."

He looked me in the eye when he said it. I did my best to get behind the politician facade, where every line is delivered with equal sincerity. I decided that I believed him.

"All right," I said. "I'll accept that." He was visibly relieved. But the problem was that it didn't really matter if the photo *was* fake. If it were published, it would become the truth. There were a lot of innocent people with ruined reputations who'd learned that lesson the hard way. "But someone's done a hell of a job here," I added. "I assume that you take this as a threat."

"Yes. It would appear that I'm being shown how nasty the campaign might get. I've never had to fight that hard. Now they're testing me. I'd say they figure that I can't take the heat."

"And can you?"

There was a lengthy pause. "I don't know," he said finally. "And that's not the issue, really. I shouldn't have to put up with something like this. There are some basic unwritten rules here. You try to cast your opponent in an unfavorable light, sure, but out-and-out lying, that's not playing fair."

It might not be fair, but it was hardly unheard of. A number of past elections had been decided when the dead suddenly rediscovered the ability to cast a vote.

"What do you want me to do?" I asked.

"I'm not sure," he said. "I want an honest campaign. What do you suggest?"

"Well, there are a couple of possibilities. I could try to persuade the opposition not to do this kind of thing. To be honest, they're not likely to respond to friendly persuasion. And I don't personally do the other sort. If you want to hire decent muscle, I can put you on to some, though."

"Good God, no," he said quickly. "I'm not going to turn myself into what I'm working against."

He seemed sincere. "All right," I said. "I could try to cut a deal with them. Do you want that?"

"I don't know. It depends on the deal."

"We're assuming one which doesn't cost you that much. I'll feel them out."

"Be—discreet, will you, Swift? I can't authorize you to make any agreements on my behalf."

"Okay," I said. "Now, about the only other thing is to try and find out where they got this photo. If I can do that, it might give you enough clout that you could dictate the terms of the deal. But I have to be straight with you—you can hire me, and I can give it my best shot, and we can still come up empty. I'd say chances are pretty good that that's what will happen. This one is a hard go."

"I'll hire you," Styles said.

We settled on my fee. He promised a nice bonus if I was able to bail him out. It sounded good to me. I slid the photo back into its envelope and took it with me. It was the first time I'd ever been employed by a congressperson.

Elwin Beasley also had an office in the little town. I walked over

36

there, enjoying the Indian-summer weather. It's a nice time of year in Virginia—still warm, with temperatures often getting into the eighties. And the air usually stays dry until the late-fall rains arrive.

I presented myself to Beasley's receptionist. I told her that I represented Stafford Styles. That was the secret word. She did a quickie phone check and informed me that I was in luck. Mr. Beasley was in and he'd consent to see me. I wasn't sure that fit *my* definition of luck.

Beasley kept me waiting for forty-five minutes. He could have been busy, but more likely it was an attempt to gain an early advantage. It didn't bother me. When you do investigations for a living, you learn how to wait or you end up in Bananaville.

I passed time reading some of the candidate's campaign literature, if you could call it that. Literacy it was not. I'm no scholar of the language, but even I could tell that the writing was full of grammatical errors and crude sentence structure. I thought that that might be intentional. Elwin was trying hard to portray himself as the hero of the common man.

Politically, he was somewhere east of Genghis Khan. He called for immediate military intervention in Nicaragua, and an invasion of Cuba as well. He favored jail sentences for anyone receiving an abortion and the death penalty for anyone performing one. He opposed affirmative action of any kind and, naturally, weighed in for federal aid to private schools. He desired that all national parklands and forests be thrown open to mining companies, foresters, and anyone else who was prepared to "put the land to use."

I was setting down one pamphlet and reaching for another when I got the call from the man.

Beasley had a spartan office. A desk and two chairs and that was it. The man himself was impressive. Not quite as tall as Styles but bigger around. A bear. He had silver hair, too, but it was unkempt. There was a good deal of it, jutting out here and there from his head, which was large. His complexion was very ruddy. I would have pegged him for a juicer if he wasn't well known for a strong stand against alcohol. He'd even gotten the folks in his home county to vote on going dry. He'd lost that one. Beasley's county was poor, and the poor don't like to drive somewhere else to ease their pain.

The candidate looked me over.

"I'm Loren Swift," I said, shaking his hand. He tried to crunch my bones but I slipped his grip before he could do any real damage.

"Sit down," he said. We sat. "And who are you, Mr. Swift?"

"I represent Stafford Styles."

"What does that mean, 'represent'?"

"I work for him."

"Ah. You must be new. I don't recollect the name."

"I am new," I said. "There are some new problems."

"Mr. Do-gooder Liberal ain't got any new problems. All he's got is the same old one. He's a pantywaist. He ain't tough enough for the job and he should step aside and let someone in who is."

"You tough, are you?"

He grinned. "You want to try me?"

I'd be giving away four inches and a good fifty pounds. But he'd accumulated fifteen or so more years. It was a stupid thing to even think about. We were supposed to be adults.

"I'll take a raincheck," I said. "It seems like there must be better ways to resolve a dispute."

"What exactly are we disputating?"

"I think you know the answer to that."

"Mr. Swift, I don't care for guessing games."

"All right. Let's say that Congressman Styles intends to run a hard but clean race and that he hopes you will be doing the same."

Beasley laughed. "I'll bet he does," he said. "I'll just bet he does. He getting worried, is he?"

"He doesn't strike me as a worrier."

"What are you offering, Swift?"

"I'm not 'offering' anything. I'm trying to find out if you're an honest man."

"Where you from, boy?" he asked.

"What does that matter?"

"I know you ain't no native Virginian. I don't believe you understand how our political system works down here."

"Mr. Beasley," I said, "I'm orginally from Boston. The system doesn't get any dirtier than it is up there. I may not know all the local ins and outs, but it'd take a lot to surprise me."

"What're you in this for, you don't mind my asking. You look like a cop."

"I work for Congressman Styles. I'm not a cop,"

You his bodyguard? . . . Naw, you're supposed to come over here, lean on me a little bit, that it?"

"We've gone over why I'm here," I said, trying to keep the annoyance from creeping into my voice. "Do you think we can come to some kind of accommodation?"

"Accommodation. Now there's a nice word. Sure, we can come to an accommodation. If *Mister* Styles decided to retire, I'd feel very accommodated."

He sat there, looking smug. His hands were folded over his ample belly. Come to think of it, maybe I'd wind up punching him out after all. "Look," I said, "either we've got something to discuss or we don't."

"Discuss," he said. "I ain't stopping you."

"You're planning on releasing some information that could be damaging to your opponent."

He shrugged. "I don't reckon I could comment on that."

"That information is false."

"I wouldn't do such of a thing."

I sighed. "All right. This not-false information hasn't yet been released. What are you waiting for, Beasley? Do you want to make some kind of deal, or what?"

"I don't really know what information you're talking about. *Mister* Styles done some things that are embarrassing to him, then he oughtn't have done them. The voting folks have a right to know who they're voting for, I say. And I don't think there's any kind of deal to be had here. We need to get the man out of Washington. If he was to leave volunteer, well—" he shrugged again "—I wouldn't be the one as to blame him."

"What's the time frame?" I said.

"Say what?"

"Ah, never mind. All right, Beasley, I get the point. But you can't win an election by lying to the public. They'll find out."

I regretted saying it, it sounded so lame.

He smiled. "Swift," he said, "if I say something's so, then it's so."

I got the number of Operation Reform, the minister's grass-roots political organization down in southeastern Virginia. It was a group that was making a lot of people nervous. If it decided to form a party of its own, there was going to be a lot of turmoil.

The folks at Operation Reform were helpful. They told me that the minister was at a speaking engagement in Richmond and they gave me the number of the Richmond office. I phoned Richmond and introduced myself as a representative of Congressman Styles. I asked for a few minutes of the minister's time. I told them it'd take me about three hours to get to Richmond. They said, well, maybe I could get a little time in the late afternoon, but how did they know who I was? I gave them the number at Styles' office and told them to check me out and call back. They did, and we set up an appointment.

I didn't much feel like driving all the way to Richmond, but I felt it was my only option. Beasley was going to wait until Styles made him some kind of offer. If he didn't get what he wanted, he'd turn the photo loose. How long this would take I didn't know, but I couldn't afford to wait around to find out. I needed to take some kind of positive action. Trying to establish if the photo was genuine seemed like the best bet.

It was a long, boring drive. It landed me up in Tobacco Town at an aging clapboard-sided house. Outside was a sign with Operation Reform's logo printed on it. The sign was in green, black, and red, the colors of the disenfranchised nation within a nation.

I wasn't quite prepared for the Reverend's physical presence. He wasn't a big man, but he had the aura of power about him that's worth any amount of size. You knew that this was a leader. I wasn't surprised that he made a lot of people nervous.

"And what exactly is it that you do, Mr. Swift?" he asked me. "The congressman's office was rather vague."

Once you got past the power, he had a pleasant, friendly face. His black hair was speckled with grey. He smiled a lot. I reminded myself that while he was a crusader, he was no violent political hothead. From all reports, his ultimate trust was genuinely in the Lord.

"Troubleshooting," I said. "I'm a troubleshooter."

He gave me an ironic smile. "You *want* something," he said.

"In a manner of speaking."

"There's no manners of speaking here. I don't see you'all from one year to the next without you want something. Sooner you get to it the better."

He was right, there was no sense in beating around the bush. I'd been tabbed as an emissary from the white establishment. Already my welcome was beginning to decay. So I handed him the photo. He looked at it and immediately burst out laughing.

"It's a fake, isn't it?" I said.

"Well," he said, "that'll be the day all right, that'll be the *day*. What did you want me to do with this?"

"Nothing. I wanted to know if it was real. Now I know."

"That be it, then?"

"Well," I said, "not really. I was hoping we could—discuss it."

He chuckled. "You people break me up," he said. "Why can't you'all just talk straight out to a black man? What is it, you think we're just that dumb?"

"No, I don't think that at all."

"You may not think it, but you sure act it. Let's see if I can't help you out. You got this picture, which I think is good for a laugh, but your boss don't see it that way. He thinks it might do him some harm when the white folks vote. So he wants to know, am I gonna do anything about it? That about cover it?"

"That about covers it. I don't care for the situation any more than you do. Nevertheless, it's the way things are. Now you might not be crazy about Styles, but, Reverend, you've *got* to like Beasley a whole lot less."

"Mr. Swift, I'd appreciate it if you didn't try to put yourself in my shoes. It's not possible, you know?" I nodded. "Good. Yes, I'm aware of the political facts of life in the Commonwealth of Virginia. Lived here all my days. That's what we're going to change, those facts. And the way to do that is not by jumping *every* time some white political asks us to. Styles or Beasley, it don't matter. What matters is building our own power base. You follow me?"

"I follow you," I said. "How about if the photo's published? Would you be willing to say it's a phony?"

"I do that, I'm still just playing their pawn, ain't I?"

"You're a hard case, Reverend. You really *don't* care who wins, do you?" He shook his head. "I believe you enjoy watching them squirm."

"Me?" He feigned astonishment. "How could you say something like that about me?" He grinned.

Damned if I didn't find myself grinning along with him.

I drove back home to Charlottesville running out of options, but I had one idea left. I called my pal Jonesy. He works for the *Daily Press* and can sometimes dig up things I can't.

"Swift," he said, "the intangible man."

"All right," I said, "all right. I realize I haven't been over to watch the O's with you in a while. I've been busy, Jones. Soon, okay?"

"Sure, sure. You need something. What is it?"

"Where could I go to get a photo retouched? I want the best."

"Hmmm," he said, "you've got me. Is it worth a six-pack of Moosehead?"

"Yeah." The man worked better when he had an incentive.

"Okay. One of our photographers knows all about that stuff. I'll ask him in the morning. Get back to ya."

Which he did, about nine the following day.

"Swift," he said, "let me ask you something. How good a job are you looking to get done?"

"I want to put two photos together so it looks like they always were."

"Okay. In that case you're gonna have to go out of town. There are some people locally who can do a nice job. But a professional could spot it. If you want it so even a pro can't say for sure, then you gotta go state-of-the-art. That's a Chromacom. Or a Scitex, one."

"What in God's name is that?"

"Digital retouching, Swift. They do it with lasers and computers now. It beats all hell out of a knife and a bunch of darkroom chemcials. All the big boys have these machines. You know—*Time, National Geo*, everybody. But the things are a bit pricey. Over a mil each. No one in Charlottesville could justify laying out that kind of bread. There aren't even any in Richmond. You'll have to go to D.C."

"What am I supposed to do, walk into your beloved *Washington Post* and ask to use their—what is it?"

"Chromacom. Naw, they wouldn't let you. Fortunately, I'm a thorough man. Got a pencil handy?" He gave me an address in Northwest D.C. "That's an outfit called Capitol Lasergraphics. They must do an awful good business, because they've got one. You can rent it if you want. If your, uh, client can afford it."

"How much?" I asked, and I nearly fainted when he told me. I thanked him and promised him a couple of six-packs of Moosehead.

Then I phoned Styles' office. He wasn't there, but I told them to track him down, give him my name, and tell him it was important. He called back in half an hour. I filled him in on my lack of progress thus far and said I wanted to go to D.C. to talk with some retouching experts. I told him I might need to rent the Chromacom and how much it would cost. He took it well. I asked him to get in touch with Capitol Lasergraphics and say that one of his aides was on the way and would they give me every possible attention. He agreed to do it.

Before leaving Charlottesville, I stopped by the *Daily Press* and had Jonesy pull me a few items from the morgue. The seed of an idea was beginning to sprout.

Capitol Lasergraphics had several floors of a shiny glass building just off Connecticut Avenue. They were doing just fine. You didn't need major-league brains to figure out how business could be so good that they'd be able to afford million-dollar equipment. The ability to manipulate information gives you access to power. And if you have access to power, you make money. Serious money. A congressional race in rural Virginia was small potatoes, relatively speaking, but what had happened there could happen anywhere, up to and including the highest levels of power. The implications were unsettling.

My guide at Capitol was a bouncy little fellow named Robert (call me Bob) Beauregard. He was short and chubby, smiled incessantly, and had almost no hair on his head.

"Congressman Styles is a fine man," Bob said. "How may we help you?"

"The congressman is concerned about the potential of the new digital retouching machines," I said. "He wants me to investigate them. Do you do any political work here?"

"I'm not sure what you mean."

"If someone wanted you to create a photo of Ronald Reagan doing the two-step with Yassir Arafat, would you do it?"

"I see," he said. "You want to know if we make judgments of content. Let me just say one thing, Mr. Swift. The law is absolutely clear in this matter. There is nothing illegal about doctoring a photograph. We do nothing illegal here. The man who makes *use* of the photograph, now *he* is open to a libel suit if that photo causes mischief, of course."

"I'm not sure that answers my question," I said.

"Perhaps not. Sure, we'd put Reagan and Arafat together. The effect would be rather humorous, and I suppose that would be the intent. We don't feel it's our function to act as censor."

"Isn't there a moral issue involved?"

"Not really. That's the business of whoever uses our services. Our business is graphics."

"And business appears to be booming."

He shrugged as if it wasn't worth mentioning. I considered what I might do next. There was a fair possiblility the Beasley people had had the work done here. It was the closest place. But Capitol's client list was undoubtedly confidential. Just as I undoubtedly could use Styles to pry the information out of them. However, I had no way of knowing what name the job had been requested under. And even if I did find that a job had come in from central Virginia, what then? Capitol would be discreet. They wouldn't keep copies of the work unless the client asked them to. In this case, there was no chance the client would have asked them to.

"Could I see the machine?" I asked.

"Certainly," said Bob.

It took up most of a small room. "This is the laser scanner," he explained, gesturing at a formidable piece of machinery. "It's the first step in the process. You lay the material to be worked on here." He pointed to a clear glass drum. "The scanner then translates that material into precise digital code, which is stored in the computer." He indicated the console. "At that point, we can call up what we have and display it on the large viewer here. Then we can do anything we want with it.

"The computer reduces the overall visual image to tiny elements called pixels. A pixel can be smaller than the grain in a photograph. Since we can make changes at the pixel level, we can obviously manipulate the image at will, and our efforts will be undetectable. Questions?"

Yeah, I thought, lots of questions. But they weren't technical ones. I handed him the folder I'd brought from Charlottesville.

"Show me how it works," I said.

For the next four hours, I watched Bob in action. In a way, it was a truly depressing experience. Because, for me, it was the end of photography as something I took for granted. I knew that I'd never again be able to completely trust a photograph.

The rest was easy. I made an appointment to see Beasley the following day and drove back down to his office. We sat across the desk from one another.

"I hope you're not wasting my time, Mr. Swift." he said.

"Beasley," I said, "I don't like you or anything you stand for. I don't know what's worse, the dirty things you do or the fact that you hide them behind pious pamphlets."

His ruddy face got even ruddier. His right fist clenched reflexively. He opened his mouth to say something.

"Just shut up," I said. "Now what I do know is that this campaign is going to be a clean one. The voters of this district may in their lack of wisdom see fit to send you to Congress, but it's not going to be due to any of your cheap lies."

I opened my folder and flipped the photograph across to him. He stared at it, uncomprehending at first. Then the lines of rage formed around his mouth and eyes.

I'd had Bob join three separate photos. The first was a stock picture of a Charlottesville motel. I'd chosen one of Beasley in which he had a somewhat surprised expression on his face. And the third was of Virginia's most outspoken feminist, a thirty-year-old woman who had fought long and hard for the ERA. Bob had done a masterful job. In the end result, Beasley and the woman were seen to be emerging from a motel room. He looked like he'd been surprised by the photographer. She was beaming at him like someone so in love she didn't care. The two of them were holding hands. That had blown me away, that the machine could perfectly interlock their hands. Bob had laughed and called it kid stuff.

"You sonofabitch," Beasley growled.

"Save it," I said wearily.

I got up. As I left, I said over my shoulder, "Keep it honest and let the voters decide."

That evening I talked to Styles. He was back in Washington. I told him what I'd done and asked him if he wanted a written report. He said no, just send the bill. I told him he'd also be getting a bill from Capitol Lasergraphics and how much it would be. He groaned, but said that it'd be worth it if Beasley played fair, because then there was no way he could win.

"If all goes well," he said, "you should get that little bonus in time for Christmas. You did a good job, Swift. I'll remember that. Though I must admit this thing cost me rather a bit."

"Congressman," I said, "believe me. It cost me, too."

Born in New York City in 1943, Doug Hornig attended William and Mary College and has lived in Virginia for the last ten years. A fulltime writer since 1984, his first novel, Foul Shot, *was nominated for the Mystery Writers of America Award as the Best First Novel of the Year for 1984. Three others have followed.*

The bored Treasury Department agent who requested field assignment discovers much more than moonshine in the hills of Lasher County, Georgia. . . .

FOUR

All the Heroes Are Dead

Clark Howard

The district director finished perusing the personnel file and shook his head dubiously. "Are you sure you've selected the right man for this assignment?" he asked his chief investigator. "We need someone to infiltrate a very close-knit bootlegging operation in Lasher County, Georgia. That's redneck country. This agent David Berry somehow doesn't seem the type for it. His background, I mean: political-science major at Yale, midwestern upbringing, interests in soccer and the theater—"

"His interest in the theater is precisely one of the reasons I selected Berry," the chief investigator said. "He's an amateur actor, belongs to a little-theater group in Alexandria. It's going to take someone who can put on a very good performance to fool those people in Lasher County."

"Maybe a better performance than you think," the director said. "The state authorities put an undercover man down there last year. He dropped out of sight and hasn't been heard from since. There are lots of deep woods and swamps in that part of Georgia. Good places to dispose of a body."

"I still feel Berry's the man for the job," the chief insisted.

"All right," the director said with a quiet sigh. "Have him come in."

The chief rose and summoned David Berry from an outer office. When the director saw him, his doubts were by no means assuaged. Berry's hair was styled, he wore a three-piece Brooks Brothers suit, and carried an attache case. He belonged, the director thought, in the bank examiners section, not in illegal whiskey.

47

"Berry, you've been with Treasury for three years now," the director said. "According to your file, all of your assignments up until now have been desk work. Do you think you can handle an undercover job?"

"Yes, sir, I do," Berry replied. "I've been eager for field work for quite some time now." His voice was precise, educated.

"You've read the Lasher County file," the director said, "so you know what the case is all about. An estimated one hundred thousand gallons of liquor is being manufactured illegally somewhere down there every year. That's not what we consider a huge operation, by any means. The government loses tax revenue on about two-and-a-half-million dollars annually based on their selling price, which is around one-third the cost of legal liquor, so we wouldn't go broke if we let them operate indefinitely. But that's not the point. The issue here is a violation of the law—manufacturing liquor without a license and distributing liquor without a tax stamp."

"Most of their sales, as you know from the file," the chief said, "are to rural residents in south Georgia and Alabama, and northern Florida. People that are commonly known as 'rednecks.' They live in and around places like the Apalachicola Forest, the Osceola Forest, and the Okefenokee Swamp. That's where we think they've got their manufacturing plant—their whiskey still: in the Okefenokee."

David Berry nodded. "Yes, sir, I noticed in the file that at one point there was nearly a six-hundred-percent increase in the sale of Mason jars in the swamp communities."

The chief smiled. "That's how we pinpointed the manufacturing site. Normally they make runs about a hundred miles away for their Mason jars, but apparently they ran out of them from their regular suppliers and had to buy locally. It was a sure tipoff—you can't bootleg hooch without Mason jars."

The director, still looking worried, sat forward and folded his hands on the desk. "Berry, I want to emphasize to you the potential peril of an assignment like this. You'll be going into a completely foreign environment, among people who are totally different from the kind you're accustomed to associating with."

"I know that, sir," Berry said. "I plan to spend a few weeks traveling around small towns in northern Georgia to learn how to act the part. I fully intend to prepare for the role."

"Your dress, you mannerisms, your speech—you'll have to change everything."

"Well, Ah don't think Ah'll have too much trouble with the speech, suh," Berry said, suddenly falling into a very good southern drawl. "Ah been listenin' to some dialect records over at that there linguistic department at the university an' Ah spect Ah'll have the talkin' down pat pretty quick like." Smiling, Berry reverted to his own speech pattern. "As for the clothes, visits to a couple of thrift shops and surplus stores will take care of that. And the mannerisms—well, just opening the beer can and drinking out of it ought to do for a start."

The chief flashed an I-told-you-so smile at the director. "We've established a complete new identity for him," he said. "His name will be Dale Barber. We chose that surname because Barber is very common in the southeastern U.S. He'll have an Alabama driver's license, army discharge, social-security card, and two membership cards to private after-hours clubs in Tuscaloosa. We picked that city because it's far enough away from where he'll be operating to make it difficult for anybody to check up on him, and it's large enough— about a hundred fifty thousand—to throw them off if they do. I think we've got all the bases covered, sir."

"It certainly seems like it." But there was still a trace of doubt in the director's voice, a gut feeling of reluctance inside him, some instinct—perhaps based on his thirty years of law-enforcement experience—that told him not to give David Berry the Lasher County assignment. It was nothing he could put his finger on and he knew if he tried to explain it to his chief investigator he would sound as if he were procrastinating. Based on the chief's recommendation and Berry's apparent ability to discharge the assignment, he was left with no choice. "All right, Berry, the job's yours," he said.

He had a feeling that he would never see the young agent again.

Three weeks later, David Berry was cruising down Highway 441, which ran parallel to the Okefenokee Swamp. He was driving a '78 Chevy pickup with a roll-bar he'd bought with agency money in Tuscaloosa. A battered suitcase and a cardboard box containing his extra clothes rode in the rear bed along with a nearly bald spare tire, a lug wrench, an empty gas can, and a six-pack of Miller's beer. In one corner of the pickup's back window was a decal of a Confederate flag. Inside the cab was a rifle rack with a .22 pump on it. A Slim Whitman tape was playing in the dashboard deck.

When David got to DeSota, the little town that was halfway down on the edge of the swamp, he circled the tiny town square once and pulled up in front of Luther's Café.

Getting out of the truck, he stretched and twisted some of the stiffness out of his back and shoulders. He knew that several people sitting by the window in the café had already noticed him, his truck, the Alabama plates. His appearance, he knew, fit the picture—old faded Levis, an inexpensive plaid cotton shirt, a blue denim vest, and a soiled yellow visor cap with an STP patch on it. The cap was pushed to the back of his now unstyled hair. On his feet he wore low-heel Frye boots.

Going inside, David sat at the counter and looked at the handwritten menu. A waitress came over to him—redheaded, well built, a sexy wide mouth, too much mascara. She wore a white uniform that had "Tommy Sue" embroidered above her left breast.

"Hi," she said, setting a glass of water in front of him.

"Hi, Tommy Sue," he said, reading her uniform. "Ah'll have three chicken wings, some coleslaw, an' fried okra. An' iced tea."

Their eyes met just long enough for them to realize it. Then David reached down the counter and retrieved the sports section of the Tallahassee *Democrat*. He pretended to read, but he was actually thinking about Eileen, his girl friend. She was working on her master's in history at Georgetown. Eileen was tall, slim, chic, and proper—almost too proper sometimes. She had not been at all pleased about this field assignment.

"Georgia!" she had said. "Really, David. Can't you get out of it somehow? The Clarys' lawn party is coming up."

"I don't want to get out of it," he had told her. "This is my first opportunity in three years to get away from a desk."

"But *Georgia!* Couldn't you get an assignment someplace close?"

"There aren't many illegal whiskey stills in Bethesda or Arlington or Alexandria," he pointed out. "We have to go where the violation is. I'm sorry about the Clarys' party."

Tommy Sue brought his food and David put the paper aside. He began to eat the chicken wings with his fingers. Out of the corner of his eye he saw the fry cook come out of the kitchen, wiping his hands on a greasy apron. "That your pickup with the 'Bama plates?" he asked.

"Tha's me," David said with his mouth full.

"Where'bouts in 'Bama you from?"

"Tuscaloosa. Ax'ly Ah'm from Coker, a little piece north. But ain't nobody ever heard of Coker, so Ah say Tuscaloosa."

The fry cook nodded. "Jus' passin' through?"

David shook his head. "Lookin' for work. Heard up in Waycross that y'all had a canning factory down here that might be hirin' on."

"Cannin' factory shut down last week. Soybeans done poorly this year. Nothin' to can."

David shook his head in disappointment and kept on eating. In a booth near the window sat three men he could sense listening with interest to his conversation with the fry cook.

"Know of anything else around?" he asked.

"Such as?"

David shrugged. "Ah ain't particular. Fillin' station, farm work, construction."

"Things is real slow right now. Maybe fu'ther south. Florida maybe."

David grunted. "Ah'm runnin' low on lookin' money. There a poolroom in town?"

"Right across the square. Leon's Pool Hall."

"Maybe Ah can pick up a couple dollars."

"Don't count on it," the fry cook said.

There was a motel called Harley's Motor Inn a mile out the highway: twelve units that usually filled up only during the legal fishing season. The season was past now and the alligators were breeding in the swamp waters, so there was no one at Harley's except a notions salesman who worked the territory between Macon and Orlando. The salesman was in Unit One, so Harley put David in Unit Two when David drove out after lunch and checked in.

"How long you be staying?" Harley asked.

"Couple days maybe. Lookin' for work."

"Things is real slow around here. Be twelve-fifty a night, first night in advance. No playin' the television after midnight."

David carried his old suitcase and cardboard box into the room and unpacked. Then he pulled off his boots to stretch out on the bed for a while. It was funny about those boots. He had expected to hate them. His taste ran to Carranos: glove-leather, Italian-made. But these Frye boots, after a week of breaking in, were as comfortable as anything he'd ever put on his feet. It was the same with the Chevy pickup. In Washington he drove a low-slung Datsun 280-Z and rode close to the pavement. The cab of the pickup was up high, above everything except motor homes and tractor rigs. You saw a lot more in a pickup cab than in a sportscar.

David spent the afternoon resting, then at sunset he showered, put on clean jeans and a striped shirt, and drove back uptown. He found a phonebooth next to the post office and called the chief on a blind telephone number with a memorized credit-card number. "I'm settled," he said when the chief answered. "I should be able to spot the delivery truck tonight. Unless you hear from me to the contrary, I'm ready for stage two."

"I understand," the chief said. "Good luck."

David left the booth and walked across the street to Luther's Café again. Tommy Sue was still on duty. "You work all the time?" he asked when she handed him the supper menu.

"Girl's got to make a living," she answered. While he studied the menu she said, "I saw you in the phonebooth. Calling your wife like a good little boy?"

"Don't have no wife. Let me have the fried catfish and hush puppies. Iced tea. Pecan pie for dessert."

"Calling you girl friend then?" she asked as she wrote down his order.

"Calling my mama. Your curiosity satisfied now?"

"Well, 'scuse me for livin'," she said huffily.

Throughout his meal David occasionally caught her glancing at him. Whenever he did, he threw her a smile or a wink. She turned her nose up at him. When he paid his supper check he said, "Next time Ah talk to Mama, Ah'll tell her you said hello."

"Don't bother."

"No trouble. Ah'll tell her Ah met this here little Georgia peach who's too pretty to even describe."

"You might's well save it, Alabama. You got off on the wrong foot with me with that curiosity crack. I was only makin' small talk."

Outside the window David saw a Buick drive up to Leon's Pool Hall, followed closely by a Dodge pickup. One man got out of the Buick, two out of the pickup, and they all went inside. They were the same three who had listened so intently to David's conversation with the fry cook at noon.

"Let's you and me start all over," David said, turning his attention back to Tommy Sue. "At breakfast."

"I don't work breakfast," she told him. "I come on at eleven-thirty."

"What time do you get off?"

"Nine-thirty—when we close. I work ten hours a day, four days a week. That way I get to spend three days a week with Lonnie."

"Lonnie?"

"My little boy. He's four. My mamma keeps him for me, over in Talbot."

"Oh." David glanced out the window again and his thoughts went momentarily to the Dodge pickup. It looked like the right truck, he thought. The one the department had come so close to catching several times.

Tommy Sue, taking his silence for disinterest, handed him his change, shrugged, and started to walk away.

"Hey, wait a minute. What time did you say?"

"What's it matter? You turned awful cold soon's you found out I had a kid. But don't feel bad, it's happened before."

"I didn't turn cold, I simply became distracted," David said, lapsing into his normal speech before he realized it. Tommy Sue frowned, staring curiously at him. David locked eyes with her for a moment, then forced a smile. "That was Tony Randall. Ah can do Johnny Carson too." His awkward smile faded. "Can Ah come back at nine-thirty? Take you for a beer?"

She shrugged. "I guess," she said. But there was now a trace of reluctance in her voice.

David went back to his pickup and drove out of town. Cursing himself for his momentary lapse of cover, he drove up and down the back roads for an hour, until twilight came and a grayness began to settle over the red dirt fields. Then he headed back uptown. It was fully dark when he parked in front of Leon's Pool Hall. Walking toward the door, he stopped at the Dodge, put his foot up on the back bumper, and pretended to pull a pebble out of his heel. While he was doing it, he palmed a miniature electronic transmitter with a magnet on the back of it, and attached it to the inside of the bumper. Then he went on into the pool hall.

Leon's was a prototype of every poolroom in every small town in the South. Six Brunswick tables so old their cushions could barely reject a ball. Drop pockets with net catchers. A shelf near each table holding a can of talcum for the cuestick shaft and blue chalk for its tip. A few rickety raised wooden benches for tobacco-chewing spectators. Half a dozen spittoons. Two pinball machines that paid off in free games that could be cashed in for money. A wooden bar with an illuminated beer-logo clock over the cash register behind it. And on the bar two large jars—one of pickled eggs, one of pigs' feet. All under a cloud of gray smoke that hung at the ceiling because it had noplace else to go.

David went to the bar and got a bottle of Bud. The three men who had driven up earlier were shooting nine-ball on a middle table. David stepped up on one of the benches and sat down to watch. Two of the men shooting were either twins or brothers very close in age. They wore jeans with leather belts that had their names tooled on the back of them—Merle and Earl. The latter, David noticed, also had E-A-R-L tattooed on the top joint of each finger on his right hand. The work didn't look professional. It was a jailhouse tattoo, David guessed. The third man was the oldest, probably fifty, with a pot-belly hanging over the waist of a pair of self-belted polyester trousers. He wore a shirt that had a western scene embroidered across the yoke. David sensed that he was studying him from under a pair of tinted lenses between shots.

David watched the progress of the game, waiting for an opportunity to interject a comment. To come right out with a remark would have been poor form and would have marked him at once as a total outsider, an "up-North" type. He had to be subtle about it. He waited until Earl, the one with the tattoos, missed a fairly easy straight-in corner shot, then he rolled his eyes toward the ceiling and groaned quietly. But not so quietly that Earl couldn't bear him.

"What's your problem, boy?" Earl said antagonistically. "Don't nobody ever miss a shot where you come from?"

"Not that kind," David said. Then he raised his hands, palms out. "Hey, Ah'm sorry, hear? Ah didn't have no call to remark. It just slipped out."

"You a pool player?" asked the older man, smiling across the table.

David shrugged. "Ah shoot a game ever' now and then." Which was a gross understatement. David had been president of the billiards club at college for five semesters.

The older man came around the table. He had a chaw of tobacco in one cheek, but instead of using a spittoon he kept a Dixie cup handy. "We heard you say at Luther's today that you hoped to win a little money over here. You care to shoot a game of rotation with Earl here? Say for twenty-five dollars?"

David pursed his lips. "That's mighty temptin'."

The man in the polyester trousers smiled. "What's your name, boy?"

"Dale Barber. From Tuscaloosa, Alabama."

"I didn't ask where you was from. My name's Billy Roy Latham. My friends call me Billy Roy. You can call me Mr. Latham." He peeled twenty-five dollars off a roll and stuck it in one of the corner pockets. "Anytime you're ready."

David covered the bet and beat Earl 67 to 53. He could have run the balls and blanked him, but he didn't want to look like a slicker trying to skin the locals. Neither did he want his thumbs broken. So he laid back and just won by two balls, the six and the eight. As he was fishing his winnings out of the pocket, Earl's brother Merle said, "Lemme have a crack at him, Billy Roy."

Latham nodded and put another twenty-five in the pocket. Merle was about in the same league as Earl. David beat him a little more badly, 71 to 49, winning with the two, three, seven, and ten balls.

After the game with Merle, Latham removed his tinted glasses and smiled an arificial smile at David. "Ah cain't decide if you're good or jus' lucky. How 'bout you and me shoot a game for the fifty you've won?"

David glanced around. A dozen men had idled up from the other tables and were gathered around watching. They were somber, leathery men, their eyes squinty from years in the bright sun of the fields. Maybe they worked for Latham, maybe they didn't. But David knew instinctively that even if he had wanted to there was no way he'd be allowed to walk out with the fifty he had won.

"How 'bout it, boy?" Latham pressed. "You an' me for fifty each."

"Whatever you say, Mr. Latham."

The balls were racked and Latham won the break. He made the six on the break, then ran the one, two, and three, and dropped the twelve off the three-ball. David saw at once that Latham was a much better pool shooter than Merle and Earl.

On his first shot, David ran the four, five, seven, and eight, tying it up with twenty-four points each. Latham made the nine and ten, but scratched on the ten and had to spot it back on the table. David then made it in the side pocket but missed the eleven-ball. Latham made the eleven. David made the thirteen, to go three points ahead, 47 to 44. Latham made the fourteen, to move up to forty-eight. Then he missed the fifteen and it was David's turn.

The fifteen was the game-winning ball. It was dead on the side rail, midway down from the end pocket. Its position did not present a difficult shot, merely a tricky one—the cueball had to hit the rail and the fifteen-ball at the same time in order to run the fifteen straight along the cushion into the pocket. If the cueball hit the fifteen first, the fifteen would be brought out from the rail and go nowhere, leaving the opponent a good shot. If the cueball hit the rail first, the fifteen would roll straight along the rail but wouldn't have enough momentum to go all the way to the pocket.

David chalked his cue-tip and bent low over the far end of the table. Wetting his lips, he took dead-perfect aim and let go a slow shot that hit the fifteen and the cushion at the same time. The fifteen rolled along the rail—and stopped four inches from the pocket.

There was a general murmur of approval from the onlookers: the stranger had lost. David shook his head and stepped back. Billy Roy Latham leaned casually over the side rail and eased the ball on in to win the game. He got more than a few pats on the back as he dug the fifty dollars out of the end pocket.

In the men's room, David and Latham stood side by side washing the talcum off their hands at a tin sink. "You could've made that last shot," Latham said quietly.

"Can't win 'em all," David said.

"You could've won that one. Why didn't you?"

David shrugged. "Your town, your people. No call to beat a man in his own town. 'Sides, Ah broke even."

Latham studied him for a long moment as he dried his hands. Then he made up his mind about David and nodded to himself. "There's a place called Joe's Pit out on the highway that's got good barbecued ribs and ice-cold beer. How 'bout havin' a bite?"

"No offense," David said, "but Ah got other plans." He winked at Latham. "Tommy Sue over at the café."

Latham grinned. "You Alabama rednecks is all the same. After the sun goes down you only got one thing on your mind."

"Yep. Jus' like you Georgia rednecks." David bobbed his chin. "See you around."

He bought a cold six-pack at Luther's and drove away from the square with Tommy Sue. "Where do ya'll park around here?" he asked.

"Out by the cemetery. It's quiet there."

"Ah reckon it would be."

She showed him the way. When they were parked, David opened both doors of the pickup and two cans of the beer. They sat holding hands and sipping the beer. Someone had burned a stump during the day and there was still a smell of scorched wood in the air. It mixed with the fragrance of hackberry plants that grew wild along the side of the road. The result was an odd, almost sensual night scent. After they finished a can of beer each, David guided Tommy Sue onto the seat and put his lips on her throat. He found himself whispering things to her that he would never have dared say to Eileen. Things that made Tommy Sue draw in her breath and entwine her fingers in his hair.

It was later, when they were having their second beer, that she asked, "Who are you anyway?"

"Jus' plain ol' Dale Barber from Tuscaloosa, honey."

"You're not 'just plain ol' anybody from anywhere," she said. "And that wasn't no Tony Randall imitation you were doing earlier. That was the real you."

David looked out at the moonlight and thought it over. "Suppose it was the real me? What would you do about it?"

"Depends on who you came here to hurt. I'm not from DeSota, I'm from Talbot, but the people here been good to me. I wouldn't stick nobody in the back."

"I wouldn't ask you to. Let's get to know each other a little better first. Then we can decide what's right and what's wrong." He kissed the tips of her fingers as he talked.

"You're so gentle," she said softly. "I can't imagine you hurting nobody." She turned her hand around. "Do that to the palm."

"Tell me about your little boy."

"I already told you. His name is Lonnie and he's four and my mama keeps him for me over in Talbot. He's just like any other little boy. Likes cowboys and trucks and beaches. I keep tellin' him we'll go down to the Florida beaches some weekend but, Lord, I never seem to find the time."

"Where's his daddy?"

"Run off with another woman. Last I heard he was on welfare out in California. He left me with Lonnie to raise. I couldn't find no work in Talbot so I come over here to DeSota. A friend of Mama's sent me to see Mr. Latham. He gave me the job at Luther's and fixed the hours so I could spend three days a week back home."

"Billy Roy Latham? He owns Luther's?"

"Sure. Luther's. Leon's Pool Hall. DeSota Market. The filling station, the canning factory, even the undertaker's parlor. He owns just about everything in Lasher County."

"When he helped you out, did he make any moves on you?"

"Not one. He's been a perfect gentleman. He's good to lots of people, and most times he don't ask nothin' in return."

A Georgia godfather, David thought. He had guessed as much from the demeanor of the men in the poolroom. But he had not imagined that Latham owned the entire county. It would be interesting to see how he reacted the following day when his illegal whiskey operation began to fall apart.

But that was tomorrow and tonight was still tonight. David slipped his hand up Tommy Sue's back under her blouse. He felt nothing except flesh.

"Where do you stay the four nights you're in DeSota?" he asked.
"Out at Harley's Motor Inn. I rent Number Twelve by the week."
"I'm in Number Two," he told her.
She put her lips on his ear. "Small world," she said.
David started the pickup.

The next day when David drove up to Luther's for breakfast, Billy
Roy Latham and one of the brothers, Merle, were drinking coffee in
a booth and looking worried. David nodded a greeting and sat at the
counter. The fry cook was in the kitchen doorway, moving a toothpick back and forth in his mouth. "Somethin' wrong?" David asked,
bobbing his chin toward the somber men in the booth.

"Revenue agents caught that fellow's brother Earl with a load of
bootleg last night. Got him just after he crossed the Florida line."

David nodded. "Oh." The fry cook's wife, who worked mornings
until Tommy Sue came on, handed him a menu. "Just grits and
sausage," David said.

While David was eating, Merle got up and left the booth. After he
was gone, Latham waved David over to join him. "Bring your plate
on over," he said hospitably. David carried his coffee and the rest of
his meal over.

"How'd you make out with Tommy Sue last night?" Latham
asked.

"Struck out," David lied. "She's a right proper girl."

"You got that right," Latham said. "Gonna make a fine little wife
for some man someday." Latham sighed wearily and took a sip of
coffee.

"Fry cook tells me you got problems this morning," David said.

Latham shot an irritated look over at the counter. "Fry cook's got a
big mouth." Then he studied David for a moment. "But he's right.
One of them boys you whipped at pool last night got caught in a
revenue-agent trap." Latham narrowed his eyes. "You know anything about bootlegging?"

"A little," David admitted.

Latham tossed down his last swallow of coffee. "Come on, take a
ride with me. Somethin' I want to show you."

They rode in Latham's Buick down Route 441 to a narrow county
road that cut east into Okefenokee Swamp. Five miles along,
Latham turned into a rutted dirt path barely wide enough for the car
to negotiate. The farther they drove, the more the morning sunlight
was shut out by the entangled treetops overhead and the more eerie
the great swamp became. A bit of fog still clung to the ground on

both sides of the car, looking wet and cold, making David think of the warmth he had left behind in Tommy Sue's bed. He shivered slightly and wished he was still there.

Before the road ended, Latham turned into a bog path and guided the car with a sure, practiced eye onto a log raft ringed with empty 55-gallon drums to keep it afloat. Sticking his head out the window, he whistled three times. Presently the raft began to float across the marsh to an island, being pulled along by an unseen rope under the murky water. The trip took only three or four minutes, then Latham, who had not even shut off the engine, drove the car onto the island and into a stand of tall pines. David saw the rope and pulley that were used to bring the raft over. A black man with enormous muscles was standing next to the pulley crank. "That's Mose," said Latham. "He can crush a man's skull between his hands." David didn't doubt it for a moment.

The car drove through the shade of the pines, and up ahead David could see the whiskey still. It consisted of several large wooden tubs and a couple of cast-iron vats with kerosene burners under them. Everything was connected by wires and tubes, and with the escaping steam and the bubbling surface in two of the vats it reminded David of the mad doctors' laboratories he used to see in the movies as a kid. Latham parked and they got out. "Come on," he said, "I'll give you the ten-cent tour."

He led David to the layout of tubs, where several lean sweating white men were pouring industrial alcohol from ten-gallon cans into the first tub, then straining it through a water-and-charcoal filter into a second one. "Tha's how we wash the noxious chemicals out of the alky," Latham said. "Over here in this tub is where we mix water with the alky, then we run it into that iron vat and cook it some, put some caramel or butterscotch coloring in it to make it look good, then run it into the last tub there to simmer and cool." He grinned sheepishly. "I usually pour a fifth of bonded rye into the final batch to give it a little extra flavor. Like a taste?"

"Why not?" David said.

Behind the last vat were several young boys filling Mason jars with the freshly cooled liquor. Latham opened one of the jars and handed it to David. Although his taste ran to very dry martinis and good brandy, David knew he had to take a convincing drink of the bootleg stuff, as if he'd been drinking it all his life. He took a respectable swallow, prepared to forcibly hold back both cough and tears if necessary, but to his surprise the drink went down not only smoothly but with a tart good taste. He saw that Latham was smiling at him.

"Smooth, ain't it?"

"Sure is, man," David admitted. "And good too."

"Ah don't make nothin' but the best for my customers," Latham bragged. He nodded toward a picnic table and benches under a low weeping willow at the edge of the clearing. "Let's set a spell." As he spoke, Latham pulled back one side of his coat and for the first time David saw that he had a pistol stuck in his belt. Glancing around, he also now saw two men armed with rifles, one at each end of the compound. "Sure 'nuff, Mr. Latham," David said easily and followed him over to the table.

"You know," Latham said, sitting down and shaking a Camel out of a soft pack, "I sometimes wonder what the ol' world's comin' to. I read in the papers and see on the evenin' news all the stories about crime in the streets, violence in the schools, poverty in the slums, crooks in gub'ment, all that sort of thing. Makes me realize more ever' day that things is changin' too fast to keep up with—and not necessarily for the better neither. Hell, even all the heroes are dead. Harry Truman's dead. Audie Murphy's dead. John Steinbeck's dead. Ain't nobody around to admire no more. Nowadays all's a man can do is hope to keep his own little part of the world protected from outside influences that might corrupt it. You take Lasher County now. It's my own little corner of the earth and I try to look after it as best I can. I own nearly all there is to own from one end of it to the other, and ever'body except the postmaster and a couple of bankers works for me."

Latham leaned forward on the table and locked eyes with David.

"I run this county like the whole country ought to be run. We don't have no welfare recipients or food stamps down here 'cause we don't need 'em. Ever'body that *can* work *does* work. An' the ones that can't, why the others takes care of 'em. Our old people and our sick people don't want for nothin'. Nobody sleeps cold in the wintertime, nobody goes hungry at suppertime, and nobody has to be afraid *any*time. We ain't got no real crime in Lasher County— no robberies, burglaries, that sort of thing. People here *work* for what they want. They work for me—in my café, my pool hall, my grocery market, my filling station, my farms, my canning factory, and ever'thing else I own. My farms and canning factory are the economic backbone of this county. And when the economy don't stay up, when crops are bad or inflation keeps me from making enough to go around for ever'body, why then this whiskey bi'ness takes up the slack. It's this right here—" he waved an arm around "—that keeps the people of Lasher County free and independent of

60

the rest of our dyin' and decayin' society." Now Latham's expression seemed to turn hard as stone. "And I'm here to tell you I'll do anythin' I have to do to keep it that way. Do you take my meanin'?"

David, his mouth as dry as old wood, managed to speak. "Yessir, Mr. Latham. I take your meanin'."

"Good," Latham said quietly. He sat back and seemed to relax a little, toying with the burnt-out stick match he had used to light his cigarette. "I don't know," he said matter-of-factly, "if it was just a coincidence you comin' to town one day and Earl gettin' caught with a load that same night. I don't know if you're really Dale Barber from Tuscaloosa or if you're a revenue agent from Washington. I know that Tommy Sue is crazy about you—I talked to her on the phone after Harley called to tell me you'd left the motel. Incidentally, I admire the fact that you said you struck out with her instead of braggin' the other way; that's the mark of a good man. Anyway, Tommy Sue says she thinks you're who you say you are."

She lied for me, David thought.

"But I'd like to hear it from you," Latham said. "For some funny reason I kind of like you. And I kind of trust you. Enough to give you the benefit of the doubt anyhow. I think I'll know if you lie to me. So I'll just ask you outright: who are you, boy?"

A montage of his own world saturated David's mind. Washington. Eileen. The Clarys' lawn party. Dry martinis. Sportscars. Italian shoes. Styled hair. A career in government.

Then the montage dissolved into another world. Lasher County. Frye boots and Levis. A Chevy pickup. Catfish and hush puppies. Tommy Sue's warm neck and the things he could whisper against it.

David met Billy Roy Latham's fixed stare with a calm sureness. "I'm Dale Barber, Mr. Latham. From Tuscaloosa."

The letter he wrote to the district director was brief and polite. He was sorry to resign so abruptly in the middle of a field assignment but he had been offered a job in private industry that he couldn't turn down. He wished the department luck in its pursuit of further leads in Lasher County even though based on his own investigation he didn't believe it would be possible to find an illegal whiskey still in the vast Okefenokee Swamp.

The letter to Eileen was also brief, and apologetic. He was leaving government service for private employment and he had to be honest and tell her he had become interested in another woman. He would always remember her fondly, he said, and was certain that, attractive educated woman that she was, she would find someone who deserved her much more than he did.

He mailed the letters in the box outside the DeSota post office, then pulled up in front of Luther's just as Tommy Sue was leaving for the night. She was carrying a small suitcase.

"Hop in," he said. "I'll give you a lift."

"I'm fixin' to catch the ten o'clock bus to Talbot," she told him. "My three days off starts tomorrow."

"I'll give you a lift to Talbot," he said.

"You mean it?"

"Sure I mean it. Get in."

She put her suitcase in the back and climbed into the cab.

"I start work for Mr. Latham on Monday," he told her.

Tommy Sue's eyebrows went up. "Doin' what?"

"Helping him run Lasher County, honey. He said a good ol' boy like me from Tuscaloosa would fit right in. Said that someday I might even take over and run it for him. How's that for a future?"

"Sounds like you've got the future all worked out. What about the past?"

"There isn't any past," David replied quietly. "There's just today. And tomorrow. Listen, let's pick up your little boy and drive down to Florida to the beach. Would you like that?"

"I'd like it just fine." Tommy Sue slid over close and curled up to him. "You're wrong about there bein' just today and tomorrow," she said.

"Am I? What else is there?"

"There's tonight."

The pickup drove out of town and into the Georgia night.

Born in Tennessee in 1934, Clark Howard was the son of a well-known bootlegger. Howard spent much of his youth in foster homes, from which he often ran away, giving him an understanding and feeling for the hunted and hounded that is reflected in his work. His short stories of crime and detection began to appear in the late 1950s in digest magazines. Howard has been nominated for a Mystery Writers of America Award four times for fact-crime, including his Six Against the Rock (1977) and Zebra (1979); and he won the Mystery Writers of America Award for the short story, "Horn Man." He received another nomination for "All the Heroes Are Dead."

The voodoo pastor who cheats his parishoners sets murder and its unexpected revenge into action in the hot New Orleans nights by the levee. . . .

FIVE

Thrown-Away Child

Thomas Adcock

The little room in back where Perry stayed was "nothin' but a damn slum the way that no-'count keeps it," according to his Aunt Vivian. She had a long list of complaints about her nephew, most of which were shared by most people who knew him. But she and Perry were still family and so she loved him, too, in a quiet and abiding way.

Vivian lived in the rest of the place, a wooden cottage of four narrow connected rooms built up on hurricane stilts, with a high pitched roof, batten shutters over the windows, and French louvered doors on either end. The front steps were scrubbed every morning with a ritual mixture of steaming hot water and brick dust to keep evil spirits at bay. The back steps led from Perry's squalor to a tiny fenced garden of thick grass, a chinaberry tree, and a lilac bush. In appearance and infirmity, the cottage was nearly the same as the forty or so others crowded into a rut-filled dirt lane between lower Tchoupitoulas Street and a levee almost crumbled away from years of flood and neglect.

The neighborhood was one of many that tourists in the city were not encouraged to visit, a neighborhood where pain and fears from the hard past overlapped a generally despairing present—a haunted part of New Orleans, some claimed. Which was why, among other customs, the front steps were washed down with brick dust every day.

On most afternoons, the people in the lane would go to the levee for the coolness of the river breezes or to catch themselves a dinner of Mississippi catfish. There, ancient Creole men and widow ladies— with *tignons* covering their hair, the Madras handkerchiefs favored by voodoo women with seven points carefully twisted heaven- ward—would talk until dusk of the old days and the old ways.

Long ago, Vivian and her husband had been terribly proud of the cottage. It was truly theirs, no thanks to any of the banks or mortgage companies—bought and paid for with the saved-up wages of a yard man and a cleaning woman whose ancestors had once been shackled to posts in the public squares above Canal Street and sold as slaves. But on a sunny day in March of 1948, Vivian and Willis Duclat took title to a little wood cottage and became the first of their families to own their own home.

It was a long way up in a perilous, hostile world and Willis and Vivian were pleased to be gracious about their ascent. Almost everyone else in the lane shared generously in their reflected joy. One who did not was a tall, sour-faced woman next door to the Duclats, a spinster known as Miss Toni. "Ain't goin' to be no comfort to you or the rest of us down here to be buyin' your own place when it's the last one that ain't owned yet by Theo Flower. Theo's wants the whole lane bad and he means to get it, one way'r other. He knows the mysteries, so that's how he'll get you yet—one way'r other."

Vivian said to pay no mind to Miss Toni. "She only says those poisonous things 'cause she's lonesome and miserable."

The pride of the Duclats was brief.

Toward the end of '48, the parish tax assessor came calling. He smiled quite a bit and seemed genuine. He shook hands with Willis, same as he'd shake a white man's hand. And he addressed Vivian properly as Mrs. Duclat. The assessor was there to explain how he had some important papers for signing, papers that would bring paving and curbing and a sewer hook-up. The Duclats didn't understand quite all of the small print on the man's papers, but since he'd been so respectful Willis and Vivian trusted him and signed where it said "Freeholder." Then by Christmas of '49, when they'd fallen impossibly far behind on the special surcharges for modern conveniences levied against them by those important papers, the Duclats' home was seized by the sheriff and put up for sale in tax-forfeiture court.

At the auction there was only one bidder—the Church of the Awakened Spirit, in the person of its pastor, The Most Reverend Doctor Theophilus Flower. At last, Theo Flower and his church owned every last cottage in the lane. Pastor Flower wasted no time. He called on the Duclats the very day he put down the cash money to retire the delinquent surcharges, plus the customary plain brown envelope full of money for his friend, the smiling tax assessor.

Pastor Flower drove straightaway from the courthouse to the Duclats' place in his big white Packard motorcar, one of the first postwar models off the Detroit assembly lines. When the neighbors saw the Packard roll in from Tchoupitoulas Street, they went to their homes and shut the doors until they knew Pastor Flower had gone away.

In the parlor of the newly dispossessed Duclats, Theo Flower was courtly and sympathetic. The pastor had no need for meanness when he bought somebody's home out from under them—the law made it all so easy and polite.

"Now, I know you can understand that our church has many missions," he said in his deep, creamy preacher's cadence, "and that among them is providing what we can in the way of housing for our poor and unfortunate brothers and sisters."

Willis sat in a caneback chair in a sort of shock, still as a stone while Pastor Flower talked. He didn't appear to hear anything. He'd hidden from his wife for days before the court sale so that he could cry, and now his eyes looked like they might rust away with grief. Vivian sat next to him and held his big calloused hands. She looked at the floor, ashamed and resigned, and listened carefully to Theo Flower.

"I surely don't want to see fine people like you having noplace to live. You see, though, how we must serve our members first? Now, I've been giving this predicament of yours a lot of my thought and some of my most powerful prayer and I do believe I have come upon a solution—"

When at last Pastor Flower was finished, he collected twenty dollars on account toward the first year's tithe to the Church of the Awakened Spirit. And the church's two newest members, Vivian and Willis Duclat, signed some important papers their new pastor happened to have with him, pressed inside the red-leather Bible he always carried. They signed where it said "Tenant."

After scratching his name to Theo Flower's lease, Willis rose from his chair and crossed the room angrily, tearing himself away from Vivian's grip on his shirt. He stood towering over the preacher and his black eyes came alive again. Duclat's huge hands, made hard and heavy from his work with shovels and stone and earth, clenched into dark fists. His voice sounded as if it were a thousand years old.

"I ain't no educated man," he said to Flower, "and I ain't well spoken like you. But I ain't simple, neither, and I can sure as hell figure you just done somethin' crooked here. I'm goin' to think on this, then I'm goin' to figure some way to bring you down for what you done to me and my wife, and prob'ly other poor folks besides."

65

The Most Reverend Doctor Theophilus Flower only smiled. When he did, Vivian saw a flash of gold at the back of his dark-brown lips. Then Flower stood up, no match in physique to Willis. He folded the lease into his Bible and answered the big angry man with the clenched fists: "It won't do to talk like that, brother. I know you're a troubled man today and I'm sorry for you, truly. But you'd best not take an adversary's tone against a man who knows the mysteries like I do. You understand what I mean, don't you, brother Willis?"

Willis understood only too well. Since he was a boy, he'd heard of Theo Flower's abilities, how he could call forth the dead from beyond, how he could "fix" an enemy, how his power came from the evil fangs of river snakes. Willis felt something cold on his neck, something like a wet wind.

Then the pastor drove off in his Packard. And later, in the silent night, Willis awoke from a nightmare with a violent fever and pains that shot through his chest and neck.

Willis never worked another day, nor did he sleep well. Then three months into the new year of 1950, on the very day that Perry was born to his younger sister, Willis Duclat dropped dead.

It happened despite his precautions. Convinced that mortal danger lay waiting in the alleyway in the form of water moccasins or copperheads that would sometimes slither up from the levee, Willis had begun a new daily protective routine. He would mix a batch of quicklime and cayenne pepper into the boiling water left over from scrubbing the front steps and pour the potion in two parallel lines along the inside of the fence that enclosed his garden. One of the old *voodooiennes* assured him he would be safe now, back as well as front.

Just before he died, Willis was sitting on a step out back, smoking a morning pipe of tobacco. Vivian was on her way to a mansion on St. Charles Avenue, where she had a job minding three children, cleaning some, and cooking for a doctor who ate far too much. Across the river, meanwhile, in the parish of Algiers, a midwife pulled an infant boy into the world from between the legs of his very young and frightened mother.

Willis's left leg dangled off the side of the pine steps and his bare foot swung back and forth, toes brushing through the dewy grass that he'd coaxed into growing from muddy soil. Then suddenly, his body convulsed with a spasm so overwhelming it threw him to the ground, where he twisted around for a few seconds in mute torture before his heart stopped. Vivian found him when she returned home in the afternoon. He was sprawled on his back in the grass, his face covered with bits of blossoms, the white and purple petals that fell from the chinaberry tree.

She ran to a confectionary shop where there was a public telephone and rang up the doctor's house. Her employer drove over right away, breaking the speed limit even though Vivian told him that Willis was dead and already cold. The doctor examined the body there in the garden and after a minute or two pointed to a blue-black welt on Willis's left ankle. "He's full of venom more than likely," he said.

"No, sir," said Vivian. "Somebody's gone and hexed my man."

The lane was never paved, nor was it ever so much as named. And through the decades, Theo Flower bought up hundreds more ragged neighborhoods in New Orleans, building up his church membership and the sort of respectability money from any source whatever buys in the entrenched power structure of a southern town.

Along about the middle 1970s, the federal government mandated sewer hook-ups for even the lowliest neighborhoods in any city that expected revenue-sharing funds. So New Orleans obliged people like Vivian Duclat, finally. For his part, Theo Flower hiked her rent since the property would become more valuable with the addition of a modern convenience.

In July of 1983, Perry Duclat was paroled out of the Louisiana State Prison at Angola after serving half of a seven-year sentence for grand theft—auto. He'd been convicted of "borrowing" a Rolls-Royce that belonged to the doctor where his Aunt Vivian worked. In his defense, Perry told the judge, "I was helpin' out my aunt one day at the big house and the man was out of town for the weekend and there was that nice big car of his just sittin' in the garage goin' nowhere. So naturally I borrowed it. How else is a man like me ever goin' to have any style in his life? I put it back right where I found it and I never hurt it one little bit, no sir." Perry had borrowed many things in the past, many of them yet to be returned, so the judge threw the book at him and lectured him on how he'd probably never amount to anything with that sort of thieving attitude. The defendant only smiled.

And even so, even though the doctor told her she could never work at his house again, Vivian took Perry in when he was released from Angola with nowhere to go. She took him in because they were family, no matter what; because he was born on that terrible day her husband died; because in the years he'd been at Angola he'd taken on such a strong resemblance to Willis.

Every day but Sunday, Vivian would get up early in the morning and go off to work someplace. Perry would get up right after that and attend to the chores, which included keeping his aunt's part of the cottage meticulously clean and scrubbing down the front steps because she believed most of the old myths even if he didn't. By ten o'clock or so, he would be back in his own room watching television.

In the three months he'd been there, Perry's room had become wall-to-wall beer cans, hundreds of them, under a film of cigarette ash. He would light cigarettes and leave them burning on the windowsill or at the edge of the dresser. Holes were burnt into the sheets of his bed, where he sat day after day watching television game shows, talk shows, soap operas, meaningless news and witless comedies and endless commercials on a portable black-and-white set with a wire coathanger for an antenna. He liked to crush the cans after draining them, then he'd toss them aside, anywhere. Mostly, he drank Dixie beer, in the white cans with red-and-yellow lettering, or Coors in the gold cans when he had a few dollars extra.

Some days he'd stroll down to the levee. But Miss Toni had whispered around that Perry was an escaped convict, so very few neighbors would have anything to do with him. The old-timers talked to him, though, especially the widows in their *tignons*, garrulous old magpies always happy to pass along the legends that meant everything to them and practically nothing to the disrespectful younger generation.

Sometimes he would tend his late uncle's garden, where Miss Toni would spy on him from a window, ducking out of sight when he turned his face in the direction of her cottage. Or he'd sit on the back steps and read a book, which Miss Toni considered most highly suspicious. Perry had two big stacks of books in his room, one on the dresser and another that filled a corner, floor to ceiling. Sometimes, too, he would write or draw in a tablet. About once a week, he would set off by foot all the way up to the library on Rampart Street.

But mostly Perry watched television, drank and smoked and drowned himself in thought. By noon, his eyes were boozy slits and his fingers stank of nicotine. He would watch the flickering idiot box until it went dark in the wee hours of the next day. He ate very little, though he did enjoy whatever his Aunt Vivian cared to cook or bake.

The two of them seldom talked. The chat was pleasant when Vivian spoke of Perry's late uncle, when she'd show him photographs of Willis or bring out a box of Willis's personal effects or tell Perry again about the day he died, what the doctor said, and how she thought that was "nothin' but medical yap." But then it would lead inevitably to the subject of Theo Flower and their chat would quickly become an argument loud enough for Miss Toni next door to hear every word of it, even without her big ears at the window.

"That nigger Flower's nothin' but an old-timey conjure man, nothin' but a slick and cussed old fraud who's got lots of little old ladies like you and Miss Toni and all scared out of your bloomers 'cause he's supposed to 'know the mysteries,'" Perry would say, eyes rolling and his voice heavy with sarcasm. "Haw! Y'all must be crazy."

To which Vivian would reply, her jowls quivering and a finger wagging up against her nephew's nose, "You best shut that sassy trap, boy! In the first damn place, we're beholden to Pastor Flower for this house we're in. And in the second damn place, well, let's just say you ain't lived near long enough to understand that precious little in this ol' world is actually what it seems to be."

She never quite told him so, but Vivian thrilled to her nephew's boisterous arrogance on the subject of Theo Flower. She supposed this might be a womanly fault of hers, enjoying the antagonisms of men at dispute where she was concerned, so she kept quiet. But when Perry would inveigh against Pastor Flower and his church, Vivian's eyes would mist over some, and through that prism of tears and remembrance she sometimes thought she was looking at her husband again. God bless poor black men for what little arrogance they dared show the world, she thought.

And Vivian didn't care a hoot whether Miss Toni heard them carrying on—which she did, and which she dutifully passed along nearly word-for-word to Pastor Flower himself, who maintained a pervasive interest in the personal lives of his home-indentured flock.

Perry's irreverance greatly disturbed Theo Flower. His unease was compounded by the unnerving physical resemblance he saw in Perry to the late Willis Duclat, who was about Perry's age when he died. Perry had taken to attending Sunday services of the Church of the Awakened Spirit and he sat right down center and never took his eyes off Pastor Flower, never registered any expression, just stood and sat down when requested. Never had a nickel for the collection plate. But there he sat anyway, unembarrassed, looking for all the world like Willis Duclat with his hot black eyes, taut olive-brown skin, high forehead, and straight hawklike nose. And those wide shoulders and thickly muscled arms, with big hammer hands folded in his lap.

"You better come do somethin' on that boy here," Miss Toni warned Pastor Flower on the telephone. "I tell you, I believe Perry's got some kind of trouble-makin' designs. I see him some days on those back steps, lookin' over to my place and starin' at me and wonderin' lord only knows what! Now, you know how we don't want no trouble here. We mean to keep in our houses, Pastor Flower. Please do somethin' on him!"

"Yes, yes. You're quite right," he told Miss Toni. "We will have to stop any trouble before it has a chance to begin."

Pastor Flower said yes to a drop of brandy in his coffee and asked permission to light a cheroot in Vivian Duclat's parlor besides. "Oh my, yes, go right ahead," she said. "My Willis was a smokin' man, you know. La, yes, he had to have that pipe of his from mornin' to midnight."

"Yes, I do recall that." Flower fired a sterling Tiffany lighter and touched the yellow-blue hiss of flame to the blunt end of his cigar. In the flash of light, Vivian saw again the gold crowns of sparkle in the back of his mouth.

It was a Sunday twilight and a heavy blackness moved across the sky, overtaking what was left of the day and the week. Perry's television set droned from the back of the cottage.

"Sister Vivian, I come here to talk with you tonight on a delicate matter, one that causes me grave concern as to your welfare."

"What in the world can that be?" Vivian had enjoyed several drops of brandy in several cups of coffee before the pastor's call and her voice was thick.

"Well, Sister Vivian, you know how people will talk. Many of your neighbors and friends are worried sick about your being all alone in this house with a man fresh out of prison, a man who I am told lives like some sort of wild animal in the back room of this cottage and who does nothing besides drink all day long. Now, I must worry about this for your sake—and for the sake of the church's property, after all."

Vivian touched her lips to hide a smile, which she thought Pastor Flower might well interpret as contemptuous. "I think I know maybe just one neighbor who'd gab like that and maybe she's over there listenin' now. Besides, if I had to worry 'bout ev'ry man 'round this neighborhood who'd ever been locked up, well, shoot, I'd be a mighty nervous old hag by now. So don't you worry none 'bout my nephew Perry, 'cause I'm sure not worryin' and you can tell Miss Toni the same if you want."

"Well, I only mean that your husband Willis was a hard-working, sober man and this Perry is a layabout. That is what I'm told." Flower coughed, then opened his red-leather Bible and spread it out on the parlor table. "You know very well from the scriptures how the devil works through wicked drinking men and other idle folks."

"Maybe I know that," Vivian said. "I do know for sure that the devil works through schemin' folks."

She poured herself another brandy and spotted it with coffee out of respect for the ministry. The ministry accepted one for himself.

"Let me set your mind at ease some, Pastor Flower. You should know a little of Perry's story, then maybe you'd understand him like I do. He's not a dangerous young man, no more than any other young man. He is sloppy, though. I'd be ashamed to have you see where he stays.

"But look here, Perry's been bruised all through his life and them bruises come one right after the other. Ain't none of them healed up completelike, which is maybe why he lays 'round all the day long. Sometimes he shows some spunk, but if he's dog-tired from life most of the time, then I figure he's got the right.

"His mother—that would be Willis's sister—was nothin' but an ignorant teenage girl livin' over in Algiers in a shack all alone near a coalyard. How d'you s'pose a girl like that made out in the world? Well, you can imagine right enough. Anyway, she gets herself in the family way and then come runnin' over here with the baby, not even knowin' her brother Willis had passed on. Not that she'd care 'bout that, mind you, not any more'n she cared for that baby she just plopped down on me.

"But I minded the child for a while and loved him. I named him, too, you know. Maybe I might have gone crazy without the baby 'round me to take my mind offa how Willis died like he did—" Her shoulders shook and she cried softly. Pastor Flowers moved to comfort her with his hands, but she backed away from his touch.

"And you know all 'bout that," she said to Flower. "Anyway, Perry's mama went up to Chicago, so I heard. She wrote how fine she was doin' up North and how she wanted to send for Perry and all. But then the man who did her come by one day with a new wife and says he wants to take his baby and raise him up over to Algiers. That's what he did, took Perry away from me and wasn't nothin' I could do 'bout it.

"But Perry started comin' back here regular when he got older, just as soon as he could get by on the ferry on his own. An' I started noticin' how beat-up lookin' he was. I got it out of him what was goin' on over to his daddy's house. His daddy's lady would be all the time hittin' him, or burnin' him with cigarettes or shamin' him in front of the other little boys by comin' after him with a belt and whuppin' his head till he'd fall over bloody, then whuppin' some more until he messed his pants.

"I tol' his daddy all this when he would come for him to take him back, and that man said his boy was possessed 'cause he wouldn't never do nothin' right or what was told him. Then he finally put little Perry in a home someplace out in the country.

"Next I heard, Perry'd busted out of that home, which was more like some prison than a home, which it never had any right to be called, and he headed north lookin' for his mamma. He found her, too. He come back and tol' me how she was nothin' but a whore and a dope addict, how she looked like death itself and didn't even know Perry was her kin.

"Well, he was right. Later on, we heard from some city health official up North how she was dead from heroin and askin' us did we know her birthday. They was so shocked to learn she was only thirty-six.

"Perry figured he'd better stay over with his father, else his daddy'd make trouble for me. But the man tossed him out soon's he showed up over there to Algiers.

"And so, you see, Perry's had trouble all the time in his life. What do you expect? He was nothin' but a thrown-away child. Least that's what he think of himself anytime he's away from here."

Pastor Flower folded his hands over his Bible. Vivian ran her fingers through her hair nervously. From the back of the house where Perry watched television came the added sound of a beer can popping open, an empty being crushed, then the clatter of it when it fell to the littered floor.

"I'm sorry for you, Sister Vivian, but I cannot stand by idly in this matter."

Her voice rising high, Vivian said, "What do you mean? Don't you be takin' my Perry away! Don't you be takin' another man from this place!"

"Quiet, woman!" Flower's voice thundered. There was stillness in the house. "What I shall do here is convene the spirits and consult the wisdom of the other side. I shall call out your own husband, Willis Duclat!"

Vivian shrieked and her cup and saucer crashed to the floor.

"Yes," Flower said, "I shall call out the spirit of Willis Duclat. He— and only he—shall guide us on the matter of your nephew!"

Pastor Flower closed his Bible and the sound of it echoed in the parlor. He stood up and moved to the door, put on his hat. "I shall request that everybody in this lane come to service next Sunday. You come, too, Sister Vivian. I know you wouldn't want to miss hearing your husband's voice."

The tall dark woman at the side of the altar began chanting in a low, melodious voice. She started in a *francais africaine* dialect—
"*Danse Calinda, boudoum, boudoum!*
Danse Calinda, boudoum, boudoum!"
Pastor Flower, in a scarlet robe covered with *gris-gris*—dolls made of feathers and hair, skins of snakes, bits of bone—rose from a pit beneath the altar in a great plume of white-and-grey smoke. Beaming at the congregants in front of him, he turned and knelt at the altar as the woman's chanting grew in volume and tempo. He rapped the floor and then lit the black crucifix-shaped candles. He turned again to face his flock and he picked up the chant himself, raising his arms, commanding all to join in the calling out of spirits from beyond life.

Bodies swayed in the pews of the Church of the Awakened Spirit and the chanting rolled in waves, the single line of African French pulsating stronger and stronger through the sanctuary and out the open door into the liquid air of a savagely hot, humid Sabbath morning in New Orleans. Hands kept time and feet moved from muffled accentuation to a steady, rhythmic pounding.

Vivian Duclat, tears streaming down her face, for she had slept little during her week of anticipation, slapped her hands together determinedly and pounded her feet. She would hear her man, maybe she would even see her Willis—it didn't matter if the image were no more real than the times she thought she saw him in Perry's face. But what would Willis say of Perry? Would he send him away from her? Would Willis, too, throw the child away?

The tall dark woman stepped forward from the altar, moved her arms in an arc, and then switched to the Creole *patois* and to the uninhibited, throaty *canga*—
"*Eh! Eh! Bomba, hen! hen!*
Canga bafio, te,
Canga moune de le,
Canga do ki la,
Canga li!"
All joined the chant, their massed voices now storming and frenzied, so full of pathos and longing that it became impossible for anyone to remain free of the swing and the narcotic influence of the

ancient words. Everywhere, people were prepared to believe it all, for the first time in many cases. The eyes of the young were no longer disrespectful, they were full of proper fright—the old-timers clung righteously to *gris-gris* charms of their own they'd brought along to the ceremony, their little "conjure balls" of black wax and bits of their own skin or bleached lizards in glass jelly jars or dried-up rooster hearts—the curious things they kept under lock and key at home, out of embarrassment and fear. Pastor Flower then began the dance of the Voudou, the leader.

He raised a bottle of brandy from the altar, dashed some of the liquid on each side of a brown bowl full of brick dust, then tossed back his head and took a long pull of the liquor. Then he started the slow hip shuffling, moved his feet backward and then forward, accelerating his movement up to the speed of the hypnotic *canga*. Without ceasing a single step of his dance, Flower poured the rest of the brandy into the bowl, then ignited it with his silver Tiffany lighter. The bowl flamed up high over the altar and still he danced the maddening *canga*, his powerful voice starting to rise up over the waning strength of all the others:

"I call out Willis Duclat! *Eh! Eh! Bomba, hen! hen!* I call out Willis Duclat! *Eh! Eh! Bomba, hen! hen!* Willis Duclat, speak through me—"

And suddenly, a tall young man covered in a brilliant red-and-black robe and hood ran crazily from somewhere in the back of the church, whirling and leaping and howling like a dervish until he reached the altar and a stunned Pastor Flower, who tripped and fell to his knees. The mysterious figure then vaulted over a railing and turned to the panicked congregation.

He tore the hood from his head, then the robe from his body, and stood before the assembly, his olive-brown body naked and oiled, his handsome face with the straight hawklike nose held high. Women screamed, but they did not avert their eyes, for the figure before them was a perfect masculine beauty. He raised his big-fisted hands and cried out over the nearly hushed church.

"I am Willis Duclat! I *am* Willis Duclat!"

And from the pew next to Vivian Duclat, a trembling Miss Toni stood up and screamed, "Jesus, Mary, and Joseph, it's him! Oh la, it's him!"

The old ladies in *tignons* began fainting away and children squealed. Men stared, gape-mouthed, unable to help the women and the young. The tall, muscular, naked man grasped the shoulders of a terrified Theo Flower and lifted him several inches off the floor,

74

then dropped him, crumpling, to a twitching heap. He turned again to the congregation and roared, "I, Willis Duclat, have come out!" He then knelt to Pastor Flower and whispered to him, "Time for you to blow town, chump, 'cause your number's up here."

He stripped Flower's robe of his *gris-gris*, which he dropped into the bowl of flaming brandy with elaborate gesticulation, so that all in the church could see he meant to destroy Theo Flower's control over them. "Be gone, the impostor's fakery!" he shouted.

He asked for silence. Then, he raised an arm and slowly directed it toward Miss Toni. "You," he said, "were in league with the impostor cowering at my feet. You placed the snake below the steps where you knew it would strike at me. You murdered me! It could have been no other way!"

Vivian sobbed.

"La, gawd-a-mercy!" Miss Toni screamed.

"Yes, yes, it was you! You and the impostor, this man called Theophilus Flower, who has oppressed you and cheated you all so cruelly for so many years since my death. It was you, Miss Toni, who killed me—to keep me from telling the truth that I do today!"

"La, mercy! Mercy! Oh la, please!" Miss Toni fell to the floor, gasping and writhing and consumed with her guilt, which took the form of what the hospital would later diagnose as massive cerebral hemorrhage.

The man then tore a lock of hair from his head and held it high over him so all could see. "Today I have destroyed the power of the impostor Theophilus Flower, who was foolish enough to call me out. I tell you all now, you must shun him! This hair I hold is the most powerful *gris-gris* of all, the hair of one from beyond. I shall give it to someone who lives amongst you. I shall plant it in his head this very night as he sleeps, and there it will grow. I shall give the power to a thrown-away child, now a grown man in my image, so that you shall always know him!"

Then he disappeared into the pit below the altar.

"Thank you for receiving me here, sir. I would have understood your refusing me."

"Well, son, I look at it this way: you done the crime and you done the time. Now that's just so much water under the bridge, don't you know. B'sides, you intrigue the hell out of me."

"Yes, sir. Thank you again." He brushed lint from the top of his sharply creased charcoal-grey slacks, part of a Parisian suit he'd had made for him by a tailor at Gauchaux's on Canal Street.

The fat man offered him one of his cigars, which he declined in favor of a pipe that used to belong to his uncle. He lit the pipe and the fat man's cigar, too, with a sterling lighter that used to belong to Theo Flower.

"Tell me," the fat man said, "how's Vivian doin' for herself these days? We all loved her so much. Damn me for casting her out like I did just 'cause of what you did."

"Nice of you to inquire, Doctor. My aunt's doin' just fine now. She had a little excitement at church a while back, but she rested lots afterward and I was able to take care of her, now that I'm runnin' the church myself and all."

"She's welcome to come back to me any time, you know."

"Thanks again, Doctor. I'll send her callin', but, you know, she likes her retirement now and she's earned it, I'd say."

"Of course, of course." The doctor shook his fleshy head. "Damn me again! Perry, I'm sorta sorry now for havin' that judge crack down on you like he did."

"That don't matter much now. You might say you straightened me out by catchin' me. I had lots of time to think things through in prison. It was sorta strange, actually. All kinds of thought just sorta took over me, and I couldn't do much more'n think, day in and day out. Finally, I figured that I had to watch close for somethin' to come along that I could grab onto to make life good for me and my aunt for a change."

"Well, sounds to me like you did a fine piece of thinkin'. Just how'd you manage to take over the church, though? I mean, Theo Flower didn't strike me as a man ready to retire, like your old aunt. All of us fellows downtown were sorta surprised when he lit out for Baton Rouge like he did, without even a bye-you-well."

Perry smiled. "He had a change of spirit, you might say. Decided on greener pastures maybe. Anyway, I was around and interested in the church, you know. Spent lots of time readin' up on it and all and figurin' how I might make my contribution. So, the moment come along when I figured I might grab on, so I done that."

He smiled again. "Of course, I had to first prove to Pastor Flower that I understood all the mysteries of his divine work. He musta been satisfied, because he signed everything over to me."

Perry emptied the contents of a satchel onto a table between him and the doctor.

"It's all legal, I didn't have to steal anything—or 'borrow,' I should say." The doctor laughed and Perry went on. "See here, it's all the deeds and titles and bank accounts—everything. That's why I come to you, sir, for some guidance in handling this all."

"You can count on me, Perry."

"I'm so glad."

"Where do you want to start?"

"Well, first thing," Perry said, "I want all the cottages down there in that lane off Tchoupitoulas deeded over to the tenants, maybe for a dollar apiece, some token like that that'd be sure to make it legal, and then—"

Thomas Larry Adcock, author of the critically well-received novel, Precinct 19, *was born in Detroit on January 5, 1947, and lives in Manhattan with his actress wife. A former police reporter for the* Detroit Free Press *and St. Paul Pioneer Press, he has also written features for the* New York Times, Chicago Today, The Minneapolis Star-Tribune, The Toronto Telegram, *and* Detroit Magazine, *among others. Currently a regular contributor of short stories to* Ellery Queen's Mystery Magazine, *he is completing a trilogy of mystery novels.*

Charlie may be old, but he knows hit men when he sees them; and they give him a reason to go on living. . . .

SIX

A Matter of Need
Wyc Toole

The girl walked across the sandy yard, sparsely covered with thin runners of brown grass, and turned up the path to a white frame house hidden in a small orange grove that was going to seed. She sang to herself as she walked. Her eyes were big and violet, and she was wearing a thin white blouse, faded blue jeans and sandals. She was deeply tanned and her tawny hair was parted in the middle and tied in full pigtails on each side of her head with pieces of bright yellow yarn. The morning sunlight that filtered through the tangled leaves of big oak trees made shifting patterns of light on her hair and face. It was still cool under the trees, but the sharp glare of the sun on the big lake behind her promised another blistering day.

The old man sitting barefooted in a rocker on the screened front porch of the white house watched the girl coming up the path and, for a moment, he smiled. Sometimes he found it hard to believe there was a girl so young and so happy and so beautiful that still came to see him. It was as if she belonged in another place and another time. Then thoughts of the real world crowded the smile off his face. He turned from her and watched a spider working its way carefully across a web after a trapped fly. He ignored the sound of her light step and the rusty squeal of the screen door as it opened and then slammed shut.

The girl stopped inside the door, hands on hips and her head tilted slightly to one side. A faint flicker of amusement played at the corners of her full mouth as she watched the old man deliberately acting as if only he and the spider existed in the world. Then, as she got a good look at him in the shadows of the porch, her smile faded and she pressed her lips together in anger, "Charlie Johnson! Just what do you think you're doing?"

The old man mumbled something unintelligible and returned her frown.

She stared back at him and snapped, "That's right! Sit there mumbling and barefooted like some old idiot cracker. See if I care! Darn you, Charlie, you haven't even put your teeth in this morning, let alone shave. I can hardly stand to look at you." She threw the last sentence at him as she stamped across the porch and into the house. In a moment, she returned carrying a glass half filled with water and the missing teeth., She thrust the glass at him and said, "Now you just fish those teeth right out of there and put 'em in your mouth. You hear me?"

The old man kept his eyes lowered as he stuck his fingers in the glass, pulled out the teeth and adjusted them in his mouth. Then he raised his head, looked directly into her eyes and said, "Hear ya! Hell, woman, they can hear ya all the way in town!"

"Don't you cuss at me, Charlie Johnson!" she said heatedly.

"I ain't cussing at you," the old man said sheepishly. "If I was, you'd have ya fingers stuck in ya ears by now." He glared.

"I know you're evil and mean. You don't have to convince me," she answered sharply. Then, as she looked anew at the old man in the chair, alone and defiant, her mood changed and she asked softly, "Have you eaten breakfast yet?"

"I don't want no breakfast!"

The girl smiled and walked behind his chair. She bent over and put her arms around his neck and rested her chin on his shoulder. Even sitting, the old man was so tall she only had to bend a little. She put her lips near his ear and whispered, "Well, you mean old man, I'm going to fix you some breakfast and you are going to eat it."

"Go ahead and waste time if ya want to, but I ain't gonna eat."

The girl rubbed her soft cheek against his rough white whiskers and said, "Ah, Charlie, you can't do this to yourself. What would Sarah say if she saw you sitting here like this?"

For a minute the old man's face softened. He sat very still, feeling the warmth of her cheek against his. Then he sniffed and rubbed his nose with a big calloused finger and said hoarsely, "Now, why you want to go and say a thing like that? Here I am, a sick ole man with not one damn thing to live for, and you come flouncing in all bright-eyed and bushy-tailed, saying stuff to make me feel bad."

The girl tightened her arms around his neck. "That's not true and you know it. Talking about Sarah is a good thing and I promised her I'd watch after you and that's exactly what I intend to do, no matter what. So don't you talk that way anymore. You've got a lot to live for and you know it."

"No, I don't know it," he said quietly.

The girl squeezed his neck again and said firmly, "Well, you do. So just hush about it . . . and you ain't sick either." She smiled. "And when I get to heaven, I surely don't want Sarah fussing with me about you sitting down here barefooted, needing a shave, with no teeth in and not eating breakfast. So you come on." She straightened up quickly, patted him on the head and walked toward the kitchen.

The old man got up and followed her. He sat down at the small kitchen table and watched her poking about in the refrigerator. He had always wanted a daughter, but not even in his best dreams had he imagined one as fine as Jan. His eyes followed her moving about the kitchen, cooking and chatting away without caring if he were listening or not. She reminded him of Sarah, and he was almost content. Lately, it seemed to him that Jan and her husband, Sam, had always lived in the small house next door; the only neighbors for miles. He felt so close to them that it was hard to believe they had moved in only a year before Sarah died . . . and she had been gone just six months.

His mind moved on, roving over things past, and he was lost in thought when Jan pushed an appetizing plate of eggs and bacon in front of him. The coffee smelled strong, pats of yellow butter melted on the hot toast, and his resolve not to eat faded completely away. As he tasted the good food, he decided that for a man who did not deserve much from life, he had been treated pretty well these past few years. Maybe God was telling him something . . . that he wasn't completely lost . . .

Jan noticed his smile and said, "You see? You get your teeth in and eat something solid and you feel—"

Charlie looked up. "Why don't you just hush, woman, and lemme eat. You are the talkin'est thing God ever made. I'm sure glad it's Sam you're married to."

Jan pretended to be angry, raised the big wooden spoon she was holding and shook it at him. "You better believe you're lucky, Charlie Johnson. I wouldn't put up with your foolishness for five minutes. You think you—"

"Jan, gal," he broke in laughing, "I believe you just naturally like to fight. If you wasn't so pretty, I'd throw you outa here so I could eat in peace."

Jan tilted her head and said seriously, "When you laugh like that, Charlie, you don't seem old at all. I bet you were a mighty good-looking young man."

"I had a couple of gals fancier than you who thought so."

"I'm being serious," Jan insisted.

"Me, too," Charlie grinned.

"You are not. You're trying to make me jealous and it won't work." She thrust her head forward and wrinkled her nose at him. "So there." Suddenly she asked, "What kind of person were you, Charlie? Sometimes your eyes get very cold and that hideous accent disappears. I don't believe you're from around here at all. Sam and I were talking the other night about how little we know about you. What kind of work did you do? Were you a good man? Would I have liked you?"

Charlie bent his head and attacked the eggs. For a while he didn't say anything and the room was still. Then he took a sip of coffee and replied thoughtfully, "I don't really know, Jan. You might have. I wasn't the best man in the world—might even have been the worst for a few years—but, right or wrong, you might have liked me. Sarah did, and she knew."

"Knew what?" Jan asked when he paused.

"Oh, I'll tell you someday when we got more time. I guess we do things sometimes we wish later we hadn't, but they're already done and you can't change 'em. Seems to me the big problem is that all our choices about the kind of life we lead are made when we're teenagers. Then as we get older, we do the best we can with the road our youth and inexperience took us down. Just takes some of us longer to switch roads than others, that's all."

Jan turned back to the stove and said quietly, "I don't understand everything you say, but I think I know what you mean. Maybe some-day I'll tell you about me. That might be the real question. Would *you* have liked *me?*" Her mood changed quickly and she laughed and said, "Too bad we'll never know. I suspect it would have been interesting."

Charlie wiped his plate with a piece of toast, put it in his mouth and mumbled, "All this serious talking done ruined my appetite, and I thought you was in such a big rush to get going this morning. That's all I heard about yesterday—taking care of that young one. Go on and get that baby over here. He's better company than you."

They continued abusing each other happily until Jan left and walked across the yard to her house. In a short while she came out again balancing a baby on her left hip and a large bundle on her right. Charlie watched her through the kitchen window and thought what a fine woman she was—built for carrying kids and having them; heart as big as the lake. She and Sam were going to have a fine life. A little hard on them now, but that didn't hurt at the beginning. He wasn't certain, but the way she was starting to poke out in front probably meant he would have two babies to watch over soon. That is, if he was still around. Seemed as though the place got lonelier every day since Sarah died. Deep inside, he knew that having Jan and Sam next door was all that had kept him from taking a long swim in the lake one night and not coming back. Even with them there, the water still looked very inviting sometimes when the nights went on forever.

Being alone was no good. That was how he had spent most of his life until, very late, he had found Sarah and they had moved out here. After that he understood what he had been missing. Being alone was a form of death itself, and with Sarah gone he wasn't sure the few years he might have left were worth all the pain that rose out of his present emptiness. It was something to think on.

He had made out a new will, leaving everything to Jan, the closest person to family he had. Just go swimming one night and let the kids enjoy themselves. He could imagine her face when she found out he owned all the land around the lake and how much money was in that bank in Orlando. It was something to consider real seriously.

When he went out on the porch, Jan was busy laying out all the equipment needed to support the baby. "You gonna be gone for a week?" he growled.

Jan shook her head at all she had brought and agreed, "Sure does look like it. But you'll be glad I brought all this stuff by the time I get back this afternoon. He's starting to eat like a young alligator."

"Mean as one, too. Takes after his ma. Don't you?" he asked the baby, bending over and rubbing the little boy's head.

"You go put your shoes on," Jan said to the old man as she moved toward the porch door, "and behave yourself while I'm gone. Probably be better with him looking after you."

She stopped at the door and Charlie walked over and took her hands in his. She looked up at his thick white hair and seamed tanned face, noticing how completely his hands engulfed hers and how much he towered over her. His shoulders were stooped, but there were still signs of power in his forearms and his eyes were a pale blue. He must have been something when he was younger, she realized, and her heart was sad.

This would be the only thing he would miss if he took that swim, Charlie mused. Yet even she added to the pain, being as far away as the moon.

Charlie shook his mind free of the terrible loneliness and said, "You run along and have a good time with Sam. You two don't get enough hours together as it is." He grinned broadly, let go of her hands and patted her stomach. "Or maybe you get too much time together, huh?"

Jan blushed. "I thought a man's eyes got bad when he was a million years old."

"I'm only a hundred and fifty, and they won't ever get so bad I can't tell when a pretty girl's in trouble." He winked.

Jan stuck her tongue out at him, turned, bounced down the steps, ran across the yard and drove off in a battered blue station wagon. Charlie watched the cloud of dust that marked the direction of the car until the light breeze carried it into the brush and the road was empty. He went back into the house, put on his shoes, came back on the porch and sat down beside the baby. It was getting hot, and he could feel drops of perspiration running down his body under the shirt. He spoke meaningless words to the baby and let the child play with one of his big fingers until the little boy fell asleep. Then he sat in his rocker and stared out at the smooth waters of the lake and thought.

He must have dozed, because he had a confused sense of the passage of time and he heard the car before he looked up and saw it parked in front of his house. It struck him as strange that as soon as his eyes focused on it he had a immediate reaction of wariness and distrust. Strange, because the car was vaguely familiar to him without any true feeling of recognition. It was a black sedan with a pronounced lack of chrome, and the sound of the engine was too big for the car itself. He rose from his chair and moved quietly toward the screen door, like an old fox that has led a long life by dodging hunters and traps. He stopped a few feet from the screen, knowing he could not be seen from the car. The light breeze blew hot on his face and for a moment he felt dizzy and the car blurred. He took a deep breath and the feeling passed and the car came back into focus.

There were two men in it. They were discussing something heatedly, but he could not hear the words. Finally, the driver got out, looked around and started walking up the path. He was a man in his late twenties or early thirties; short, broad and solid, and even in this heat he wore a dark sport coat and gray slacks. He was hatless, and

84

his hair was thick, black and cut very short. His face was hard to distinguish because he wore large sunglasses. Charlie did not recognize the man, but the walk and the way his coat was cut around the shoulders stirred a lot of old memories.

Charlie moved silently to the door, opened it carefully and stepped out into the bright sunlight. The heat fell on his shoulders like heavy hands. He eased the door closed so as not to wake the baby and started walking down the path to meet the man. As he walked, he stooped a bit more than usual and shuffled his feet unsteadily. The walk added another ten years to the large number he already carried.

"Morning," he said to the man. "Whatcha need?"

The man stopped a few feet from him and smiled without warmth. "Not a thing, dad. Just looking for somebody that lives around here."

Despite the heat, Charlie felt a cold spot growing in the small of his back. The three boats he could see on the lake were far away—too far away. He suddenly realized he should not have left the house without a gun, but it was done now. He was careless and the heat was making him feel tired. "Not many folks live 'round here. Who you want?"

Charlie waited for the man to give him a name from out of an almost forgotten past, but to his surprise the man replied, "Mrs. Semmes—Jan Semmes. I was a friend of hers in Miami. She live here?"

The old man tried to see through the dark sunglasses, failed and made a decision. "Don't know any Semmes."

"That's strange," the man said evenly, "because down the road they said she lived up this way. A little girl, blonde, built real good, but maybe you don't notice things like that anymore, dad."

Charlie was beginning to dislike the man intensely.

"She's got to live in one of these two houses," the man said.

As Charlie was deciding what to say next, the car door opened and the second man got out. He moved slowly up the dirt path, his head to one side, looking intently at the old man's face. Charlie watched him come. He recognized this one, but was unable to come up with a name. He silently cursed himself.

The man stopped in front of Charlie and said, "Dan Hedron! You're supposed to be dead! Hell, you must be a hundred years old!"

The old man started to speak, made another decision and said in a weak voice, "You got good eyes and a better memory. I don't do so well anymore. Help me out."

"You are getting old, Dan. You never forgot a face or a name. I'm Harry Worstam." The name registered and the hair moved on the back of the old man's neck. "You should remember me—New York and once in Chicago."

"Yeah, I remember you. It was a long time ago," the old man agreed.

"You know this old buzzard, Harry?" the short man asked.

Harry nodded his head in wonder. "Yeah, I know him, Tom. You're a little young, but right in front of you is what's left of the best in the business."

"You gotta be putting me on," Tom replied, looking the old man up and down with contempt.

"No, he's Dan Hedron. I only saw him three times, but I never forgot him. The best in the country in his day. Worked only high-priced jobs; on his own, a real loner. Had everybody scared of him. When nobody else could get to a man, he could. And those were rough times," he said admiringly. "One day in the early fifties, he disappeared. He was supposed to be about fifty then and the word was he just got old and slow and somebody took him. I was a kid almost, running errands for Bill Bondy. You remember Bill, don't you, Dan? Hell, you were my hero," Harry said, reaching out and patting the old man on the shoulder.

Charlie heard Worstam's words, but his mind was busy elsewhere. Jan was in trouble. These men were a cleanup detail. They hadn't come to warn or frighten, but to kill. He shook his head to clear away the waves of dizziness. He had no idea how long he had slept. Jan could be returning any time. He had to get the men into the house where he could maneuver. It had been a long time since his mind had worked on such problems, but he already knew what he had to do. The harsh sound of Tom's voice brought him back to the yard.

"Well, that's right exciting, Harry," the stocky man said impatiently. "And maybe when you finish playing old-home-week you can ask your hero about the Semmes dame so we can get done and bail out of here. This damn hot place doesn't show me much."

The old man grinned at Harry and said, "This your boss? I thought you'd be doing better after all these years. I was gonna ask you in for a beer, but I see you got a real pistol twisting your tail. How high you supposed to jump when he hollers?"

He watched Harry stiffen with anger and say coldly to his partner, "Shut up, Tom. When I want you to talk I'll tell you. You just do what you're told." He turned back to Charlie and shrugged. "Cheap guns. All mouth. Let's go get a beer." He started toward the house, studiously ignoring the stocky man. Charlie limped along beside him. Tom hesitated and then took up the rear. "Where is that Semmes gal, anyway?" Harry continued.

Charlie pointed with his thumb. "Lives next door, but she's out for a while. You got plenty of time. What's she done to get you on her? Seems like a nice kid."

Harry shook his head and replied, "Not me, Dan. Saw her once or twice, but she's nothing to me. You remember George Hefer— used to call him Big George because he was so damn small?"

Charlie nodded.

"Well, he really is 'Big' George now. I work for him. He runs a lot of stuff around Miami and Lauderdale. Best I can gather, George saw her dancing in a show over on the beach and got all fired up. Took her out one night and somehow during the evening she saw something she shouldn't have. She was smart enough to get out and start running, but George is real careful about loose ends these days. Image thing, you know. So he put out a call on her. Been looking for almost two years now. He thinks it's that important. She really ran a crooked trail, but we got a lead in Tallahassee and here we are. Don't want to cause you any trouble, Dan, but that lake out there looks like a good place to handle it. A boat accident shouldn't stir up the police too much."

The three men went up the steps and onto the front porch. The sight of the sleeping baby brought Harry to a halt. "What in hell is this, Dan? You got a baby?" he asked.

"Not mine," Charlie replied. "Belongs to the Semmes gal. Just watching it for her."

Harry said, "That's too bad; really too bad she's got a kid."

"Pregnant too, Harry. You got a lot of killing to do."

Harry swore. "That damn stupid female should have known better. She knew George was after her."

"Person's got to hope and live," Charlie growled. He bent over and picked up the baby. "I'll put him back in the bedroom and get some beer."

The old man was gone for several minutes. When he shuffled back to the porch carrying three bottles, he heard Tom laughing and saying, "You two sound like a couple of old ladies." Tom looked at Charlie and, taking the beer, asked, "You ever worry about kids when you were working?"

Charlie hesitated and his eyes seemed more pale and icy. "The ones I killed were too mean even to have mothers. I never went in for old men, girls, and kids."

Tom grinned. "You're still pretty sharp, dad. I figured a nice boat accident with the three of you would solve a lot of problems. Seems like you got the same picture."

Harry glared at Tom and said sharply, "That's not very funny."

Tom glared back at him and snapped, "I didn't mean it to be funny. Your old buddy here got the picture quick enough and you say he was the best. How do you plan to handle him?"

"We don't have to worry about Dan. He knows there's nothing personal in this. You just take care of the girl. That's what we came for. He's no problem. Are you, Dan?"

The old man looked up at Harry and wiped his mouth with the back of his hand. Before he could answer, Tom broke in. "He's a problem, all right. You aren't using your eyes, Harry. Look at him. He likes that female. Don't you, dad?"

Harry asked, "Dan?"

The old man took a long swallow out of the bottle without taking his eyes off the men. Then he set the bottle on the table and stuck his hands in the side pockets of the old jacket he was wearing. He hunched his shoulders and leaned back in the chair.

"Harry," he said thoughtfully, "there was a time when nobody walked in my territory, and even though a lot of time has passed and they call me Charlie now, things haven't changed all that much. This is my place and you ain't gonna dirty it. Now, the best thing for you to do is finish your beer, get back in your car and go tell George I don't want anybody else messing around out here. That gal ain't gonna bother him, if he don't bother her. And I won't cause any trouble either, if he lets us be."

Tom exploded. "Do we have to sit here and listen to this old fool ramble on?" He jumped up and shouted, "Get realistic, you old idiot. You can hardly walk, let alone cause anybody trouble."

Charlie ignored the outburst and said to Harry, "And you be real persuasive with George, because if he don't believe you and he bothers Jan again—I'm gonna kill him and then you. Understand what I say?"

"I don't care who he was or what you say, Harry," Tom said. "I'm going to—"

Charlie shot him twice without taking the gun from the right-hand pocket of his coat. For a moment, Tom's face showed that he did not believe what had happened. By the time he did, he was already dead.

In the bedroom, the baby began to cry. Harry's eyes were wide and frightened and he said in disbelief, "You killed him."

Charlie shifted his position slightly so the pocket with the smoking hole in it was pointed at Harry. He stuck out a big foot and prodded Tom's body, then nodded in agreement. "Sure did. Looks like one shot was enough, too. Always was cautious. Good to know I haven't changed in that way."

"You're crazy," Harry said. "You know that? You're crazy! Do you think you can get away with this?"

"Bet Tom thinks so." Charlie grinned without mirth. His eyes narrowed as he leaned forward in his chair. "Now, Harry, you listen good and don't miss my point. I killed that idiot because I wanted you to know I was serious. You weren't paying any attention before. Also, I didn't like him and his big mouth. Since I don't like you any better, you got any idea why I ain't killed you yet?"

Harry shook his head nervously, his hands flat on the arms of his chair. He was trying to speak, but his throat was too dry.

"The only reason I ain't shot you is because I want you to deliver my message to George, like I told you. And you better make him listen, because when I'm a hundred and five and only got one eye, you still don't have a man that can take me out here. So, anybody comes, they go back like Tom, here, and then I'll be after George. And he better hope Jan's the healthiest gal in Florida, because if she even dies of pneumonia I'll probably decide he had something to do with it. There won't be no place he can hide, because if I can't get there I'll put a price on him so high his brother would kill him to collect. You got all that straight?"

Harry nodded frantically.

"Then you take your garbage and get out of here," Charlie said evenly.

"What will I do with him?"

"I don't really care, Harry. You brought him. You take him. And of course I'd be mighty upset if the police ever came out this way. No telling what I might do to you. Don't let my age fool you none. I may have a few extra years to carry around, but they taught me enough to make up for a little speed. You convinced, or do I have to shoot you a little to get the idea through your head?"

Harry was already dragging Tom's body out the door. "I'll tell him, Dan. I'll tell him. But what if George won't listen?" he asked.

"Just show him Tom and tell him I plan to live longer than he does."

"The screen door slammed and Charlie went in to soothe the baby. The child stopped crying in time for Charlie to hear the car drive away. "Well, young man, been a full morning. Hope I got that settled. Just have to keep our eyes open and watch your mother real close for a while." The baby laughed and Charlie gave him a bottle to chew on.

It was late afternoon when the station wagon pulled into the drive next door. Charlie could hear Jan and Sam laughing as the car doors slammed and they started across the yard. He stood up stiffly from the bush he was clipping and pushed the big straw hat to the back of his head. "It sure is nice to have rich neighbors who run 'round having fun all day while some of us work," he yelled at them.

Jan ran ahead of Sam and threw her arms around Charlie. "We have a kind friend that takes care of us," she explained happily. "And we did have fun, Charlie. Thank you," she said hugging him tighter.

"That's right, woman," Charlie said, loud enough for Sam to hear. "Keep on, till your husband gets mad enough to shoot me. I don't know what I ever did bad enough to get saddled with you."

Jan started to answer, and them looked down at the ground. "What in all manner of heaven are you doing here, Charlie?"

"Digging a flower bed, if it's any of your business. Lord knows, if a man has to live forever in this hot sandy place, he can at least have a few flowers."

"And you shaved!" Jan said happily, reaching up and rubbing her hand over his lined face. Her eyes became serious and she said softly, "It's good to have you back again, Charlie, because I sure need you."

"Yeah," Charlie said, rubbing his nose. "I guess you do at that, little girl."

Wyc Toole (born in 1927) was born in Augusta, Georgia, and grew up in Maine. A retired Rear Admiral in the Navy, he is currently in construction real estate in Florida and has been writing mystery short stories since the mid-60s. Toole's stories are focused solidly in the psychology of his characters. "A Matter of Need" is a case in point.

After Grandpa Eller wills his tobacco farm to nagging cousin Myrtle and her dog-killing-mean husband, nobody knows who begins stealing corn—one bag at a time—or why. . . .

SEVEN

The Corn Thief
Guy Owen

I hadn't used up but one week of my month on Grandpa Eller's farm when the corn thief came for the first time. I was the first one to find it out, too. That morning I got up early and put on my blue jeans and new chambray shirt. Already I heard the catbirds and mockers fussing in the chinaberry tree, and somewhere in the pasture towards the old sawmill site a mourning dove was calling.

I slept on a cot in Grandpa's room, so I moved about easy and slipped out to the back yard barefooted. I was twelve years old and nothing in the world pleased me more than having my grandfather brag on me.

But when I went to the corncrib to shell the corn for the domineckers in the chicken run, I let out a whoop that must have waked up all of Cape Fear County. The lock had been pried off the facing and the door was flung wide-open. Wolf, the old one-eyed German shepherd that always smelled of mange medicine, was sniffing about the crib door, whining.

"Grandpa," I hollered, "come quick. We've purely been robbed!"

"What's come over you, Joel?" He was already hurrying across the back yard, stopping under the worm-eaten catalpa tree to hitch the galluses on his blue overalls. Without his felt hat on, his thin hair was white as snow in the morning sunlight. His face was seamed and old—all except his periwinkle eyes—and his short legs moved like a beagle's. I remembered then what Mama had said about him being too old to look after me, especially since he'd already had a stroke.

Ransom Martin, the new hired man, came scurrying out from the packhouse behind Grandpa, stretching his long legs. "What's all the commotion about?"

When Grandpa leaned in the crib door, he wasn't much taller than me. His sleepy eyes squinted, studying the pile of unshucked corn. "He didn't take much," he said, "whoever he was. Not more than a sackful he could tote on his back." His voice was matter-of-fact and he didn't seem excited at all.

"Let's call Sheriff Slade, Grandpa," I suggested. "If he can't come he'd be sure to send a deputy."

"Shoot, boy," Ranse spoke up quick. "Make him drive all the way from Queen City for one sack of weevily corn?"

Grandpa agreed that it wouldn't be necessary to call the Sheriff from the county seat.

"What you aim to do, Cap'n Jim?" Ranse asked, cornering his greenish eyes at my grandfather.

"First thing I figger to do," Grandpa said, calmly looking at the tall hired hand, "is get me a brand-new lock. A big one. And I reckon I'll tie old Wolf someplace close by tonight."

"I could stand guard with my new twenty-two," I volunteered.

But they didn't pay me any mind, Ranse and Grandpa.

"That old dog," Ranse said, "he ain't no 'count." He spat tobacco juice toward the scalding barrel where a few chickens were scratching in last season's hog hairs and new mule-hoof paring. "He ought to be shot and put out of his misery."

When I turned around, Grandpa's housekeeper was standing by Ranse. Myrtle's face was puffy and she acted as if she was mad from being waked up by all the hollering and whooping. Ranse told her about the stolen corn.

"I'm not surprised a bit in this world," she said. "I heard something. I kept hearing something the whole enduring night." Then she looked at Wolf and made a face. "He's too old to keep any thieves away. He's not fit for anything but to eat biscuits and carry fleas."

Grandpa stooped to pat Wolf. "You live long enough, you'll be old too one day," he said to Myrtle in a low voice. "Just because something's old don't mean it's worthless."

"I brought my rifle, Grandpa," I broke in. "I could stand guard on the back porch tonight."

"We'll wait and see, Joel."

Before we turned away, Ranse said, "I know a way to stop that thief."

"How's that, Mr. Martin?" I asked. For some reason I didn't like to call him "Mister." I'd seen the way he had of rubbing against the housekeeper when he thought they were alone.

But Grandpa was walking away. "I reckon me and Joel here'll get that lock."

Which is what we did. That evening, after we finished grading tobacco in the packhouse, we rode to the store at Eller's Bend in Grandpa's rattletrap Studebaker and bought the biggest lock that Uncle Sam Eller had in stock.

"Jim, you trying to keep something in or out with that all-fired lock?"

Since there were a few customers in the store, Grandpa didn't say anything, just sort of smiled. He bought me a nickel sack of peppermint sticks and a box of shells for my .22. Then we drove on back and I helped him nail the new lock on the crib door.

For all the good it did. Because next morning we saw that the corn thief had come again and made off with another sack of corn. And Wolf, who was tied close by, hadn't barked once. It was puzzling. I knew the German shepherd was getting blind; maybe he was almost deaf, too.

"What'd I tell you, Cap'n Jim?" Ranse said with a knowing grin. "If that sorry no-'count dog was mine I'd shoot him, sure."

That night I slept in the barn loft with Grandpa, waiting for the corn thief to return. Lying awake on the sweet-smelling oats, I did a lot of thinking. One thing I decided, quick enough, was this: I wouldn't write Mama about the thief that plagued us, slipping about the farm so quiet in the night that Wolf wouldn't even bark at him. I wouldn't tell her because she didn't want me to spend July with Grandpa in the first place, since Grandma had died and Grandpa had been in the hospital and had to hire Myrtle for his housekeeper. But I reasoned that Grandpa needed me more than ever and in the end I convinced her.

It wasn't Grandpa's idea to sleep in the barn loft; it was Myrtle's notion. She kept pestering him about it, in that scratchy voice of hers, until he gave in, maybe just to get some peace. And, of course, I went along. The truth of the matter is, I sort of sided with Myrtle— though I didn't like her at all, even if she was Mama's second cousin once removed. She was too bossy and sulky, and she never kept tea cakes in the stove warmer the way Grandma used to do. Not to mention coconut pies and pound cake in the food safe.

But Ranse Martin, the hired hand that slept on a cot in the packhouse, had his own plan. "You listen to me now, Cap'n Jim. I'll fix a trap with that double-barrel twelve-gauge of yours that'll take care of the lowdown thief."

The housekeeper was clearing away the supper dishes. "You might pay Ranse some mind now, Jim Eller," she said. She was a

93

short woman, with frizzly hair dyed the color of cornsilk, except for the dark roots. Like Grandma, she dipped snuff, but she wasn't clean with it. Sometimes her lips and teeth were stained with Sweet Society snuff.

"I wouldn't want to harm a man just for a shirt-tail full of corn."

Nor for the whole cribful, I thought. That's the kind of man Grandpa is. He was a gentle soft-spoken man.

Anyhow, when it was good and dark, we took our two guns and a flashlight and climbed up the ladder in the aisle of the barn. We took two old raggedy patchwork quilts and some of the tow-sack sheets used to spread over the cured tobacco, and made ourselves beds. Grandpa raked up a thick mattress of oat hay and we put two bales of peanut hay in front of our heads at the open loft door to rest our guns on. Grandpa said we'd keep our shells in our pockets; we wouldn't load unless we heard the thief coming.

Then we stretched out, talking low for a little while. I watched the fireflies blink on and off and the heat lightning off in the distance towards Clayton. Millions of stars were out like shiny bits of mica and the moon was like a quartered cantaloupe. The light was so clear I could see the corncrib, which set off a little ways from the big barn, almost like it was day. I aimed my .22 towards the board window, pretending it was loaded and clicking my tongue against the roof of my mouth for a shot.

"You think the thief will come back, Grandpa?"

"I don't know, son," he said. "It's not likely he'll come tonight. Some other night maybe."

"If he comes, we won't shoot him, will we?"

"No, we won't shoot. It would be a terrible thing to shoot a man for a few bushels of corn. A man whose family may be hungry."

"Ranse, he doesn't think it would be wrong to shoot him."

"Every man to his own notions."

"We'll just capture him, then, won't we, and holler for Myrtle to call Sheriff Slade?"

"That sounds like a mighty good plan. But you ought to get a little sleep now. You've got a lot of tobacco to take off the sticks in the morning. We've got to get that curing ready for the auction."

But I couldn't begin to sleep. "Don't you think we ought to keep guard, I mean stay awake in shifts so we wouldn't miss him—if he comes?" That was the way they did in all the books I read.

But Grandpa said it wasn't necessary. He told me he'd propped some old tin cans against the door. If anybody broke in the crib, we'd be bound to hear and wake up.

But I made up my mind I'd stay awake all night by myself, and for a long time I did, after Grandpa was asleep on the oat mattress. Once when the quartered moon was way up high, I thought I heard something in the barnyard. I gripped my rifle and peered over the bale of hay. But it was nothing but a barn owl looking for mice.

After that I eased back down and scrooched under the quilt. A breeze was rising from the Cape Fear River and it was cool. For a while I lay awake on my back, smelling the oats and listening to the breathing of the brindled cow in the stable below.

Towards midnight in the hayloft I started getting sleepy. Then, before I knew it, it seemed like a hoot owl had lifted the woods up and was carrying them far, far away . . .

Grandpa woke me, shaking my shoulder. "Joel," he called gently. Then we went down the cobwebby ladder together. I pumped a basin of water, then we washed up. Just as Grandpa always did, I sloshed the cold water on my face, drying with the towel hanging on the nail

"We'll sleep out again tonight, won't we, Gramp?" I asked.

"Maybe. We'll wait and see, son." He looked tired and there were worry lines around his pale eyes.

When we went in to eat breakfast, Ranse Martin and Myrtle were already sitting at the kitchen table. Like Myrtle, Ranse was from Queen City, and she had hired him herself on the spur of the moment when the old hired man quit while Grandpa was in the hospital. I suppose Josh Shipman got tired of Myrtle's sharp tongue or hard biscuits, maybe both.

Anyway, she sent for Ranse to help her tend the crops, claiming him for her dead sister's brother-in-law. One thing sure, he didn't know anything much about farming. He told me he'd been in the transportation business, but I found out all he did was drive a taxi. I heard Uncle Sam Eller say he probably sold a little moonshine on the side.

Now the hired man smiled and put his coffee down on the checked oilcloth. "He come back?" he asked. When he smiled you could see his stained teeth, and his reddish mustache bristled beneath his hawk's nose. He wore his dark hair long and combed it so it covered a bald spot on the crown of his head.

Myrtle heaved up then and got our eggs and grits from the stove warmer. They were cold, but the biscuit toast was good and the coffee was strong and hot.

Pouring my coffee, she said, "I bet a silver dollar you two went to sleep before ten o'clock out yonder. A thief could—"

Grandpa saucered his black coffee and said, "Well, at least there's no corn gone."

The new lock hadn't been touched.

"Sure we went to sleep. We didn't have any notion he'd come back again so soon." I set to eating then, hungry from staying awake to guard the corncrib.

But Grandpa just picked at his breakfast like there was a spider in his plate. I could see he was pondering something.

"Well," Myrtle fussed, "I'd like to know what you figger to do."

"Maybe he's got all he needs now," Grandpa said.

"Maybe he heard us in the barn loft," I chimed in, "and will stay away for good." I started to tell them about the big barn owl but I thought better of it.

Myrtle just snorted.

Ranse commenced, "Look here now, Cap'n Jim, me and you just better set us that trap this evening when we knock off." He seemed to grin and his lips were pulled back from his gums.

"No, not yet. I wouldn't want to harm—"

"Hunh, I think it's a time you listened to Ranse, Jim Eller, and quit being stubborn as a iron-headed mule."

"It's just a few bushels of corn, Myrtle," I said.

"Who pulled your chain, Mr. Big Britches?"

"That's it," Ranse persisted. "That's all it is now, but mind you when a thief gets to stealing like that, there's no telling what he'll wind up taking. To my way of thinking he's got to be stopped."

"And I'm not going to set still," Myrtle said, her voice rising "while some low-lived scoundrel steals us out of house and home, I'm not about to."

She sounded like she already owned the place, which someday she would. Grandpa had willed the house to her after he got sick so he would have someone to take care of him and wouldn't be a burden to his daughters. I had heard Mama fussing with Papa against it, though Myrtle was her own blood kin.

"I'm glad she's no kin of mine," Papa had said.

Myrtle commenced to pout but Grandpa didn't appear to pay her any mind.

But we had to listen all over again to Ranse telling about how him and his uncle once cured a corn thief. How they rigged up a shotgun in the crib, and when the man opened the door that night, it blew one of his legs nearly off.

"Simple as shooting a dove on a fence post," Ranse said, winking at me.

I gave him a sharp look. Grandpa had taught me never to shoot a bird unless it was on the wing, never to take unfair advantage of any creature, wild or tame.

Grandpa pushed back from the table. "I'll give it some thought." He stood for a minute in the doorway studying the two of them his face older than I'd ever remembered it being.

"You do that thing, Cap'n Jim," Ranse said, slapping the table. "I tell you there's more than one way to catch a thief."

That night we slept in the hayloft again and this time I sneaked a bullet in the chamber of my rifle.

When we woke up, it was long past daylight. My mouth dropped open when I saw the door to the corncrib was open. The thief had pried open the new lock, maybe with a crowbar, just like before. But that wasn't all: along with the corn, a power saw was gone from the tool shed. And we hadn't heard a whimper out of Wolf.

Ranse Martin was standing on the back porch grinning at us when we came down. "What'd I tell you all yesterday? You wouldn't listen to me before. I reckon you will now." He actually seemed happy the thief had come back again.

All that morning I worked hard in the packhouse. I had a notion I wanted to try out. I took the tobacco off the sticks as fast as I could, throwing the empty sticks out the window and piling the bright leaves beside Grandpa. He was grading the tobacco near the open door, holding the spread leaves up close to his eyes before dropping them into one of the three piles on the grading bench in front of him.

When I had taken off enough tobacco to last until past noon and swept up the broken stems and twine, I told Grandpa I was going to take the .22 and look for a rabbit over by the old millpond.

"You better be careful in them woods, boy," Ranse said. "I'd stay out of them woods if I was you. I seen a great big rattler near that dam, not more than three days ago." He was sitting near Myrtle, tying the tobacco in big awkward hanks.

"Your mama told me she didn't want you traipsing around—" the housekeeper began. She was tying the best grade, wearing a white sack apron to keep the sand off her flowery dress.

But I caught Grandpa's eye, and I didn't pay them any attention.

"Here, Wolf," I called, standing in the packhouse door.

Then the dog and I struck out across the pasture towards the woods. Grandpa knew I wasn't just out for any rabbit. Wolf must have sensed it, too, from the way he wagged his tail and kept his gray muzzle to the ground, sniffing and whining. Anybody would have thought he was a spry pup and not an old half-blind, nearly toothless dog.

We tracked the corn thief for nearly a mile. I could have done it without Wolf, the signs were so clear. I could see where he'd gone down the side of the cow lane, mashing down a fennel here and there or rabbit tobacco or ragweed. When he got to the woods behind the barn, he climbed the fence and turned north, headed, I guessed, for the old sawmill road that led to the Wilmington highway.

Presently Wolf sniffed all around in a clump of sumac and blackberries, then, looking back at me, headed up the dry creek bed, into the woods towards the old sawmill. I gripped my rifle and trotted after him, scaring up a hermit thrush.

In ten minutes we left the scrub oak and poplar and ran into the cut-over pine. I was glad I'd put on my straw hat then, because the sun was hot. Sweat trickled down my ribs and the pine needles felt warm and soft under my bare feet. They were good to smell, too. A squirrel fussed at me, but I just waved and smiled at him.

When we came out into the clearing, Wolf barked and dashed ahead. I ran after him, crossing the old lumber yard. A blue-tailed lizard sat gulping the sunshine on the pile of rotting slabs and a catbird flew up from eating blueberries.

When I walked around the slab pile, you could have bowled me over with a feather.

There was the stolen corn!

I took off my hat and squatted down, putting my arm around the dog's neck. His nose was wet and he was panting, with his tongue hanging out. "You may be old," I told him, "but you can still track a thief."

All the corn was there. The thief had dumped it in a sucken place at the foot of the sawdust pile and raked down sawdust over it. But he hadn't nearly covered it up. I guess he figured nobody would look for corn in an old sawdust pile. Either that or he was in a big hurry. The dog and I searched all around, under strips and old slabs covered with vines, but we didn't find Grandpa's power saw.

That evening, after we'd packed the graded and tied tobacco down and covered it with old quilts, Grandpa and me took our guns and headed for the sawmill site. The gun were just for show, because we decided to keep my discovery a secret.

Grandpa stood watching Wolf scratch at the pile of stolen corn. He took off his sweaty felt hat, scratched his head, and spit a glob of tobacco juice onto the sawdust pile.

"Don't that beat bobtail?" I said. "What do you make of it, Gramp?"

He just grunted and studied the situation a while, his eyes disturbed.

"Ain't that some kind of funny stealing?" I asked.

Grandpa said maybe whoever it was intended to hide the corn there until he had a wagonload. Then some night they could cut the wire fence and drive a wagon in and take it out by the old logcart road.

On the way back he said, "Then again, maybe they didn't really intend to steal that corn, Joel."

Which was a puzzle to me. But I didn't have time to ask any more questions, because just then Myrtle was calling us to supper, her voice as screechy as ever.

At the supper table Ranse said, "I reckon you'll listen to me now that thief has stole something worth as much as a power saw. I already got the stuff ready to set our little trap."

As usual Myrtle set in to backing him up, fussing and whining. I figured one reason Grandpa gave in finally was to get a moment's peace from the two of them.

"It might be the best thing after all," Grandpa said, looking away from me. "I just hope he won't come back."

I was sure surprised to hear him agree to the trap. It wasn't like him to do such a thing.

"Now you're talking sense for once," Ranse said, squinting at Myrtle, whose lips were quirked in a smile.

I guess Ranse Martin expected to get his way, sooner or later, because he had all the stuff ready. He'd nailed a board to a stanchion in the middle of the corn pile, with a V sawed in it to cradle the shotgun barrel. The stock rested on the corn. He had another board with a spoon contraption fixed to it.

When Grandpa climbed up on the dwindling pile of unshucked corn and settled the gun, Ranse tightened the strong twine he had braided that ran to a staple in the door and slipped the loop over both triggers. Then he shifted the old twelve-gauge shotgun until it aimed where he wanted it.

"Now, boy, you slip out that window and open the door."

I did. And when I eased the crib door open I heard the two clicks, one right after the other.

Grandpa took the claw hammer then and knocked the board with the V in it loose and nailed it back six inches lower. That way, if the shotgun went off, it would hit the thief in the legs, not in the chest. All this time he never looked me in the eye.

At least, I thought, he's showing that much mercy.

Ranse squatted close by, his bald spot under a string of red peppers dangling from a rafter. He watched Grandpa with narrowed eyes. "Suit yourself, Cap'n Jim. You're the boss, but I sure wouldn't show him no mercy, a thief like that."

Grandpa said, "The Bible tells us to temper justice with mercy."

"Well, get me them shells now," Ranse said gruffly.

"I'll get them Grandpa," I volunteered.

"Yeah, let Big Britches there fetch 'em."

"No," Grandpa said. "I'll get them myself, Joel. I know where they are."

"Hurry now," Ranse said. "We'll get ourselves a thief if he dares come back. I tell you, the time me and my uncle . . ."

But Grandpa had already gone, walking towards the house on his short legs, the back of his shirt stained with sweat.

It was almost dark now and the last domineckers had already gone to roost. The hired man and I waited in the corncrib about 15 minutes, not saying anything. Somewhere in the pile of corn a mouse was gnawing steadily.

Finally Ranse took to popping his knuckles. "What in the name of the devil's keeping him?"

"I hear him coming now."

"The Cap'n just gettin' old," he said. "He's old like that mangy dog, livin' on borrowed time."

"Grandpa's not old," I said. "He's not as old as you think, leastwise."

When Grandpa came back with the two shells, Ranse was fidgeting nervously with the gun.

"What kept you so long?" he said, reaching for the shells.

Grandpa didn't answer him. Instead, he clambered up the pile of corn. "I'll load it myself," he said.

I watched closely as Grandpa squatted and slipped the two shells into the chamber and flicked the safety catch off.

Ranse stooped and adjusted the gun until the twine was stretched as tight as a guitar string. "I double guarantee you that won't miss."

Then we slid down the corn pile and climbed out of the window. Grandpa swung the heavy board window to and twisted the wooden latch.

"What if he comes in the window?" I asked.

"Heck," Ranse said. "Ain't he always come to the door?"

"Maybe he's got all the corn he needs," Grandpa said quietly.

That night, of course, we slept in our beds for a change. There was no reason to guard the corncrib. Grandpa turned out the light, after reading a chapter in his old Bible, and pretty soon I heard him snoring away.

In a little while the housekeeper and Ranse turned off the radio in the parlor and went out on the front porch. I heard them talking and laughing, kind of low, rocking on the end of the porch shaded by the chinaberry tree.

I sneaked to the window, and when I peeked out I saw Ranse and Myrtle sitting close together in their rocking chairs. He had his arm on her shoulder.

As soon as Myrtle turned the lights out after Ranse, I slipped out of the cot and put on my shirt and blue jeans. Grandpa was breathing quietly and I didn't disturb him.

On the back porch I picked up my .22 and tiptoed out into the moonlit yard. I put my shoes on sitting on the back steps. Then I climbed the ladder up to the barn loft and stretched out on the oats, with my rifle resting on the bale of hay. If any thief came, I made up my mind I'd capture him first, before he got blown to smithereens by Ranse's devilish trap.

I reckon my intentions were good, but, like before, I dozed off sometime before daybreak. And that made a lot of difference.

Anyhow, when I woke up it was good daylight. I guess what woke me then was Grandpa's brogans, because when I looked down he was walking towards the corncrib, his face half hid by his old felt hat. He stopped at the crib door and tested the lock. I saw that it hadn't been broken. Then he walked slowly around to the board window.

I was just about to surprise him and call out, when I stopped. What made me keep still was this: I happened to glance towards the smokehouse, and there was Ranse Martin squatting down and looking over the stacks of stove wood. It looked curious. I couldn't puzzle out what he was hiding for, so I scrooched back under the oats beside my rifle.

But I could still see Grandpa standing by the crib window. He didn't open it right away. The shoats in the pigpen commenced squealing and I heard him speak to them gently. Then he looked all around, finally towards the packhouse where Ranse slept. He spit out some tobacco juice and reached for the latch on the board window.

The minute he put pressure on that latch I sensed something was wrong. Out of the corner of my eye I glimpsed Ranse Martin stand up by the smokehouse, and I felt the hackles on my neck rise. But it was too late to warn Grandpa.

Because as soon as he pulled on the window the shotgun exploded near his head and the shot echoed in the woods behind me. For a second Grandpa seemed to clutch at the window sill. His fingernails scrabbled against the rough boards as his body slumped down, and then he sprawled out beside the crib. One arm was flung over his head and his old felt hat was still on. He didn't budge.

My heart was thumping against a button and I was weak as skimmed milk. I just lay still for a minute, listening to the pig squealing and the mules stamping below in their stalls. Then I told myself I had to go down. If Grandpa wasn't dead, I would have to help him.

That's when I saw Ranse, and I ducked my head back and kept still as a mouse. He was walking past the woodpile, his shotgun held down by his side. His eyes looked puffy, and there was a smile on his thin lips.

For a minute he stood in front of the corncrib. I heard a door slam, and then Myrtle was running across the back yard. "Is it all right, Ranse?" she cried.

He waited for her. "Hush now," he said. He put his arm around her waist and together they walked around the edge of the crib with Ranse keeping the shotgun down by his side, away from the pudgy housekeeper. I watched them studying Grandpa's body. I could hear every word they said, and it was enough to turn my blood cold.

"Well, Myrt, what'd I tell you now?"

"I don't want to think of anything going wrong, hon."

Ranse patted her on the rump. "All you got to say is the old man set the trap and then forgot about it and killed himself. Everybody knows he's not been himself since that stroke. Leastwise, nobody's going to guess I turned the gun to cover the window instead of the door. And that house there is all yours—ours."

"I reckon you know best. But I feel so sorry for—Oh, I do hope nothing goes wrong."

"There's nothing to go wrong, I've been tellin' you."

"But what about the boy? He saw you-all—"

"I've thought about that, too," Ranse said, tapping his head with a finger. "I'll just say the old man changed his mind and we reset the trap to cover the window."

Then I heard her scream. Ranse put his hand up to her mouth, but it didn't help. She cut loose as loud as the shotgun had, louder.

But what made her holler was enough to stop the tears in my eyes.

It was Grandpa. He was getting up. I saw him rise to his knees, and then he stood up, with the two of them gaping at him and Myrtle's shoulders shaking.

He turned to face them, but he wasn't in any hurry to speak. I watched him brush the dirt off his work shirt and khaki trousers. There was a little smile on his lean face as he took off his felt hat and wiped the white hair away from his forehead. He was standing up straight, and in the morning light he didn't look so weak or old any more.

Ranse blurted out, "We—Cap'n, we thought you was shot. I'm mighty glad—"

"I reckon I know what you thought, Ranse Martin. You, too, Myrtle." Grandpa looked at the window where the gun had gone off near his head. "Mighty lucky thing for me I took all the shot out of them shells," he said.

Ranse rapped out, "What do you mean? What the hell's going—"

"You're going," Grandpa said calmly. "That's what's going, Ranse. The both of you are going to Queen City this morning." His jaw was set in that stubborn Eller way that Ma always remarks on when I act up. "I may be old, but I'm not blind. Not yet I'm not."

"That's what you think, old Cap. There's more than one way to skin a cat." Ranse swung his shotgun up then, holding it at his waist, aiming it right at Grandpa's chest.

"No, Ranse!" Myrtle cried. "I back out now. That weren't in the bargain."

"You'll back out of nothing. Shut your damn mouth."

Grandpa didn't flinch. He just got a little smile on his face.

"No, Ranse," Myrtle said. "I mean it."

Grandpa said, "You've not got to worry, Myrtle. Ranse here's been talking about killin' something ever since he came on this place. But I've got him pegged. He wouldn't kill a tick unless he could set a trap and go off somewhere and hide while the dirty work was done."

"Is that so?" Ranse snarled, steadying his gun.

That's when I stood up in the barn loft. I aimed the rifle at the corn thief, and I didn't tremble a bit. "Drop it, Ranse," I said, "Drop that gun now."

Ranse swiveled his head around and up, his eyes almost as wide as Myrtle's.

"You'd better do what he says," Grandpa advised. "I taught Joel how to handle that rifle, and he don't miss." He smiled up at me. "Come on down, son."

Ranse just let his shotgun fall out of his hands, his shoulders slumping.

I scrambled down the ladder. When I got there Grandpa was holding the shotgun, not pointing it at anybody. Myrtle was whimpering and Ranse looked like a suck-egg dog that had eaten an egg with red-devil lye in it. He even looked blue around the mouth. Wolf was sitting by the crib door looking at them with his one good eye, puzzled.

"I'll go call the Sheriff, Mister Jim," Myrtle said in a low voice.

"I hope this teaches you a lesson, Myrtle," Grandpa said.

From the look on her face it had. I almost felt sorry for her myself.

Ranse turned to walk towards the house with her. He didn't say a word more to us.

"Another thing," Grandpa called after them. "Joel and me are goin' fishing. When we get back, if that power saw has turned up, I won't mention it to Sheriff Slade."

I guess that's what's meant by tempering justice with mercy. Anyway, when we got back from the Cape Fear River, with a string of perch a yard long, there the power saw was on the back porch. And Myrtle and the corn thief had gone and turned themselves in to the law.

Born and raised in Clarkton, North Carolina, Guy Owen (born 1925, died 1981) is the author of four novels. Journey for Joedel *was a Pulitzer Prize nominee, and* The Ballad of the Flim-Flam Man *was made into the film* The Flim-Flam Man, *starring George C. Scott. Owen received his Ph.D. from the University of North Carolina at Chapel Hill and served as instructor and writer in residence at Davidson College, Stetson University, Appalachian State University, and North Carolina State University at Raleigh. He was editor of* The Southern Poetry Review.

*Once Adger Hillman tires of being shot and shot at because of a line fence feud,
he sets in motion the Hatfield and McCoy events of a modern Romeo and Juliet
story. . . .*

EIGHT

Hell's Acre
Jesse Stuart

"What are you sittin here for, Adger?" Ma asks. "Can't you hear
the guns a-boomin at the fur-end of the pasture field? Why aint you
a-helpin out?"

Ma stopped sweeping the floor and looked at me. She looked at
me with her gray hawk-eyes. The weight of the pipe on the long
stem sorta jimmied the pipe in Ma's mouth since she's lost some of
her front teeth. Ma stood in front of me solid as an oak tree. She
looked mean out'n her eyes when she spoke to me.

"You know why I aint out there," I says. "You know I was jest a
boy when I first picked up a musket and went out there to fight the
Sturgins. I didn't know how to fight. That was in 1929. I've had
enough of that damn war over a line fence. We've been fightin all
this time and we aint got a thing settled."

I laid my pipe down on the bottom of a hickory split-bottomed
chair. I pulled up my overall leg above my knee.

"Here is part of what I got," I says. "This aint nigh all. I was shot
through the hip. I was shot in the shoulder blade and the bone was
nicked. You can see the fat part on my right ear is shot off. Ma, I've
had enough of this war. I've been thinkin about some sort of peace."

Ma took her pipe out'n her mouth. It was too hard to hold in her
mouth while she talked. She looked down on my leg at the tiny scars
that glistened like white-soup beans from my ankle up above my
knee. It looked like there's two hundred tiny scars on my leg.

"I was shot down with a autermatic," I says. "Kam Sturgin
pumped six loads of buckshot at me. If he'd a-been ten yards closter
to me I'd a-been a gone-goslin. I'll never forget how I felt when I's
shot. Jest seems like the props went from under me all of a sudden."

"You was shot in the leg in 1930," says Ma.

"And I was shot through the hip in 1933," I says. "My shoulder blade was nicked in 1935. My ear was shot off in 1936. I've been sprinkled with shot so many times I don't mind it any more than I do a light shower of April rain."

Ma put her pipe back in her mouth. She took a draw on her long pipestem. The fire was out in Ma's pipe. She reached in her apron pocket and got a match. She struck it on the jamm-rock above the fireplace. Ma lit her pipe again.

"Don't sweep around me, Ma," I says. "Leave the dirt on the floor around my chear."

"You talk crazy, Adger," says Ma.

"That aint crazy," I says. "If you don't sweep around me it is a sign I'll get married."

Ma laughed and laughed. She thought I was crazy. I was glad to see Ma laugh. She laughed more than she had laughed the past nine years. I'll tell you since we've been at war over the line fence there aint been much laughin at our house.

"You air old enough to get married," says Ma. "If you live unt'l next August you'll be twenty-two."

Ma swept around me. She left a circle of dirt around my chear. I sat before the fire and baked my scarred leg. Heat felt so good to it. Seemed like it lost a lot of feeling in it since Doc Holbrooks spent two days picking the buckshot out. Some are left in my leg. I can feel them under the skin. They feel like hard dry grapes. I put my overall leg down atter my leg was baked until it was red by the wood fire.

"You aint very stiff in that leg, air you?" Ma ast. "None of the jint water run out'n your knee, did it?"

"Nope," I says. "The buckshot didn't go in deep enough."

"Listen to the guns this mornin," says Ma.

"I've been settin here listenin," I says. "That aint nothin. We hear 'em all the time. Pears like the fightin is the hardest in February and March when the ground is froze and we can't plow. I'd better get my gun and get out there."

"Be careful, Adger," says Ma. "Your body is a wreck now. Don't get shot any more. You'll not be able to stand many more bullets in your body."

"My body's good fer a lot of bullets yet," I says. I picked up Hulda. Hulda is my long-range single barrel. She's thirty-six inches in the barrel, a ten-gauge, and full choked. Use super shells loaded with two extra grams of powder and chilled buckshots. Sometimes I ring the shell so it'll shoot like a rifle when I'm shootin at a Sturgin at long range. I put Hulda across my shoulder, I sorty dragged my stiff leg and walked out'n the house. Ma came to the door with her broom in her hand to watch me go.

"Do be careful, son," says Ma.

"I've been there too many times," I says. "I'll watch what I'm doin."

I walked out past the barn. Then I went around the path through the wood's pasture to the fur-field. The wind blowed lonesome-like in the bare oak-tops above my head. The winds made a lonesomer sound in the pine-tops. The closter I got to the fur-field the louder the guns got. I clim to the top of the yaller clay bank. I looked over at the cedar tree. There was where Pa give his men orders. I whistled our signal—two longs and a short whistle. Pa answered me with two short whistles. That was the signal that all was well. I crawled on my belly over the frozen ground down to the hole where Pa was under the cedar tree.

"They air takin pot shots at us from that beech grove down yander," Pa whispered. "The damn dirty cowards air in the timber on us. We're jest shootin enough this morning to keep 'em back. We can't hit 'em in all that timber. We've skint a lot of trees around 'em though."

Pa was layin down in the hole chewin his home-twisted burley terbacker. He had two big sand rocks above him and his musket was pinted between the two sand rocks. Pa had a pot of coffee on a little fire down in the hole. Smoke went out'n the hole and up among the limbs on the cedar tree.

"The Sturgins can see your smoke here," I says. "They'll get you, Pa."

"They know who's in this hole," says Pa. "This is the place they can't get. I'm upon this little rise here. I can look every way and give my men orders. I think I put another bullet in old Kam Sturgin this morning. If I did, this makes eight times I've shot 'im. He's a hard booger to kill."

"Spat——"

The cedar bark flew over us. Pa opened fire with his musket toward the beech timber. Pa shot until his musket was hot. He shot from between the sand-rocks. Our men opened fire plum across the end of our pasture field. They knowed the Sturgins were trying to get Pa.

"The Sturgins can't take my land," says Pa. "Our war started in 1918. We fit 'em with the courts until 1928. I've sunk fifteen hundred dollars with lawyers' fees and court costs. Then the Supreme Court give the Sturgins that acre of ground. They've lost nearly all their land payin lawyers' fees to get it and they aint got it yet. I jest decided powder and lead was cheaper than lawyers' fees and court costs. That's the reason we've been fightin another ten years fer that acre of land."

Pa put Hulda between the sand-rocks. Pa started feedin 'em the ringed shells from Hulda's muzzle, and we heard 'em screamin and hollerin. They thought we'd turned a cannon loose on 'em that shot buckshot.

"We'll win this fight with this kind of a gun," says Pa.

"Did the Hillmans ever fight their kinfolks?" I ask Pa.

"Never in my lifetime, Son," says Pa as he opened fire with Hulda at the beech grove. Pa jest talked like nothin had happened and kept shootin. "Never in my lifetime, Son. We respect our own people. We've had little fist fights among ourselves but they don't amount to nothin. We've never used a gun or a knife. We've never even used a rock or a club when we had our little skirmishes with our own folks."

"Gee," I says, "that's fine!"

I jumped out of the hole and started over the bank. I think every Sturgin's gun barked at the same time when I hit the open field bent over half-double, runnin. The bullets hit all around me. They wheezed over my head. One went through the elbow of my coat-sleeve.

"Take kiver," Pa hollered. "What's the matter? Have you gone batty? You'll git shot again."

"I aim to end this damn war," I says.

I leaped over the yellow clay bank safe from the flyin bullets. I can't tell you how I felt. I took down the hollow to Kam Sturgin's farm. I took down the hollow behind the winter-fern-kivered bluff. I was safe from their battle lines. I was soon behind the Sturgin lines. I could still hear the guns boomin over toward our house. I walked down the hollow with a pipe of terbaker until I come to Kam Sturgin's big log house. I'd allus wanted Effie Sturgin. I would get her.

The hound dogs run out to the gate and started barkin through the palins at me. The palins were tall and the tops sharpened so a body couldn't climb over the fence. Kam was fixed fer us so we couldn't attack his house. I was goin to make an attack a different way.

"Howdy-do!" I hollered. "Is there anybody at home?" I could peep through the palin cracks. I could see eyes peeping from the winder glasses at me. No one dared to come outside the door.

"Kam Sturgin and his men have been whopped," I hollered. I thought that would bring somebody out'n the house. It did bring somebody out'n the house. It brought Effie Sturgin out'n the woodshed. She walked out with her sleeves rolled to her elbows. She looked like an angel to me.

"You might say Pa is whopped," says Effie, "but I don't believe it. He will never be whopped by the infernal Hillmans and their click. They might kill 'im but they won't whop 'im. Is that you, Adger Hillman?"

"Yes, mam, this is Adger Hillman," I says. "This is all that aint been shot away by Sturgin bullets."

"What are you doin here?" she ast.

"I've throwed my gun down and quit fightin," I says. "I'm tired of fightin."

"Have the others quit fightin?" she ast.

"Hell, no, Honey," I says. "Can't you hear the guns crackin? I'll tell you what is wrong with the Sturgins. They can't shoot."

"They can shoot," says Effie. "They are good marksmen."

"They couldn't hit me," I says. "I was runnin fast as a rabbit."

Effie looked at me and I looked at her through the palin fence.

"I've got to get back to washin clothes," says Effie.

"Let me hep you," I says.

"I can't let you come in here," she says.

"Yes you can," I says.

"Ma would take the top of the house off is she's to see you come in at this gate!"

"Aint there another way around?" I ast.

Effie stood and looked at me. She shivered in the February wind. She stood a minute before she answered me.

"I don't believe you are up to a trick, Adger," she says. "You know we aint on good terms with your people."

"I'll cross my heart," I says, "that I aint up to a trick."

"Jest don't let Ma see you slip behind the woodshed," says Effie. "There's a trap door there. I'll open it. Come in from the backside."

Effie walked back in the shed as if nothing had ever happened. I slipped along beside the palins. I slipped up behind the woodshed. Effie opened the door from the inside. I walked in the woodshed. The palin fence tied onto each side of the woodshed and that made it part of the fence.

"Thank you, Effie," I says as I walked into the shed. "I've come to see you. I have something to tell you."

"What?" Effie ast.

"We can stop this war among our people," I says.

"How can we do it?"

"Get married," I says, "if you love me enough."

"You've ast me too suddenly," says Effie.

"Honey, we can," I says. "You know we can. All that's ever kept us apart has been our people. Your people hast nearly got me four different times. You see me limpin, don't you?"

"Yes," says Effie, "what is the matter?"

"Your Pa filled my leg full of buckshot."

"Pa did?"

"Yes, your Pa did," I says. "Kam Sturgin shot me."

"I can't hep it if he did shoot you," says Effie. "You was out to get Pa."

"You can hep it," I says. "You can kiss me for every buckshot that went in my leg."

Effie didn't answer me.

"You know kinfolks don't fight each other here," I says. "We won't fight our kinfolks. Do you fight yourn?"

"You know we don't," says Effie. "You know that kinfolks don't fight each other here."

"Then we can stop this war."

"Yes."

Effie put her arms around my neck. I helt her close. I kissed her and she kissed me. We jest let the washin tub of clothes stand. We loved and loved in the woodshed. I'll tell you she's the purtiest woman I'd ever seen. Her tiny white wrists was just about the size of my middle-finger and my index finger put together. Her eyes were green like a cat's eyes. Her lips were clean and purty and red with bloom as the petals on a spring pink. Her teeth were white as grains of corn when the shuck has just been stripped off. She was nearly as tall as I was.

"I can't love you all afternoon," she says. "I've got to get my washin out on the line."

"I never washed clothes in my life," I says, "but I'll hep you. I'd rather wash clothes than carry a gun and fight all the time."

I couldn't wash clothes very well. I washed them the best I could. I'd work awhile then I'd hold Effie in my arms. I washed clothes and loved Effie all afternoon in the Sturgins' woodshed. It was the best way to end a war I'd ever seen. I jest wondered why I hadn't thought of it before. I'll tell you it was a pleasant way to end a war. Effie wondered why she hadn't thought of it before. I never even thought about my brothers, cousins, uncles, brothers-in-law over there layin in the broom-sage on the frozen ground on their bellies and poundin away over an acre of land. I didn't even think about Pa in the hole under the cedar tree drinkin coffee and chewin terbacker fer his nerves. They could all fight and be damned. If it did or it didn't stop the war—I was marryin Effie Sturgin and taking her out'n the mess and gettin out'n it myself. You don't know what one of these damned long fights is until you've been in one. I was gettin out and stayin out.

"You'll haf to go, Adger," says Effie. "It will soon be dark and our men that are alive will be slippin back through the woods to their homes to do up their work. A lot of them will never slip back. Pa has been shot seven times. He's still alive and fightin. Uncle Charlie was shot in the leg. He's got white swellin in his leg now and he hast to drag it along. Cousin Eif, Charlie, Bill and Van sleep on the hill—brother Cy and Mort sleep beside them. Uncle Dave, Uncle Martin, Brother-in-law Did kilt—nearly all the men hast been shot sometime or the other—or they've been skint with bullets."

"We aint been shot up that bad," I says—"I've lost one brother, four cousins, one uncle and a brother-in-law. They are buried on the hill jest across from the hill where your people are buried."

"What kind of a place is it where they are fightin?" Effie ast me.

"You've got your pasture fence set behind the line fence five acres deep and ten acres long," I says. "We've got our fence set back the same way. We're losin fifty acres of our best land. You're losin fifty acres of your best land. Our bull was shot through the brisket with a stray ball behind our lines. We've had two calves and a cow shot. We're jest fightin on it to get one worthless acre. Look at the money spent in the courts and look at the men kilt and plugged. Men that will never fight again and the men that will never be able to work again. Look how our neighbors air gettin ahead of us over behind the ridges. They are raisin terbacker and corn while we are raisin hell. When we marry, Effie, it will be ended. We'll all be kinfolks then."

"Give me time to think," says Effie. "You know I love you, Adger. I've allus loved you. I've been afraid to go with you. I hate your last name. I'll allus hate the name of Hillman. It's a mean name. It's the name the Devil wants it to be. You must come and see me. Come when you can. Give one long whistle. I'll leave the door unfastened to the woodshed. Don't let anybody see you. You must go now."

"I'll see you," I says.

I pulled Effie close to me. I kissed her purty face over and over. I was fightin a different kind of war now. I loved this kind of war.

"Good-by, Honey," I says. I grabbed my cap and I went out at the trap door. I hit the road runnin with my cap in my hand. I took up the crick the way I'd come. I heard people talkin around the bend in the road. I jumped over the bank and hid behind a rock. I hadn't more than got behind the rock until I saw about a hundred men comin down the road with their guns on their shoulders. The men in front were walkin fast and a-cussin the Hillmans.

"I'd soon shoot a Hillman as a rabbit," said a tall bearded Sturgin.

"They air a bunch of polecats," says a small man walking beside of the tall bearded man, "and we got to get 'em thinned out when the green gets back in the trees and we can snipe 'em from the cliffs."

Then I heard a man groanin and hollerin. Four men were carryin him. Two men walked behind and carried a leg a-piece. Two walked in front and carried an arm a-piece. They had their muskets strapped around their shoulders. The man's head was bent over with his face turned toward the sky. He would groan when the men shook him. His long red beard stuck out from his chin like the handle of a cane. The wind moved his beard as the men walked. His clothes around his waist were red with blood.

"Oh, my side," he would groan.

"Don't go on so, Kam," says one of the men a-hold of his leg. "We can't let the Hillmans know you've been plugged again. It gives them a fresh start. They'll be right over on our side of the fence tearin up the dirt. Old Tarvin Hillman will have his hole dug over on our side the fence blastin us with buckshots."

"Oh, if you'd been plugged through and through like I have," Kam moaned, "you'd groan too. You know I'm tough. I can take it. This is eight bullet holes I have in me. I'm plugged through and through and that silk handkerchief feels funny in my stummick."

"It's in place though, Kam," says a short stocky Sturgin carryin one of Kam's arms. "I know it is fer I pulled it through the bullet hole and tied a knot in each end so it couldn't slip out. Take it easy. We'll soon have you home. We can give you some hooch and you'll feel better. It's three-ply hooch and it will put the spirit in you."

"Hooch, hell," Kam mutters—"I'm hurt. Old Tarvin Hillman plugged me with a rifle. I know he plugged me. I saw a cloud of smoke under his cedar tree the second I's plugged."

I was glad when that crowd of Sturgins got past me. I changed my path. I went over Sturgin land to the acre of land we'd been fightin over. It got a little dark before I got there and I got afraid. I thought I might meet the spirits of the dead men that had been kilt by Hillman bullets. I'll tell you the trees over in Sturgins' pasture field clear back to the second fence was riddled by our bullets. The bark was all skint off'n the trees. It was a ugly dark field. You could feel empty cartridges all over the ground with your feet. You could find holes dug out everyplace. Our side of the line fence wasn't shot up half as bad as the Sturgin side. We must a-had better guns. In all our war with the Sturgins Pa had jest lost one finger and had been plugged in the thigh once when he crawled out'n a hole. I had sad thoughts though as I dragged my numb leg across the pasture-field of brown broomsage in the moonlight.

It was before daylight when Pa took his men and went to the field to shoot at Sturgins across the line-fence. I stayed behind to hep Ma feed the hogs, milk the cows, carry in water. I made up my mind not to go to the pasture field anymore and shoot across the line fence at the Sturgins. When I thought about the Sturgins I couldn't hate that name. It was a good name to me anymore since I'd seen Effie Sturgin. I could see her cat-colored eyes looking at my beardy face. I could see her purty hair and her purty white teeth. I could feel her soft hair in my hand and her tall body clost to me when I loved her. Hell, I didn't want to fight anymore. I'd had enough fightin. I didn't ever want to fight again. I wanted to get out'n it. I wasn't a-goin to get kilt over an acre of old poor worthless land when there was a girl in the world as purty as Effie Sturgin.

As I set on a milk stool and milked Old Roan, I could see Effie Sturgin in a little house. I was fur away from our pasture field. It was out'n the range of the bullets. It was over in Hog Hollow. I could see her washin her clothes and my clothes under the shade of a big oak tree in our yard. I could see hollybocks bloomin by the door of our shack. I could see geese, pigs and chickens about our door. I could see some little Hillmans running around loose in the yard—free as the wind that blows. That was what I could see when I looked over our barn lot and zigzaged two streams of milk into the three-gallon zinc bucket.

"What's the matter with you, Adger," Ma ast, "that you aint goin out there anymore and heppin your Pa fight the blasted Sturgins?"

"I'm on furlough," I says, "and it's goin to be a long furlough too. It's goin to be forever. I'm through."

"What's the matter?" Ma ast. "Hast the color of your blood turned from Hillman red to Sturgin yaller?"

113

"Nope," I says, "my blood is still Hillman red but my heart has changed."

"Who's the gal?" Ma ast me.

"Effie Sturgin," I says.

"My Lord," says Ma—"a Sturgin—"

"Yep," I says—"a Sturgin."

"She can't come under my roof atter I've lost a boy by the Sturgin guns."

"They've lost more than we have," I says. "They are crippled up. If you'd see their men hobblin along the road then you'd know. Looks like they've all got the jake-leg. Old Kam Sturgin has been plugged eight times. He's still alive and fightin. Look at me Ma! I'm a cripple fer life if some feelin don't get back to my leg."

"A Sturgin gal in the Hillman family," says Ma as she reloaded her pipe and lit it with a match. "You ain't standin by us, Adger."

"I'll end this war," I says, "and it's right now time it was ended. The trees hast started gettin green. You know what that means. It means bush-whackin."

I couldn't hep it. I jest set the millk bucket down in the barnlot. I jumped over the fence. I never said another word to Ma. I left her talkin to herself in the barnlot. I'd been goin to see Effie a month now. I'd been slippin around the battle lines. I'd been slippin like a fox when he goes to get chickens. I had to come back in the dark. I had to dodge the Sturgins all the way. They'd be comin home car-ryin their dead 'r heppin their wounded. I could allus smell their terbacker smoke and hear 'em cussin Hillmans before they got nigh me. Now I was makin my last trip.

I whistled fer Effie behind the palins. She come to me. Effie looked like a queen when she come through the trap door of the woodshed. We didn't do any talkin. We jest helt hands and run like two turkeys up the road. We walked five miles to town and got our license. We walked six miles back to Brother Tobbie Bostick's and jumped the broom.

"I'm glad to see this," says Brother Tobbie, "fer I believe it will end that fightin over there. I've heard guns over there jest like a field of men huntin rabbits. I've preached the funerals on both sides. I've prayed a lot over that trouble. I hope this will end it."

"We haf to be goin," I says to Effie. "We got work to do."

We left Brother Tobbie prayin over our family troubles. We took up the sand-rock path, and over the cow-path hill to the hollow. We could hear a gun now and then. We walked up the hollow to where the little crick branched off the main hollow. We slipped up this crick toward the beech grove. We slipped up behind the Sturgin lines.

"You'd better holler, Honey," I says, "to one of your men. We might get shot."

"Oh, Pa," Effie hollered. "This is Effie. Please don't shoot."

"Take kiver, youngin," said a coarse voice. "What air you doin here nohow? This aint no place fer wimmen folks!"

Jest somehow the guns stopped barkin on our side of the fence. Guess our men heard a woman's voice and bad as they are to shoot they'd never shoot at a woman. We didn't take kiver. We walked up in the beech grove.

"Papa," says Effie.

Effie walked toward Kam Sturgin. He was propped up behind a big beech tree smokin his pipe and givin orders to his men. He had bandages and plasters all over 'im.

"What brings you here?" Kam ast, "and who might that young man be?"

"My husband," says Effie—"Adger Hillman!"

"My God," says Kam—"you married a Hillman!"

"Yes," says Effie—"I married a Hillman. We want you to stop shootin right now. We want this war ended."

"Atter I've lost this much blood," says Kam. "I'll lose the rest of my blood or win this fight and my acre of ground."

"How about dividin that acre of ground, Pappie Kam?" I ast.

"Don't Pappie me," he says. "I'll plug you on the spot."

"No you won't," says Effie.

"I'll Pappie you too," I says.

"Stop your men from fightin," says Effie.

"We'll stop the Hillmans," I says. "We don't fight our kinfolks. Aint that a rule among you?"

"Come to think about it, that's the rule among our people," says Kam. "I jest hate to be licked."

"We aint licked," says Effie.

We turned and walked down the hollow. We heard two short whistles. We didn't hear anymore guns.

"That's our signal fer retreat," says Effie.

"Let's hurry and get to the other side," I says.

We run down the beech grove hollow. We kept under cover by the fern-kivered bluff. The trees had started to put out their new spring coats of leaves. March was nearly over. April would soon be here. We hurried to the top of the yaller-clay bank.

I gave Pa two short whistles. Pa answered me with two longs. We jest walked over into Pa's headquarters. He was makin coffee.

"This is my wife, Pa," I says.

"Son, wasn't you afraid to bring her out into the open? Don't you know what is goin on here?"

He had his musket pinted between the sand-rocks. Pa didn't pay us no minds.

"We aint afraid," says Effie. "There won't be anymore shootin from the other side. It's all over."

"I thought something funny," says Pa—"We heard a woman's voice down there awhile ago. I signalled my men not to shoot that way. Then the guns stopped. Who might your wife be, Adger?"

Pa turned and looked at me. He twirled the corners of his mustache with his big fingers.

"Effie Sturgin," I says.

"A right purty gal," says Pa, "but I don't like that name, Sturgin. Child, you've changed it fer a better one. And this is the reason, Adger, you've been layin down on the job since last February—right when we've been doin the hardest fightin. We lost three of our best men last month. I know Sturgins lost five men last month."

"Pa, you'd better give a signal fer the men to come in," I says. "The Sturgin men have gone home. You know we don't fight our kinfolks."

"You air right, Adger," says Pa, "but what air we goin to do about that acre of ground?"

"Divide it."

Pa give three long whistles again. Not a man stuck his head up out'n the broom-sage.

"They will come," says Pa.

Pa give 'em seven long whistles. Effie didn't know what it meant. It was our victory signal. Men popped up all over the field. They started talkin. A lot of our men limped as they walked toward the cedar tree. They looked beardy and tired. Effie was afraid when she saw their muskets.

Effie put her arms around me. We loved and loved above the coffeepot. We could see the long line of men trailin around the path fer home. I could feel the life comin back to my own leg now.

Jesse Stuart was born in a log cabin in Riverton, Kentucky, in 1907. At age three, his father, who could hardly write his own name, carried the little boy three miles to the schoolhouse and told him, "You

*must have booklearning. . . . You must not grow up like a weed."
Stuart worked his way through Lincoln Memorial University (B.A.,
1929). A collection of his poems,* Man with a Bull-Tongue Plow
(1934) brought him fame; Taps for Private Tussie *(1943) brought
him fortune. He traveled and taught worldwide until a stroke con-
fined him to a wheelchair in 1971. He died in 1984. Nearly all his
thirty-plus books and more than three hundred short stories celebrated the lives and people of the red hills of Kentucky.*

In the days before West Virginia seceded from Virginia, Squire Randolph and his friend Abner ride high into the Blue Ridge Mountains to remonstrate with the notorious adventurer Doomdorf and discover a mysterious murder that defies everyone, for awhile. . . .

NINE

The Doomdorf
Mystery
Melville Davisson Post

The pioneer was not the only man in the great mountains behind Virginia. Strange aliens drifted in after the Colonial wars. All foreign armies are sprinkled with a cockle of adventurers that take root and remain. They were with Braddock and La Salle, and they rode north out of Mexico after her many empires went to pieces.

I think Doomdorf crossed the seas with Iturbide when that ill-starred adventurer returned to be shot against a wall; but there was no Southern blood in him. He came from some European race remote and barbaric. The evidences were all about him. He was a huge figure of a man, with a black spade beard, broad, thick hands, and square, flat fingers.

He had found a wedge of land between the Crown's grant to Daniel Davisson and a Washington survey. It was an uncovered triangle not worth the running of the lines; and so, no doubt, was left out, a sheer rock standing up out of the river for a base, and a peak of the mountain rising northward behind it for an apex.

Doomdorf squatted on the rock. He must have brought a belt of gold pieces when he took to his horse, for he hired old Robert Steuart's slaves and built a stone house on the rock, and he brought the furnishings overland from a frigate in the Chesapeake; and then in the handfuls of earth, wherever a root would hold, he planted the mountain behind his house with peach trees. The gold gave out; but the devil is fertile in resources. Doomdorf built a log still and turned the first fruits of the garden into a hell-brew. The idle and the vicious came with their stone jugs, and violence and riot flowed out.

119

The government of Virginia was remote and its arm short and feeble; but the men who held the lands west of the mountains against the savages under grants from George, and after that held them against George himself, were efficient and expeditious. They had long patience, but when that failed they went up from their fields and drove the thing before them out of the land, like a scourge of God.

There came a day, then, when my Uncle Abner and Squire Randolph rode through the gap of the mountains to have the thing out with Doomdorf. The work of this brew, which had the odors of Eden and the impulses of the devil in it, could be borne no longer. The drunken negroes had shot old Duncan's cattle and burned his haystacks, and the land was on its feet.

They rode alone, but they were worth an army of little men. Randolph was vain and pompous and given over to extravagance of words, but he was a gentleman beneath it, and fear was an alien and a stranger to him. And Abner was the right hand of the land.

It was a day in early summer and the sun lay hot. They crossed through the broken spine of the mountains and trailed along the river in the shade of the great chestnut trees. The road was only a path and the horses went one before the other. It left the river when the rock began to rise and, making a detour through the grove of peach trees, reached the house on the mountain side. Randolph and Abner got down, unsaddled their horses and turned them out to graze, for their business with Doomdorf would not be over in an hour. Then they took a steep path that brought them out on the mountain side of the house.

A man sat on a big red-roan horse in the paved court before the door. He was a gaunt old man. He sat bare-headed, the palms of his hands resting on the pommel of his saddle, his chin sunk in his black stock, his face in retrospection, the wind moving gently his great shock of voluminous white hair. Under him the huge red horse stood with his legs spread out like a horse of stone.

There was no sound. The door to the house was closed; insects moved in the sun; a shadow crept out from the motionless figure, and swarms of yellow butterflies maneuvered like an army.

Abner and Randolph stopped. They knew the tragic figure—a circuit rider of the hills who preached the invective of Isaiah as though he were the mouthpiece of a militant and avenging overlord; as though the government of Virginia were the awful theocracy of the Books of Kings. The horse was dripping with sweat and the man bore the dust and the evidences of a journey on him.

"Bronson," said Abner, "where is Doomdorf?"

The old man lifted his head and looked down at Abner over the pommel of the saddle.

"'Surely,'" he said, "'he covereth his feet in his summer chamber.'"

Abner went over and knocked on the closed door, and presently the white, frightened face of a woman looked out at him. She was a little, faded woman, with fair hair, a broad foreign face, but with the delicate evidences of gentle blood.

Abner repeated his question.

"Where is Doomdorf?"

"Oh, sir," she answered with a queer lisping accent, "he went to lie down in his south room after his midday meal, as his custom is; and I went to the orchard to gather any fruit that might be ripened." She hesitated and her voice lisped into a whisper: "He is not come out and I cannot wake him."

The two men followed her through the hall and up the stairway to the door.

"It is always bolted," she said, "when he goes to lie down." And she knocked feebly with the tips of her fingers.

There was no answer and Randolph rattled the doorknob.

"Come out, Doomdorf!" he called in his big, bellowing voice.

There was only silence and the echoes of the words among the rafters. Then Randolph set his shoulder to the door and burst it open.

They went in. The room was flooded with sun from the tall south windows. Doomdorf lay on a couch in a little offset of the room, a great scarlet patch on his bosom and a pool of scarlet on the floor.

The woman stood for a moment staring; then she cried out:

"At last I have killed him!" And she ran like a frightened hare.

The two men closed the door and went over to the couch. Doomdorf had been shot to death. There was a great ragged hole in his waistcoat. They began to look about for the weapon with which the deed had been accomplished, and in a moment found it—a fowling piece lying in two dogwood forks against the wall. The gun had just been fired; there was a freshly exploded paper cap under the hammer.

There was little else in the room—a loom-woven rag carpet on the floor; wooden shutters flung back from the windows; a great oak table, and on it a big, round, glass water bottle, filled to its glass stopper with raw liquor from the still. The stuff was limpid and clear as spring water; and, but for its pungent odor, one would have taken

121

it for God's brew instead of Doomdorf's. The sun lay on it and against the wall where hung the weapon that had ejected the dead man out of life.

"Abner," said Randolph, "this is murder! The woman took that gun down from the wall and shot Doomdorf while he slept."

Abner was standing by the table, his fingers round his chin.

"Randolph," he replied, "what brought Bronson here?"

"The same outrages that brought us," said Randolph. "The mad old circuit rider has been preaching a crusade against Doomdorf far and wide in the hills."

Abner answered, without taking his fingers from about his chin:

"You think this woman killed Doomdorf? Well, let us go and ask Bronson who killed him."

They closed the door, leaving the dead man on his couch, and went down into the court.

The old circuit rider had put away his horse and got an ax. He had taken off his coat and pushed his shirtsleeves up over his long elbows. He was on his way to the still to destroy the barrels of liquor. He stopped when the two men came out, and Abner called to him.

"Bronson," he said, "who killed Doomdorf?"

"I killed him," replied the old man, and went on toward the still.

Randolph swore under his breath. "By the Almighty," he said, "everybody couldn't kill him!"

"Who can tell how many had a hand in it?" replied Abner.

"Two have confessed!" cried Randolph. "Was there perhaps a third? Did you kill him, Abner? And I too? Man, the thing is impossible!"

"The impossible," replied Abner, "looks here like the truth. Come with me, Randolph, and I will show you a thing more impossible than this."

They returned through the house and up the stairs to the room. Abner closed the door behind them.

"Look at this bolt," he said; "it is on the inside and not connected with the lock. How did the one who killed Doomdorf get into this room, since the door was bolted?"

"Through the windows," replied Randolph.

There were but two windows, facing the south, through which the sun entered. Abner led Randolph to them.

"Look!" he said. "The wall of the house is plumb with the sheer face of the rock. It is a hundred feet to the river and the rock is as smooth as a sheet of glass. But that is not all. Look at these window frames; they are cemented into their casement with dust and they are bound along their edges with cobwebs. These windows have not been opened. How did the assassin enter?"

"The answer is evident," said Randolph: "The one who killed Doomdorf hid in the room until he was asleep; then he shot him and went out."

"The explanation is excellent but for one thing," replied Abner: "How did the assassin bolt the door behind him on the inside of this room after he had gone out?"

Randolph flung out his arms with a hopeless gesture.

"Who knows?" he cried. "Maybe Doomdorf killed himself."

Abner laughed.

"And after firing a handful of shot into his heart he got up and put the gun back carefully into the forks against the wall!"

"Well," cried Randolph, "there is one open road out of this mystery. Bronson and this woman say they killed Doomdorf, and if they killed him they surely know how they did it. Let us go down and ask them."

"In the law court," replied Abner, "that procedure would be considered sound sense; but we are in God's court and things are managed there in a somewhat stranger way. Before we go let us find out, if we can, at what hour it was that Doomdorf died."

He went over and took a big silver watch out of the dead man's pocket. It was broken by a shot and the hands lay at one hour after noon. He stood for a moment fingering his chin.

"At one o'clock," he said. "Bronson, I think, was on the road to this place, and the woman was on the mountain among the peach trees."

Randolph threw back his shoulders.

"Why waste time in a speculation about it, Abner?" he said. "We know who did this thing. Let us go and get the story of it out of their own mouths. Doomdorf died by the hands of either Bronson or this woman."

"I could better believe it," replied Abner, "but for the running of a certain awful law."

"What law?" said Randolph. "Is it a statute of Virginia?"

"It is a statute," replied Abner, "of an authority somewhat higher. Mark the language of it: 'He that killeth with the sword must be killed with the sword.'"

He came over and took Randolph by the arm.

"Must! Randolph, did you mark particularly the word 'must'? It is a mandatory law. There is no room in it for the vicissitudes of chance or fortune. There is no way round that word. Thus, we reap what we sow and nothing else; thus, we receive what we give and nothing else. It is the weapon in our own hands that finally destroys us. You are looking at it now." And he turned him about so that the table and the weapon and the dead man were before him. "'He that killeth with the sword must be killed with the sword.' And now," he said, "let us go and try the method of the law courts. Your faith is in the wisdom of their ways."

They found the old circuit rider at work in the still, staving in Doomdorf's liquor casks, splitting the oak heads with his ax.

Bronson," said Randolph, "how did you kill Doomdorf?"

The old man stopped and stood leaning on his ax.

"I killed him," replied the old man, "as Elijah killed the captains of Ahaziah and their fifties. But not by the hand of any man did I pray the Lord God to destroy Doomdorf, but with fire from heaven to destroy him."

He stood up and extended his arms.

"His hands were full of blood," he said. "With his abominations from these groves of Baal he stirred up the people to contention, to strife and murder. The widow and the orphan cried to heaven against him. 'I will surely hear their cry,' is the promise written in the Book. The land was weary of him; and I prayed the Lord God to destroy him with fire from heaven, as he destroyed the Princes of Gomorrah in their palaces!"

Randolph made a gesture as of one who dismisses the impossible, but Abner's face took on a deep, strange look.

"With fire from heaven!" he repeated slowly to himself. Then he asked a question. "A little while ago," he said, "when we came, I asked you where Doomdorf was, and you answered me in the language of the third chapter of the Book of Judges. Why did you answer me like that, Bronson?—'Surely he covereth his feet in his summer chamber.'"

"The woman told me that he had not come down from the room where he had gone up to sleep," replied the old man, "and that the door was locked. And then I knew that he was dead in his summer chamber like Eglon, King of Moab."

He extended his arm toward the south.

"I came here from the Great Valley," he said, "to cut down these groves of Baal and to empty out this abomination; but I did not know that the Lord had heard my prayer and visited His wrath on Doomdorf until I was come up into these mountains to his door. When the woman spoke I knew it." And he went away to his horse, leaving the ax among the ruined barrels.

Randolph interrupted.

"Come, Abner," he said; "this is wasted time. Bronson did not kill Doomdorf."

Abner answered slowly in his deep, level voice:

"Do you realize, Randolph, how Doomdorf died?"

"Not by fire from heaven, at any rate," said Randolph.

"Randolph," replied Abner, "are you sure?"

"Abner," cried Randolph, "you are pleased to jest, but I am in deadly earnest. A crime has been done here against the state. I am an officer of justice and I propose to discover the assassin if I can."

He walked away toward the house and Abner followed, his hands behind him and his great shoulders thrown loosely forward, with a grim smile about his mouth.

"It is no use to talk with the mad old preacher," Randolph went on. "Let him empty out the liquor and ride away. I won't issue a warrant against him. Prayer may be a handy implement to do a murder with, Abner, but it is not a deadly weapon under the statutes of Virginia. Doomdorf was dead when old Bronson got here with his Scriptural jargon. This woman killed Doomdorf. I shall put her to an inquisition."

"As you like," replied Abner. "Your faith remains in the methods of the law courts."

"Do you know of any better methods?" said Randolph.

"Perhaps," replied Abner, "when you have finished."

Night had entered the valley. The two men went into the house and set about preparing the corpse for burial. They got candles and made a coffin and put Doomdorf in it, and straightened out his limbs, and folded his arms across his shot-out heart. Then they set the coffin on benches in the hall.

They kindled a fire in the dining room and sat down before it, with the door open and the red firelight shining through on the dead man's narrow, everlasting house. The woman had put some cold meat, a golden cheese and a loaf on the table. They did not see her, but they heard her moving about the house; and finally, on the gravel court outside, her step and the whinny of a horse. Then she came in, dressed as for a journey. Randolph sprang up.

"Where are you going?" he said.

"To the sea and a ship," replied the woman. Then she indicated the hall with a gesture. "He is dead and I am free."

There was a sudden illumination in her face. Randolph took a step toward her. His voice was big and harsh.

"Who killed Doomdorf?" he cried.

"I killed him," replied the woman. "It was fair!"

"Fair!" echoed the justice. "What do you mean by that?"

The woman shrugged her shoulders and put out her hands with a foreign gesture.

"I remember an old, old man sitting against a sunny wall, and a little girl, and one who came and talked a long time with the old man, while the little girl plucked yellow flowers out of the grass and put them into her hair. Then finally the stranger gave the old man a gold chain and took the little girl away." She flung out her hands. "Oh, it was fair to kill him!" She looked up with a queer, pathetic smile.

"The old man will be gone by now," she said; "but I shall perhaps find the wall there, with the sun on it, and the yellow flowers in the grass. And now, may I go?"

It is a law of the story-teller's art that he does not tell a story. It is the listener who tells it. The story-teller does but provide him with the stimuli.

Randolph got up and walked about the floor. He was a justice of the peace in a day when that office was filled only by the landed gentry, after the English fashion; and the obligations of the law were strong on him. If he should take liberties with the letter of it, how could the weak and the evil be made to hold it in respect? Here was this woman before him a confessed assassin. Could he let her go?

Abner sat unmoving by the hearth, his elbow on the arm of his chair, his palm propping up his jaw, his face clouded in deep lines. Randolph was consumed with vanity and the weakness of ostentation, but he shouldered his duties for himself. Presently he stopped and looked at the woman, wan, faded like some prisoner of legend escaped out of fabled dungeons into the sun.

The firelight flickered past her to the box on the benches in the hall, and the vast, inscrutable justice of heaven entered and overcame him.

"Yes," he said. "Go! There is no jury in Virginia that would hold a woman for shooting a beast like that." And he thrust out his arm, with the fingers extended toward the dead man.

The woman made a little awkward curtsy.

"I thank you, sir." Then she hesitated and lisped, "But I have not shoot him."

"Not shoot him!" cried Randolph. "Why, the man's heart is riddled!"

"Yes, sir," she said simply, like a child. "I kill him, but have not shoot him."

126

Randolph took two long strides toward the woman.

"Not shoot him!" he repeated. "How then, in the name of heaven, did you kill Doomdorf?" And his big voice filled the empty places of the room.

"I will show you, sir," she said.

She turned and went away into the house. Presently she returned with something folded up in a linen towel. She put it on the table between the loaf of bread and the yellow cheese.

Randolph stood over the table, and the woman's deft fingers undid the towel from round its deadly contents; and presently the thing lay there uncovered.

It was a little crude model of a human figure done in wax with a needle thrust through the bosom.

Randolph stood up with a great intake of the breath.

"Magic! By the eternal!"

"Yes, sir," the woman explained, in her voice and manner of a child. "I have try to kill him many times—oh, very many times!—with witch words which I have remember; but always they fail. Then, at last, I make him in wax, and I put a needle through his heart; and I kill him very quickly."

It was as clear as daylight, even to Randolph, that the woman was innocent. Her little harmless magic was the pathetic effort of a child to kill a dragon. He hesitated a moment before he spoke, and then he decided like the gentleman he was. If it helped the child to believe that her enchanted straw had slain the monster—well, he would let her believe it.

"And now, sir, may I go?"

Randolph looked at the woman in a sort of wonder.

"Are you not afraid," he said, "of the night and the mountains, and the long road?"

"Oh no, sir," she replied simply. "The good God will be everywhere now."

It was an awful commentary on the dead man—that this strange half-child believed that all the evil in the world had gone out with him; that now that he was dead, the sunlight of heaven would fill every nook and corner.

It was not a faith that either of the two men wished to shatter, and they let her go. It would be daylight presently and the road through the mountains to the Chesapeake was open.

Randolph came back to the fireside after he had helped her into the saddle, and sat down. He tapped on the hearth for some time idly with the iron poker; and then finally he spoke.

"This is the strangest thing that ever happened," he said. "Here's a mad old preacher who thinks that he killed Doomdorf with fire from Heaven, like Elijah the Tishbite; and here is a simple child of a woman who thinks she killed him with a piece of magic of the Middle Ages—each as innocent of his death as I am. And yet, by the eternal, the beast is dead!"

He drummed on the hearth with the poker, lifting it up and letting it drop through the hollow of his fingers.

"Somebody shot Doomdorf. But who? And how did he get into and out of that shut-up room? The assassin that killed Doomdorf must have gotten into the room to kill him. Now, how did he get in?" He spoke as to himself; but my uncle sitting across the hearth replied:

"Through the window."

"Through the window!" echoed Randolph. "Why, man, you yourself showed me that the window had not been opened, and the precipice below it a fly could hardly climb. Do you tell me now that the window was opened?"

"No," said Abner, "it was never opened."

Randolph got on his feet.

"Abner," he cried, "are you saying that the one who killed Doomdorf climbed the sheer wall and got in through a closed window, without distrubing the dust or the cobwebs on the window frame?"

My uncle looked Randolph in the face.

"The murderer of Doomdorf did even more," he said. "That assassin not only climbed the face of that precipice and got in through the closed window, but he shot Doomdorf to death and got out again through the closed window without leaving a single track or trace behind, and without disturbing a grain of dust or a thread of a cobweb."

Randolph swore a great oath.

"The thing is impossible!" he cried. "Men are not killed today in Virginia by black art or a curse of God."

"By black art, no," replied Abner; "but by the curse of God, yes. I think they are."

Randolph drove his clenched right hand into the palm of his left.

"By the eternal!" he cried. "I would like to see the assassin who could do a murder like this, whether he be an imp from the pit or an angel out of Heaven."

"Very well," replied Abner, undisturbed. "When he comes back tomorrow I will show you the assassin who killed Doomdorf."

When day broke they dug a grave and buried the dead man against the mountain among his peach trees. It was noon when that work was ended. Abner threw down his spade and looked up at the sun.

"Randolph," he said, "let us go and lay an ambush for this assassin. He is on the way here."

And it was a strange ambush that he laid. When they were come again into the chamber where Doomdorf died he bolted the door; then he loaded the fowling piece and put it carefully back on its rack against the wall. After that he did another curious thing: He took the blood-stained coat, which they had stripped off the dead man when they had prepared his body for the earth, put a pillow in it and laid it on the couch precisely where Doomdorf had slept. And while he did these things Randolph stood in wonder and Abner talked:

"Look you, Randolph . . . We will trick the murderer. . . . We will catch him in the act."

Then he went over and took the puzzled justice by the arm.

"Watch!" he said. "The assassin is coming along the wall!"

But Randolph heard nothing, saw nothing. Only the sun entered. Abner's hand tightened on his arm.

"It is here! Look! And he pointed to the wall.

Randolph, following the extended finger, saw a tiny brilliant disk of light moving slowly up the wall toward the lock of the fowling piece. Abner's hand became a vise and his voice rang as over metal.

"'He that killeth with the sword must be killed with the sword.' It is the water bottle, full of Doomdorf's liquor, focusing the sun. . . . And look, Randolph, how Bronson's prayer was answered!"

The tiny disk of light traveled on the plate of the lock.

"It is fire from heaven!"

The words rang above the roar of the fowling piece, and Randolph saw the dead man's coat leap up on the couch, riddled by the shot. The gun, in its natural position on the rack, pointed to the couch standing at the end of the chamber, beyond the offset of the wall, and the focused sun had exploded the percussion cap.

Randolph made a great gesture, with his arm extended.

"It is a world," he said, "filled with the mysterious joinder of accident!"

"It is a world," replied Abner, "filled with the mysterious justice of God!"

Melville Davisson Post was a Southern gentleman of the old school. Born in Rominee Mills, West Virginia on April 6, 1871, he graduated

*from West Virginia University (B.A., 1891; L.L.B., 1892). He prac-
ticed criminal and corporation law for eleven years before turning to
writing as a career. His first short story, "The Corpus Delicti" (1896),
gained him national fame; in it he showed how to commit the perfect
murder (the legal flaw he exposed was later corrected). Most of his
work consisted of short mysteries with legal backgrounds. Post died
on June 23, 1930, in his West Virginia home.*

If his client died of suicide, McGavock wonders, why did someone try to garrote him as he poked around the premises. . . .

TEN

The Turkey Buzzard Blues

Merle Constiner

1: Murder Valley

A soft spring river-wind blew in through the open windows, riffled the papers gently on McGavock's desk. McGavock yawned. The janitor, puttering about the waste basket, straightened, leaned on his broom. "And then," the janitor explained, "after I'd done burnt this here corpse with pine knots, I'd sift the ashes fer little stuff—buttons and teeth and sich. I'd take this little stuff and cram 'er down my ole muzzle-loading shotgun and fire the charge straight up in the air. By golly, whur's your *corpus delicti* now? It's a perfeck crime!"

"The shotgun," McGavock warned. "We've got to dispose of the shotgun. Let's see. You could cut off the barrel with a hacksaw, thread the ends and screw it into your plumbing system somewhere. The gunstock you could whittle into a—" He rolled his eyes. "Sh-h-h! We're being eavesdropped!"

Miss Ollinger, the chief's secretary, drew herself up in affronted dignity. "I'm not interested in your diabolic small-talk." She made a prim, Pekingese mouth at him. "Something very important has broken. Mr. Browne wishes to consult you in his office immediately."

McGavock looked stupid. "Wishes to consult who? Him?" He pointed at the janitor. "Or me?"

"And I'd advise you to hurry."

McGavock got lazily to his feet, sauntered across the room and entered the chief's sanctum.

Old man Atherton Browne greeted his ace detective with an expression of abject misery. "They're going to make me retire, Luther,"

131

he said in a low whisper. "The doctor tells me I have a mighty bad heart." His ancient cheeks wrinkled in rivulets of self pity. "I'm a gonner!"

McGavock was taken aback. "You retire? In a pig's eye! When is this coming off?"

"Who knows?" The old man was vague. "Now, Luther, you and I are just like father and son. Here's my problem—and it's confidential. If I leave, I'm going to have a look over the staff and select a sort of general manager to take my place." He coughed politely. "You've been much in my mind. I was wondering if—"

"So that's it!" McGavock hooted. "You're trying to sell me a load of goods! I don't catch what you're getting at but I don't want any part of it. Me, your new manager. Haw! Pete Coyle's the pet around here—and you know it. He's respectable, he shaves three times a day and carries a pocket shoe-shine kit. I'm just riffraff, I don't even have a decent contract with you!"

The oldster studied him with tragic, mucous-rimmed eyes.

McGavock was a small man, wiry and tough. His coarse black hair was cut in a short pompadour and there was a tweedy sprinkling of gray about his temples. He had a taunting, selfish quality about him that aroused instant animal antagonism in total strangers. At some time or other he'd been with about every major agency in the country. A genius at getting results, he was a hard man to take. He'd never felt at home until he'd hit this Memphis outfit.

His employers liked what he brought in but didn't want to know too much about his methods. He worked under a roving license— an agreement that the agency could repudiate if things got too hot. This one-sided arrangement was a constant gripe to him.

He leaned his sinewy shoulders against the wall. "You sent for me," he announced coldly. "Why?"

Atherton Brown sighed. "Something has come our way, son, that has all the earmarks of being dynamite. Something big. And it's going to take real talent to crack it." The old man was benign. "There's a bonus in it for you if you'll handle it."

McGavock was silent, wary.

The oldster produced a cream-colored envelope, slipped out a sheet of folded paper and waved it in the air. McGavock took it wordlessly from his fingers. A note, written in the tiny shaded letters of another era. It read:

Atherton Browne, Detective Agency
Memphis, Tennessee.

Dear Mr. Browne:

As I understand it, you people have commercial policemen for hire.
I would like to rent one as I have a situation here which the local law
refuses to consider seriously. I've got tramps in my girls' dormitory.
Please send me a man to put an end to this irregularity.

I am willing to pay anything up to, and including, ten dollars if I am
completely satisfied with your results.

Yours respectfully,

Simon Tetcherall Layton, M.A. Litt.D.
Pres., Layton's Female Academy
Rockton.

McGavock laid the paper on the desktop, grinned. "So this is your
dynamite? He pays anything up to ten bucks—and you're going to
split me a bonus out of it! Furthermore, that letter's dated three
weeks back. What is this? A rib?"

The chief was grave. "No, Luther, it's no rib. I've heard of the
Layton's back in Rockton. They're a powerful and wealthy clan.
There's big money in this—but we have to earn it. I want you to go
down there and, ahem—insinuate yourself into a generous fee."

McGavock was savage. "Not me! You don't catch me fooling
around with any girls' dormitory!"

The chief chuckled. "Layton's Academy has been out of existence
for thirty years. The old buildings still stand, I believe, but the college
passed its vogue and closed its doors at least three decades ago." He
became persuasive. "Do what I advise, Luther. Give it a go. I'm a
southerner. I know the pulse of these people. Something, a sixth
sense, tells me there's something pretty devilish stewing back there in
Rockton." He leaned forward. "We may be late already. To be perfectly frank, I smell murder!"

McGavock was impressed in spite of himself. He asked dubiously:
"How do you get murder out of—"

"Instinct, Luther. An old man's instinct." The chief was firm.

McGavock faltered. "O.K." He bared his teeth. "But this time
you'd better be playing it on the square." He wheeled, slammed out
of the room.

Miss Ollinger, from her desk in the corner, cleared her throat self-righteously. "Mr. Browne, I don't wish to appear officious—but I'm afraid I've caught you in a lapse of memory."

The chief smiled evilly. "How so?"

"You showed Mr. McGavock the *old* letter—but you forgot to mention the *new* one, the one we received this morning."

The oldster put on a great display of exasperation. "By Gad, you're right! Oh, well, I guess there's no harm done." He slid a second letter from beneath his blotter pad, clipped on his glasses and reread it:

Atherton Browne, Detective Agency
Memphis

Gentlemen:

About three weeks ago my aged father sent you a note requesting the services of a detective. You quite sensibly ignored it. Today, in arranging my father's papers, I came across several drafts of this communication to you.

I am writing you to ask you to take my father's letter out of your files, to destroy it, and to consider the correspondence closed.

I regret to inform you that my father was mentally unwell at the time of the writing and, having taken a turn for the worse in the meantime, has since hanged himself.

Yours truly,

Doxie Layton
Rockton.

"No," the chief repeated. "There's no harm done. Mr. McGavock's an exceptional man, Miss Ollinger. He works much better when he's—er—unburdened with trivia."

The town of Rockton, buried in the hill-country, was no cinch to reach by rail. Three times, in the scant hundred miles, McGavock was forced to change trains. He was tired and grimy and irritable when the one-lunged local finally churned its way up the spur track to the dingy depot. The station platform was deserted. McGavock picked up his oversized Gladstone and headed for Main Street and a hotel.

The burg was a lethargic, easy-going Southern community of the type so familiar to him. A little larger, maybe, than the average—he guessed its population around four thousand, a county-seat. The town's business section formed a scattered rectangle, two blocks deep, around court square. Where Main Street faced the courthouse the pavement was roofed by one long, continous marquee supported by gas pipe stanchions set in the cement curb. It was suppertime and the sidewalks were abandoned. In the purple quiet of the spring evening, hounddogs, slumbering in shadowed entranceways, awoke to the sound of his footsteps and stretched—dipping their forelegs at him in formal canine bows. His nostrils caught the woodsmoke scent of kitchen ranges, the faint lemon fragrance of bursting magnolia blooms. This was the sort of town he understood, this was the sort of town he liked.

The hotel was a squat, boxlike building of discolored brick. An ancient sign above the door said: *Simmons House.* McGavock swung his travelling bag across the threshold. The quaint, old-style lobby was fresh and pleasant. The small room was a rotunda in the best classical design, circular and domed, two stories high, and galleried about the second floor was a mahogany railing. A portly, frowzy man in an uncreased black stetson and with cigar ashes on his rumpled vest was piddling with a newspaper behind the desk.

McGavock set down his Gladstone, said: "Am I addressing Mr. Simmons?"

The portly man laid aside his paper. He had a puffy sallow face and protruding, china-blue eyes. He proclaimed ponderously: "Mr. Simmons was killed in eighteen fifty-four hunting buffalo in the Nebraska Territory."

"I hadn't heard." McGavock rocked back on his heels. "Are you the clerk?"

The frowzy man smiled paternally. "I, suh, am Robertus M. Leach. Sometimes referred to as the Honorable. In my impetuous youth I did a short hitch in the Legislature at Nashville. At the present time, however, I am, more or less, a man of leisure. I—"

"Swell. Fine. I want a room. Can you register me?"

The puffy Mr. Leach was overcome with regret. "That I cain't do, suh. Harvey, the gentleman who officiates over this hostelry, is up to the Gipsy Tearoom having himself a coke-and-ammonia. He will no doubt return within the next few hours."

"So soon?" McGavock was sugary. "In that case I'll just sit here on the stair-step and wait for him. No—on second thought, I won't." He ambled toward the door. "I think I'll look over your town."

Mr. Leach, the Honorable, nodded. Suddenly he screwed up his face and called: "Loosahatchie!"

McGavock came to a dead stop. "What say?"

"I hear," Mr. Leach shouted, "that the spring rains have flooded the Loosahatchie River!"

"I'm not surprised." McGavock was polite. "Heavy rains have a way of doing that to rivers. Is it serious?"

"Oh, no. Not serious."

McGavock waggled farewell, stepped out on the sidewalk.

A telephone directory at the corner drugstore said: *Layton, S.T. r 721 Ashwood Ave.* That was his man. A bit of indirect conversation with the garrulous young pharmacist behind the counter gave him pointers on locating Ashwood Avenue.

Number 721 Ashwood was an angular, slate-roofed cottage. There was a scholarly, precise atmosphere about the place. The neat, velvety lawn was enclosed by a low box hedge, the shrubbery at the gate had been trimmed to square pillars surmounted by geometrical spheres. McGavock strolled up the turfed brick walk. The porchlight was on, there was a brass plate on the door: *Dr. Simon Tetcherall Layton, M.A., Litt. D.* There was something else on the door, too—a big, showy funeral wreath.

McGavock glared. "Our client's dead! Wait until old Atherton Browne learns of this!" He clanged the old-fashioned lever bell-pull.

The door was opened by a waspish little fellow with a cut-away chin and droll, squinty eyes. He wore a rose-colored dress robe, a calabash pipe drooped from the corner of his mouth. He made a fork of his index and second fingers, lifted the pipe from his lips, exclaimed cordially: "A human! Why bless your heart! I'm in the mood for company."

"I want," McGavock announced loftily, "to enter my niece in your female academy."

This struck his host as vastly humorous. "That, friend, will take a bit of doing. Who do you think I am?"

McGavock spat. "You're Doc Layton." He gestured to the name plate. "I can read, can't I?"

The fellow in the dressing room robe grinned. "I'm afraid you're a little twisted. This is Dr. Layton." He touched the wreath with his pipestem. "The late Dr. Layton. I'm Charlie Lusk, his amanuensis and general handyman. Come in and sit down." He stepped back. "You can help me keep the cat away—those rascals."

McGavock stepped inside. It was a house of death, all right, and there was just one word for it: spooky. The soft-carpeted hallway with its dull, dark woodwork was illuminated by a single dim night bulb. A rubber plant, hat rack and a crockery umbrella-stand were lined along the wall. Lusk jerked his thumb toward the parlor. Through partly open sliding doors, the detective could see a casket on sawhorse trestles, could glimpse a mound of musky, odorous lilies and tuberoses. "There he lies," Lusk declared jocularly. "Waiting for tomorrow's festivities. Burial at ten. Would you like to look at him?"

McGavock walked forward, gazed down at the tranquil face of his client. There was nothing extraordinary about the professor—winged collar, shoe-string necktie and long silver hair. Nothing extraordinary except his bulbous forehead. "He had a big brain," McGavock observed. "What happened to him?"

"Two days ago he hanged himself in the attic." Lusk's friendly casual voice seemed ghoulish in the hollow, high-ceilinged room. "I myself found him. It gave me quite a start." He arched his eyebrows courteously. "May I pour you a snifter?"

On a card table in the corner of the room was a cut-glass decanter, a high-ball glass and a platter of sandwiches. Charlie Lusk had been having himself a one-man party. McGavock remarked: "You don't appear too cut up over it."

"I'm not." The secretary was amiable. "Why should I be? I'm standing this deathwatch tonight because I'm getting paid for it. The family simply isn't interested. I'm serving Dr. Layton in death just as I served him in life—for good old frogskins. You're obviously a man of the world, you get my point of view."

McGavock was bland. "Yes. I do. What's this about the family not being interested?"

"I was referring to the son, Doxie, and his wife. They're interested in the demise, I guess—they're the ones who inherit." Lusk picked up a hardboiled egg, sprinkled it with salt and pepper. "They just can't be bothered with the functional details of the obsequies and interment. They stay holed up in that big white house of theirs out at the end of Locust Street and let me handle the funeral duties. I swear, they'd have had me embalm the body if they could have gotten away with it. Those people really pinch pennies." He stowed a bite of bread in the side of his mouth, and said: "You can't enroll your niece at the female academy—it's been closed for thirty years."

McGavock looked disappointed. "That's what I get for putting it off!" He paused, asked: "What made the professor hang himself?"

"Just before his suicide he went stark, raving mad."

McGavock looked skeptical. Lusk said breezily: "It's the truth. And how! Living around with him like I did, I saw signs of it every day."

McGavock pursed his lips sententiously. "Old folks are funny."

"Professor Layton wasn't funny—he was downright potty. Stuff like this: a couple of weeks ago, on a warm day, I come into his study. He has a roaring fire going in the fireplace. He shoves a broomstick into the coals, drags it out and stares at it—like he was reading a thermometer! I ask, 'What goes on?' He says, 'Charlie, it's just right, just hot enough.' What do you think he did then?"

"'Tis an engaging tale, indeed," McGavock declared. "What did he do then?"

"He took out his dentures, upper and lower plates, and tossed them on the fire. They were old-timers, made of hard rubber, and they blazed away to a fare-you-well. I was bug-eyed. I said, 'Dr. Layton, why did you do that?' What do you think he answered?"

"I give up."

Charlie Lusk shook his head. "He said that he was tired of masticating with substitutes, that he was going to grow himself a set of the real McCoy—and him eighty years old. He said he was going to do it through sheer willpower! That was the first time I realized he was nuts. Two weeks later he went up in the attic with a piece of clothesline and hanged himself."

McGavock put on his hat. "Well, I'll be wandering along. If you'll see me to the door, I'll let you get back to your wake."

Lusk was reluctant to see him go. The secretary lingered on the front porch, said cheerily: "Thanks for the pleasant visit. It's been a long time since I've talked to a city-man. If you're going to be around town—look me up."

McGavock nodded vigorously: "That I certainly shall."

Main Street was coming to life. Already the citizenry was straggling to town from its supper tables. Here and there, a few townsmen in their shirt sleeves and broad-brimmed hats gathered on sidewalk benches and collected in court square to enjoy the gentle spring evening in communion with each other. Little moppets in pigtails and starched calico, and chuckle-heads with shaved craniums galloped, knee-high, up and down the pavements trying out their lungs. Womenfolk were home over their dishpans; later they, too, would appear, in modest, protective groups of twos and threes.

McGavock foraged up and down the side streets, located a general store that catered to rural trade, and entered. An adenoidal, fuzzy-faced youth was sitting on a nail keg, greasing his brogans with a scrap of bacon rind. He gaped at the detective's approach, showed a mouthful of mossy green teeth, said: "He's to home, doggone him, a-eatin' his way through a mess of hog jowl and hoe-cake."

"Who?"

"The party yo're a-wantin'." The buck went back to his greasing. "I'm jest the boy."

"Oh, come now." McGavock was stern. "That's the wrong psychology. You're breeding an inferiority complex. Hitch your wagon to a star, put your shoulder to the wheel, look at the world through rose-colored glasses—and get me a spool of white darning thread."

The youth got to his feet, lumbered behind the counter. "Thur you are, mister." He laid the item on the glass showcase. "Spools of thread, I kin git. Hit's beans and rice and stuff that has to be weighed out that throws me. Them dum scales shore gives me a wrassle. Oncet—"

"I know just how you feel." McGavock was sympathetic. He turned, waved his hand in the vague direction of court square. "I'm a stranger here. What's that big building I passed, the one with the clock? Is that Dr. Layton's female academy?"

The buck was horrified. "No sirree! That's we'uns brand new co'thouse! The old academy hain't nothing but a batnest down on the river road. Hit's nothing at all! Anything else?"

McGavock walked to the front of the store. There was a display card on the counter and clipped to the card was an assortment of tawdry, imitation pearl necklaces. The printing read: *Genuine Imitation Simulated Pearls—25¢*. McGavock detached a strand from the card, paid the boy. "I'll take these, as well."

The youth considered this a good buy. He said: "Them's as purty as a red shoe, hain't they?"

McGavock nodded. He fastened the necklace around his throat, started for the door, stopped. "How do they look?" He suddenly unclasped them, dropped them into his coat pocket. "I don't believe I'll wear them after all."

The buck was slack-jawed with relief. "That's better, mister," he said earnestly. "Them ain't fer fellers—them's fer gals!"

The river road looped out past the cemetery, descended a shaley grade at the corporation line, and wound its serpentine way into the brush and scrub of the dank, lush bottomlands. It was here, in a fetid saucer-like depression, that McGavock found Dr. Simon Tetcherall Layton's academy for females.

There were three buildings in the clearing—one a squarish two-story affair, and its mate, a slightly larger edifice with a cupola. Gaunt and bulky in the night, they were dismal reflections of the buffeting of time and neglect. "Rot and decay," McGavock muttered. "But oh-so-lovely in the sight of Professor Layton, M.A." The wreck with the sagging cupola, the detective decided, would be the old recitation hall. The squarish building, then, must be the female dormitory. The two structures were set facing each other. Behind the dormitory, at the edge of the brush, was a ramshackle woodhouse. Just these three specter-like relics of another day.

2. The Ghost Strikes

McGavock started across the spongy swampgrass, and a light sprang up within the dormitory building.

A soft, shifting light—the beam of a hooded flashlight. The yellow gleam began at the front downstairs and then, progressively, it began a tour of the floor, room after room—a window lighting, then darkening, and the next in succession in its turn.

Someone, McGavock realized grimly, is searching for something. The torch came abruptly to a halt in the last window. And now, McGavock thought, he's found it.

Rapidly and silently, the detective crossed the clearing. He advanced on the old dormitory from the rear. He groped his way along the narrow passage between the woodhouse and the building, circled the corner. His eyes swept the brick facing.

The flashlight lay outside the window, on the window ledge. A big coon-hunter's torch. Its lens was muffled with a bandana. It lay so that its beam was through the grimy window, into the room. McGavock went suddenly taut. He'd been trapped and he knew it—but the realization came too late.

Things began to happen.

Out of the shadowed entrails of the woodshed behind him, an avalanche of flailing arms and sweaty clothes threw itself upon his back—a bestial tornado of frenzied fury. Bubbles of fiery pain burst beneath McGavock's eyelids. In the flash of a split second, he felt his consciousness slipping from him. He was being beaten and kicked in an effort to drag him from his stance, but the black pain in his body was so excruciating that the blows felt as though they were coming from far away—from another world.

Blindly, in a haze of torture, McGavock got his elbow under his chin, and pivoted. He slammed out, backhand, with everything he had. His knuckles sank into soft flesh, there was a jarred grunt. Battling now, entirely in animal reflex, he let loose with both barrels, fists and feet.

And then, suddenly, it was all over. Somehow he was alone, on his hands and knees in the swampgrass, fumbling at his throat. He slipped the noose from his neck.

The garrote was a slender thong of green rawhide. He got stiffly to his feet, tossed the contraption into the weeds. For a long moment, he stood in the silence of the night—regaining his strangled breath.

The deathtrap had been simple and effective. He'd been expected, possibly he'd even been followed. When he'd appeared at the edge of the clearing, his attacker had started laying his bait, had walked down the far side of the building, flashing his light into each window as he passed, creating the illusion that he was prowling around inside. At the last window, he had placed his torch on the sill and hidden himself in the woodshed with his rawhide thong. It was foolproof, it couldn't miss.

McGavock tucked in his shirt, straightened his collar. "And Doc Layton died of strangulation. My, my." He patted his pocket to make sure he hadn't lost his necklace and thread. As vitality crept back into him, he became bullmad. He gave the old dormitory a venomous, farewell glance. "What's here will have to wait. I want to talk to people. I want to talk to this Doxie Layton. And I mean now!"

Anyway one turned it, McGavock decided, it came out murder. There was too much throttling going on to be anything else. "I don't know what it's all about," McGavock simmered. "But I'm going to find out. He made one big blunder—and that was when he put the tap on me. I'm going to have this baby's hide if I have to pay the freight myself!"

Charlie Lusk had said that the professor's son, Doxie Layton, lived with his wife in a big white house on Locust Street.

McGavock hit Locust, kept going until he reached the end of the pavement. The house, on a small wooded hillock, was white all right, and plenty big. A showy, many-columned Georgian affair, it was overloaded with verandas and wings and porte-cocheres, like a debutante's wedding cake. McGavock pulled down the corners of his lips in distaste. "Me, I'd rather live in a nice, dark cave." A brass carriage-light was bracketed to the gatepost and a procession of similar lights, winding along the gravelstone drive, lit up the broad lawn. McGavock struck out across the yard, dead center, in a beeline for the porch. He took the porchsteps in a lope, clanged the knocker on its escutcheon.

The Honorable Robertus M. Leach opened the door and bowed him in. McGavock pulled up in the foyer, arms akimbo. Inch by inch, his cold eyes flicked over the ex-politician, took in his bloated dewlaps, the rippled vest with its smudged cigar ashes. "Up at the hotel this evening you were an ex-Senator—" McGavock put a lunatic tremor in his voice. "Now you're Doxie Layton! A quick change artist, bedad." He recoiled, said imploringly: "Don't tell me you were the corpse I saw in Professor Layton's casket."

The frowzy man waggled his hands and head in violent denial. "Wait a minute, let me get a word in. I was Robertus Leach uptown, I'm Robertus Leach here. Mr. Doxie's in the library."

McGavock followed him down a lavish hallway, glittering in baroque gilt and prismatic chandeliers. Leach paused at an ornate, iron-studded oak door, dipped his shoulder. "After you, suh."

The mansion's library reeked wealth. The powder-blue rug had a two inch nap. The walls were pressed leather and the rare colonial furniture gave off a lustrous, shimmering patina. There were alabaster figurines and oriental vases and busts of famous poets—but, as far as McGavock could observe, there were no books in the Layton library. Two easy chairs sat face to face by a cribbage board, on an inlaid taboret. A man leaned forward out of one of these chairs, looked directly into—and through—McGavock. He screwed up his face, asked petulantly:"Who was it, Bobby?"

Mr. Leach shrugged. "Just a person, Doxie. I brought him in."

"Well, take him out."

McGavock flattened his lips, said roughly: "You're Doxie Layton. I'm Lute McGavock, from the Browne agency. About three weeks ago your old man wrote us a letter asking us for a detective. I, my friend, am he."

Layton picked up the deck of cards, gave them a dexterous one-handed cut. He was a rugged, handsome man in his middle-fifties, broad-shouldered and lean-flanked. His cheeks and ears were bronzed and weathered. One of these thousand-acre plantation owners, McGavock decided—this man had ridden many a rough mile on horseback. He was one of those strange mixtures of the metropolitan and the rural that you find among the landed elite. His madras shirt and soft flannel coat were right off Park Avenue but there was a white patch of skin at the nape of his neck where his black hair had been hacked off in a country-boy haircut. He said coldly: "I wrote your agency two days ago cancelling my father's request."

"Well, your letter never arrived." Even as he said it, McGavock realized he'd been finagled. There sprang into his mind's eye the vision of old Atherton Browne saying: *It's my sixth sense, Luther. I smell murder.*

Layton smiled frostily. "I sent it and you received it. Please leave."

McGavock controlled himself. He declared woodenly: "Layton, as of this moment, your father lies in his casket, a murdered man. Murder is my trade. I'm ready to pick up from here and go to work for you. What do you say?"

Layton turned his stony face from McGavock, addressed Leach. "Laroux, down at New Orleans, predicts a whacking good year for cotton, Mr. Bobby."

Leach puckered his forehead. "Maybe so, Mr. Doxie, maybe so. If the grass doesn't take it."

McGavock was sugary. "This is a wonderful town, this Rockton, where an old gentleman like Professor Layton can get knocked off and no one bothers about it." He grinned maliciously, weighted his words carefully. "Tell me, Layton, is this ex-politician a personal friend of yours?"

The plantation owner smiled. "What is the man talking about, Mr. Bobby?"

Leach shrugged. "That, I couldn't say, Mr. Doxie. Perhaps, Mr. Doxie—"

McGavock blew up. "Stop giving me that Mister Gallagher-Mister Shean routine." He purpled. "Don't bat me around like I'm a frog in a churn. Say you did write my boss voiding your father's request about it. I came down here in good faith to help you people out of a jam." He began to shout. "If you don't want to do business with me, O.K., it's up to you. But don't get hoity-toity with me, I can't use it!"

McGavock's voice snipped off in mid-air. There was a dead silence. Woodsounds of the spring night came, muted, through the open casements: the shrill purring of tree-frogs, the lonesome ululation of a mating bobcat. Layton rolled a wheat-straw cigarette in tanned, blue-veined hands. "Why," he asked meticulously, "why did you ask me if Mr. Leach, here, is a friend of mine? You see him in my home. You see him playing cards with me."

"You'd play cards with an acquaintance. He'd have to be an intimate friend before you'd let him read your mail."

Leach said: "If you're walking towards town, suh, I'd be delighted to join you."

"Wait until you hear what I have to say—maybe you'll have a change of heart." McGavock went into detail. "You, Layton, showed

Leach the note you wrote to us cancelling your father's request for services. You thought your letter would keep us away. Leach is a little foxier. His guess was that it would bring us on the run. He figures out mailing time, decides if I show at all I'll show up today. For some reason, it's important to him to know if a detective is on the job. He checks train schedules from Memphis, knows I'll have to stay at the Simmons House. He's there to give me the onceover when I pull in. He made the error of treating me like a yokel—I'm not. I'm a damn good detective."

Layton studied the fire on his cigarette, his hand was as steady as a rock. He said: "I didn't let Bobby read the letter to you. He was in my office the other morning just as I was finishing it. He was headed for the postoffice and kindly offered to take it along with him. I gave it to him—flap sealed."

The Honorable Robertus M. Leach laughed awkwardly. "Watch yourse'ves, gentlemen, the play is getting a little rough."

"Why horse around?" McGavock was insolent. "You opened the man's letter—why not admit it? You were in the Simmons House, waiting for a stranger from Memphis. When I came in, you thought you had spotted me but you had to make sure. You uncorked your Loosahatchie gag. You asked me if the Loosahatchie River was flooded by the spring rains. The Loosahatchie throws an arc around the Memphis area about twelve miles out of town. To get here on the railroad, I had to cross it. If I'd answered definitely, yes or no, I'd have given myself away." He winked at Layton. "That's just a free-gratis sample of my wares."

Layton's neck corded. He said calmly: "I like the sample. I'll have to have more of same, Mr. McGavock. May I consult you tomorrow morning at your hotel? Thank you." McGavock started for the hall. The frowzy Mr. Leach retrieved his blackthorn walking-stick from the floor by his chair, said: "Goodnight, Mr. Doxie, let's not jump to hasty conclusions. Let's sleep on this mare's nest, all of us. As my old grandmother used to say, the morning's wiser than the evening. Mr. McGavock, will you permit me to accompany you as far as—"

Layton's voice was icy. "Goodnight, McGavock. Leach, you stay. I'd like a chat with you."

McGavock had a problem and, as he saw it, it was going to prove a tough one. He'd tackled many a case where there was suspicion of homicide, but no body. In this set-up, conditions were reversed; he had the corpse and no one seemed much interested. Sooner or later, he realized, he was going to find himself confronted with a scoffing

144

version of the local law. He decided to take the bull by the horns and get it over with.

The big clock on the courthouse steeple said eight twenty-five, the sidewalk throngs were thinning out, townsfolk were herding their families, heading for home and bed. McGavock crossed the square, ascended the broad steps and entered the courthouse.

It was a new building, smelling of unseasoned plaster and aromatic varnish. McGavock ambled down the unlevel cement corridor, located a frosted glass door pane marked: *LUDLOW CHILDRESS, Office of Sheriff.* The door was open and McGavock sauntered in.

The room was tidy, efficient-looking. The one window was heavily barred and the gray walls were bare except for a single cartridge calendar depicting a sunset scene of a voluptuous Indian maiden in a birchbark canoe. On the floor, along one wall, was a row of six two-gallon pottery jugs. Sheriff Childress sat behind a shiny, golden oak desk. He was a husky, big-boned man in a pony-skin vest—he had the dewlaps of a bloodhound and there was an expression of apathy on his stolid face. He sat like a man frozen. He watched McGavock breeze in, said tensely through motionless lips: "Take it slow and easy, good friend, for God's sakes. You're a-fixin' to bring back my misery."

McGavock introduced himself, presented his credentials. The sheriff waved the papers aside. "I cain't read no writin' now. I gotta keep a good firm holt on myself. Any minute now, my misery she's due to come back on me."

McGavock said persuasively: "This is water down the old sewer— but I'll make a go of it. Heist yourself up out of that swivel chair and strap on your gun. There's been a murder."

"My gun's already strapped on. I ain't never without it," Sheriff Childress rebuked him. "Now about yore murder, let's reason hit out. Whenever they's been a killing, I always hear about it. I'm sheriff, someone always tell me. Q.E.D. Logic *ad mandamus* tells us they hain't been no murder. If they had been a killing, son, I'd of heered about it." He looked smug.

"You're hearing about it now." McGavock was patient. "That's what I'm doing now. I'm trying to tell you—"

"Who, according to you, has been kilt?" The sheriff smiled paternally.

"Simon Tetcherall Layton. And don't laugh."

"I cain't he'p it!" Sheriff Childress grinned. "Old Doc Layton kilt hisself, that ain't no crime. Yo're a stranger, friend. Fellers in town has been pranking you. Hyuh-hyuh-hyuh!" The sheriff rolled back in his chair, closed his eyes and broke into a bellowing guffaw. "Yes, 'y doggies, some 'un's done sent you to me on a foolish errand. They wasn't nothing—" The sheriff stopped in mid-sentence. His features went rigid, contorted in pain. "For Heaven's sakes," he said hoarsely. "We've went and did it. We brought back my misery."

Sheriff Childress groped in a desk drawer, produced a cigar box and opened the lid. McGavock stared inside and flinched. The box was alive with about two dozen scurrying beetles, shiny black bugs with elongated, jointed bodies. McGavock had seen just such bugs in rotted logs. The sheriff studied the scampering insects, caught one deftly between the ball of his thumb and forefinger. He tilted his head, inserted the beetle in his ear and—to the horror of McGavock—*squeezed*. McGavock licked his dry lips. "What—?"

"Earache. I got me a spanking mean earache." The sheriff closed the boxlid, sighed. "They ain't nothing like the juice of a betsey-bug for a ear misery."

"It's a new one on me!"

"Mebbe so, son, mebbe so. But mountainfolks has used them for years. Now kindly evacuate and lemme alone. I'm a sick man."

McGavock was resigned. "I guess I'm going to have to use the pearls, after all." Sheriff Childress wiped his fingers fastidiously with a fluffy purple handkerchief. McGavock said pleasantly: "Well, brother, don't say I didn't warn you. When things begin to crack, don't come to me with a high pressure gripe. I've offered to co-operate, I've laid the dope on the line—and you've given me the brushoff. I'm going back to the hotel. I will say this before I leave: tomorrow at ten in the morning, they're burying the old professor. At precisely that moment, while the cottage is empty, I'm going to be in Doc Layton's house turning it off for whatever I can find in the way of clues. I leave you this option—you can either pick me up there for breaking and entering—or you can use your noodle and hop onto my wagon."

Sheriff Childress sat motionless, his eyes went glassy. "Praise Jehovah," he whispered. "She's a-easing up on me. Go away, friend, go away."

It had been a waste of time, just as McGavock had suspected it would be. He didn't much like the looks of it. It was going to be pick-and-shovel work from the very beginning. He was in a nettled mood as he walked the lonesome street toward his hotel. The shopfronts along Main Street were already burning their nightlights behind grimy, flyspecked windows. The wooden awning above his head made a half-tunnel of shadow across the pavement. He pushed through the door of the Simmons House, strode with angry clicking heels across the tiles to the desk.

McGavock registered. The clerk, an amiable, mild-mannered specimen with crescent eyeglasses, blotted his signature, said courteously, "Your room is 207." He handed the detective his key. "I've had your bag taken up. They tell me that tannic acid will do in an emergency."

McGavock started for the stairs, walked six steps and stopped dead still. "What was that crack about tannic acid?" He turned. The clerk was nowhere in sight. Halfway up the stairway, he heard the clerk's detached voice addressing him again.

"Tannic acid," the voice called genially, "is for bad burns. You're playing with fire, suh!"

The second floor gallery was horseshoe-shaped. A murky corridor, covered with straw matting, led off the mezzanine into the vitals of the old building. McGavock, his fingers splayed on the mahogany bannister, paused a moment at the head of the stairs, peered down into the well of the rotunda. Potted plants, clean tiles, shabby furniture—it was a peaceful, lethargic scene. That little lobby was Rockton in a capsule: *too* peaceful. Nothing, come murder and mayhem, could cause a ripple in the even tenor of its ways. He cursed, shook his head, and started for room 207 and his gun.

It was then that he saw the girl.

She'd been standing in the shadows, behind him, before a closed door. Just a faint shimmer of filmy voile in the dark mezzanine. He pretended to ignore her, wandered casually past her, but she stepped directly into his path, blocking his way. He shoved roughly into her, threw her off balance with his shoulder, said: "Whoops. Excuse it please."

The girl's hand dropped to the doorknob. "Just step inside, if you will." Her voice was low, commanding. "I'm in trouble."

McGavock made gurgling, derisive noises. The girl's tone became steely. "And don't be lewd. I'm Hallie Layton. This is not a bedroom—this is the music room."

"Why didn't you say so!" McGavock arched his eyebrows. "I'm a sucker for a fugue." He followed her across the threshold. She shut the door and faced him.

They were in one of those special parlors that old-time hotels reserved to protect their female guests from the ribald inspection of a masculine world. The Victorian wallpaper was printed in great clusters of violent lavender grapes, there was a broken-down pink plush sofa, a battered piano with a dime-store table lamp on it, and a miscellany of tattered brocade chairs. "So you're Doxie's old lady?" McGavock teetered back, gave her a harsh, unfriendly inspection.

Mrs. Layton was well worth an ocular tour. Svelte, long-legged and graceful, she was a gal with poise. Her lipstick had been put on with a brush and her blue-black hair, falling back from her white forehead, lay about her shoulders in glossy, waxen symmetry that spelled time and care—but it was McGavock's shrewd guess that here was a kid that would rather knock down a quail or saddle a horse than open a vial of imported perfume. In the first place, she was pretty, in the second, she was expensive. Her dainty, white frock was childishly simple—but it had cost somebody plenty scratch. She showed her wealth in her manner, too. McGavock gauged her age at about nineteen-point-zero, yet she stood before him with the self-assurance born and bred in a heavy wallet. She arched herself haughtily, said: "I've told you I'm in trouble. You're a detective. Will you help me—or won't you?"

"So you know I'm a detective." McGavock ogled. "Could it be you were listening at the keyhole when I was in conference with your husband and Leach?"

She shrugged it off. "Who cares. Yes, I admit it. I'm scared. I heard you say that Father Layton had been slain. I know what that means, it means the extermination has begun."

McGavock waited, deadpan. The girl amplified. "It's Fiddler Joplin. He's always in trouble with the law—and he blames it on us Laytons. He comes up for trial next court-day for taking fish illegally—he probably blames that on us, too."

"Malarky!"

"It's true. I'm making it sound silly but it's really something deep and hateful. To get the right idea, I'll have to give you a few facts. Don't think I'm boasting. The Laytons—my husband, my late father-in-law, and myself—control about two thousand acres—"

"Yoicks!"

"It's large, but there are many larger plantations." She took a deep breath. "Half of this was owned by my late father-in-law, half by my husband and myself. We ran it like a commercial enterprise. My father-in-law managed his section, we managed ours. The whole was under the supervision of my husband. We had periodical auditings and so forth."

"How does this Joplin fit in?"

"Most of our land is fertile bottoms but part of it is hill country." She was embarrassed. "Joplin is a squatter. He has a small hill farm called Joplin's Mill. We own the title to the property but the Joplins have lived on the land for a hundred years. About a month ago, Daddy Layton—for some strange reason—suddenly took Fiddler to court and tried to eject him from the land. Fiddler claimed title by prescription and adverse possession, which means he'd been using it and had actually settled on it. The jury upheld Fiddler, as it should have, and my husband and myself were in sympathy, but you see it was Daddy Layton's land."

McGavock was bleak. "That's bad. But it doesn't quite add up. Evictions give shootings in barbershops. They don't give tricky murders like the old professor's."

Her lip curled. "You don't know Fiddler Joplin. He's a schemer. He's cunning. The squatter affair wasn't all, either. About a week before the attempted eviction, Daddy Layton tried to get through a true bill accusing Joplin of 'shining.' The sheriff had him in jail three days questioning him. It was this seeming persecution, coupled by the fact that Joplin's Mill had been in the family so long, that made the jury uphold the defendant."

"There you are." McGavock grunted. "I've never seen anything like the deep south hill country for lawsuits." He rubbed his jaw. "I'll work for you, sister. Who is this Charlie Lusk?"

Distaste showed on her fine features. "He's an outsider."

"So am I."

Pretty Mrs. Layton exhibited the first signs of snobbery. "I mean he hasn't any connections. Any family or anything. Sometime ago, Daddy Layton took it into his senile brain to get a personal secretary. He wanted a girl, but we put our foot down on that. What would Rockton say, a young city female living with the old professor? We put an ad in the Nashville paper and it brought us Charlie Lusk. Daddy only wanted to pay him six dollars a week, Charlie held out for fifteen, so we made up the balance in secret to him."

McGavock asked politely. "Are you and Mr. Layton going to the funeral tomorrow?"

"I suppose so. Certainly."

McGavock was urgent. "The old man was killed. There's some clue, some place in that cottage of his, which will clinch it. I tried to get in tonight but this menial Lusk wouldn't let me past the threshold. Can you get him away in, say an hour, and keep him away for twenty minutes?"

She considered. "Yes, I can. I'll call him up from the drugstore and tell him that effective from the moment of Daddy Layton's death his salary was cut automatically to the original six dollars." She smiled. "That'll bring him flying out to Doxie with his mouth full of argument."

"Swell. Now, two things more. How does this Robertus M. Leach tie up with you folks, and where can I get a drink of whiskey?"

"Since Anderson went back to Arkansas, Mr. Leach has taken over his place as sort of a stop-gap. Mr. Leach's position is only temporary." She noticed McGavock's knotted forehead, explained. "I keep forgetting that you're a stranger. Anderson was our business advisor. He worked with Doxie but had nominal charge over the entire Layton acreage. He planted, jockeyed for proper prices with the buyers and so forth. A month or so ago his mother died and he went back home to Arkansas. My husband's more of a farmer than a businessman. He picked up Mr. Leach to keep his ledgers until he could locate a—er—more competent person." She met his eyes squarely. "That's the whole story. We've got Scotch, rye and bourbon at the house. I'll have a bottle sent around to you when I return."

McGavock shook his head. "It won't do. I got a galvanized stomach. I favor popskull moonshine."

She stared at him in uneasy pity. "I've heard that private detectives were like that. Well, there's a place in the cellar back of the old abattoir, but I don't recommend it. It's a low and dangerous crowd. It's run by an ex-convict named Pokey."

"Fine!" McGavock was ecstatic. "Just the thing. I'm only dregs myself."

Room 207 was neat and antiseptic-smelling. There was a brass bed, a framed magazine print of Sam Davis, the boy martyr, on the wall, and a huge cupboard-like wardrobe. McGavock stepped through the door whistling. He stood for a moment in the center of the room, taking in the comfortable surroundings. He cocked his thumb and forefinger at the wardrobe, hissed: "Come out of there Jesse James, and you too, Frank, I got you'uns covered." He walked to the window, tested the latch.

The big Gladstone was by the foot of the bed. He laid out his pajamas and dressing slippers, fumbled around and located his revolver. McGavock was funny about his gun. He didn't like to carry it unless he thought he might actually need it. A gun, the way he saw it, was just a tool of the trade. He wouldn't have carted it around with him twenty-four hours a day any more than he would have carried a Stilson wrench or a pair of wire clippers—just on the off-chance they might come in handy.

150

McGavock's gun was designed for heavy duty. It had a short barrel and a heavy bore, the walnut grip was battered and worn. It'd seen plenty of action. It was a tight case, he reflected, he'd seldom gotten away to a tougher start. But things were breaking at last. The wiry little detective was an opportunist, an expert at pushing his luck. It's like a pebble on a hillside, he decided, you get one small rock pried out and, *whambo!* down comes the landslide.

He killed five minutes by his wristwatch to give the gal time to clear out of the hotel. At the end of this period, he stuck his gun behind his belt buckle, turned out the lights and locked the door behind him.

3. Moonshiner's Hide-out

Pokey's Place was a bit hard to find. In the alley back of Main Street, a ramshackle loading-platform ran the full length of the block, each merchant having his own back-door outlet to it. Built in the old days, this platform was wagon-high, about four feet from the ground. By careful use of his flash, McGavock discovered that beneath each shop, back under the platform, was a door leading to what had once been the merchant's storeroom. Rot and decay had changed that custom. The doors on many of the basements were completely missing, others were sagging from disuse.

The red-clay alley was rutted, foul with the dung of mule and horse, and as black as a cave. McGavock made his way down the line. At the end of the row, the final building perked up his interest. An almost obliterated sign said: *Thos. Barlow & Son, Fresh Meats.* The old abattoir. It was foul, dilapidated; its windows were gaping with broken panes.

McGavock beamed his torch under the platform. The basement door was new. It was a strong affair of two-by-eights, of white pine, fastened to the jamb with barn hinges. McGavock bent his back, stepped under the platform and swung it open.

The dive was low and mean. McGavock knew these small town deadfalls for what they were: dynamite. There were just three men in the cellar—two customers and the proprietor. The place was vile, musty, the brick walls sweated to patches of fungus mold, the bare earth floor was spongy from age. The proprietor lolled behind a short packing-box counter at the front of the room, chatting with one of his customers, the other customer was spread-eagled on his back in a tangle of filthy bedclothes on a cot in the corner. His jaw was canted at a rigid angle—he was drunker than seven hundred dollars.

McGavock paused in the doorway and admired him. He was a big man, six feet three or four, and his greasy carrot hair was shaggy and matted. With McGavock's sudden appearance, the proprietor and his companion clammed up like they'd swallowed alum.

McGavock touched his hat brim. "Salutations, good brethren." He advanced casually into the room, leaned his elbow on the packing-box counter. There was a stony silence. McGavock said breezily: "Well, here I am, boys. The man you've been waiting for."

The proprietor was brutish, unshaven, with evil little eyes. Like his two customers, he was dressed in overalls. "We ain't wantin' nobody, mister," he drawled. "Jest turn yourse'f around and go right back out that door." McGavock glanced at the customer by his elbow. A small, wrinkled hillman with the pointed face of a field-mouse. The detective addressed him. "How about a dram of nice charred whiskey? Would you take a drink with me?"

There was a moment of confusion. The mouse-faced man was in a spot. It was an invitation that you don't refuse unless you wish to infer an insult. The hillman thought it over. He remarked carefully: "If you got her, stranger, I'll drink her." He passed the buck right back to McGavock.

"Fair enough." McGavock showed his teeth. He said to the proprietor: "You're Pokey. This is a blind pig. I want a pint of your best rye. I want something that's been charred in a heart keg to a natural red. I don't want any green stuff that's been colored with manure or iodine. I don't want anything that's been touched up with lye to give it a gag. I want something that's come from copper, not tin, and—"

Pokey's face broke into a beam. "You shore want a lot. And durn iffi'n I hain't got it." He went to the cot, rolled back the drunk, produced a pint bottle from under the mattress. He set the container on the counter, drawled: "One dollar, please."

McGavock was astounded. "You never saw me before. You're taking a chance, aren't you?"

Pokey's eyes were cruel. "Hit's you that's taking the chance, poddner If you're an alcohol-tax-man sombuddy's in fer some hell-raisin'."

McGavock uncorked the bottle, shoved it across the counter to the mouse-faced man. The hillman tilted it back, took a five-ounce drag and choked. "'Scuse me," he said politely. "That last swaller, she went down my Sunday pipe." McGavock offered the bottle to the proprietor who took the traditional, courteous sip, and returned it. McGavock completed the ceremony.

The ritual finished, McGavock remarked convivially: "I'm a hunter and a fisherman, gentlemen. Zooks, how I love wildlife! You've got some fine hills hereabouts. They must be loaded with game."

The mouse-faced mountainman hiccoughed, nodded. "They is at that. They reely is." He took an althea toothbrush from his pocket, sprinkled a pinch of snuff on his lower gum, and rubbed the powder into the flesh. "Yes, sir," he declaimed when he'd finished the operation. "They's fish and I kin take y'all to 'em. Was you wantin' a guide?"

"Maybe yes, maybe no." McGavock looked sly. "He'd have to be the right man. I'm after gray foxes and I use chemicals and smokers."

There was a silence. The mouse-faced hillman was shocked. "A fellar cain't take fox this time a year, and chemicals and smokers'll get you a trip to Nashville. They're a violation of the Fish and Game Act. Fox is out, but if you want trout—"

"Swell." McGavock prepared to leave. "Meet me at the Simmons House tomorrow morning. I'll have the jugs."

Again that strained silence. Pokey said: "You'll have the what?"

"The jugs. We'll jug them," McGavock explained. "You know how it's done. You put a little lime in the jug, make a small hole in the cork, drop the jug in the trout pool and *powie!* up they come. Blast them out, that's my style."

"You got a hellacious style if you don't mind my sayin' so." The little hillman was suddenly distant. "Yo're cryin' for a ball and chain."

McGavock argued. "We won't get caught, we'll be slick about it. They tell me Fiddler Joplin's been getting away with it for years. If he can jug fish, so can we."

That did it. The faces of McGavock's companions were drawn in coarse, livid anger. Pokey spoke and his voice was dull and dead. "It all comes out now. You ain't no alcohol-tax man, yo're a sneaky game warden. Well, yo're wasting your time, yo're jipper-jawing around tryin' to get evidence on Fiddler Joplin." The proprietor's unshaven cheeks contorted in contempt. "The rich folks, the Laytons, have got a grudge agin Fiddler. They're tryin' to frame him into prison."

McGavock sneered. "But I saw the jugs this evening in the sheriff's office. That's evidence, isn't it?"

"It ain't enough to convict him and Sheriff Lud Childress durn well knows it. Fiddler Joplin takes game and fish like anyone else, but he takes it in season and he takes it legal. He had him those jugs fer another purpose."

McGavock broke into a raucous laugh. That's a good one. I could see the holes in the corks—they'd been limed."

Pokey looked puzzled. "They was all set to explode, I know that. But he won't tell nobody what he was going to use them fer. Game warden, take my word fer it, he's innocent."

"O.K., McGavock agreed. "I will. Take my word for it—I'm no game warden."

McGavock stood in the shadow of a foamy crape-myrtle tree and subjected Professor Layton's slate-roofed cottage to a cautious scrutiny. By now, if Hallie Layton had carried through her agreement, Charlie Lusk had shed his luxurious dressing-robe and had left the house. It was an eerie picture: the porchlight burning like a death lamp, the curtained windows, the funeral wreath swaying gently against the door panel in the fitful spring breeze.

McGavock swung from the sidewalk, through the box-hedge gateposts, up the glazed brick wall. He clanged the lever bell-pull, waited. There was no response. He tested the knob, found the door unlocked, and entered.

Systematically, he made a quick, thorough prowl of the ground floor. Off the corridor, to the right, was the old headmaster's study. To the left was the parlor. The parlor was just about as McGavock had last seen it. The decanter on the card table was about empty and the platter of sandwiches nearly consumed, but otherwise everything was the same—the center of interest was still the trestled casket with its heap of sultry flowers. At the end of the hallway was the kitchen, which McGavock passed up. Flanking the kitchen, on its left and right, respectively, was the cubbyhole which served the secretary as living quarters, and the larger, more comfortable master's bedroom.

Lusk's tiny room was cramped, but somehow cozy. There was a Spanish daybed, a small bureau and a friendly-looking, broken-down Morris chair with a shelf of books beside it. Three thread-bare suits hung from a broomstick bar in the corner. The detective picked up the books, examined them one by one. The first was a paperback affair titled: *1001 JOKES, Fun for Young and Old.* The four others were instructional volumes on how to become a self-taught cartoonist. The flyleaf of each volume bore the scrawled signature: *Leslie Anderson, Little Rock, Arkansas.*

"Leslie Anderson?" McGavock muttered. "Layton's business manager, eh? The lad replaced by the incumbent Mr. Leach. You're going places, Luther."

He got his big surprise of the evening when he flipped down the toggle and turned on the overhead light in old man Layton's master bedroom. The walls and floor jumped at him in almost blinding illumination. McGavock boggled. The bulb in the professor's ceiling fixture was at least two hundred watts in strength. Abruptly, he grinned. "Oh ho! So that's the way the land lays."

Working swiftly and efficiently, he began a minute search of the old man's quarters. The collar compartment of the cumbersome dresser paid off with an interesting document. A curt, arrogant letter. He unfolded the paper, read:

Dear Dr. Layton:

In response to your repeated conversations with me on street corners, in court square, at church—in fact wherever you encounter me in public—in response to these persistent conversations, I have finally been driven to take the matter up with your son, and my employer, Mr. Doxie Layton.

You say that you are old and infirm and that you wish Mr. Doxie to assume your holdings and acreage and that you are fully prepared to relinquish all title in his favor. You indicate that account-keeping and business management of so extensive holdings are, at your age, difficult and onerous.

I have, as I have indicated above, conferred with Mr. Doxie on this point. He wishes me to state flatly and finally for him that the idea of your deeding your property and estate to him at this time is not acceptable to him. He says that you are sufficiently vigorous and fully competent to handle your own affairs and that he hopes you will disabuse your mind of any doubts on this subject.

Mr. Doxie Layton has asked me to put his position in writing to bring an end once and for all to the matter. To be blunt: Mr. Doxie will keep his property and you will keep yours.

Sincerely,

Leslie Anderson
Manager, Layton Farms

"He's finally done it," McGavock said softly. "He's found a way to relinquish deed and title." He thrust the letter into his breast pocket.

The signature on the paper was in careful, angular script. The same name—in the front of the cartoon books in Charlie Lusk's room—had been round and fancy, almost illiterate. You didn't have to be a graphologist to note the dissimilarity. McGavock went back to his prowl.

It was then that he made his big discovery. It was so cleverly concealed that he nearly muffed it. Three old quilts were stowed in the bottom drawer of the dresser. McGavock lifted them out. The drawer was lined with old newspapers. McGavock removed the papers. Cut in the wooden panel of the drawer-bottom was a hole. A small, rectangular hole, about four by eight inches. Just a hole. McGavock could look through it to the carpet beneath the dresser. For a moment, he was nonplussed. A strained, attentive expression grooved his face, brought out the network of wrinkles about his tired, wise eyes. He clicked his tongue, said: "For Gosh sakes!"

He replaced the quilts, shut the drawer, and stood up.

Professor Layton's room was a primer in crime. The two-hundred-watt bulb in the ceiling fixture, the ridiculous, huffy letter in the collar compartment, the squarish hole in the dresser drawer—they all fitted together to produce iron-clad evidence to convict a murderer. McGavock's lips thinned. He was reforming his opinion of the old absent-minded professor.

He groped in his pocket, located the spool of thread and the imitation pearl necklace. "Now," he said, "a little hocus-pocus in the attic and then tally-ho for bed."

The attic stairs were at the rear of the hall, by the kitchen. The detective ascended a steep, narrow flight of steps, and found himself in a hot, stuffy cubicle. He heard the scratching scurry of startled mice and flicked on his torch. Two frightened bats took off from the rafters above his head and slapped their way frantically through the open louvers.

The garret was floored and represented the space between the main story and the roof. Overhead, the timbers arched and pyramided into hips and gables. The place was bare, but for one article of furniture: an old leather-covered, claw-and-ball piano stool. McGavock caught the stool in his light, threw the beam directly upward. Hanging down from a rafter, over the piano stool, was about ten inches of cotton clothesline. "So this," McGavock declared, "is where they cut him down." He was hardly interested.

The garret floor was a patchwork of odds and ends of planking. The detective selected a spot about three yards or so from the pedestal of the stool, dropped to his haunches. He took off his hat, dented the crease at a forty-five degree angle. He placed his pencil flash in the crease so that it struck the floor before him in a pool of light. He probed in his vest pocket with a hooked finger, came out with a small cylindrical object that resembled a tire-pressure gauge: a machine tool jimmey with a telescopic handle.

He picked a floorboard at random, a warped three inch plank about two feet in length, inserted his jimmey and pried. It came loose with a squeak. On the lath and plaster bottom of the cavity thus disclosed between the joists, he spread a one dollar bill. He produced his spool of thread, broke off a length about ten inches long, laid the piece across the aperture at right angles to the elongation. With the chisel-blade of his tool, he withdrew the nails from the plank and refitted it in its original position. He dropped the spool into his pocket, tossed the bent nails over his shoulder, and inspected his work.

Everything seemed normal. Except that section of white thread. It ran along the floor for a couple of inches, disappeared by the edge of the plank, reappeared at the opposite joint and once again advertised its presence.

McGavock got to his feet, put on his hat. "Don't fail me, baby" he said."I'm depending on you." His eyelids were hot and stiff. It had been a long, hard day.

Outside, on the street, he headed for the hotel and fresh, clean sheets. The sweet wood-scents from the crested hills swept in soft, soporific gusts through the little town. McGavock was asleep on his feet by the time he reached his room.

Things started off with a bang the next morning while McGavock was at breakfast.

The ground floor of the Simmon's House was T-shaped. The lobby, or crossbar of the T, fronted the sidewalk and jutting back at right angles to the rotunda, behind the staircase, was a succession of utility and service rooms culminating in the hostelry's old-fashioned kitchen. The dining-room was located at the left of the hallway, immediately in the rear of the manager's office.

The room was high-ceilinged, airy and pleasant: curtains arched and billowed by the open windows and the morning sunlight, lemon-colored, splashed on white linen cloths and glinting silverware. Floor and woodwork gave off a faint sanitary smell from frequent scrubbings with lye-and-ashes. McGavock selected a small table by the wall and placed his order.

There was an open window by his shoulder and, constantly and persistently, throughout the meal, the curtain flicked and furled across his line of vision. He'd just demolished a platter of meal-fried

157

drum fish and was topping the job off with sweet yellow tomato jam and beaten biscuits when suddenly, on an impulse of exasperation, he leaned forward and anchored the curtain to the table with the sugar bowl. To do this, he was forced to rise partially out of his chair. For a split instant, he had a good, clear view of the outside. That was how he saw the trespasser.

Directly beyond the window, possibly eight feet below him, was a small enclosed courtyard. Two sides of the courtyard were formed by a tall board fence, the inside L of the hotel constituting the remaining walls. A man came through a gate in the fence, from the alley. He was carrying his shoes in his hand.

It was the shoes-in-the hand stuff that aroused McGavock's interest. The detective canted his chair, settled back where he could watch without being seen.

The man was a giant—six feet three or four—with tangled carroty hair. He wore faded overalls. McGavock placed him instantly: the lad at Pokey's, the big drunk who had sprawled in alcoholic stupor, spreadeagled on the cot in the corner.

The man stood for a second in the center of the cobblestone court and studied the row of second-story windows. He had the appearance of a man who was confronted with an emergency and didn't like to make snap judgments. A low coalhouse nestled in the crotch between the hotel and the fence. The man hid his shoes carefully in a stack of oak stove wood, frowned apishly. Abruptly, he raised his arms, grasped the coalhouse eaves in enormous, knotty hands. His shoulder muscles bunched. With lithe, unbelievable grace, by sheer strength of his biceps, he drew his monstrous hulk up from the ground onto the shed's roof.

McGavock was fascinated. In an animal crouch, the man ascended the slanting tin roof, to the row of second-story windows. He reared back on his hunkers, began waving his finger at the sashes, working his lips. He's counting, McGavock decided.

Finally the big man made his choice. He produced an iron tire tool, forced the window catch, and crawled out of sight into the building. McGavock closed his eyes, visualized the layout of the second floor. He counted windows himself—and smiled bleakly.

The big man had entered room 207, McGavock's room.

McGavock was deep in reverie when a pompous, blustering voice cut loose about six inches from his eardrums. "Well, well! I thought I'd find you here, suh! Partaking of ye old inn's matutinal edibles, I perceive. I'd like to join you, suh, but I have already enjoyed gustatory fulfillment. I will, however, accept one of yall's toothpicks." A pudgy hand suddenly grasped the china toothpick holder, upset the spindles in a heap on the tablecloth, pawed through them, selected one. McGavock turned his head, stared into the puffy, unctuous face of the Honorable Robertus M. Leach.

"Up bright an early, I see." McGavock was deliberately insulting. "Whose letters have you been snooping into this morning?"

Leach pulled up a chair facing the detective, lowered himself ponderously, in jelly-like convolutions. "You cain't make me mad, Luther." He chuckled. "I like you and besides I'm too all-fired happy, everything's bluebirds with me this lovely spring morning."

McGavock sneered. "I catch. Layton was going to tie the can on you last night and you talked him out of it. Is that what you mean?"

The puffy man looked offended. "You got the hatefullest way of saying the most simple things." He smiled serenely. "Essentially, suh, you done named the facks. I threw myself on his mercy. I explained to him that when I broke into that communication to you people in Memphis I didn't have anything but his interests at heart. I said, 'Mr. Doxie—if I'm your business manager it behooves me to manage your business and I cain't do that lest I know everything about everything.'"

"And he fell for it?"

Leach looked foxy. "Doxie Layton has what you might call the rich landowner psychology. His big obsession is land and raisin' crops. He don't like to be bothered with any kind of details that he can't figure out in terms of land or crops. When I saw he was writing a detective agency, I was afraid he was in trouble. It was my obligation to take the burden off my employer. I explained it to him last night after you left and he understood. I was just doing my duty, Luther."

"Don't call me Luther." McGavock's voice was creaky. "You're snake-eggs in my book!" He controlled himself, asked: "Do you really have Boss Layton's interests at heart? O.K., then. Answer me a few questions. Who was this Lester Anderson, what did he look like, and what were the circumstances of his so-called resignation?"

Mr. Leach looked mildly astonished. "So Les is involved in this? I'm not surprised. I never liked the man." He pressed his finger deep into his fat cheek, went through the motions of deep thought. "Les didn't resign, he hightailed. One dark night he just up and skedaddled, left Mr. Doxie stranded—that's how I came into the picture. What did he look like? Let's see. If I were describing him in court, I'd say that he was middle-aged, handsome, a good dresser, and all-fired cold-blooded. What I call the northern-type business man, the kind that would put his grandmother out picking cranberries if it would show black on the family ledger."

"A northerner? I thought he came from Arkansas."

Leach disgorged his toothpick. "So he said, but who knows? That's my description of him, would you like my *impression?*"

"Very much."

Leach was solemn. "I can put it in a single word: skittery."

McGavock was silent.

"Here's what I mean," Mr. Leach explained. "You'd be in a room and all of a sudden Lester Anderson would step out of the closet. It gave me the chills. I never visited Doxie but he pulled it on us. We'd be talking, and suddenly he'd pop out on us."

McGavock threw his voice deep in his chest, said in a hollow baritone, "Robertus M. Leach, the Honorable, I'm going to ask you to make a statement. Last night there was a scuttleful of cigar ashes on your vest, a condition which had the appearance of being habitual with you. However, this morning I observe that they have vanished. I am a detective; such details intrigue me. What became of those ashes, suh?"

Leach batted his eyes. "I brushed them off." He drew himself up like a pouter-pigeon. "You're a mighty sorry detective, suh, if you think my vest has anything to do with this-here affair. I'm going to Dr. Layton's buryin'. I always make a particular point of brushing off my vest whenever I go to a buryin'."

"Spoken like a true gentleman." McGavock pushed back his chair, got up. "Expect a large crowd at the funeral?"

"Just the four of us. Mr. Doxie and Miss' Hallie, Lusk and yours truly."

McGavock cocked an eyebrow. "How's chances of crashing the convention?"

"It could be done, but I wouldn't advise it. Frankly, you wouldn't be welcome."

McGavock said viciously: "You folks wait until I throw a funeral, and you want to come! You'll be sorry then!" He slammed out of the room, left Mr. Leach in a befuddled stupor.

McGavock walked heavy-heeled down the matting-floored upstairs corridor. He came to a noisy halt by the door of 207, rattled his key against the escutcheon and listened. There was no sound. He inserted the bit in the lock, threw the bolt, and entered the room.

The barefooted giant was standing awkwardly in the center of the carpet. He was a hard-looking specimen. His shaggy, uncut hair fell in tangled tufts almost to his collar. His unshaven, slab-like cheeks were stiff in sullen anger. McGavock asked crisply: "Who are you and what do you want?"

The man spoke in a wooden whisper. "I'm Fiddler Joplin, and I'm aimin' to find out yore weight. I'm fixin' to slap you back to whur you come from."

"You've been standing here, waiting for me, for twenty minutes? Why didn't you sit down? There's plenty chairs and a nice soft bed!"

Joplin flushed, indicated his mud-caked overalls. "I ain't wantin' to mess up nobuddy's furniture."

"Well!" McGavock was speechless. "Think of that!" He grinned. "Don't get too rough with me, that gives blood on the nice clean rug."

The red-haired man dug in a hip pocket and came out with a claspknife, a wicked implement with a sheepsfoot blade. Joplin laid the knife on the washstand. "I'll put her here," he said reluctantly, "or elst I'll be cuttin' on you. When I start to fight, my elements gits up."

McGavock said gently: "What have you got against me, Fiddler?"

"Hit's been know-rated to me that yo're a durn, skunky spy." He spoke without particular malice. "Pokey says you was in his place last night, whilst I was asleep, that you was tryin' to work up some crooked evidence on me. Let me pose you this, are you taking money from then Laytons?"

"Not yet, but I hope to."

"Why don't you folks leave me alone?" Dark, turbulent anger, the dangerous, desperate rage born of long brooding, surged into his stolid face. He spoke in a low, monotonous mumble. "Why do high-class rich folks like the Laytons pick on a poor honest farmer? I'll tell you why: they got the black blood of Satan in 'em. For months now, they been persecutin' me. Here am I, out on my hungry-feedin' farm not harmin' nobuddy, mindin' my own business. Doctor Layton, which was that ole dragon, the Devil, and the pappy of the brood—as hit sayeth in the Gospel—Doc Layton, he gets the idee to persecute me. First he sets Lud Childress on me as a 'shiner.' The sheriff throws me in jail and questions me for three days. They ain't nothin' to hit, so he has to let me go."

McGavock listened to the cascade of hate. Joplin went on: "That was just the beginning. A week later the old professor tries to evict me, hails me into court. The Joplins have done live at the Mill since before Jefferson Davis, I reckon. The court upholds me. The old man gets a-plottin' and a-plannin'—and lays a new snare. They're tryin' to jail me for juggin' fish!"

"I saw six jugs in the sheriff's office," McGavock declared amiably. "They were yours, weren't they?"

"That's right. But—"

"And they were limed, they were all set to blast?"

"I reckon." The giant began to sweat, beads of moisture gathered on his low forehead. "It looks like they got me redhanded, but they ain't. I'm innocent." His eyes were furtive, cornered. "I cain't tell you no more. Don't crowd me." He took a deep breath. "I'm gonna whip yore britches," he said placidly. "Then pack up your satchel and git yorese'f Memphis-bound. Yo're a trial and a tribbelashun!"

McGavock made the mistake of arguing. He said: "Now hold on, Fiddler. There's two sides to every question—"

The big man came at him. He came at him in a lunge. He took three nimble, running steps, like a bobcat on a tree branch, came to a sudden stop and unloaded a haymaker. The attack was so unorthodox that it caught McGavock flatfooted. When the red-haired man rushed, McGavock's reflexes falsely warned him that he was in for an eye-gouging wrestling match. The detective lowered his fighting guard, and Fiddler Joplin swung. It was a woodsman's swing, the swing of an axman. The giant's fist, launched in a great downhand arc, caught McGavock in the cup of his shoulder. The mighty impact drove him backwards and down, threw him flatly against the wall.

Just that one terrific blow. Joplin made no attempt to follow it up. McGavock, his shoulder throbbing, crouched taut and tense—infuriated at himself for his blundering misjudgment, his posture was that of a man dazed and badly hurt.

A queer change came over Fiddler Joplin. The network of capillaries on his flat cheeks burned fiery red, his eyes went dull and slaty.

He said lifelessly, "I cain't help myself, amen," and reached for his clasp-knife.

McGavock clinched. He knocked the knife to the floor, kicked it under the bed. Joplin threw clumsy, bearish arms around him and McGavock hit him three times below the heart. The hillman staggered. McGavock disengaged, laid an eight-inch pile driver at the hinge of the big man's jaw, measured him with a final heartpunch as he sagged. He was out before he struck the floor.

The wiry little detective went to the washstand, bathed his hands and face, dried them on the sleazy hotel towel. He paused a moment, gazed with moody, unseeing eyes at his handiwork—two hundred and forty pounds of it—on the gay, floral carpet. He said to himself, "Fisticuffs, good old-timey fisticuffs!" without realizing that he was speaking.

He left the room, locked the door from the outside, and tossed the key through the open transom. He heard it jingle as it hit the bed.

4. Gala Funeral

His eye caught sight of two familiar figures as he descended the broad, sweeping stairs into the lobby. Doxie Layton and the secretary, Charlie Lusk, were perched side by side on a red leather sofa, beneath a dusty rubber-plant—waiting for him.

They were dressed, each according to his tastes, for the burying. The landowner was garbed in fine black cheviot, his vest was piped with silver braid and he wore high black shoes which had the suspicious appearance of being hunting boots beneath his trousers. He watched McGavock approach with thoughtful eyes, as though he were judging the staple of a very inferior bale of cotton. For Charlie Lusk, the funeral was obviously an outing. The secretary was rigged for a bullfight: his jacket was of goose-track tweed, his flannel slacks were vivid chocolate. His single contribution to the sobriety of the occasion was a mourner's armband. He leaned back, behind Layton's range of vision, and gave McGavock a wry wink.

They arose simultaneously as he advanced on them. He flagged them off. "Some other time, boys," he said. "I'm behind schedule."

Layton was nonplussed. "That's a rather brusque way to greet a client, isn't it? Last night you offered yourself to me for hire. I'm prepared, sir, to retain you." He pointed to the clock above the desk: it said a quarter to ten. "Do you wish to deal with me? Answer yes or no. I, too, am occupied this morning. The funeral procession leaves in fifteen minutes."

McGavock pretended amazement. "Not from here, not from the hotel! That explains a lot. First Leach and now yourself and Charlie, here. I wondered why the kith and kin were congregating at the Simmons House."

Layton was unperturbed. "You're a strange and irritating personality, Mr. McGavock. Large cities incubate queer hybrids, don't they? Nevertheless, I've come to a decision. I'm prepared to pay you twenty-five dollars, cold cash, if you prove to me that my father was murdered."

"O.K. Follow these instructions: take out the oldster's stomach, chop it up and make a solution from it. Analyze that solution. He was given sleeping powders—and then hanged." McGavock pushed his hat onto his forehead with the flat of his hand. "Twenty-five dollars, please. Just forward it to your favorite charity—if any. Now step aside."

Layton said coldly: "I'd amputate my living hand before I'd desecrate my father's mortal remains. I've talked enough with you, sir."

McGavock fumbled in his breast pocket, located the letter he'd discovered in the drawer of Dr. Layton's dresser. "Here's an exhibit," he remarked, "that I'd like to hear a little more about." He handed the paper to Lusk. "You were the old man's secretary. Did you ever see this thing before?"

Charlie Lusk scanned the page intently. "No," he answered. "No, I never have. The old man was trying to give away his property, eh? Well, well."

"Let's take a look at that." Doxie Layton whipped the paper from the secretary's fingers. He read: . . . *you wish Mr. Doxie to assume your holdings and acreage and are fully prepared to relinquish all title in his favor . . . Mr. Doxie wishes me to state flatly and finally for him that the idea is not acceptable to him! Signed: Leslie Anderson, Manager, Layton Farms.* For a moment his poise cracked. "What rigmarole is this?"

McGavock asked blandly: "Is the signature genuine?"

"Of course it's genuine. But that means nothing at all." Layton got organized. "Why blast that Leslie Anderson! I was lucky to get rid of him. He was obviously involved in matters concerning me without my knowledge!" He wheeled on Lusk, lashed out: "Did you know anything about all this, Charlie?"

Lusk said calmly: "No, I didn't. But I will say this. The old man was crazy—though not about money. Maybe Anderson suddenly jumped his trolley—"

"And talking about Anderson," McGavock put in, "what's this I hear about him hiding in closets?"

"That's right." Layton was grave. "It got to be quite an embarrassing stunt in that period just before he left us. He was eavesdropping on me, there was no doubt about it. The butler's pantry was his favorite. You can hear the conversation in the parlor quite well from the butler's pantry. I caught him three times while I was entertaining guests. I asked him what he was doing. He said he was counting the jams and jellies, that a good business manager checked up on everything. He was guilty, flustered—"

"Shelf-conscious, eh?" McGavock grinned. "Am I a comic? Wow!" He nodded. "I'll be seeing you."

Layton said angrily; "When Anderson comes back, I'll cut his salary. Just to hold him in line. He was a good manager, you know."

McGavock took three paces to the door, turned. "*Was* is the right word. Leslie Anderson will never pop out of another closet. He's deader than a dime's worth of chitterlings."

Dr. Simon Tetcherall Layton's tiny, slate-roofed cottage had undergone a change of aspect. In the bright crystal wash of a blue-and-silver sky, it seemed a different place altogether, it seemed cheerful, cozy. The specter of death had vanished. The curtains had been pulled back, the wreath was gone from the porch, and the casket of Daddy Layton was, at that very moment, rolling along over red clay backstreets to its final resting place. McGavock strolled up the glazed brick wall, tried the knob. The house was locked.

An ordinary skeleton key did the trick. He stepped inside, kicked the door shut behind him.

A heavy hand reached out from behind portiers, laid itself on his shoulder. The booming, complaining voice of Sheriff Ludlow Childress broke the tomblike silence. "Mister McGavock, I as an authenticated representative of law and order for Tilden County, do here and thereby arrest you for breaking and entering!" The dewlapped sheriff, ponyskin vest and all, materialized in the hallway, dangling a pair of rusty handcuffs. He was puffing. "You said you was gonna do it, but I jest couldn't believe it. Hain't you ashamed o' yorese'f—breaking into a corpse's domicile! Jest wait till the jury sits on you! Don't they respect the dead back in Memphis?"

McGavock grinned. "Hi, Ludlow. How's the ear-misery?"

"Hit's went away, thank you, but you cain't sweet talk yore way out'n this. This-here's a criminal act."

McGavock hardened. "So it's going to be that way, eh? You're siding with your constituents. Doctor Layton was murdered—and I'm prepared to prove it to you. But you don't want to listen. You're covering for someone. You don't want a homicide case—you'd rather have a breaking-and-entering charge against an outsider like me. O.K. You're the sheriff."

Sheriff Childress lowered his eyelids. "Yo're jest a-goadin' me into idle speech. Bob Leach warned me agin you. He said yo're slicker than a vixen, and dangerous. I ain't covering up no murder and you mighty well know it. You come here from Memphis, on your own, without no client, and are going around fomenting, trying to stir up a sitshiation, hoping the good Lord will drop a juicy fee in yore lap. Jest like Bob Leach was a-sayin'—we hain't needin' no trouble-makers in Rockton."

"Sure, sure." McGavock appeared to be in deep meditation. He asked, apropos of nothing. "What kind of a knot was it?"

"What kind of a knot was what?"

"The knot in the rope in there—" McGavock pointed toward the attic. "How was the rope tied, the rope that hanged old man Layton?"

"Just tied to a rafter. Just an ordinary knot, I guess." The sheriff was tolerant. "Why?"

"I have a feeling you've passed up some very valuable evidence." McGavock was grave. "We do things differently in the city. We study the knot. If it's a bowline, a sailor tied it; if it's a carrick bend, a carpenter tied it; if it's a timber hitch, a lumberman did it. And so on." He closed his eyes, reminisced dreamily, "How well do I re-member that time we found an old man all trussed up with lover's knots. A dead giveaway. We scouted around and arrested his house-keeper. Yes, sir, they were having a secret romance—"

Sheriff Childress was uneasy. "A knot is just a knot to me. Mebbe we'd best step up and have a look."

"It'll pay you in the long run," McGavock promised. "That, I can guarantee."

The tiny garret was sepulchral, still. The golden morning sun-shine, beating through the louvers, cut the shadows in a crisscross of moted, lucent rays. The halflight was weird, other-worldly. McGavock's searching gaze swept the floor in quest of his thread, found it, continued casually to the piano stool. Sheriff Childress clicked on his flash, beamed it at the length of clothesline dangling from the rafters. "There you are," he declaimed. "What do you make of 'er?"

McGavock went through the pretense of studying it. He looked flabbergasted. "I'm stumped! I never saw anything like it." He walked abruptly to the window, turned his back to the room, and stared morbidly through the slatted louver down into the little yard with its velvety lawn and frothy, lacey lilacs.

Sheriff Childress' plaintive voice said miserably: "Don't do me this-a-way! You get me higher than a kite—and then you go and let me down. Is this really murder, McGavock? If so—what are we gonna do?"

McGavock wheeled from the window, faced him. "We'll have to use the pearls, Sheriff. It's trickery, I admit, but we're in a hole. We simply have to use them. It's a ruse I've relied on over and over again—and I've always found it highly successful. Shall we give it a go?"

Sheriff Childress asked dubiously: "What pearls?"

"These." McGavock dug in his pocket and produced the imitation pearl necklace. He grasped the string loosely in his hand, so that his thumb held the strand between his first and second finger. Mr. Childress studied them warily. He asked: "Is them genuwine?"

"No, they're fakes. This whole business is a fake. Now you take this necklace—" He wedged his thumb deftly through the strand, exclaimed: "Oo-o-ps! They broke!" The beads cascaded in the air, they rattled and bounced about the floor.

Sheriff Childress said: "Oh, my gracious!" He bent his portly frame, began picking them up. McGavock joined him, he went to the far side of the room, leaving the sheriff to work in the corner where he had planted the plank and thread. Results came quickly. Sheriff Childress grunted with astonishment, said excitedly: "You run on downstairs, Mr. McGavock. I gotta be alone."

McGavock, without looking up, asked: "Why?"

Sheriff Childress' voice trembled. "This ain't no time to ask questions, Git out'n here. I got a inspiration. And when I get a inspiration, I gotta be alone."

"About these pearls—" McGavock protested.

"Forgit them durn pearls," the sheriff ordered, "and leave this attic now! Wait for me down in the parlor."

"O.K." McGavock was amiable.

He stood up, strolled to the door.

He started down the stairs, heavily. He went down five steps and, without pausing or altering the rhythm, stamped back up again.

Sheriff Childress was on his hands and knees, staring goggle-eyed at the floor. As McGavock watched, the good sheriff grasped the ends of McGavock's thread, lifted the plank, and his jaw dropped. He reached into the pseudo-hiding place and took out the one-dollar bill. McGavock said breezily: "Find something, Sheriff?"

Childress started. He blew out his cheeks, got awkwardly to his feet. "I tole you to leave me alone!" he quavered in rage. "I do swear, I hain't never, no time, seen nare a snooper like you!"

"What's that in your hand? It looks like a dollar bill."

"It is a dollar bill," the sheriff spluttered. "You done forced me into confiding in you, you done ketched me." He controlled himself. "Let bygones be bygones, Luther. I'm ready to co-operate with you. Facks is proving you're right; they's more to this than a mere suicide. It's murder, it's murder and robbery, it all comes to me like a visitation, I see the whole thing in my mind's eye. Charlie Lusk kilt ole man Layton."

"Take it slow," McGavock objected. "I don't quite see—"

"It's as plain as day. This dollar bill proves it." The sheriff spoke pontifically. "This here hole in the floor is a hiding place, ain't it? Why, sure. Old man Layton fixed it up. He took out this board and laid that thread under it so he could find 'er when he wanted 'er. Now, nobuddy would go to all that trouble just to hide a little ole one-dollar bill."

McGavock didn't like the way things were developing. He said: "Here's the way I see it—"

Sheriff Childress ignored him. "I say that Doc Layton had a treasure trove in that hidey-hole. He was a miser. Mebbe they were thousands and thousands of dollars there. Lusk, living here in the house with him, caught on to it. He gives the old professor some kind of a sleeping powder or something, takes him upstairs, and hangs him. In his greed, when he rifles the cache, he gets careless and leaves this one-dollar note—that would be easy to do." The sheriff gazed on his companion benevolently. "Thanks to you and yore meddlin', we finally got us a clue."

"That dollar bill," McGavock announced pleasantly, "is suspicious. It's an indication of some kind of guilt, perhaps: At this stage, it's a little perilous to go any farther. It is an opening, it does put you on some kind of a trail. It substantiates what I've been repeating: that there's dirty work in Doc Layton's demise." He beamed, reached out suddenly and shook the sheriff's hand. "Good-bye, old pal. It's been great knowing you."

Sheriff Childress looked troubled. "What do you mean, good-bye?"

"It's heigh-ho and off to Memphis for me, I guess." He smiled sadly. "This is turning out to be one of those cases I can't resist—I've solved dozens of them. But, as you and Bob Leach say, there's no place for me here in Rockton. I'm not needed. Good-bye—and good luck with your visitations."

"Now hold on there." Lud Childress cleared his throat. "Bob Leach ain't my boss. Stick around a few days. I claim Rockton needs you." He grinned suddenly, an honest, boyish grin. "And I know durn well I do."

"That's better," McGavock said quietly. "You've made a smart choice. I've got this case practically solved. It'll be over by eight tonight, and I'll see that you get full credit." He started for the door. "Look me up this afternoon. *Don't forget.*"

When McGavock came out into the porch he circled the cottage, passed through the backyard, and left the premises by the rear. The little home was out at the end of Ashwood Avenue. Beyond the low hedge which marked the property's limit was sloping, rock pastureland. McGavock's problem, as he saw it, was to reach Simon Tetcherall Layton's dilapidated female academy. And to reach it, if possible, without causing to much fuss or commotion. The path he took the night before had led him by the cemetery—so that was out.

He looked with distaste at the rough countryside, paused a moment to get his bearings—and started his hike. It started bad, and got worse. Using the town water-tower as a landmark, he skirted the corporation line. The first quarter-mile was tough going. Spanish needles and pricklypears, and then, as he descended through a network of dry gulleys, it got increasingly meaner. Finally he reached the river level. Here the ground was vivid in bright green grass, treacherous swamp grass, alive with small metallic leopard frogs and cut by sluggish, muddy sloughs. McGavock kept a cautious watch for copperheads. He pushed his way through a tangle of hazel and sumac and found himself in the clearing.

The dismal buildings stood dank and dreary against their background of water-oak and looping muscadine. McGavock, with no attempt at concealment, made directly for the dormitory. The front door, sagging on its rotted sill, was ajar. The detective swung the panel on its squeaking hinges and entered amongst the cobwebs and mold. He found himself in what had originally been the reception parlor. The small, bare room had but two doors: the entry and a door leading back into the dormitory proper. The layout of the building was extremely interesting from a historian's point of view. McGavock had heard of such queer floor plans. The architecture was a relic of those days when females, under the guise of chaperoning, had been herded like sheep. Immediately beyond the parlor was the first bedroom. This, when the academy flourished, had been the bedroom of the house-mother. It, like the front room, had but two doors. Behind the house-mother's room was the first student bedroom, with two doors. And so on—back the entire length of the edifice. The arrangement was such that when Simon Tetcherall Layton's gals went to bed at night—they stayed there. The rooms were linked chain-fashion. The only way a student could indulge in nocturnal courtship was to parade through a sucession of chambers, climaxing in the house-mother's room.

McGavock shuddered. "How did the poor chicks ever get themselves husbands? They didn't. They graduated, went home, and settled down to a life of gilding cat-tails and painting pansies on china pintrays."

Each cubicle was like its neighbor—an east window, a west window, and a fireplace. It was the final, end bedroom that paid off.

This room was an exact facsimilar of the others except for several extraordinary details. Something new had been added. On the mantelshelf, above the fireplace, was a granite washbowl half full of dirty water, a filthy scrap of towelling, a bar of yellow laundry soap—and a cheap mirror. McGavock smiled. This was spoor that had so excited Dr. Layton, the evidence which had driven him to write his 'tramps in the girls dormitory' letter to the Browne Agency.

McGavock worked, and worked fast. It took him just two minutes to find it. He could have pretty well described it before he found it. Up in the fireplace, back on the chimney ledge, he located the bundle. A newish, gray garment, tightly rolled. He laid it gingerly on the floor and spread it out. It was a one piece suit of jumper-type coveralls such as mechanics and farmers use—smeared with smudges of clay and stiff with great blotched stains that could only be dried blood. In the center of the roll was a small hammer and a little black leather kit. He realized that he'd found the murder weapon: a stubby, vicious brickmason's hammer—the short hickory handle was streaked and red. McGavock was careful not to touch it.

He picked up the black leather kit, opened it. It was an expensive masculine toilet set. There was a pair of military brushes, an ivory-handled nail file, and an empty leather loop. "Swell!" McGavock exulted. "Everything here but the comb!" The name of the owner, gold-stamped within the kit's cover, said: *Leslie Leroy Anderson.*

McGavock rolled up the coveralls as he had found them, replaced them in the fireplace. He said: "You will try to strangle me, eh? I've got you now, friend. You're a gone goose."

It was high noon, the sacred hour of spareribs and okra, when McGavock returned to Main Street. Mankind had vanished from the pavements. The hot sun, directly overhead, burned down on court-square in a dry, tremulous haze. There was a scattering of wagons and surries up and down the block. A mountain child in a tattered buggy, guarding his pappy's property from the world of outlanders, munched parched corn and watched McGavock with saucer-like eyes while the buggy's blue mule, following its young master's example, ripped off great sections of the hitching post and masticated them with moody delight. The eyes of mule and boy were on McGavock as he passed, and he saw in each the same tired wisdom of the ageless hills.

McGavock took off his coat, unbuttoned his collar. The thermometer in front of the Simmons House said ninety-one as he swung into the lobby. The mild-mannered clerk with the crescent eye-glasses greeted him pleasantly. McGavock said apologetically: "Brother, I owe you moola. I hate to admit it, but I've lost my room-key."

"You left it in your room," the clerk said genially. "The chambermaid found it there about a half an hour ago." He took a key from the rack behind him and laid it on McGavock's palm, his manner offhand and casual.

"Whoa!" McGavock objected. "There's a mistake here. The key is number 209. I'm 207."

"You were 207." The clerk smiled placatingly. "You are 209 now. Sheriff's orders."

"Does the sheriff tell people where to sleep in Rockton?"

The clerk laughed good-naturedly. "If the exigency demands, yes. About thirty minutes ago the chambermaid tried your door. It was unlocked so—"

"But I left it locked!"

"That was your impression. However, as I have stated, your key was inside. As I was saying, the chambermaid entered and found your key on the bed. She found the body on the floor."

"She found the what on the floor?"

"The body." The clerk soothed him. "Don't get jumpy. All hotels have them at some time or other. This was a man known as Fiddler Joplin, he had a rather unsavory reputation. There's no need for alarm, you're not suspect. The killing must have happened at least an hour after you left. The sheriff, nevertheless, would like to talk to you if you can spare him the time."

McGavock's voice was bleak when he spoke. "What happened to this Fiddler Joplin?"

"He was strangled with a rawhide noose. By a confederate, most likely. He was a big man, we don't understand how it was done. It's quite a mystery." He paused, screwed up his face. "May I give you a tip?"

McGavock nodded.

The clerk said confidentially: "Cook tells me he has some mighty fine river-caught sturgeon. Just say that I recommended it and they'll do it up extra-special for you."

McGavock observed sweetly: "Just pack a little in a lunch pail and I'll take it with me." He started briskly for the door, stopped abruptly when he was half way across the lobby and turned to observe. "From now until eight tonight—I'm going to be long-gone."

5. The Noose Tightens

Hallie Layton received McGavock in the conservatory.

The detective was about halfways up the gravelstone drive, headed for the mansion's templelike veranda, when the girl appeared for an instant by a flowering crabtree at the corner of the building and beckoned to him. She did it with a great show of secrecy. It was pretty obvious that she had been waiting for him, that she was trying to divert him before he reached the porch.

He left the drive, cut across the lawn, and followed her wordlessly into a great glassed-in solarium.

It was a domed airy enclosure, mill-roofed with small paned windows—as large as a ballroom. There were rows and shelves of exotic plants and ferns, running certainly into the hundreds, and so much sunshine—refracted at a dozen angles by the slanting panes—so much hairy greenery and waxy foliage, numbed McGavock's senses. The heavy fragrance of the sullen blossoms layered the atmosphere in strata of musky perfumes. Hallie Layton stood before him, stared at him fixedly.

Long-legged and graceful, she was truly a beautiful woman. Her soft jet hair was caught at the nape of her neck with a little-girl ribbon. She was garbed in a loose knee-length frock of oxblood and thread-of-gold and wore tiny spike-heeled velvet pumps. McGavock gave her an intense, personal scrutiny, said: "Well, well. So this is the way folks get themselves up for buryings in Rockton!"

She flared. "Don't be absurd. I wore black at the funeral. When it was over I came home and dug out the wildest clothes I owned. You know, like you'd rinse out your mouth when you'd swallowed a fly."

McGavock asked calmly: "You didn't like the old man?"

"I loved him. You don't understand. It was just the coffin and the big hole in the ground and everything." She bit her lip. "I'm funny. I can't stand the thought of a living creature losing its spark of life. I guess it's something psychological with me."

McGavock made his voice insolent, pointed. "Do you hunt?"

The door was open to the yard. Six white peacocks, in a snowy line, paraded through the archway into the room from the lawn, wandered aimlessly in and out among the potted ferns. "Of course I hunt." The girl flushed angrily. "I see what you mean—but hunting is entirely different." She tried to explain. "Death, like anything else, comes in degrees. Some deaths are tragic, some are logical and essential. Every time you drink a glass of fermenting wine or eat a slice of moldy cheese you're actually destroying life, but you think nothing of it, do you? What I'm saying is—"

McGavock watched the peacocks. "For your essay on death," he declared, "a great big phooey. Why did you flag me in here?"

She parted the fronds of a drooping bracken, took out a businesslike checkbook and a tiny gold pen. "How much do I owe you?"

"Why worry?" McGavock was vague. He said conversationally: "I've listened to some funny yarns about the old professor. Someone, I believe it was Sheriff Childress, was remarking that the oldster burnt up his teeth just before he died. They say that he was going to grow himself a real set—just by will power. Had you heard the story?"

She nodded. "Yes. It's a fact. Daddy Layton himself told me all about it. He was sitting before his fire one day and he suddenly got exasperated with his dentures. He decided he'd raise a set himself—mind over matter. He took out his plates and tossed them into the fireplace. It sounds strange but who are we to say that he didn't know what he was doing!" She shook the checkbook. "How much do I owe you?"

McGavock noticed that each of the peacocks had one big-jointed toe. It had been bothering him. He asked: "Why is it that those birds each have a swollen toe?" He pointed at the nearest snow-white fowl.

For a minute, she didn't understand. "Oh, that." She smiled. "Peacocks have a tendency to roam. When you buy them, you smash one of their toes and from then on they'll never so much as leave the grounds."

"Just up and smash it, eh?"

That's what I said." She bridled. "Don't look so righteous. It sounds brutal, and maybe it is. But it's an old traditional preventive and I can't see that it's any of your business!" She went into a cold rage. "You're reared in a city and you come out here and try to tell us how to run our lives. Of course, we Laytons are just half-civilized, but we manage to subsist—"

"I guess you do. Two thousand acres!"

She said frostily: "Last night I lost my head. I went to the Simmons House and retained you. All right, that's a contract. This morning Daddy Layton was buried. That terminates our relationship." She put pen to paper. "How much do I owe you?"

"Five thousand dollars."

Mrs. Layton recoiled. "Are you joking? No, I see you're not. Why that's preposterous. You haven't done a thing."

"I've been pleasant company, haven't I?" McGavock grinned. "Five grand is the toll."

She recapped her pen, folded the checkbook, thrust it in her pocket. "That does it. You don't get one red penny. Maybe that'll teach you a little courtesy. We make a fetish of manners here in the wilds, you know." She gave him a thin, tigerish grin. "I'll buy your ticket back to Memphis—and leave it for you at the station."

He lifted his hat from his knee, patted it onto his head, stood up. "The only trouble with owning two thousand acres, as I see it, is that you're subject to delusions of grandeur. Don't lay that bullwhip on me, sister, you don't see any ox yoke around my neck. You and I have a contract and you can't break it by just snapping your fingers. You're twisting facts a little, aren't you? Last night, at the Simmons House, you didn't hire me to solve the death of Professor Layton. You were afraid of bodily harm; you contracted with me to protect you. That agreement was certainly not unilateral, it takes two to break it. If you were in danger last night, you are in danger now, I refuse to release you."

She scoffed. "Try to collect a cent!"

"You no doubt know all about Irish setters and walking-horses, but I happen to be fairly well acquainted with the law of the land. By your own admission, Layton Farms is a partnership. If we can't collect from you, we'll put the pressure on your husband. If it's no soap there, we'll sue the estate of old Doc Layton. And when Atherton Browne sues, newspapers get out their red headlines."

She was saying something over and over, underneath her breath, and he couldn't make it out. He asked: "What are you mumbling about?"

She whispered sulphurously: "You dog, you mangy, mangy dog! You dog—"

He nodded in solemn agreement. "I'm afraid it's true. And now, if you'll excuse me, I'll depart from this charming bower of ever-blooming delight. And see a man about some jugs."

Charlie Lusk in his chocolate slacks and goosetrack tweed jacket—minus mourner's armband—was coming down the broad stone steps of the courthouse as McGavock turned into the square. The secretary was a changed lad. His breezy, cocksure attitude evaporated. His shoulders were slumped and he was dragging his feet like a man walking on skates. McGavock called, "Hello!" and Lusk, observing him, made a futile attempt at putting on his old happy-go-lucky routine. He fanned his fingers, waved, said, "Hi, sport." His voice bent, his eyes were confused, stunned.

McGavock chuckled. "I know just what's going through your mind. It's a dismal world, isn't it?"

Charlie Lusk licked his lips, choked up. "You're not kiddin'. The outlook is very black."

The impact of the sun was terrific. McGavock stopped in the chalky-blue shadow of a fluted pillar. "The high sheriff wants to pin a homicide on you, eh?"

"He's got the wrong person. It seems that while we were at the funeral, Childress was searching Dr. Layton's home. Up in the attic, he found some sort of a hiding place with a one dollar bill in it. He claims it was a big money cache. He said that I killed my employer and robbed him of his secret savings. All that Sheriff Childress wants me to do is, first, to admit premeditated murder; second, to confess that I stole thousands and thousands of dollars, and lastly, to restore the money. That's a brief sketch of my immediate future. It doesn't appeal to me." He tried to smile. Abruptly, he looked mildly astonished. "How did you know?"

"I was with him when he searched the house," McGavock answered. "I'm a detective, you know. Which brings to mind a detail that has us puzzled. We happened to turn over your bedroom along with the rest of the house. I noticed that you're something of a bookworm and that your tastes run to cartoon books and jokes. The subject matter is beside the point, what I can't get is the signatures on the flyleaves of these volumes. Everyone bears the signature: Leslie Anderson, Little Rock, Arkansas. Did you borrow them from—"

Layton looked scared. "The books are mine. I don't know who put that name in them—or why. I noticed it three days ago. It must have been done just after the old man hanged himself."

McGavock said thoughtfully: "The names are forgeries all right. No man would sign his address just Little Rock. He'd say 1066 Gashouse Terrace, or something like that, he'd give the street address. Are the books valuable?"

The whole batch, secondhand, is worth maybe three dollars and a half."

McGavock frowned. "When do they read the will?"

"The what? Oh, the will. Tomorrow afternoon. It's just a formality. The relatives all have copies. The Layton family is kind of a business corporation. Everything goes back automatically into Layton Farms. Even the old man's reputation. Haw!"

McGavock frowned, wagged his head slowly. "It's a mess, Brother Lusk, it's a real mess." He turned on his heel, took the steps two at a time, and entered the courthouse.

Things were transpiring in the office of the sheriff. Mr. Childress was entertaining.

When McGavock first walked into the room, he didn't get it. He thought Mr. Childress had suddenly been struck loony. The big sheriff was tilted back in his swivel-chair. He had an unlit cigar clamped in his dewlapped jowls, he had taken off the paper cigarband, had placed it on his ring finger, and, at arm's length, was admiring it in melancholy gravity. He twisted his hand back and forth, studying his finger, clucking his tongue in outraged bewilderment. "Horrible," he said. "Positively horrible." He looked strained. "Would you mind saying that again?"

McGavock stopped, hard-heeled. "I didn't say anything."

Sheriff Childress was annoyed. "Oh, come in, McGavock. I wasn't speaking to you. Now that you're here, come in." He spoke past McGavock's shoulder. "I'd like to hear that story again—from beginning to end."

It was then that McGavock observed the sheriff's guest. He was sitting modestly back in the corner, behind the door. He was a little difficult to recognize at first—and then McGavock placed him. Pokey, the ex-convict that ran the bootleg dive under the old slaughter-house. He'd come out of his hole and he was dressed for society. He'd shaved and washed, he was wearing ministerial blue serge and was immaculate in white shirt and black tie. The lines in his brutish face were deep in sullen, anti-social anger. "I'll tell you again," he said. "But I don't expect you to do anything about it. Folks like Fiddler Joplin and me don't throw much 'fluence. We don't do much candidating for sheriff, come election-time."

Childress exclaimed reproachfully: "Now, that ain't so, friend. I'm a pore man's sheriff!"

Pokey's eye lit up sardonically. "If you say it, I guess that makes it a fact." He addressed McGavock. "And you, accordin' to my notion, hain't any better. Fiddler was a friend of mine. He was found dead in your room up at the Simmons House. How do I know you didn't do it?"

"Answer him gentle," the sheriff advised McGavock. "He's a tolerable good boy, all-in-all, but he's got a bur under his saddle and a gun in his pocket. Fiddler's demise has upset him, he'd kill you at the wink of an eye. Tomorrow, he'll be all right."

McGavock said pleasantly: "Goodness! This is just like a cutback to old Arizona. What's bothering you, Pokey?"

"I'm scared and I'm mad."

The sheriff coaxed. "Tell him about it, Pokey."

"Something's going on around this town that's mighty, mighty bad. I don't know what it is, but Fiddler Joplin did. He got to broodin' over it. I tried to pump him but he wouldn't loosen up. I figured it was something to do with him and the Laytons, something to do with them persecutin' him. Maybe a lawsuit or something like that. Last night I learned different."

Sheriff Childress spoke from the corner of his mouth. "Listen to this, McGavock. It's horrible."

Pokey continued: "Last night Fiddler come into my—er—establishment loopin' drunk. He was talkin' wild about Doc Layton, calling him Satan, that old dragon. Well, he stumbled around for a little and fell down on the bed—passed out cold. He was in a stupor. Doggone, if after a time he didn't begin talking in his sleep. He kept sayin' one thing over and over agin. It chilled my blood to hear it. He said, *Splashed with blood from eye to bosom!* Just that one sentence. I bet he said it a hunnert times!"

Sheriff Childress walled his pupils at McGavock. "Get that? Splashed with blood from eye to bosom. Who was he referring to?"

McGavock declared soberly, "Now listen, Pokey, I'm after Fiddler's slayer—and I'm going to get that very party. But I want you to be honest with me. You claim that Joplin wasn't jugging fish. You, if anyone, should know." He indicated the jugs along the wall. "How do you explain those?"

Sheriff Childress cut in petulantly, "Of course he was a-juggin'. I got a phone tip and went out to his place when he wasn't to home. I found those jugs under his bed. The corks is pierced, they's lime in 'em, they're already to go to town." An idea stuck him. "Are you intimatin' that they were planted there? That he was framed?"

"No," McGavock declared. "They were his jugs, all right. Weren't they, Pokey?"

Pokey nodded. "They was his jugs, he admitted it to me, but he wasn't set on takin' no fish with them." He got to his feet, stood a moment in the doorway. "If the law had any gumption, it'd know he was telling the truth. Where would he use them? They ain't nothing but shaller branches out in them hills. His place is fifteen miles from the river, it's too far. And if he had a notion to jug the river-pools, he would-a takened them down there at night and limed them when he got there. He wouldn't have toted all that evidence fifteen miles." He sauntered from the room, closed the door behind him."

Sheriff Childress was impressed. He said quietly: "The man is right. I never thought of it that way. Which makes things considerably balled up for heavens' sakes!"

"Get out your car," McGavock ordered. "We're heading for the hills. I want to take a look at Fiddler Joplin's cabin. And I mean quick!"

Joplin's little farm was eight miles, dead center, back in the very heart of the Blue Rock country. Blue Rock was a name loosely applied to a wild, almost impenetrable maze of wooded ridges directly east of town. The drive was just eight miles, but it took them an hour and a half to make it. The trip started out a slow, tedious crawl, and got progressively slower.

They left the city limits, hammered along the macadam pike at a creeping fifteen miles per hour. McGavock spat, said nervously: "What the matter with this buggy? Can't we do any better than this? We're investigating a murder, you know."

Sheriff Childress said complacently: "If I'd open her up, she'd bend the needdle. Good cars are hard to get. I've had this baby ten years and I'm aimin' to keep her ten more." The ragweed and roadside sumac rolled by in a slow-motion panorama. McGavock closed his eyes, attempted to doze, when he was jolted forward in the seat. "We turn here," Sheriff Childress explained. McGavock could see no turn, only the long, straight highway.

Childress, suiting action to the words, whipped his steering wheel abruptly to the left. The car groaned, slowed off the pike, over the berm and shoulder ditch, into a cornfield. "They's more ways to get back into the Blue Rock country," Childress remarked, "than a razorback has ticks. But this-here is the shortest."

178

They drove along a fence-line of mock orange for a quarter of a mile and headed up a gentle hillside. Three times in fifteen minutes the sheriff dismounted and opened up gates, and they passed through herds of sheep and grazing cattle. The angle of the grade increased, the shale and prickly pears gave way to holly and scrub cedar. An unpainted frame one-room church appeared on the hillside. Six wagon trails, like spokes of a wheel, led off from the church. The sheriff selected a particular trail, fitted the car wheels in the ruts and grinned. "We can't miss hit now. We're on our way to the ridge."

"As I get it," McGavock said slowly, "Fiddler didn't live in a cabin. He lived in part of the old mill. Am I right?"

The sheriff nodded. "That's true. But how did you . . ."

McGavock yawned, said: "Pokey just told us so, in your office, didn't you hear him?"

The sheriff objected. "Pokey didn't say nothing about . . . Well, here we are!"

Joplin's Mill was in a little tree-locked hollow. Looking down on it from the ridge, it was a mournful, shabby scene. At one time, it had been a tiny, mountain gristmill, thriving and busy, and now, its roof-line sagged, its shingles were warped and mossy. The woody, encroaching tendrils of the forest had reached into the clearing. McGavock asked smugly: "What's that big pool of water just behind the building?"

Sheriff Childress said absently: "That's the old millpond, Luther." He suddenly looked thunderstruck. "Oh, golly! Fiddler was going to jug fish in his own millpond!"

"Let's get down there," McGavock ordered grimly. "We're wasting time."

The building had long ago been partially dismantled by the insistent plucking of the fingers of time. The old mill was little more than a heap of tinder, the back half had buckled completely and lay in a vine-covered mass of helter-skelter timbers and planks. There was evidence, however, that the fore-end of the building had been inhabited. A window had been cut into the siding, a new cut cedar log had been laid as a doorstep. Some of the old mill machinery had been salvaged from the wrecked structure and lay rusty and neglected under a crude lean-to behind the living quarters.

McGavock, like a homing pigeon, made straight for the lean-to. He asked: "Where's the millstone?"

Sheriff Childress pointed to a great circular rock that rested against the warped clapboards. There was an ugly blackish stain on its sandstone surface. The sheriff bent forward. "'y doggies! That's blood!"

"Of course, it's blood." McGavock was cross. "What did you expect? Sorghum? Let's go inside."

It was a pretty shiftless excuse for a home, McGavock realized. There was plenty of timber on the place, if Joplin had wanted to build himself something comfortable—but evidently Fiddler simply didn't crave comfort. The room was crudely furnished, the walls were papered against the wind with old newspapers, the floor was unevenly pieced of odds and ends of scrap lumber. In one corner, there was a primitive stove fashioned from an old oil drum, in another there was a clumsy homemade bunk. Two broken chairs and a rough-sawed table completed the furnishings.

It was the object on the table which drew their gaze, eclipsed everything else. Smack in the center of Fiddler Joplin's table sat a birdcage. The cage was a beautiful example of mountain craft, ornately woven of white oak withes.

In the cage was a buzzard. It was the first buzzard that McGavock had ever seen so closely—and it wasn't pretty. Huge, gawky, and nauseating, it was hard to look at. Out of a blackish clump of tousled feathers, stuck its serpentine neck of reddish, wrinkled skin ending in an evil-eyed, big beaked head. Its odious, predatory feet were the exact color of pale human flesh. It studied them with stupid unconcern.

Sheriff Childress gagged. "My Redeemer! What did he want to go and keep a thing like that as a pet for?"

"How did he catch it?"

"They're easy to catch. Just bait a snare-noose. Kids in the hills catches 'em and puts paper collars on 'em. But this is different!" The sheriff purpled. "Cagin' 'em and keeping 'em is—"

"Sure, sure." McGavock walked to the corner of the room. There was a scuttle of ashes by the stove. He lifted the scuttle, set it out a couple of feet, and scuffed the floor with his shoe sole. Sheriff Childress frowned, asked: "What are you looking for? More blood stains?"

McGavock was curt. "Nope, no blood today." He picked up the bird-cage, stepped out into the open, and released the captive.

The vulture loped a few crazy yards, took off with great sweeping strokes of its wings. They watched it disappear into the sky. "And now," McGavock said, "we'll take a quick gander at the millpond—just to keep the record straight."

The pool back of the building was stagnant, foul. Brush and scrub grew down to the very edge of the scummy surface. A blue-black moccasin, as meaty and thick as the sheriff's wrist, sunned itself on a rotting log, waterspiders circled and zigzagged through the slimy algae. "How deep," McGavock asked curiously, "did they dig these ponds?"

Sheriff Childress was restive. "Now that," he declaimed ponderously, "I never did hear tell." He took out a big gold watch. "Shall we be gettin' back to civilization?"

6. Triple Killer

On the slow drive home, Sheriff Childress was morose. Once, on the ridgeroad, with an expansive view of the valley below them, McGavock broke the silence, "So all this country is Layton Farms?"

"That's right, Luther." The sheriff was glum. "Every-which way you look. As far as you can shoot a 30-30—and a heap sight farther. They're mighty fine people, the Laytons."

For nearly an hour, neither of them spoke. They reached the little church in their backtracking, passed it, began their itinerary through the endless pastures.

Finally, McGavock spoke. "What's wrong with you? I haven't heard a chirp out of you since we left the hills. Don't tell me your ear-misery has come back on you!"

"It's worse'n ear-misery, Luther, if you can imagine such a thing. I got me a bad case of the blues."

"The blues?"

"I'm subject to 'em. God pray you never get 'em, Luther. Hit's like yore heart is laden with worms and gallwood. I cain't get that buzzard off'n my worried mind. I got the turkey buzzard blues."

The car lunged out of the cornfield, onto the macadam. They passed the red painted cotton gin, entered the outskirts of town.

"The blues, eh?" McGavock remarked finally. "I know just what you mean. And I've got the cure for them. Meet me tonight at Doxie Layton's. At eight o'clock. Bring Charlie Lusk along with you, and your friend, Bobby Leach, the Honorable. Bring your handcuffs, the ones that you've been trying to snap on me all day. I've got a murderer for you. And one thing more—be sure that you have a brand new percussion cap on your shooting iron. Quite frankly, I expect a fracas."

Sheriff Childress said in a hurt voice: "My pistol doesn't use percussion caps. It uses cartridges just like all these new-type revolvers!"

Gradually, as the minutes ticked off, the light changed. Of the three of them in the lavish Layton library—McGavock, the master of the house and his wife—only McGavock seemed comfortably at ease. At seven-thirty the sun went down, splashing the honeysuckle on the window, laying a filligree of rose-and-gray on the shiny pressed-leather walls. Hallie Layton sat bolt upright, taut. Across from her, her husband, his lean weathered face half obscured by shadows, relaxed in his favorite overstuffed chair. The sun went down. And as the moments passed, the rose-and-coral of its rays faded from the luxurious carpet, faded to violet. There was a quivering instant of half-light, of afterglow, and the room was plunged into the diaphanous surge of spring twilight.

The plantation owner reached into the shadows, clicked on a table lamp.

McGavock said: "And from Las Vegas I went to a little place called Worthington, Indiana—my what wonderful adventures! From there I went to Miami and helped an old lady find her emerald necklace. Out in Colorado, some goof was cutting up people and putting them in beer barrels, so—tally-ho—out I got to Colorado—"

The clock on the mantle struck a quarter to eight. Doxie Layton remarked coldly: "We can see you've had an interesting life, Mr. McGavock. It's good of you to entertain us. But just what is the point of this call?"

"Just whiling away the tedium," McGavock explained. "Waiting for eight bells. At eight, we're going to nail your father's murderer. Didn't the sheriff mention it to you?"

He obviously hadn't. They didn't seem too jubilant at the prospect. Layton picked an imaginary speck of lint off the lapel of his Park Avenue coat, scrutinized it intently. The brunette twisted forward in her chair, her eyes were hot in anger but her voice was soft and reproachful. "Do you consider this the time and place for coarse dramatics, Mr. McGavock?" A note of personal hostility crept into her tone. "The earth is still fresh on Daddy Layton's grave. Why not postpone this until tomorrow—after the reading of the will?"

"That would be too late. We must do this now, or we'll never again get the chance."

Layton rolled a brown paper cigarette. "You've been talking out of the corner of your mouth ever since you arrived in Rockton. Whispering mysterious nothings." The plantation owner spoke peacefully, softly, but there was steel beneath his words. This is, McGavock realized, this is the showdown. Layton said lazily: "Explain yourself, and fully, before I throw you out."

"Some time ago," McGavock declared, "your father wrote us in Memphis. He'd found what to him appeared to be evidences of tramps in his old Academy dormitory. It was that letter, coupled with a bit of personal investigation on his own part, that caused his murder. Yes—don't screw up your face. Professor Layton was murdered. We'll never be able to prove it, of course, as long as you refuse permission for an exhumation and post mortem. However—"

"However, baloney!" Layton scoffed. "If you can't prove it why go further? Frankly, I must advise you that I consider you a charlatan. You're here simply as an opportunist. You realize that you've failed—"

"I can prove that Leslie Anderson was murdered. I can produce the body. I can prove that the party that killed Anderson had plenty good reason to kill Professor Layton. How does that sound?"

Layton laughed. "You're really fighting for a fee, aren't you?"

From the front door, the knocker clanged and banged on its plate. "That," McGavock observed, "sounds like some kind of a sheriff." The girl arose and left the room. She returned with her unwelcome guests.

Sheriff Childress came through the door like a man made new. The scent of action was in his nostrils, his face was flushed in excited anticipation. He looked upon McGavock with the trusting, happy gaze of a child at Christmas. Beside him walked Lusk, and a little behind him, to one side, tagged Robertus M. Leach. The frowzy man peered past the officer's shoulder, smiled, bowed and nodded at the assembly.

Grimly, McGavock watched them approach. "Now we can get this over." He pointed. "Sheriff, arrest that man. Watch out!"

The big sheriff moved like a lynx. He pivoted, grabbed Leach by the forearm, wrenched it up behind his shoulders. The frowzy man spluttered and thrashed. Charlie Lusk jumped into the fray, he clutched Leach's flailing arm, anchored it.

McGavock said fiercely: "Not that one, not Leach! Charlie Lusk's our man!"

It took three of them, McGavock, Layton, and the sheriff, to put on the manacles. The little secretary ranted and raved. Sheriff Childress eyed his prisoner uneasily. He said: "It was did, jest like I knowed all along—by a doggone outlander! How'd he do it, Luther?"

Layton said amiably: "Now this, McGavock, is a different story. I somehow felt—er—that you were trying to frame me into it. Tell us about it."

Raising an eyebrow, McGavock said: "It'll cost you five grand." Layton gave the go-ahead sign of a buyer at an auction, said: "Shoot!"

McGavock nodded. "And, I might add, it'll save you many thousands. O.K. Here's the set-up. It's pretty transparent—I'm surprised that you people didn't catch it yourselves. Lusk, here, as the old man's secretary, has been embezzling from his employer. That's the background. Anderson is the spark that touched off all this killing. Some weeks ago, when the time came for the annual auditing of the Layton Farms books, Anderson, as was the manager's duty, checked up on Professor Layton's. He found them deficient. He knew the old man wasn't stealing from himself, so he accused Lusk. Lusk admitted it, asked for time to make restitution. Anderson agreed. I'm guessing about this—but as you'll see, it can't be any other way."

Hallie Layton exclaimed: "Then it wasn't Fiddler Joplin after all?"

"Fiddler Joplin had his place, and it was an important one." McGavock laid it on the line. "Lusk's plan was devilishly simple. His scheme was to lure Anderson to his place of death and murder him. The death-place, selected by Lusk for the scene of his crime, was Joplin's Mill. He worked on old man Layton, told him that Fiddler was moonshining. The old man had Fiddler thrown into jail for questioning. That was to clear the premises for the killing. Anderson met Lusk at night at Joplin's Mill and was by him slain, yassuh!" He paused. "Lusk became worried. Fiddler suspected that something was wrong."

"I see." Layton's eyes were slaty. "The body is at the mill. Lusk then worked on my father, afraid that his crime would be discovered, prodded my father into attempting to evict Fiddler as a squatter!"

"Exactly. To no avail," McGavock continued. "Fiddler had good reasons to believe a murder had been committed at his place while he spent the weekend in the hoosegow. He—"

Sheriff Childress was skeptical. "How could he know?"

"He saw blood on the millstone. Remember what he said in his drunken sleep—'Splashed with blood from eye to bosom?' He was using old miller's terminology, handed down to him by his pappy. The hole in the center of the stone is the 'eye' and the depression is the 'bosom'. He suspected that Anderson had been slain on the place, he set out to locate the body and to thus vindicate himself in the estimation of his friends and neighbors. His methods were crude and primitive. He figured that any corpse on the place would logically be submerged in the old millpond. He caught himself a buzzard as sort of a feathered bloodhound to smell out the body—and set to work. He limed some jugs. In his handy-man way he was going to use these jugs exactly as folks use dynamite, he was going to blast in the pond to bring the body to the surface."

Lusk said hoarsely: "I'm no embezzler. I wouldn't know how to go about it!"

"Oh no?" McGavock scowled. "You're an A-1 forger, you know all the expert tricks. Your books on how to cartoon are a cover-up in case anyone catches you with trick pens and inks. You forged Anderson's true signature to that letter in the old man's collar drawer as an *exemplar* and then scribbled his name in those volumes in your room as a red herring. You use a high-powered shadow-box in your forgery. You've constructed a dandy. You've cut a hole in the bottom of the old man's dresser drawer; this is your box. You take that two hundred watt bulb out of the ceiling fixture—I bet you made the old man keep it—and put it under the drawer. A plate of glass goes on the hole, and you're all set to trace anything that comes along!"

Doxie Layton said slowly: "So he killed my father, too. Why?"

"As I said, he made a murder-appointment with Anderson out at Joplin's Mill. He expected mean, bloody work. He prepared a washbowl and towel in the old, abandoned girl's dormitory. After he'd dispatched Anderson, he searched him, he took from his body, along, doubtless, with his wallet—Anderson's comb case. Lusk then returned to the dormitory, slipped out of his coveralls, washed, and combed his hair with the dead man's comb. The old academy, Mr. Layton, was your father's pride and joy. He was prowling around and found the wash bowl. That was why he wrote us. On a later trip he found more. He found definite evidence of murder. He found the weapon—and he found Leslie Anderson's comb."

Robertus Leach, the Honorable, puffed. "What has a comb got to do with this?"

"It caused the old man's death. I suspect that he recognized two kinds of hair on it, and placed one kind as that of his secretary. He brought it home with him and confirmed it. He quizzed Lusk in a roundabout way and Lusk got suspicious. The oldster got scared. He built a big fire in his fireplace and burned the comb. Just then Lusk, snooping, popped into the room. The old man was a quick thinker. He tossed his teeth into the flame so that the hard rubber of his plate would cover the odor of the burning comb. It didn't save his life though."

Layton was convinced. "That was why Les Anderson kept popping in and out of closets. He suspected his life was in jeopardy."

"Precisely. And—"

"If I've been embezzling," Lusk said slyly, "why didn't I pull out while I was in the clear?"

"No hurry," McGavock explained. "The books won't be balanced again until after the will is read. You've still got a couple of days. I bet your suitcase is packed right now."

Sheriff Childress was getting an idea. His face jerked and contorted. At last he spoke. "Now, Luther, you done a right good job. And we're shore thankful to you. I'm gonna dredge that millpond tomorrow and seine up Les Anderson. As I see our case, it depends on our finding Les Anderson's corpse. I hope to heaven hit's thur!"

Lusk gloated. "It won't be. Anderson's in Little Rock."

"It won't be," McGavock repeated. "But Anderson's not in Little Rock. There are new nailheads in the ashes of Joplin's bedroom. Anderson's buried under the floor—and you can bet he's down deep."

There was an instant of horror. Silence held the room momentarily.

Sheriff Childress protested. "That cain't be, Luther. When you and me was out there this afternoon, the buzzard in the cage was half asleep. If they'd been a cadaver around, he'da been all hysterical and excited. He'd certainly a-smelled it."

"Lusk buried his victim under Fiddler Joplin's floor. Didn't you?" The secretary crumpled. McGavock ignored him, said: "And now to finish off with a brief lecture on natural history. Most folks think buzzards smell carrion. They don't. Believe it or not, they're guided entirely by sight. They have eyesight many times more powerful than man, they're kin to hawks. They can be so high in the sky that a human can't see them, yet they've picked out maybe a tiny fieldmouse on the ground. Their eyesight is truly marvelous. Their sense of smell, ladies and gentlemen, is greatly overrated. Any questions from the audience?"

Merle Constiner has been a frequent contributor to the short story and paperback original market. Perhaps best known for his western novels, Constiner is the creator of such series detectives as Luther McGavock, of the Brown Detective Agency of Memphis, Tennessee, and Dean Rock Wardlow, an expert on almost everything. His stories are ingeniously plotted and told with a gentle, almost tongue-in-cheek humor. Set in Tennessee, his stories show a deep love and understanding of the people and the land, as well as an acceptance of their traditions.

Instead of an easy way to riches, two crooks discover that kidnapping can be a very poor bargain indeed. . . .

ELEVEN

The Ransom of Red Chief

O. Henry

It looked like a good thing: but wait till I tell you. We were down South, in Alabama—Bill Driscoll and myself—when this kidnaping idea struck us. It was, as Bill afterward expressed it, "during a moment of temporary mental apparition"; but we didn't find that out till later.

There was a town down there, as flat as a flannel-cake, and called Summit, of course. It contained inhabitants of as undeleterious and self-satisfied a class of peasantry as ever clustered around a Maypole.

Bill and me had a joint capital of about $600, and we needed just $2000 more to pull off a fraudulent town-lot scheme in Western Illinois with. We talked it over on the front steps of the hotel. Philoprogenitiveness, says we, is strong in semi-rural communities; therefore, and for other reasons, a kidnapping project ought to do better there than in the radius of newspapers that send reporters out in plain clothes to stir up talk about such things. We knew that Summit couldn't get after us with anything stronger than constables and, maybe, some lackadaisical bloodhounds and a diatribe or two in the *Weekly Farmers' Budget*. So, it looked good.

We selected for our victim the only child of a prominent citizen named Ebenezer Dorset. The father was respectable and tight, a mortgage fancier and a stern, upright collection-plate passer and forecloser. The kid was a boy of ten, with bas-relief freckles, and hair the color of the cover of the magazine you buy at the newsstand when you want to catch a train. Bill and me figured that Ebenezer would melt down for a ransom of $2000 to a cent. But wait till I tell you.

About two miles from Summit was a little mountain, covered with a dense cedar brake. On the rear elevation of this mountain was a cave. There we stored provisions.

One evening after sundown, we drove in a buggy past old Dorset's house. The kid was in the street, throwing rocks at a kitten on the opposite fence. "Hey, little boy!" says Bill, "would you like to have a bag of candy and a nice ride?"

The boy catches Bill neatly in the eye with a piece of brick.

"That will cost the old man an extra five hundred dollars," says Bill, climbing over the wheel.

That boy put up a fight like a welterweight cinnamon bear; but, at last, we got him in the bottom of the buggy and drove away. We took him up to the cave, and I hitched the horse in the cedar brake. After dark I drove the buggy to the little village, three miles away, where we'd hired it, and walked back to the mountain.

Bill was pasting court plaster over the scratches and bruises on his features. There was a fire burning behind the big rock at the entrance of the cave, and the boy was watching a pot of boiling coffee, with two buzzard tail-feathers stuck in his red hair.

He points a stick at me when I come up, and says, "Ha! cursed paleface, do you dare to enter the camp of Red Chief, the terror of the plains?"

"He's all right now," says Bill, rolling up his trousers and examining some bruises on his shins. "We're playing Indian. We're making Buffalo Bill's show look like magic-lantern views of Palestine in the Town Hall. I'm Old Hank, the Trapper, Red Chief's captive, and I'm to be scalped at daybreak. By Geronimo! that kid can kick hard."

Yes, sir, that boy seemed to be having the time of his life. The fun of camping out in a cave had made him forget that he was a captive himself. He immediately christened me Snake-eye, the Spy, and announced that, when his braves returned from the warpath, I was to be broiled at the stake at the rising of the sun.

Then we had supper; and he filled his mouth full of bacon and bread and gravy, and began to talk. He made a during-dinner speech something like this:

"I like this fine. I never camped out before; but I had a pet 'possum once. I hate to go to school. Rats ate up sixteen of Jimmy Talbot's aunt's speckled hen's eggs. Are there any real Indians in these woods? I want some more gravy. Does the trees moving make the wind blow? We had five puppies. What makes your nose so red, Hank? My father has lots of money. Are the stars hot? I whipped Ed Walker twice, Saturday. I don't like girls. You dassent catch toads unless with a string. Do oxen make any noise? Why are oranges round? Have you got beds to sleep on in this cave? Amos Murray has got six toes. A parrot can talk, but a monkey or a fish can't. How many does it take to make twelve?"

Every few minutes he would remember that he was a pesky redskin, and pick up his stick rifle and tiptoe to the mouth of the cave to rubber for the scouts of the hated paleface. Now and then he would let out a war whoop that made Old Hank the Trapper shiver. That boy had Bill terrorized from the start.

"Red Chief," says I to the kid, "would you like to go home?"

"Aw, what for?" says he. "I don't have any fun at home. I hate to go to school. I like to camp out. You won't take me back home again, Snake-eye, will you?"

"Not right away," says I. "We'll stay here in the cave a while."

"All right!" says he. "That'll be fine. I never had such fun in all my life."

We went to bed about eleven o'clock. We spread down some wide blankets and quilts and put Red Chief between us. We weren't afraid he'd run away. He kept us awake for three hours, jumping up and reaching for his rifle and screeching, "Hist! pard," in mine and Bill's ears, as the fancied crackle of a twig or the rustle of a leaf revealed to his young imagination the stealthy approach of the outlaw band. At last, I fell into a troubled sleep, and dreamed that I had been kidnapped and chained to a tree by a ferocious pirate with red hair.

Just at daybreak I was awakened by a series of awful screams from Bill. They weren't yells, or howls, or shouts, or whoops, or yawps, such as you'd expect from a manly set of vocal organs—they were simply indecent, terrifying, humiliating screams, such as women emit when they see ghosts or caterpillars. It's an awful thing to hear a strong, desperate, fat man scream incontinently in a cave at daybreak.

I jumped up to see what the matter was. Red Chief was sitting on Bill's chest, with one hand twined in Bill's hair. In the other he had the sharp case-knife we used for slicing bacon; and he was industriously and realistically trying to take Bill's scalp, according to the sentence that had been pronounced upon him the evening before.

I got the knife away from the kid and made him lie down again. But, from that moment, Bill's spirit was broken. He laid down on his side of the bed, but he never closed an eye again in sleep as long as that boy was with us. I dozed off for a while, but along toward sunup I remembered that Red Chief had said I was to be burned at the stake at the rising of the sun. I wasn't nervous or afraid; but I sat up and lit my pipe and leaned against a rock.

"What are you getting up so soon for, Sam?" asked Bill.

"Me?" says I. "Oh, I got a kind of pain in my shoulder. I thought sitting up would rest it."

"You're a liar!" says Bill. "You're afraid. You was to be burned at sunrise, and you was afraid he'd do it. And he would, too, if he could find a match. Ain't it awful, Sam? Do you think anybody will pay out money to get a little imp like that back home?"

"Sure," said I. "A rowdy kid like that is just the kind that parents dote on. Now, you and the Chief get up and cook breakfast, while I go up the top of this mountain and reconnoiter."

I went up on the peak of the little mountain and ran my eye over the contiguous vicinity. Over toward Summit I expected to see the sturdy yeomanry of the village armed with scythes and pitchforks beating the countryside for the dastardly kidnappers. But what I saw was a peaceful landscape dotted with one man ploughing with a dun mule. Nobody was dragging the creek; no couriers dashed hither and yon, bringing tidings of no news to the distracted parents. There was a sylvan attitude of somnolent sleepiness pervading that section of the external outward surface of Alabama that lay exposed to my view.

"Perhaps," says I to myself, "it has not yet been discovered that the wolves have borne away the tender lambkin from the fold. Heaven help the wolves!" says I, and I went down the mountain to breakfast.

When I got to the cave I found Bill backed up against the side of it, breathing hard, and the boy threatening to smash him with a rock half as big as a coconut.

"He put a red-hot boiled potato down my back," explained Bill, "and then mashed it with his foot; and I boxed his ears. Have you got a gun about you, Sam?"

I took the rock away from the boy and kind of patched up the argument. "I'll fix you," says the kid to Bill. "No man ever yet struck Red Chief but he got paid for it. You better beware!"

After breakfast the kid takes a piece of leather with strings wrapped around it out of his pocket and goes outside the cave unwinding it.

"What's he up to now?" says Bill, anxiously. "You don't think he'll run away, do you, Sam?"

"No fear of it," says I. "He don't seem to be much of a home body. But we've got to fix up some plan about the ransom. There

190

don't seem to be much excitement around Summit on account of his disappearance; but maybe they haven't realized yet that he's gone. His folks may think he's spending the night with Aunt Jane or one of the neighbors. Anyhow, he'll be missed today. Tonight we must get a message to his father demanding two thousand dollars for his return."

Just then we heard a kind of war whoop, such as David might have emitted when he knocked out the champion Goliath. It was a sling that Red Chief had pulled out of his pocket, and he was whirling it around his head.

I dodged, and heard a heavy thud and a kind of a sigh from Bill, like a horse gives out when you take his saddle off. A rounded-off rock the size of an egg had caught Bill just behind his left ear. He loosened himself all over and fell in the fire across the frying pan of hot water for washing dishes. I dragged him out and poured cold water on his head.

By and by, Bill sits up and feels behind his ear and says, "Sam, do you know who my favorite Biblical character is?"

"Take it easy," says I. "You'll come to your senses presently."

"King Herod," says he. "You won't go away and leave me here alone, will you, Sam?"

I went out and caught that boy and shook him until his freckles rattled. "If you don't behave," says I, "I'll take you straight home. Now, are you going to be good, or not?"

"I was only funning," says he, sullenly. "I didn't mean to hurt Old Hank. But what did he hit me for? I'll behave, Snake-eye, if you won't send me home, and if you'll let me play the Black Scout today."

"I don't know the game," says I. "That's for you and Mr. Bill to decide. He's your playmate for the day. I'm going away for a while, on business. Now, you come in and make friends with him and say you are sorry for hurting him, or home you go, at once."

I made him and Bill shake hands, and then I took Bill aside and told him I was going to Poplar Cove, a little village three miles from the cave, and find out what I could about how the kidnapping had been regarded in Summit. Also, I thought it best to send a peremptory letter to old man Dorset that day, demanding the ransom and dictating how it should be paid.

"You know, Sam," says Bill, "I've stood by you without batting an eye in earthquakes, fire and flood—in poker games, dynamite outrages, police raids, train robberies, and cyclones. I never lost my nerve yet till we kidnapped that two-legged skyrocket of a kid. He's got me going. You won't leave me long with him, will you, Sam?"

"I'll be back some time this afternoon," says I. "You must keep the boy amused and quiet till I return. And now we'll write the letter to old Dorset."

Bill and I got paper and pencil and worked on the letter while Red Chief, with a blanket wrapped around him, strutted up and down, guarding the mouth of the cave. Bill begged me tearfully to make the ransom $1500 instead of $2,000. "I ain't attempting," says he, "to decry the celebrated moral aspect of parental affection, but we're dealing with humans, and it ain't human for anybody to give up two thousand dollars for that forty-pound chunk of freckled wildcat. I'm willing to take a chance at fifteen hundred dollars. You can charge the difference up to me."

So, to relieve Bill, I acceded, and we collaborated a letter that ran this way:

EBENEZER DORSET, ESQ.:
  We have your boy concealed in a place far from Summit. It is useless for you or the most skillful detectives to attempt to find him. Absolutely, the only terms on which you can have him restored to you are these: We demand $1500 in large bills for his return; the money to be left at midnight tonight at the same spot and in the same box as your reply—as hereinafter described.
  If you agree to these terms, send your answer in writing by a solitary messenger tonight at half-past eight o'clock. After crossing Owl Creek on the road to Poplar Grove, there are three large trees about 100 yards apart, close to the fence of the wheat field on the right-hand side. At the bottom of the fence post, opposite the third tree, will be found a small pasteboard box.
  The messenger will place the answer in this box and return immediately to Summit.
  If you attempt any treachery, or fail to comply with our demand as stated, you will never see your boy again.
  If you pay the money as demanded, he will be returned to you safe and well within three hours. These terms are final, and if you do not accede to them no further communications will be attempted.
                                                    TWO DESPERATE MEN

I addressed this letter to Dorset, and put it in my pocket. As I was about to start, the kid comes up to me and says, "Aw, Snake-eye, you said I could play the Black Scout while you was gone."

"Play it, of course," says I. "Mr. Bill will play with you. What kind of a game is it?"

"I'm the Black Scout," says Red Chief, "and I have to ride to the stockade to warn the settlers that the Indians are coming. I'm tired of playing Indian myself. I want to be the Black Scout."

"All right," says I. "It sounds harmless to me. I guess Mr. Bill will help you foil the pesky savages."

"What am I to do?" asks Bill, looking at the kid suspiciously.

"You are the hoss," says Black Scout. "Get down on your hands and knees. How can I ride to the stockade without a hoss?"

"You'd better keep him interested," said I, "till we get the scheme going. Loosen up."

Bill gets down on all fours, and a look comes in his eye like a rabbit's when you catch it in a trap.

"How far is it to the stockade, kid?" he asks, in a husky voice.

"Ninety miles," says the Black Scout. "And you have to hump yourself to get there on time. Whoa, now!"

The Black Scout jumps on Bill's back and digs his heels in his side.

"For heaven's sake," says Bill, "hurry back, Sam, as soon as you can. I wish we hadn't made the ransom more than a thousand. Say, you quit kicking me or I'll get up and warm you good."

I walked over to Poplar Cove and sat around the post office and store, talking with the chaw-bacons that came in to trade. One whiskerando says that he hears Summit is all upset on account of Elder Ebenezer Dorset's boy having been lost or stolen.

That was all I wanted to know. I bought some smoking tobacco, referred casually to the price of blackeyed peas, posted my letter surreptitiously, and came away. The postmaster said the mail carrier would come by in an hour to take the mail on to Summit.

When I got back to the cave Bill and the boy were not to be found. I explored the vicinity of the cave, and risked a yodel or two, but there was no response.

So I lighted my pipe and sat down on a mossy bank to await developments.

In about half an hour I heard the bushes rustle, and Bill wobbled out into the little glade in front of the cave. Behind him was the kid, stepping softly like a scout, with a broad grin on his face. Bill stopped, took off his hat, and wiped his face with a red handkerchief. The kid stopped about eight feet behind him.

"Sam," says Bill, "I suppose you'll think I'm a renegade, but I couldn't help it. I'm a grown person with masculine proclivities and habits of self-defense, but there is a time when all systems of egotism and predominance fail. The boy is gone. I sent him home. All is off.

There was martyrs in old times," goes on Bill, "that suffered death rather than give up the particular graft they enjoyed. None of 'em ever was subjugated to such supernatural tortures as I have been. I tried to be faithful to our articles of depredation; but there came a limit."

"What's the trouble, Bill?" I asks him.

"I was rode," says Bill, "the ninety miles to the stockade, not barring an inch. Then, when the settlers was rescued, I was given oats. Sand ain't a palatable substitute. And then, for an hour, I had to try to explain to him why there was nothin' in holes, how a road can run both ways, and what makes the grass green. I tell you, Sam a human can only stand so much. I takes him by the neck of his clothes and drags him down the mountain. On the way he kicks my legs black and blue from the knees down; and I've got to have two or three bites on my thumb and hand cauterized.

"But he's gone"—continues Bill—"gone home. I showed him the road to Summit and kicked him about eight feet nearer there at one kick. I'm sorry we lose the ransom; but it was either that or Bill Driscoll to the madhouse."

Bill is puffing and blowing, but there is a look of ineffable peace and growing content on his rose-pink features.

"Bill," says I, "there isn't any heart disease in your family, is there?"

"No," says Bill, "nothing chronic except malaria and accidents. Why?"

"Then you might turn around," says I, "and have a look behind you."

Bill turns and sees the boy, and loses his complexion and sits down plump on the ground and begins to pluck aimlessly at grass and little sticks. For an hour I was afraid of his mind. And then I told him that my scheme was to put the whole job through immediately and that we would get the ransom and be off with it by midnight if old Dorset fell in with our proposition. So Bill braced up enough to give the kid a weak sort of a smile and a promise to play the Russian in a Japanese war with him as soon as he felt a little better.

I had a scheme for collecting that ransom without danger of being caught by counterplots that ought to commend itself to professional kidnappers. The tree under which the answer was to be left—and the money later on—was close to the road fence with big, bare fields on all sides. If a gang of constables should be watching for anyone to come for the note they could see him a long way off crossing the fields or in the road. But no, sirree! At half-past eight I was up in that

194

tree as well hidden as a tree toad, waiting for the messenger to arrive.

Exactly on time, a half-grown boy rides up the road on a bicycle, locates the pasteboard box at the foot of the fence post, slips a folded piece of paper into it, and pedals away, off again back toward Summit.

I waited an hour and then concluded the thing was square. I slid down the tree, got the note, slipped along the fence till I struck the woods, and was back at the cave in another half an hour. I opened the note, got near the lantern, and read it to Bill. It was written with a pen in a crabbed hand, and the sum and substance of it was this:

Two Desperate Men:

Gentlemen: I received your letter today by post, in regard to the ransom you ask for the return of my son. I think you are a little high in your demands, and I hereby make you a counter-proposition, which I am inclined to believe you will accept. You bring Johnny home and pay me $250 in cash, and I agree to take him off your hands. You had better come at night, for the neighbors believe he is lost, and I couldn't be responsible for what they would do to anybody they saw bringing him back. Very respectfully.

Ebenezer Dorset

"Great pirates of Penzance," says I; "of all the impudent—"

But I glanced at Bill, and hesitated. He had the most appealing look in his eyes I ever saw on the face of a dumb or a talking brute.

"Sam," says he, "what's two hundred and fifty dollars, after all? We've got the money. One more night of this kid will send me to a bed in Bedlam. Besides being a thorough gentleman, I think Mr. Dorset is a spendthrift for making us such a liberal offer. You ain't going to let the chance go by, are you?"

"Tell you the truth, Bill," says I, "this little ewe lamb has somewhat got on my nerves too. We'll take him home, pay the ransom, and make our getaway."

We took him home that night. We got him to go by telling him that his father had bought a silver-mounted rifle and a pair of moccasins for him, and we were to hunt bears the next day.

It was just twelve o'clock when we knocked at Ebenezer's front door. Just at the moment when I should have been abstracting the $1500 from the box under the tree, according to the original proposition, Bill was counting out $250 into Dorset's hands.

When the kid found out we were going to leave him at home he started up a howl like a calliope and fastened himself as tight as a leech to Bill's leg. His father peeled him away gradually, like a porous plaster.

"How long can you hold him?" asks Bill.

"I'm not as strong as I used to be," says old Dorset, "but I think I can promise you ten minutes."

"Enough," says Bill. "In ten minutes I shall cross the Central, Southern, and Middle Western States, and be legging it trippingly for the Canadian border."

And, as dark as it was, and as fat as Bill was, and as good a runner as I am, he was a good mile and a half out of Summit before I could catch up with him.

O. Henry (William Sydney Porter) was a master of the short story. Born September 11, 1862, in Greensboro, North Carolina, he was reared by his father. When his first short stories began to appear in local newspapers, he was working in Houston, Texas, as a clerk, draftsman, and bank teller. Indicted for bank embezzlement, he fled to South America until his wife's illness brought him back to Texas and a five-year term in the Ohio State Penitentiary. Released in three years for good behavior, O. Henry spent the rest of his life writing the stories that made him famous. He died of tuberculosis on June 5, 1910.

While three people descend deep into the Arkansas cave, only two will return. . . .

TWELVE

The Virgin Cave
Bryce Walton

Professor Ernst Albracht fussed with the winch motor over the cave opening while his favorite graduate student, Gerard Middleton, finished unloading the Jeep. Then Gerard, with careful efficiency, began filling up three haversacks with equipment and supplies for the big drop; he continued to move with an apparent easy calm, but he wondered how long he could bear the strain of waiting.

Nylon sleeping bags. Flashlights. Butane stove kits. Portable ladders. Hammers. Acetylene lamps. K-rations . . .

Gerard frowned. He wished Ellen wouldn't sit over there in the shade that way, smugly watching and singing. Albracht must not, of course, suspect anything, so they had to act natural. But Ellen shouldn't sing. She shouldn't act happy about what would soon happen to Albracht. She must have had some love or respect for him once; she had married him.

"Shake it up, Gerard," Albracht said in his kindly voice, as soothing as a doctor's. "This day'll be a scorcher, but nature's finest air-conditioning awaits us below."

Gerard smiled dutifully. He avoided looking at Ellen who kept sitting over there singing in the shade of eroded rock and wild cucumber vines. Gerard didn't have to look at her. He saw her with his eyes closed. But he couldn't stand looking and not being able to touch her whenever he pleased. Because of Albracht, of course. He had to control himself a while longer. Then Albracht wouldn't be around. Never be around again.

Albracht had said he'd seen a small hole in the rocks no bigger than a varmint hole. He'd stuck his walking stick in, and the hole crumbled away to reveal a virgin cave. Now the opening was four feet wide. A winch had been built over the hillside hole, for they had to make a 600-foot drop by cable. A gray, taciturn hillbilly named

Landaff was hired to stay topside and handle the winch motor. Albracht was helping him fuss with an ornery carburetor.

Gerard felt a sudden chilling burst of sweat as the motor abruptly kicked loose, then kept pounding away in a steady dependable rhythm. He took a deep breath, then hooked the haversacks to the winch cable, and, as Landaff prepared to lower them one by one, he joined Albracht and Ellen in the ritual of putting on appropriate clothing for the drop. Woolen shirts and socks, spike-soled boots, rubberized suits, spun-glass helmets with headlamps attached, and earphones with attached microphones.

No one said anything. They had to keep acting natural. Gerard usually avoided talk, while the Albrachts had given up trying to communicate with each other years ago.

Albracht clipped webbed shoulder harness to the cable hook, slid down, and watched the lever controlling the cable spool until he was supported entirely by the creaking wire. Landaff revved up the motor.

Gerard and Ellen smiled down at the Professor. The Professor, pinkfaced with boyish excitement, his graying hair fluttering slightly, smiled up at them around his pipestem, then suddenly sank out of sight into the earth.

Landaff squatted by the winch motor watching them, so Ellen and Gerard avoided intimate glances. She was lowered next.

Gerard felt heat building up inside his rubberized suit. It had been a long wait. But then, when he was being lowered after Ellen, he realized that he hadn't really allowed himself to feel the accumulated tensions before.

The cozy secret meetings with Ellen, the exciting, dangerous whispering and planning—all of it suddenly exploded like one of his beautiful daydream bubbles. A chilling reality closed in around him, as cold and black as a grave.

But he could go through with it. He had to. But something seemed to be wrong with his face. He had lost control of it. He knew that his expression wasn't right. The comfortable, safe old mask had slipped off. It might even look real, he thought, the way he actually felt inside. Albracht mustn't see that. He might become suspicious.

Gerard worked on his face all the way down the chilling darkness. He fitted the old safe mask back on—the one that never showed anything.

Later their headlamps made three tiny stifled glimmers of light in a vast and absolute blackness, as they half slid, single file, down a high shale hill. Albracht took the lead. Gerard followed Ellen.

"This haversack hurts my shoulders," Ellen said. "Is all this boy scout equipment really necessary?"

"Yes," Albracht said. "It's all necessary. Caving is a dangerous sport. The loss of any item in your haversack could mean your death down here."

"You know a better way?" Ellen said, and giggled.

You shouldn't do that, Gerard thought. For you it's natural, but under present circumstances it isn't right, it's in bad taste.

As they explored along, Albracht stuck strips of red phosphorescent plastic tape to rocks. If necessary, it would guide them back in total darkness to the winch cable. It would lead rescuers to them in case of trouble, to any one of them. Just another thing Gerard had to keep in mind. It must happen in such a way that rescue would be impossible. If he botched this, he could hardly expect a second chance.

Although it must be done without a hitch, it was impossible to figure the exact method in advance—not in a virgin cave. But there were a number of excellent possibilities. A person could be crushed by a falling rock, pinned down to expire slowly; fall down a rocky shelf; get stuck in a fissure or crevice; fall into a bottomless pit; freeze, drown, or get lost; or be sucked into an underground river's flume. A person might build a fire in a cavern that had insufficient fresh oxygen and die from carbon monoxide poisoning. Cave deaths have even resulted from untimely explosions of bat guano.

But all these possibilities shared a common virtue—they appeared accidental. Ellen had taken out two double-indemnity policies on Albracht.

So he must stay alert, ready to seize exactly the right moment and select exactly the right place—and then act with pan-flash decision.

Ellen stopped suddenly. Gerard bumped into her and felt his stomach twitch as Albracht yelled up at them. He yelled again through megaphoned hands, this time in all directions. Measuring the cave's size, he explained, by timing the returning echoes of his voice. Then he said very quietly. "Seems to be a tremendous cavern. A real find."

"Congratulations," Gerard said.

"It always gets to me," Albracht said. "The feeling that no one's been here before you."

"Why should anybody ever be here?" Ellen said. "Why would anyone rather be a mole than a man?"

"So let me suggest again, most sincerely, my dear—" somehow Albracht always maintained a gentle tolerance—"that you go back up and wait for us."

"One thing is more boring than crawling about in a hole," Ellen said. "Being alone in an Ozark cabin on a hot summer day."

"You never minded before."

"The television worked."

But Gerard knew the real reason she had insisted on making this drop—to be sure he did the job, and did it properly.

"A tremendous erosion pocket," Albracht said. "Seems cathedral size."

"They'll name it after you, dear," Ellen said. "You'll be immortal. I can see it now—Ernie's Hole."

Albracht moved on without comment, his body a gesture of tireless forebearance. He managed skillfully to find ways through boulders and stalagmites. But it seemed to Gerard, depressingly, that they only made a large erratic circle without finding another exit. Still there has to be one, Gerard thought, his mouth dry. It had to happen to Albracht in some remote cavern or labyrinth, not here where Landaff would know at once if there was trouble.

Albracht sank to his knees. He flashed his light into a small opening through a wall of sparkling limestone crystal. "Cold draft coming," he mused aloud. "Probably another cavern at the other end. Seems short, no more than fifteen feet, I'd say, judging from the sound of running water coming through. Might be a tight squeeze, so you may have to push your haversacks through ahead of you. I'll go first. If it's clear I'll give you the word to follow."

Albracht was still talking with boyish enthusiasm as he wriggled away out of sight.

Ellen gave Gerard a sly, conspiratorial wink. He smiled back, but slightly past her direct gaze, and found his sight going out into infinite blackness. He felt a quick sharp squirm of fear.

Her whisper exploded in the vast stillness like a paper bag. "This caving is so childish and stupid!"

"So are a lot of things," Gerard said.

"But he hasn't really cared about anything else for years. Why?"

"I know facts," Gerard said. "You want to know how these erosion pockets are formed out of limestone, okay, I can tell you. But—"

"You're already beginning to talk like a damn professor—like *him!*"

Albracht's sudden sepulchral voice came out of the rock. "All right now, Ellie. It's about twenty feet. Careful."

She smiled at Gerard, then squirmed out of sight. He shivered. It wasn't just her eyes or her smile. But whatever she said, the way she stood or sat or walked was an invitation and a promise . . .

200

He had been most grateful for her smile. At first he had been grateful only to Albracht. The professor taught botany and speleology, and the latter was also his hobby. When not lecturing or writing treatises and popular articles on caves, he explored them. Every summer he favored one graduate student with an invitation to share the Albrachts' vacation in their Ozark cabin. Relaxation was combined with speleological field work around Lake Tanacomo.

Albracht had first invited Gerard to his house near the campus to share a faculty tea. Gerard had been deeply grateful for Albracht's recognition. He met Ellen that afternoon and she smiled at him. Few women had ever smiled at Gerard, and none had ever smiled at him quite that way. In all his life no woman like Ellen had ever really looked at him. Attractive, sophisticated, much younger than Albracht who was 50, Ellen had a genuinely hypnotic charm.

Gerard's gratitude was measureless. Too many of his 25 years had been fevered away during lonely nights with books, ambitions, and dreams instead of human beings. Too many years alone, quietly bitter, secretly angry for always having to work his way, he had every reason to be a bottomless well of gratitude. Grateful for Albracht. Grateful for Ellen and her smile. Indescribably grateful for what came after the smile during those secret cozy meetings. Most grateful for her promises.

Gerard had been hungry all his life.

They stood on a dangerously narrow ledge about twelve feet long. And Albracht studied the rent in Ellen's rubberized suit made by a snagging rock. Ellen's face was pale. In the beam of Albracht's headlamp the gash in her suit looked like a jagged, perhaps mortal wound.

Albracht kept insisting that Ellen turn back at once because of the torn suit. But Ellen insisted on continuing what she called "this most fabulous exploration of the century." Gerard caught part of a supposedly clever remark about her being a beautiful icicle or the greatest of all tourist attractions, a stalagmite shaped like a girl.

But Gerard was more concerned with the sound of the river gurgling below. The beam of his headlamp caught the water's dark shine swirling deep and deadly through ice-coated rocks. It can happen here, he thought, here and now. Albracht could fall into the river. No, it must be absolutely certain. Albracht could fall into the river— but only if it was certain he would drown.

Ellen leaned toward Gerard. "What's that chirping?"

Gerard moved his flash and focused it in a tiny crack. "Cave cricket."

"What was that, young man?" Albracht asked, assuming a deliberately exaggerated professorial tone.

"*Ceuthopilus,* sir." Gerard said in mock apology. "Similar to the cricket found in cellars. After a few generations born in total darkness, their eyes become useless and are bred out. They also lose their color. No need of protective camouflage in total darkness."

"Very good," Albracht said. "Yes, my favorite pupil."

"Mine too," Ellen said. "But that awful cricket. I hate it. White like a little slug and with no eyes."

"But it's happy with no light," Albracht said. "It loves and lives and sings."

"It shouldn't," Ellen said. "It shouldn't want to sing or be alive here at all."

She stepped back in disgust and would have fallen from the ledge if Albracht hadn't caught hold of her. But she let out a high sharp yell. It disturbed thousands of bats hibernating somewhere up in the darkness.

Albracht shouted a warning. Gerard covered his eyes with his arms as a hot stinking mass squealed around him. He remembered that cave bats' teeth were usually not strong enough to break skin, and they used their "sonar" to fly, so they were never likely to get in your hair. But they could take out your eyes.

Gerard uncovered his eyes at Ellen's second scream. He saw her topple backward into the misty blackness as the last of the bats fluttered away. Her headlamp and helmet flew off and when the light left her, her body seemed to dissolve in a black paste. It fell in a strangely stiff way except for her arms that went round and round twice like pale lily stalks.

Then she toppled end over end, as rigid as a display-window mannequin.

Albracht shouted. Gerard felt paralyzed with the horror of feeling his mask of control slipping. But he didn't lose control. The mask remained—the thin boyish look, diffident and shy, the wide and guileless blue eyes, the odd lack of animation.

He ran to help Albracht. He lunged out of fear and in an agony of release at the thought of Ellen dissolving into nothing. It was as if a spear had been jerked out of his pierced belly.

He got out the portable ladder—nylon cord with aluminum rings attached. He got the cord hooked to a spike, and the spike hammered into a crack below the ledge. Albracht climbed fearlessly down the ladder and plunged to his armpits in the vicious current. He slipped, went under, reappeared, spun away, and then clung helplessly to a rock.

Gerard got there fast, but he was frightened now. If Ellen, was really gone, he'd be alone with it—alone in the darkness. The current dragged at him. But he was still in control, going slow, testing his spike-soles on the slick bottom. He knew now that they were all an eyewink away from death.

As he worked along toward where Ellen's pale face and black hair bobbed like a matted cork, he saw, only thirty feet downstream, the river boiling suddenly down under a limestone wall in a seething whirlpool. Ellen was struggling weakly in a kind of backwash in the rocks. He finally managed to get the nylon line hooked to her webbed belt, and then Albracht helped him reel her into a large eroded pocket he had found in the limestone wall on a level with the rushing river.

Then she sat shivering on a bed of fine gravel bleached as white as dried salt.

"Anything else wrong, Ellie? Broken bones or anything?"

Her blue lips worked until she finally stuttered faintly, "Just—just cold."

The icy water had entered through the tear in her suit, and she could freeze to death in minutes.

"We'll fix that up," Albracht said. "You'll warm up in the sleeping bag while we dry your clothes over the stove." He looked up at Gerard. "Get out the butane stove and set it up." Then he began unrolling Ellen's sleeping bag.

Gerard got the stove assembled and as he lit it, he looked up. Something in his stomach turned completely over. Albracht was taking her clothes off. Gerard shivered, looked quickly away. He heard Albracht say, "Take a look over there where the river goes under the wall, Gerard, please. Maybe we can find a way through."

But Gerard didn't find a way through the wall. He worked back through the erosion pocket about 50 feet, but found no opening. He didn't want to find one. Albracht evidently wanted to keep on exploring if he found a way, but Gerard was finished. His nerves wouldn't stretch an inch farther.

He stood motionless in a forest of helectites, those stony formations that curl and twist in grotesque patterns. He saw through them to where, just beyond a thicket of icicles about 30 feet away, Ellen lay in the sleeping bag near the river. The scene was a weird frozen

203

stillness, a small bowl of light locked in infinite blackness where nothing moved. Ellen didn't move. The propped flashlight was still and unblinking. No air stirred. The flame of the butane stove didn't flicker even slightly in the dead air.

And where was Albracht?

Gerard felt one of those recurring, engulfing needs to be with Ellen, to be close to her, as close as to his own body. When he'd been with her before, in that wondrous secrecy, she had made him feel heady, reckless, willing and able to do anything.

He got to her as quickly as he could and knelt beside her sleeping bag.

"Where's Albracht?"

Her little mocking smile had come back, but there was apprehension in her eyes as she pointed.

Gerard flashed his headlamp over through the rocks and listened.

"You don't look so good," she said. "Better get on with it, before your feet get colder than mine."

Albracht's sudden shout jerked Gerard around and seemed to pinch at his stomach. Albracht's face, illuminated by his own flashlight, glowed suspended over the black water like a luminescent ceremonial mask. He was neck-deep in that treacherous tide, at the very edge of the whirlpool.

Ellen cried out in genuine disbelief. "Ernie, what are you doing there?"

Albracht yelled for the end of the nylon line. Gerard tossed it out. Albracht hooked it underwater to his belt. "If I don't come back, haul me in," he said.

"What are you doing?" Ellen almost screamed.

"Don't worry," he shouted back, his face wet and shining with spray. "There's an airspace up there and if I don't slip I can get through without getting my face under. There's another big chamber on the other side of this wall. The river may come up again over there."

Then he waved, and his head dissolved in foam. Then darkness . . .

Half an hour later, Gerard still held the frayed broken end of the nylon line he had reeled in. There was still no sight or sound of Albracht.

"He must be crazy," Ellen whispered. "He wouldn't have that kind of nerve."

"Any caver has to have guts," Gerard said heavily. "Even him."

"But what's happened to him?"

"We don't know," Gerard said.

"We have to know."

"Yes. River might come up again over there, might not. Might have taken him down to hell."

"He must have thought he would come up somewhere."

"He must have. But he couldn't be sure."

"We have to make sure."

"We ought to," Gerard said.

"We have to *know* what's happened to him. He may be hurt. Broken bones, or something. He may still be alive. Maybe help can reach him. We don't *know*. Maybe he's all right, and can get out some other way. We have to make sure."

"You mean I have to make sure." Gerard rubbed his hands together.

"Make sure he'll never be found—or not be found too soon."

Fear surged through Gerard's body. But it didn't show. He stood up. The fear was worse than other recent moments of near terror. But Ellen had enabled him to do what he could never have done anywhere else except in his dreams. And anything, any risk, was better than the dull, empty, unpromising loneliness he had always known before.

He hooked a nylon line to his belt, tied the other end around a stalagmite, and waded into the river.

"Wait for me here," he said. Then his spike-soled shoes slipped out into sickening softness, and the current dragged him down. A black mouth sucked and swallowed him. It chewed, it gurgled, it ground him down through a rocky gullet. He struggled, like a helpless, futile bug flushed down a drain.

His webbed belt snagged. He kicked, he strained, he screamed inside, bursting and suffocating. His belt tore free and he shot away and down, free of it, but leaving everything attached to it—knife, ax, first-aid kit, matches. Helmet and headlamp ripped away with some of his scalp. His tortured lungs, bursting, pried open his mouth. An icy paste of sooty black poured in to drown and freeze his soul . . .

He lay on corrugated rock somewhere near the river. He concentrated on maintaining control, his one dependable protection. Especially his breath. He kept his breathing low, slow, easy. If his breathing got loud, it echoed, and he would hear it even above the sound of the river. He didn't want to hear that again, not that loud erratic blood-thump in his ears. He didn't want to hear himself at all

205

again. It was only a reminder of all the sound there was now, or ever could be.

The river had spewed him up again, but there was no way of knowing where. A 600-foot drop, then a walk and a climb down several hundred more feet, then the river had sucked him down—no way to figure how much farther down, or to where.

There was no way out from wherever he was—no way but the river. He didn't want to make that terrible drop again. He could never bring himself to go that way again.

His shattered wrist watch was a phosphorescent smear on his arm. He had opened his eyes in pitch-blackness. There was no sound. Nothing turned. No light went off and on. Nothing stopped and started anywhere. There was no more time.

He knew he could have been wherever he was for hours, for weeks, for months. But he had no idea how long he could stay, how long he could keep himself alive.

He concentrated on holding himself in one rigid integrated piece. The stillness was without end, the blackness absolute. He had bulged his eyes hopefully at first, strained and popped them at the dark trying to find light somewhere, even the tiniest light. But pure blackness pressed over his face, muffled his nose and mouth, suffocated him.

He merely existed in the dark. A worm, he thought. A blind worm or one of the first amoebas that ever lived on earth.

He had hated his life. To change it into something else, anything else, he had been ready to kill a man. A man whom he respected, a man who cared for him. But now the bitterest memory he had of that hated past was a vision of paradise. Sights, sounds, memories kept thumping at his brain, almost but never quite getting in, like bugs hitting lighted windows.

Now he could only lie blind and breathing in the dark. He had crawled in carefully measured circles trying to find a way out. He had explored every inch, squirmed into every hole and over every rock. And he was sure now: there was no way out—no way but the river.

There were only little potholes, slightly warm from subterranean springs. Pools in which food bred, lived brief blind cycles. Where salamanders crawled, totally blind, with layers of skin pulled by eons of evolution over the remnants of eyes they no longer needed.

Now Gerard felt blindly about—he grabbed, fumbled, lost, retrieved. The great blind hunter. He learned slyness and skill. Little crayfish, panarian worms, isopods, hydras, water sponges, even a few mollusks, slugs, and snails.

He caught and crushed them to watery pulp in his numbed fingers. He seemed to have eaten thousands of times, devoured thousands and thousands of salamanders, snails, slugs, crayfish—all as blind and white as he—but he knew that it would end sometime, that when he reached into the potholes and found them empty, found he had eaten them up faster than they could breed, it would all be over . . .

Slowly he opened his eyes. Silently he listened for that very tiny sound that had gone through him like a shiver of glass. Blackness. No change. He held his breath, waited, hoped. Only silence.

His gaze kept going out, meeting infinite layers of darkness. He started to raise his hand to his face, but there was no way to keep his eyes from seeing out and out—into nothing.

He started to run.

His body thumped. It battered. It bounced and went down. Little violent explosions went off in his head—

But he was free now. Even if there were eyes here, the eyes of judges, juries, the condemning eyes of all his enemies, they couldn't harm him. They couldn't see his face to know how he felt, to know exactly where and how he was vulnerable. So they could never again attack, laugh, jeer, humiliate, beat, and murder him. He was safe now. No one ever again would see him exposed, and naked and helpless.

He had thought he was alone and safe before, hiding behind his expression, his perpetual mask. Now he knew what being alone really was. Oh, it was safe all right. And he knew something else— there were things more horrible than being alone, than not being quite safe. No matter where you are there is always a much worse place. No doubt of that. A much much worse place—

He laughed.

Things seemed to break loose inside him. He began to yell—a monotonous, low, oddly controlled yelling as he beat the rocks with his fists . . .

He kept grinning up at the light. He smiled at it. He kept hoping it was a real light, a light that would never go away. He prayed. The light stayed, and, yes, that was the Professor—dear old Albracht! No mistaking that face shining under the headlamp's beam—that familiar, kindly face of Ernst Albracht.

The light stayed and shone down with that unearthly luminescence of angels seen in church windows. The professor's voice was gentle too—just like the touch of his hand reaching down, lifting up.

"Let's go now, Gerard. I'll help you."

Yes, sir, yes, sir—

Albracht led the way without hesitation. He seemed to know exactly where he was and where he was going. But Gerard knew that he would never have the vaguest idea how they got through—through a maze that would have bewildered rats. Along narrow ledges, through narrow crevices, down shale slides, down slopes of fluted limestone, through tunnels of ice . . .

When they got there he knew at once where they were. He knew when Albracht started peeling off the phosphorescent strips of plastic tape. It was the route Albracht had once marked, and was now dissolving behind them.

Gerard recognized the cathedral-like stillness, the steep high rockslide of glittering shale where the suspended cable gleamed like a strand of iridescent cobweb. And there was the cave opening 600 feet above his head. Gerard stood quivering below that bar of familiar light. It sliced down into his eyes, across his cheekbone and jaw, with a thin bar of fire.

He stumbled up the shale like a drunken mole in strong light. It was such a short way from where he had lain, where he had died over and over in the darkness. He just hadn't known the way. But Albracht knew. He seemed to have known all the time.

Gerard felt a cold charge of fear.

Albracht's eyes were close to him now, like drops of clear dark water, fixed and unblinking.

"This isn't a virgin cave," Gerard said. "You've been here before. You knew where we were going. You knew exactly where I was all the time."

"I've known about you and Ellen, too, for some time," Albracht said gently. "And I knew what you had planned for me." He took a slow drag at his pipe. "But let's go on up now, Gerard. We've got to break the news of the tragic accident to Landaff."

"Accident?"

"Oh, yes, she fell into the river, remember? A search party will be down here inside an hour. We'll all do our best to find Ellie, of course, but no one ever will. No one knows where the river goes."

"We could—" Gerard's voice broke.

"You think you could find her?" Albracht asked. "No, believe me, you can't. No one can ever find her now."

"Why?" Gerard whispered. "Why have you saved me?"

"You're a fine scholar, Gerard, with a great potential to do good. I have always felt responsible to correct in what little ways I can the faults of miseducation."

Albracht smiled around his pipe stem. "I left you there for seven hours, my boy, hoping it would bring about a vital change in you—for the better. As an experience, you know—a learning experience . . . a lesson for the future."

Bryce Walton has written most types of fiction, although he is best known for his science fiction novel for young people, Sons of the Ocean Deeps *(1952) and "The Sleeper Is a Rebel" (1948). Born in Blythdale, Missouri, on May 31, 1918, he held a series of interesting jobs (including gold miner and sailor) before serving in the Marine Corps as a combat correspondent (1942-45), where he won a Special Citation from Admiral Nimitz for his coverage of the Iwo Jima invasion. He has published more than 1,000 stories. An avid skin diver and spelunker, Walton's stories of exploring the dark depths of earth and ocean are based on personal experience.*

Much more than romance in the starry night is in store for the arrogant hunter who stumbles upon the sullen, but beautiful, hill woman and her much older husband. . . .

THIRTEEN

The Lady-Killer
Wilbur Daniel Steele

Bo J. (Bee Jay) Cantra butted through a belt of sumac, head down, wind sobbing. Bullbriar ripped another gap in his thirty-dollar gunning-shirt. He didn't know. If he had he wouldn't have cared. Bee Jay was lost, and he was deathly scared.

The foliage gave way and he saw a quiet pool at his feet, no bigger than a bathtub, fed by a ferny trickle from some spring. Thirst grabbed him. First, to prove himself collected, he thought to lay his gun down carefully; it was imported. He discovered he had no gun. When had he thrown that away?

He sank to his knees and leaned forward on his hands. The water made a mirror to give his face back. Panic had creased it and dirty sweat lined the creases. It made him look of a sudden forty-seven years and five months old.

What would Eleanor Wye have thought? What would Sonya Seely have thought? Or—what-was-her-name?—the brunette bit of youngness last week, Harriday's party at Twenty-One, and afterwards—what would she have thought to see him now, anybody's forty-seven?

But still most pressing, what would Eleanor Wye have thought? He remembered Grand Central, him and Bert Wye and Harriday with their guncases bidding their wives goodbye. And Bert saying how he'd have to be back in town in time to catch a train for Chicago Friday to sell a bridge. And with that, Eleanor's glance crossing with Bee Jay's, swiftly, privily, yet plainly: "Did you hear that? Friday evening, then."

Apple-cheeked Bert, so long a side-kick, so suddenly a sap.

Damned creased face! The man broke the image by plunging his mouth into the water. When he'd sucked up all his belly would hold he remained there on all fours, drips falling down off his chin.

211

"Friday"! What a bloody joke now! Friday, Bert might be off for Chicago all right, but where would B. J. Cantra be? But no—no Chicago for Bert—to hell with a bridge sale, he'd be right here in the wilds of Carolina, along with the posses, the rangers, combing the woods with failing hope, good old Bert.

"Friday"? . . . Thursday, Wednesday, Tuesday. Could this be only Tuesday? The half-dozen hours since he'd found himself separated from Bert and Harriday seemed weeks. Still Tuesday.

Words hardly noted at the time came back. About now, at home, Eleanor would be with Harriet—"for cocktails and a dish of dirt, Eleanor dear." Harriet had made the date laughingly, there at Grand Central. With Eleanor, of all people, innocent-sweet, knowing one bit of dirt she wasn't likely to dish out to Harriet Cantra!

A sudden illogical fury filled the man. He saw his wife as he hadn't seen her for how many years, still something the stranger, pretty with youth, preoccupied with her "two boys"—him and the baby—no time yet, no need yet, to know what was what and learn the answers. And now that an outside woman should have it over Harriet in cynical secret—

Bee Jay went to pieces. "Harriet, I'm a bum!" He wailed aloud: "Harriet! *Do* something! I'm lost! Hear me? I'm going to die! Lost in the woods!"

No-no-no! He staggered up, turning round and round, hollering with his raw throat: *"Bert! Hy-eeee! Harriday! Somebody!"*

Embarrassment born of hysteria hushed him. In the silence came a whisper near at hand among the ferns that hid the feeding trickle. Even as he jerked his eyes it ceased. A flat triangular head lifted and hung. A moccasin had been lying coiled there all the while.

Bee Jay inched backwards, heel by heel. Brush laid hands on him. He broke out bleating: "O God—oh please—"

He whirled and fought the brush, broke through, ran at stumbling random. "O God I'll be good!" A cloud of aspen blinded him. He pitched across a ribbon of light, landing in a bunchy darkness of jack-pine. "O Jesus—O Harriet—"

By and by a limb of naked deadwood barred him. He stood and gaped at it. He grabbed it and hung on, realizing what it was, the rail of a snake-fence zigzagging through the woods.

He followed along, hardly daring let go. The woods fell away. Down across scraggly pastureland he saw two paintless cabins, one a house and one a barn. He leaned on the fence and laughed aloud.

"This is one on you, Bee Jay! This is one for the book!"

Hysteria? Not a bit. Shame? No. That but minutes ago he'd been stumbling in circles, fighting trees, bleating prayers, soaking his clothes with sweat till they stank of terror, was all rubbed right out. Houses! B. J. Cantra had the world by the tail again.

It was going to be too good to keep. Already he could hear himself, maybe over old-fashioneds for two in a hotel nook, or maybe, towel-swathed, in the locker-room at Agwamis: "For one while there, till I happened on that fence, Baby was I lonesome!"

Across the glimpse between house-cabin and barn-cabin a figure passed. Instantly Bee Jay took his elbow off the fence. He got out a handkerchief and went over his face and neck, hard in the creases. He laid his thinning top hair back where it belonged with a comb of fingers. By edging his shoulderblades together in back, in front he lifted and flattened the bag of stomach muscles below the rib-arch. All this mechanical. You tauten a string and a tin monkey climbs.

The glimpsed figure down there wore a skirt.

The skirt had once been turkey red, but wear, work and weather had turned it a dungy brown. Milk spattered it now, though the wearer had hiked it up over her knees to keep it out of the pail under the lean cow's belly. She was barefoot because of the barn dirt.

It took Bee Jay a minute to get all this. What light there was came in at the doorway in which he stood; piled fodder-corn stopped the one window. And even outdoors it was growing dusk.

The girl, or woman, whichever she was, had glanced at him once, around the cow's rear, and returned to her milking.

"Well-er—" He twinkled to himself, re-cleared his throat. "Waal now—howdy, lady."

Once more she tipped her face in sight, eyes small, widely set, heavy cheekbones and chin.

"He's to Hebers. He' be back."

Bee Jay was thinking: what an animal; though, come to look at it, that neck of hers isn't so worse—if someone would take a scraper to it. "Pardon, what did you say? He? Who? Where?"

"To Hebers. He' be back. You quit that." The last, all of a stolid piece, was to the restless cow. And on with the milking.

"But see here—look here—I'm in a bad fix."

Chee-chee, chee-chee, jets in foam was all he got for answer. This was something new for B. J. Cantra. Involuntarily he wet a thumb and tried to iron out the worst of the V-shaped tears in his Abercrombie shirt. But then he came to, and was amused.

He turned out of the doorway and studied the yard, naked red earth, its only adornment chicken-traces. The dwelling, built like the barn of mill-waste from which bark hung like hair, was plainly of but a single room. Bee Jay had to smile. "Primitive" was a word people tossed around. Eleanor was addicted to it. A lot she knew! He'd have an earful for her Friday night and a good laugh.

The thought of Friday, three days off, brought him back to where he was. Better than lost in the woods, yes. But still! Moreover, he was hungry. Moreover, damn it all . . . Uneasy rancor pulled his shoulderblades together, repairing his silhouette. A palm did something mechanical to his under-chin. Who the devil did she think she was, to go on pumping at a cow in there, when plenty of dames that were really something—

But she had finished. She stood in the doorway, pail in hand.

He spoke sharply. "Now listen, honey, look at me."

She looked somewhere else, no more expression than a turnip.

"I'm hungry, I'm tired. If you'll tell me how I get from here to Jones Camp, Mayburg—Are you listening? *Look at me!*"

Less than a turnip, a sack of meal. She hung her head, eyes on her feet. The feet were the color of old brown shoes, and the down on her legs gave the stain that faded up them the look of fancy stockings. One great-toe fumbled out to touch the other. Then the other did the same by it. Bee Jay had a brain-wave: *She's afraid of me.*

Life bloomed again. He was tickled. No, doggone it, he was thrilled. It made him think, somehow, of his first try of canned rattlesnake; though it had brought his gorge up it had thrilled him. Bee Jay knew so many weary females whose main play was being "frightened." But here was the real thing. As real as rags and red clay. This was primitive.

Compassion filled him. "See here, my girl." He laid a hand on the hair of the bent head, tied back out of the way with a flannel string like a horse's tail on a muddy track. (He'd been right; it did feel like horse-hair.) "See here, don't be silly. Can't you say something?"

"Thur he comes," she said.

"What's that?"

"Thur he comes."

A wagon come in sight, clear of the house corner, drawn by a mule and a pony. They approached and halted of their own accord. The driver threw the reins over them, unhunched himself, climbed down and started to unhook the many-mended traces from the near singletree.

"My name is Cantra. B. J. Cantra."

"Hunh? . . . Keep care o' the wire off that trace, Cath."

From the off-side, where she'd gone to unhitch, Cath said: "My husband's a little bit deef in the ears."

Bee Jay felt like laughing. Undersized, mean in health, a mite wry-necked and "deef in the ears" to boot, the fellow gave Bee Jay a sense of personal bigness and muscularity. Primitive stuff. *I could break him with my hands. Dumb as she is, she must see that.*

He bent with complacence and raised his voice. "I lost my way in the woods . . . Wait a second there, before you unharness—I want to get you to take me to a place called Mayburg, Jones Camp."

The man went right on. "Mornin', mebby. They're tuckered."

"Now see here! I'm paying for this, you understand, Mr.—er—"

"Judah," Cath supplied. "Jess Judah." She too went right on, throwing the traces over the pony's loins.

"When I say pay, I mean pay well. Listen—good God, man!"

"Been a furr piece. They're wore down, I tell yuh. Giddap!"

The animals moved a step and let the pole drop. The hames were unlinked. The harness was stripped and thrown into the wagonbed. Judah slapped the mule on the croup. "Go 'long!" The creature wandered off, the pony following. In the barn the cow lowed. Cath reentered, brought her out and sent her after the draught-beasts, already grabbing at rags of grass up the hill. Taking the milk-pail she went into the house, and light appeared at the single window. Her husband stood. He got out the remnant of a twist of chewing and bit off a piece. Night had come down, dark enough for the first stars.

Bee Jay quit holding in. "This is a swell fix, this is pretty!" He went skyhigh. "What the hell do you think I'm to *do?*" He shut his mouth tight, drummed the earth with a sole. "I don't suppose it would put you out *too* much, Mister Judah, just to tell me the *way*. I'll *walk*."

"Mayburg? Kinda furr piece. Mite tricky after dark, 'thout you know the road. Got a flash?"

"Don't make me laugh."

"I ain't got one."

"That's too bad." Bee Jay sat himself on the wagon-pole, one knee over the other. Here he was. It was up to Judah.

The stars brightened. Somewhere a bullbat whirred. Judah moved off, merging with the shadow of the house. There came a sound of tinware and slop of water. He returned bearing a basin.

"Thur's fodder in the barn 'll sleep yuh. I don't doubt Cath'll find yuh a bit to eat, such as it is. Aim to wash?"

The single room had a stove, a table, two chairs, and an iron bedstead. Two pots simmered on the stove.

"Set, and we'll eat." Judah pulled himself a chair and propped his elbows on the table, his brow between his hands. Like his beasts, he too was wore down. "How 'bout it, Cath? . . . *Cath!*" He looked up and around the room. "Where's Cath?"

He rose and went to peer out of the door, this way, that way.

"Cath! Where yuh at? . . . I never seen her go out, did you?"

"No," said Bee Jay. She hadn't been there when they came in.

Judah came back and sat awhile, head in hands. He got madder and madder. He stormed up, got spoons and plates from a box nailed to the wall, and was about to go at the pots, when Cath's feet were heard approaching the door in shoes. And stockings.

"Fer gawwww sake, where you been, Cath?"

More wooden than sullen: "Down to the crick."

"This time o' night!"

"'Twarn't cold, in."

"And us-all waitin' supper!" Judah appealed to Bee Jay. "What's got into her?"

Bee Jay flattered himself he knew what had got into her, poor clod. Funny as it was, still he was moved. He *was*. Doggone it, this got under his skin. He tried to catch her eye as she clumped to the stove, to reward her by showing he was wise, and pretending she'd made a hit with him.

Why bother? Well, why not? You'd do that much for a dog. Moreover, hung up here in godforsaken nowhere, what else had he to work on? It amused him to philosophize: nine chances in ten a banker cast away on a desert isle would fall to adding up seashells, partly to kill time and partly to keep his hand in.

From one pot came cornmeal mush, from the other a watery mess of greens in which stray bits of sidemeat made oily rings. The sight of it was too much for Bee Jay. But so was hunger too much for him. Spoon by spoon he got some down, keeping his face away from the bed corner where Cath had withdrawn with her plate.

Why show her his disgust of her providing? You wouldn't do that to a dog. On the other hand it was too much to ask of Bee Jay that he should hold out on any female by keeping his face from sight too long. Especially when there were two birds to be killed.

So he turned in profile, and it was Judah at his feeding that revolted him, anyone could see. Heavy-hung head right down over his slop; worse than a hungry pig, a sleepy pig! A thing like that—

216

Oh dear! Visibly, Bee Jay caught himself. He turned abashed eyes toward the corner, full of a suave dismay that said as plain as plain: "You're mistaken; I admire him immensely; great fellow. Even though *you* know and *I* know what a ghastly tragedy for such as you to be tied to a thing like that."

The trouble was, Cath wasn't looking, so the whole play misfired. Bee Jay explained it: "Devil, she was too quick with her eyes." But no, why kid himself? She was just a vegetable. A man like him should worry!

Judah had finished. He got up stretched, yawned, lighted a lantern and went to wait in the doorway. "When you're through," he said, without even looking back.

Bee Jay got to his feet. "I'll be right along."

Cath came from the corner, bringing her plate to put in the dishwash bucket, crossing behind Bee Jay.

He lowered his voice. "Nice feed. Nice girl." He pawed out back, caught her free hand and stopped her. She stood like a held horse. It was all playful impulse with Bee Jay, just to see what would happen. He squeezed. The hand hung loppy on its wrist, so much dead beefsteak. . . . To hell with her!

Bee Jay didn't sleep in the barn. He hadn't been there in the fodder five minutes after Judah left with the lantern before he knew it was no go. It wasn't the ribby lying so much as it was the ammonia. He had to get out in the air.

There was the wagon. He took the harness out of the rough board bed and draped it at the front end, hanging down over the doubletree. Returning into the barn he brought out all the fodder he could carry. Three trips and he had enough. He climbed in over a wheel and lay flat, looking right up at the stars. They began to weaken. A new pallor was spreading. Somewhere the moon was going to rise.

Bee Jay was cold. He tried to pull some of the cornstalks over him, sitting up to get at them. He stopped and studied the cabin. Human hog-house, black-asleep.

Asleep, like fun! The *man* might be. If he wasn't quite yet, that explained it; she was waiting till he was. Lying there, still as still, heart thumping, breath held, thinking of the handsome stranger in the barn. No? Bee Jay could smile. You couldn't fool Bee Jay about the way it was with women.

He sat there watching and waiting for what seemed the devil of a while. His smile thinned and rancor rose. All right, *let* her come out! All the good it would do her! Ho-hum, baby, go take yourself a walk,

217

I'm not interested. . . . It might do her good, at that. Deflate her turnip-swollen ego.

He lay down again. He set himself to think of Friday evening. Beginning at the beginning. The elevator. The penthouse bell. The maid "Yes, Mr. Cantra, Mrs. Wye is in." The hall. The drawing-room. Gladioli, and with their faint scent a fainter scent of "Nuit de Paris." Eleanor would be coming forward, hand coolly out. "Ah, Bee Jay—couldn't Harriet come?" (For the maid wouldn't be quite out of hearing yet.) And he'd take the hand in his and give it a squeeze . . . (dead beefsteak)!

Up Bee Jay sat, glowering over the wagon-side at the cabin. Homely, smelly, hairy-legged lump, who did she think she was? The moon was nearly up, but the end of the cabin toward the wagon was still too dark to make out whether the door was shut or left open.

"The hell with her! I'll give her one minute more."

Again he lay down. He yawned. He'd give her two more minutes, then he'd go to sleep. He counted slowly, "One—two—three—" A hundred and twenty it would be. "—thirty-one—thirty-two—" Look out! he'd be asleep before he finished if he didn't take care. It acted like sheep. "—forty-seven—"

He'd lost it. Where had he been? The moon was up. Lifting on an elbow he looked at the house. The door *was* open. . . . There may have been a sound he didn't know he heard. Turning his head quickly he saw her in moonlight at the barn, hesitant, peering in at the door. The heart lifted and sang within him. Who was loony now?

Unaware of him, she hesitated still a moment. Then she stole in a step (she was barefoot again, though otherwise clothed as she had been.) Cut in two by moon and shadow, she stood peering, listening. Another step and she was gone in the dark inside. The first she knew of Bee Jay was when she turned to find him behind her in the doorway.

"Well, well, well! Look who's here."

"I—I got thinkin', mister—" She took a wadded blanket from under an arm. "Yuh might be chilly."

"Now if that isn't too sweet! I call that service. Honest, you don't know what it does to me, to think of a girl like you worrying her pretty head over a poor lost bum—Or wait a second!" He put a twinkle in it, so she'd know he was on to how things were, and only kidding. "Or was it *hubby* thought of it?"

"Unh-unh. He's asleep."

Wise chuckle. "Isn't that just too bad. Sleep sound, does he?"

"Un-huh. 'Count he's deef. . . . I gotta go back in now."

Right out of the book, the cue for dismay. "Aw now listen, Beautiful, have a heart!"

"I gotta go in now." No more come-back than putty. She held out the blanket, looking neither at it nor at him. "Case yuh might be cold."

Talk about primitive! that one had whiskers. Okay, he'd play.

"Cold! *Brrrrr!* I was just about to give up and freeze to death." He took the blanket, laughing low. "Yeah?" He tossed it away. "Listen, baby, look at me."

"I'm goin' in now." She advanced one heavy pace toward him and the door, the slant moonlight climbing up her to the waist. Of a sudden his brow wrinkled with a wild and weazening misdoubt. What if she had in fact come out just to bring him a blanket! He wouldn't put it past the dumbhead. And him the city sucker with a sign on, "Kick me!"

Another step she came, moonlit almost to her averted eyes. And now Bee Jay saw something he hadn't seen before; hung around her neck a string of pearls, five-and-ten cent. . . . Oh yes? That fixed it.

"So you've got to go back in to hubby, have you, you pretty thing?"

"Uh-huh."

"Okay." He took down his barring arms with a knowing grin, stepped in past her, lay back at ease on his elbows on the hill of fodder. He watched her move; waited till she was right in the doorway. "Now Angel, quit fooling."

"Hunh?"

"Shhhh! not so loud. Come back in, nearer. You don't want him waking up and out with a gun, do you? . . . Has he a gun?"

"Uh-huh. Got no loads fer it though."

"Isn't that just too bad?" It was something off the mind, all the same. *I could break him with my hands.* This primitive stuff, by God it got you. Even the barn-stink. Like learning to like anchovies. Bee Jay patted the corn beside him.

"Come on back, hear me?"

"Unh-unh." She came, though, halfway, and stood with her back to him, looking nowhere. "It's time I gone in."

He just laughed, patted the fodder. "Right this way. Come sit down. Have a nice talk or something."

"Unh-unh." Nothing stirring. "Talk about what?"

"Pshaw—anything. You and me on a desert island, what?"

It mustn't be thought that B. J. Cantra always talked like this; at a board-meeting, say. Nor was it now because Cath Judah was a hick and a moron. Bee Jay knew the type of jitterbug slanging the women fell for, right away up to the very best of them. They might try to go penthouse-Radcliffe on him to start with, but he'd yet to know the time it didn't work out in the end.

"Think of it, poor us, all alone on a desert isle. Nothing but white sands and a tropic moon and palms sighing in the sea-breeze—not a thing on our minds—ho-hum! Eh, Cath? Does that sound—"

Bee Jay broke off. Deaf, dumb, dead-weight, she made it sound like so much nothing. What would she know about a desert island?

"Or gay Paree!" Bee Jay got off his elbows, sat up to the job. "Imagine you and me—" How could she imagine Paris? Damn her! Wasn't there anything could penetrate, waken her excitement?

"I gotta go in, mister."

Bee Jay rose from the fodder, went around and planted himself in her way. It had become suddenly hard work to be playful.

He'd damn-well do it, though. "You fraud! I bet you're Cinderalla in disguise. Come out of it, Booful! That sort of thing's all right in Holly—Hey! *Hollywood!* . . . Know what you and I would be doing this minute out there, my pretty maid? Well, it just happens there's a party on, out at Clark's. You know, Clark Gable. I know Clarkie well. Joan, Gary, Bette, Myrna—just the regulars—not a *big* party. Whaddaya say, honey heart? Of course we don't *have* to go, if we don't—Hey! Whoa! First we'll see Adrian, what? You know *Adrian.* . . . *Cath, look at me!*"

"I'm goin' along in, I reckon." Eyes on the door, mouth half open, more with the look of adenoids than of any interest.

He forced a comedy wail. "Don't you *like* Hollywood?" Perspiration wet his temples. "*Adrian*—you know, Cath—he dresses all the stars. He'll do anything for a sweetheart of mine. Well, let's see now. How about something in dark, dark gold, to match my lady's eyes? And slippers—we're going to make this a knockout from feet right up. . . ."

From the feet right up, Bee Jay dressed her. Dressed her in beauty. Beauty that grew and grew, there in the moon-shadow of the cow-shack, till it obsessed him. There's where the trouble had been till now; tongue in cheek, you'll never sell a passion. You've got to let it get you yourself. See it vivid. Be obsessed.

Fury broke right out of the middle of it. "For God-sake shut that *mouth*, can you? Do you have to look like—"

He caught himself, appalled. Now he'd done it! He begged of her: "I didn't mean—honest—I'm sorry—" His hand went out. By chance it tangled with the five-and-ten-cent pearls. "Pretty necklace, pretty neck," he stalled.

With that she came alive. For the first time she flashed a look at him, then jerked her eyes back away, far as she could get them over a shoulder. Under his touch on her throat he felt a little paroxysm pass. The sob of a caught breath.

What a sap he'd been; all this bother with desert isles and Paris and Hollywood!

"It *is* a pretty neck. Pretty, be damned! It's beautiful!"

"Unh-unh—'tain't—very."

Sap! The minute he'd seen that what she'd put on was a necklace he should have had the tip-off.

"Not very? Don't be a silly. You know as well as I do, Cath, what a lovely, lovely throat God gave you."

"Naw I don't . . . 'Tain't nothin' so much . . . I gotta go in. . . . Unh-unh—naw, mister—naw—"

You couldn't fool Bee Jay. He drew her by the shoulders, bent, dragged a slow kiss up the throat, up the chin.

"Unh-unh—naw—"

He stopped her mouth with his mouth. Her lips lay flaccid. But you couldn't fool Bee Jay . . .

When she'd gone back in the house, Bee Jay lay on the corn in the wagonbed with the blanket over him. Peace possessed him. Sleep came toward him. He didn't want it; he wanted to dream awake a while. Begin at the beginning. The switchboard girl: "You're to go right up, Mr. Cantra." The elevator. The bell. The maid: "Yes, Mr. Cantra, Mrs. Wye is in. . . .

Small noises and jouncings worked at him; growing bigger they waked him up. It was the gray before dawn. It took Bee Jay a moment to know where he was and what the shakings and clackings were. The wagon was in motion, to a sound of hoofs.

His first thought was: "He's certainly early at it." Then, with further recollection: "Fine! This works out fine." Rolling on an elbow he craned up at the driver's back and saw who it was. He could have killed her.

She had on a coat, faded to the color of lichens, and a felt toque. The thought came to him: "I'm going to throw up."

He was too mad, though. He felt like shouting at the unconscious back: "Here, you, I'm paying your husband to do this; what's the big idea *your* taking it over? You're not doing it *to do the nice thing,* my God!"

He was so mad he was helpless.

Glancing back she caught him with his chin hanging, crimson.

"You waked up?" Her eyes went stolidly somewhere else. "I meant you should sleep yer sleep out."

"And I meant you ditto. I supposed it would be your husband—"

"Tha's all right . . . Whoa."

She got out and disappeared ahead. There came a sound of bars being lowered. At a clucked command the mule and pony went on through the gate and stopped. Over the wagontail Bee Jay watched her putting the bars back. Beyond and above her the two cabins stood out against the mist of the further slope and the still higher woods. Redness touched the roofs, from the east. But it didn't seem to brighten or warm them any.

Cath came along, climbed up, gathered the reins. Bee Jay got to his knees. It was time he did something. He got to his feet and laid a hand on her shoulder.

"See here, I'd rather your husband—"

"Tha's all right, I keep tellin' yuh . . . Geddap!"

The start unbalanced him, made him hang on the harder.

"It's not all right. Stop, turn around, let's go back."

"Don't keep sayin' that!" She hit the mule a lick with the reins. "Keep care o' them eggs," she said over her shoulder.

Under the seat there was a wooden bucket of eggs, and shoebox tied with string.

The trees closed in, making a tunnel of the rut-road.

Presently, Bee Jay: "Is it far to Mayburg?"

"Mayburg? Not a great piece . . . Are your things there?"

Bee Jay sat back on the wagon's high side-board. A hundred yards to the rear a doe and fawn came out to cross the road. The fawn leaped straight in the air at sight of the wagon and nearly turned a somersault getting back into the growth. It was comical. Bee Jay wanted to hold his sides and hear himself roar with laughter . . . *Are my things there? This is one for the book!*

Up he sprang. "Listen, now, wait, I want to get this all clear." He had money out of a pocket, a five and a twenty. To hell with the five! this was no time. He thrust the twenty around in front of her face. "Let's get this all straight. Is that okay? Or wait." He added the five.

She didn't seem to understand. "Unh-unh," she shook her head. She pushed hand and money back on him. "I ain't much used to handlin' money. You go on handle the hull of it. It's goin' to be a furr piece to Hollywood."

Apparently the pony missed a step, bumping the pole.

"Quit lookin' at me!" she cried, without turning to see that Bee Jay was. Now it was the mule that swerved, head reared, hauling the pony sidewise. Bee Jay realized suddenly it was her hand on the reins was doing it. "Give me those!" He reached over her and got them away.

Her face was gray-green. She slithered down over a wheel and he saw her running off into the underbrush to the left . . . He saw himself getting down the other side, running off into the cover the other way. Saw himself bumping into trees, tearing through bullbriar, through anything, anywhere . . . So he saw himself. But still he was right here, leaning awkwardly, holding the reins, when she came back.

"All right," she said, taking them from him, starting the team. By and by: "I been nervy, kinda. It's good I got it up and over with. Here we come to Heber's . . . Hy-yah, Heber."

An opening on a dim crossroad. Shanty store. Shanty store-keeper.

"Hy-yah, Cath . . . Day to yuh, stranger."

"He's Mister Cantra. He got lost. Here's yer eggs I brought along down, save yuh the trip up there."

"That's obligin' . . . How's Judah?"

'Good. He's gone to Spartanburg a spell, wanted I should tell yuh . . . Come boys, geddap!"

On across the crossroad.

What was B. J. Cantra doing here in this wagon?

"Good I thought of it bein' Wednesday, warn't it."

"Wednesday?"

"Egg day. He won't have no call to go pryin' up around there now 'fore Friday, anyway."

The trees closed in, making a tunnel again.

Born in Greensboro, North Carolina, on March 17, 1886, Wilbur Daniel Steele turned to writing in 1912 when his first short story was sold to the Atlantic Monthly. *After serving as a Navy war correspondent off the French and English coasts in World War I, he became* one of America's best-known authors of short stories. He won five O. Henry Awards for excellence in this field, including such stories as "The Man Who Saw Through Heaven." Many of his stories are about crime and its detection. He died on May 26, 1970.